Broken Sky

John Harvey

BROKEN SKY
Copyright © 2020 John Harvey
john@johnharvey.net

Published 2021 by On-site Creative
OnsiteCreative.ca

ISBN: 9781777720025

FOR MICHELLE

Prologue

The blaze started in a wastebasket—a humble beginning for a fire that would soon burn on the other side of the world.

There was nothing special about the portable office trailer. On a humid summer night, the one-room building sat on a slope in an unlit corner lot of a Louisiana fuel refinery. The trickle of smoke escaping from its open window into the polluted sky was the first sign of trouble.

A battered white pickup waited beside the trailer with its nose pointed downhill. When the burning wall collapsed into the truck's cargo bed, it landed on a pile of items carefully chosen to increase the fire's heat. The blaze would not die easily.

The driverless truck lurched down the gravel slope and rolled into an open-ended Quonset hut, where the flames illuminated a maze of pipes. An insulated supply line jutted from the ground, feeding aviation fuel into a network of smaller pipes, which ran through clusters of gauges, then into high-pressure manifolds. And from there …

Chapter 1

Two Weeks to Newton

Not again.

Jack Scatter dangled his feet over the edge of a rocky cliff, on a world one-hundred and eighty-six million miles from the inferno in Louisiana. He considered hurling himself off the ledge—again—just to see what would happen.

Instead, he flicked a pebble into the nearby creek and leaned forward to watch the water carry it away. The stone tumbled down the steep face, following a familiar path. Far below, the stream twisted through a grassy field saddled between two mountain peaks.

Jack knew he was dreaming.

But this time I'll do something about it.

For as long as he could remember, he'd been having the same dream. Every detail repeated exactly, except for the ending. From the bare rock he sat on, to the thin clouds in the sky above, to the song of a bird in a nearby bush, he always knew what to expect from one moment to the next.

"It's time to go, Jack," the man standing beside him said.

Jack didn't turn to face the speaker; it was pointless. "What would you do if I just sat here?"

The man replied. But as always, his words became jumbled and muted, as if the answers he'd given in hundreds of dreams had melded into overlapping syllables. It didn't matter though. Jack already knew; he'd simply walk away and the dream would end.

"We're somewhere in the Spine," Jack said. A narrow line of four-mile-tall, snow-capped mountains faded into the distance ahead. "But I can't find *that* on any map."

Round, crater lakes were common on Earth, but the one he pointed to in the nearly featureless plain on his left shouldn't exist at all on Cirrus. He'd never traveled to Earth—and never would—but the dream was so vivid, so detailed, it had to have grown from a memory. He'd searched maps of both worlds but never found matching terrain. Dark green lines meandered from opposite sides of the lake, suggesting a river course, and the lake itself held a perfectly round island, exactly in its center.

The anonymous man spoke again with a hundred voices that mingled to obscure all meaning.

Jack flung another stone into the abyss. "Why can't you just once answer a question without sounding like you're underwater?"

The man walked away. This was the moment Jack was waiting for.

Through the years, repetition had taught him to hold his conscious mind at a level just below waking. That practice now enabled him to dream lucidly—to know when he was asleep and to have partial control over his dreams. Most of them. He'd tried so many things to alter the flow, but this dream always ended in the same spot.

Not this time.

He turned and focused not on the man walking away, but on the forest ahead.

Concentrate. Instead of following the man, he'd try for the forest. He needed to run, but not think about running. If he moved his real limbs, he'd startle himself awake. He fixated on the path bordering the stream, recalling the egg-shaped boulder hidden among the thousands of saplings beyond the meadow. He imagined himself leaping over the knee-high stone.

And then he was there—jogging through the short, evenly spaced trees.

I did it. I skipped ahead.

He'd bypassed half the uphill journey and was nearing the end of the hanging valley where steep walls converged to a point. He swerved through a cleft in a bus-sized boulder and—

The stranger stood below a natural dam, a moraine-like pile of fallen stone, exactly where he'd be if Jack had followed. He pointed to the top of the heap. "... answer."

"Answer to *what?*" Jack shouted. "What's the question?"

The man climbed, leaving Jack and the familiar disappointment at the base of the wall.

"That's not fair. *I beat you.* Something should have changed."

The climber didn't respond. Jack delayed until he was almost at the summit, wondering if it was worth the effort. But he'd changed part of the dream, maybe this time he could maintain control until the end. He decided to try.

Damp lichen coated the rocks and water seeped from a dozen fissures, but he remembered where the best footholds were. The man was waiting by the mouth of a cave formed by enormous blocks of fallen stone. He spoke again as Jack approached. "… inside."

Beyond, the valley ended with a small lake surrounded by steep walls on three sides, but it was the sheltered opening that drew Jack's attention.

Last chance to walk away.

He crouched beneath an overhanging lintel formed by a massive slab of gray rock, knowing he had to surrender control to move beyond this point. If he took the next step, he wouldn't be able to escape, no matter what the dream showed.

At least that's how it usually goes.

His stomach knotted as he moved closer, felt cool air at the cave's threshold, smelled damp moss. It was all so real. He struggled with the balance between dreaming and waking.

And then he was a spectator once again.

Usually, as he entered, voices swarmed from the darkness—indistinct murmurs of hundreds, possibly thousands of people at a great distance. That alone was enough to make him hesitate, but this time was different. This time there was—

Fire.

His dream self pulled back instinctively from the roar and the heat, even though he couldn't see a flame. *It's just a dream. Just a dream.* A shrill alarm pulsed nearby—not a fire alarm, a warning tone. *Ignore it.* He focused on the cave and smelled gas and oily smoke. *It's so close. Just inside.* The enfolding voices grew louder as he leaned farther, reached into the darkness and—

Woke up.

Every. Single. Time.

He'd never been able to stay asleep, to continue dreaming and discover what waited in the cave or learn who the man was. He was certain that these were important, things he once knew but had forgotten. Always, the answers hid from him like a word on the tip of his tongue.

His heart was pounding. He took several deep breaths to calm himself. The dream had seemed more real than ever; the sensation of fire was almost painful. In the darkness, he rubbed his fingertips, checking for burns. His fingers were fine but he was shaken by the sense of urgency the dream conveyed; something he'd never felt before. Equally troubling, it was occurring more often. It had gone from being an occasional event to almost monthly. This was the second time in just the past week.

Now that his breathing and pounding heart were under control, he lay quietly in his bed and listened. No sound came from within the house but a drone passed in the distance, overwhelming the song of a nocturnal bird in the hedge below his window.

It's huge, Jack thought. *I haven't heard a drone like that in … I've never heard one like that.* The machine thwupped more like a helicopter than a smaller, unmanned aircraft.

The large drone sounded as if it was heading for the family workshop in the industrial park. But the familiar rhythm of spinning blades carried an added vibrato. *It's got a chipped rotor. I guess I'll be replacing that first thing in the morning.*

His tiny second-floor bedroom overlooked the fields, not the street. It was small enough for him to roll over and flip the curtain aside without getting out of bed. *No landing lights.* Instead, he groaned when he spotted the dim numbers on the clock; dawn was still hours away. He wouldn't get back to sleep; he never did after one of these dreams. Fortunately, school break had already started and he didn't need to be alert in the morning.

He got up, dressed, and crept down the stairs, even though his mother was a light-sleeper and probably heard him. But she knew he sometimes went to the shop in the small hours, so his stealth was mostly for his father's benefit.

Instead of using the street, he left the townhouse through the back door and descended to the unlit dirt path that bordered the fields. The temperature never dropped to freezing in Fairview, but his breath clouded the predawn air. He turned up his collar and tucked his hands into his jacket pockets as he hiked the empty mile to the workshop.

- - - - -

There was something unsettling in the way Danny Kou observed people. When Pieter Reynard, CEO of Armenau Industries, entered his top-floor Seattle office, his chief engineer, Simon, was already suffering under that gaze.

Simon had once confided that he believed Danny was a *Hopper*, someone who could predict a person's movements seconds before they happened. Pieter had dismissed the idea and warned Simon against such speculation. After all, he knew Danny's secret; the man could only see half a second into the future.

As Pieter passed without offering a greeting, Simon lowered his eyes and shuffled his feet. It wasn't just the scrutiny of the head of security making him nervous; he'd brought bad news. But he'd have to endure his misery a while longer—Pieter would not be rushed in his own office. He hung his bespoke suit jacket neatly on the coat stand, brushed a fleck of dust from the sleeve, then poured himself a coffee. Finally, he sat at his desk and motioned for the engineer to speak.

Simon glanced at Danny before handing a tablet to Pieter with the results from the predawn test. "Thirty-seven aircraft were actively refueling on the ground, and one in-flight. It had to make an emergency landing near Lord Howe Island, but no one was hurt." He wiped his sweaty palms against the seams of his trousers.

Pieter had been scrolling through Simon's data. A tiny furrow appeared on his brow when he read the comment about the Australian floatplane but he just said, "Continue."

"The equipment we chose for—" Simon faltered under Pieter's glare. "That, *I* chose, for this test, had to be operational. It met all our criteria, but I hadn't anticipated that the owners might not be using it properly."

Pieter said nothing. Simon would get to the point faster that way.

"The aircraft was over forty years old and not certified for in-flight refueling." Simon fidgeted with his buttons. "If they make a public complaint, they'll lose their permits. They're upset, but there's no reason for them to check the portal crystals before they ship the old units back to us."

Pieter's family had been in the transportation business for generations. He understood why the tour company had risked fines: profit. A full tank at take-off reduces cargo weight and therefore the number of paying passengers. In theory, an aircraft with a wormhole-based refueling system could fly indefinitely, but was legally required to carry enough reserve fuel to reach the nearest airport.

Simon continued. "The pumping station in Louisiana was destroyed as … as planned. No injuries there." He subconsciously shuffled a half step back from the desk. "But the roof collapsed and tore the fuel manifold apart before the final phase. That was unexpected, and it briefly exposed the wormholes, which led to small fires in several other cities, but only minor smoke damage."

Pieter had been reading as Simon talked and had already finished the section covering the secondary fires. He considered the news for only a moment. "It's unlikely anyone will link the events. Our official position is unchanged—the fire forced us to cut the fuel supply as a precaution. Pass requests for information directly to me and prepare for the next round of tests." He said this casually, but an underlying tone made it clear he would tolerate no more delays.

Simon hesitated. He glanced at Danny, standing silently behind Pieter, and retreated another half step. Danny, like Simon himself, was of average height, but muscled like an Olympic gymnast. That and his unrelenting glare made him more intimidating than Pieter, who was broad-shouldered and stood six inches taller.

"There was a second problem," he finally said. "Our instruments recorded every crystal shattering as expected, only not until the pressure rose slightly higher than projected."

Pieter had skipped the actual measurements. He understood the principles but left the details to the engineers. "What caused that?"

"It may just be an instrumentation error, except ... well ... except that the extra pressure works out to be precisely what it would be if there were two more crystals."

"Another active pair?" Pieter's voice was controlled but menacing. "Where?"

"Now that they've been destroyed, there's ... there's no way to tell." This time it was a full step back. "I'll keep working on it and let you know as soon as I have an answer."

Pieter dismissed the engineer but called him back before he reached the door. "Wait. The floatplane. It says here they're grounded until they get the new fuel module."

"That's right. The courier has already delivered the upgrade package to their hangar. They're just waiting for one of their other aircraft to become available."

"We have a helicopter in Sydney. As a courtesy, pick up their mechanic and fly him out to the island. Have our pilot collect the old modules while they're finishing the repair."

Simon smiled, unable to hide his surprise. "That ... that's very generous. I'm certain that'll go a long way to smoothing things over." He was still smiling when he left the room.

Pieter waited for the door to close. "Make sure that airplane never makes it to the mainland."

Danny nodded and began typing on his phone. A whiff of oily smoke drifted from his clothes.

Pieter picked up a gleaming sphere of white quartz from a wooden pedestal on his desk, then spun his chair to face the window. Despite the persistent haze, he'd have a fine view of Lake Washington from the ninety-sixth floor when the sun came up—few buildings in the city were equal to or taller than his own. Except for the conference room, his office and other private spaces took up the entire floor, but the view from this corner was his favorite. Even his overbearing father would have been impressed.

He raised the sphere to examine it more closely. "The extra crystals. Can you track them?"

Danny lowered his phone. "If there are records, I'll find them. Do I have your approval?"

Approval. The meaning between them was clear. For Danny, making an aircraft and its crew disappear was trivial—the waters were deep enough off the coast. But when he asked for approval it meant he expected to hire external contractors through multiple layers of secrecy in order to hide the connection to Armenau. The operation would be expensive.

"Just clean up loose ends," Pieter said. "We can't afford delays."

Danny nodded again and left the office without a word, moving silently over the polished hardwood floor. Only the soft click of the door latch marked his passage.

Pieter shifted the tennis ball-sized stone between hands, weighing both it and his options. He'd already come so far on a difficult journey, liquidated many of his most treasured assets, and trimmed thousands of jobs. He hadn't made that decision lightly—it had taken a decade to replace those assets.

"Call Simon," he instructed the office AI.

As he waited for the connection, Pieter rolled the stone, feeling the carved dimples that mapped locations of mine shafts and pumping stations. *Such a simple thing.* The stone wasn't just any rock, but a scale model of the icy planetoid in the Oort Cloud that was the source of his wealth. *Enough fresh water to last a thousand years.*

Simon, still in the elevator, answered his phone seconds later.

"Move the resonance test up to the thirteenth," Pieter said.

"That's not … that's only two weeks."

Pieter tossed the stone and spread his fingers as it fell. With only a thought, he made it stop and hover inches above his hand. "Is that a problem?"

"We can't … I had planned for a lot more time to

prepare."

Pieter was used to gambling. He'd risked his billion-dollar inheritance on an unproven concept and parlayed that success into a business empire that now controlled vast resources on Cirrus—the world-sized space station that produced a quarter of Earth's food. And he'd done it despite the contempt of the thousands of Cirrus-investors who claimed to have built their own fortunes from the ground up.

"Will it work?" He twirled his fingers. The hovering stone began to spin.

"Yes, but …"

"But what?" The stone spun faster.

"It's a big step."

Bigger than you can possibly guess. Armenau Industries' earnings were still firmly grounded in portal-based water delivery. Giving up that stability was a huge risk, but it was too late to stop. "I'm ready."

Pieter clenched his fist.

The stone shattered.

Chapter 2

When Jack reached the cluster of drab, concrete-walled structures a mile from town, he found that all their lights were off except for one.

"Morning, Jack," a familiar voice called. "You're up early."

Jack veered off the path and climbed the short rise to the neighboring shop. "That big drone woke me. I thought I'd get started on it before whoever owns it calls." He spotted a cluster of spilled washers next to the open garage door and stooped to gather them.

"Heard it coming in myself." The older man eased himself down from the engine compartment of a huge green combine harvester. "From the west."

"West? Are you sure?" More than a hundred miles of the most productive farmland in the sector lay between Fairview and the sea; a drone as large as the one they'd heard had no purpose out there.

The man swung his arm to describe the flight path. "Passed overhead and turned around over the field."

"That's really strange." Jack returned the box of washers to its proper spot; he knew this workshop almost as well as his own. "I know one of its rotors is damaged. Maybe that's throwing off its airspeed sensor and it overshot."

"You'll figure it out. You always do." He wiped his grease-marked hands on a rag, then pulled an envelope from his pocket and offered it to Jack.

"What's this?"

"For the actuator you fixed last week and the distributor the week before. I told you, I'm paying you from now on." He jabbed the envelope at Jack.

"You don't have to do that, sir."

"And you don't have to always call me *Sir*. Call me Stan."

"Yes, sir. I will." Jack accepted the money.

"'Bout time the others started paying you for your work around here too." He cast a glance over his shoulder. "You know Hank over there is taking advantage of you. The sensor

11

array you done for him last week would've cost him four hundred for a rebuild in Port Isaac."

Jack shrugged. "I'm learning a lot. The practical experience is worth more than that. I plan to open my own shop someday, in Caerton."

"You need to be saving up for college."

"I'm ..." He looked down and nudged another carton into place with his foot. "I'm not sure I'm going."

"Hmm. Your parents think you are."

"I'm already doing what I want. I don't need more school to learn what I already know."

"Education makes the most of opportunity. Got a master's degree in engineering." Stan slapped the giant machine beside him. "You think I need that to repair this beast?"

"No."

"But if I didn't, I'd be stuck on Earth, doing the same job in a crowded and polluted city for half the wage. The fresh air alone is worth the degree. You don't know what choices you'll be facing. Keep your options open."

"Yes, sir."

"Your parents have told you the same thing, haven't they?"

"Yes, sir."

He lowered his gray-stubbled chin to look over the rim of his glasses. "It's Stan."

"Yes ... sir." Jack failed to suppress a grin.

Stan returned the smile. "Well, I won't push the matter. You'll make the right decision when the time comes." He reached down and picked up an oil-stained cardboard box. "You call Hank *Sir*?"

"He's not ... I mean, you're ..."

"Got a few more gray hairs than he does. Is that it?"

"Yes, sir."

"That's 'bout all they're good for, then." He passed the box to Jack. "Look at this steering servo for me. If you can fix it, tell me how much time you put in. I'll pay you proper."

"Yes, sir. Thank you."

"*Stan.*"

- - - - -

Jack carried the steering controller the short distance to the back door of his family's own shop and switched on the lights. Unlike Stan's garage, built to house two harvesters side-by-side, their building was long and narrow. An office occupied the front third below a second-floor mezzanine, but Jack spent most of his time in the back, which was divided into storage and a workshop. Steel racks housing hundreds of drones and spare parts filled the warehouse half of the room to the twenty-foot ceiling. He skirted these on his way to his workbench, where he emptied the box and spun the servo's motor shaft, sensing the telltale noise and vibration.

The encoder has broken loose. But I'm more interested in that drone.

He'd take the mechanism apart to confirm the problem before ordering parts, but felt confident with his diagnosis; he was always correct about these things. Pushing the servo aside, he climbed the steel ladder at the back of the room and popped the roof hatch.

The landing pad was empty. *Crashed?* He hurried to the far edge of the flat roof and checked the space between the buildings. The alley was empty, so he ran to the side overlooking the street. That was clear too. *I definitely heard a drone. So did Stan.*

The neighboring rooftops were the same height as his, and the drone was on none of them. There was no movement and no sound, but a faint glow reflected off the fields behind a warehouse across the street, the largest on the block: *Hank's place.*

He scurried back to the alley side of the building, leaned over the short raised wall next to the scupper drain, then vaulted off the roof. Hanging from the edge of the wall by one hand, he reached over to grab the downspout below the drain, then shifted his weight to the pipe.

Mom would totally freak if she caught me. So would his father. But Jack could tell exactly how strong the connections were and how much weight the pipe could bear by the way it flexed. The bolts securing the plastic drainpipe to the wall may as well have been extensions of his own fingers.

After sliding down the first section of pipe, he paused at

the bracket to make sure it was sound, then swapped his hands below the support to continue his descent. He landed lightly on the hard-packed gravel, stepped out of the alley, and crossed the street.

There was definitely a light ahead. *Voices too.* It sounded as if the back door to Hank's warehouse was open. Jack crept through the alley, hoping to find the drone without bothering anyone. Then a motion sensor turned on the overhead light, casting a long shadow past the building's edge.

Hank stepped into the light, surprisingly swift for a man who fooled no one with his claim of weighing only two hundred fifty pounds. "What are you doing sneaking around at this hour?"

"I'm not sneaking." Jack leaned to look past, but Hank's ample waistline blocked much of the view without him even trying. "I was looking for a drone. I think it crashed near here."

Hank sidestepped to block Jack. "I haven't seen anything. It's not here."

Jack said nothing. *He's lying.*

A faint voice sounded from Hank's phone. He raised it to his ear and nodded several times, then said, "You should head home, Jack. You don't want people to think you're up to no good. I'll let you know if your missing drone turns up."

Another lie. He wanted to take two more steps, to see the drone he suspected was there, but said, "Sure. Thanks." There was little to be gained by proving Hank was lying. He turned and walked away without looking back. Though he was soon too distant to hear Hank's conversation clearly, he distinctly heard the man say 'Jack Scatter' into his phone.

What's he hiding? Jack wondered as he climbed the ladder to the workshop's roof. *And why did he give my name?*

Everyone in town knew Hank considered himself a powerful man. Jack, fifteen years old and only half of Hank's probable true weight of three hundred pounds, would get no respect and no answers from the self-important businessman.

Hank saw that drone, I'm certain of it. It might even be just across the street in his warehouse. But what it was doing there and why Hank lied were things he could only guess at.

As he watched, the light behind Hank's building faded away.

Chapter 3

Jack was still at the workshop, inspecting a faulty gearbox, when the sun rose. Despite the steady stream of cold air that spilled through it, he'd left the roof hatch ajar, hoping to hear the missing drone again. The first rays of sunlight were reflecting through the gap and scattering across the cluttered workbench when his phone rang. He smiled and tucked it between his shoulder and ear so he could continue working.

"Ethan, what's up?"

"Hey, I don't have much time. I just wanted to let you know that I'm coming to Cirrus."

"Yeah, I know. Next year."

"No, today."

"*What?*" Jack set his screwdriver down and held the phone in front of him, activating both his and his cousin's cameras.

Ethan grinned as his image filled the screen. "My parents' jobs got bumped up. We flew into New Mexico last night. We'll be lifting off in a few hours."

"That's, uh, great. Why are you whispering?" Jack had automatically lowered his voice too.

"No reason. How do you spell, *sedative*?"

"What are you doing?"

"There are a couple of jerks who've been bullying the younger passengers. I found their medical records and put them both down as being highly susceptible to wormhole-sickness."

"*Found?*" Jack focused on the gap between Ethan's head and the edge of the screen. "Are you in the server room?"

Ethan shrugged. "Maybe. There are a lot of computers here. Anyway, the ship's doctor has already met them. She'll be happy to learn she can dose their meals."

"Oh, they're going to be pissed."

"Actually, no. I already thought of that. What's the name of that tube they shove … you know what I mean."

"Are you talking about a *catheter*?"

"That's it. With any luck, they'll sleep through the entire

trip."

"Uh, are you sure you want to do that?"

"Already done. Oops. Someone's coming. I gotta run." The video blurred. "See you in two weeks."

The last thing Jack heard before Ethan disconnected was a keyboard clattering on a desk and feet slapping the floor.

Two weeks. Jack set his phone on the workbench. *Why didn't Mom or Dad tell me?* He and Ethan had grown up together—virtually. They'd never met in person but had spent countless hours together online.

He considered calling home, but it was still early. The gearbox would only take twenty minutes to clean, reassemble, and reinstall. He decided to finish his work first.

Repairing drones was an unpaid job he did on weekends throughout the school year. Given the chance, he'd have worked every night of the week—the order and predictability of machinery was calming—but his parents insisted homework was the top priority.

Jack was already skilled enough to apply for a full-time job in a larger city. He could identify the problem with any mechanical device in minutes, grasped hydraulics as well as his father, and was rapidly learning electronics. His only reservation was that he didn't like to be around many people. The anxiety he suffered in crowds wasn't disabling, but it could be overwhelming. He recalled the unease he'd felt in last night's dream—a reaction to the sound of all those voices.

Sunlight was streaming through the window in the workshop's back door when he finished the repair. He set his tools down and considered the open roof hatch.

If Hank is hiding that drone, he's not going to fly it in the daytime.

Jack climbed the warehouse ladder, closed and latched the overhead panel from below, then headed home for breakfast. And answers.

- - - - -

"We just found out ourselves." Jack's mother, Emily, slid a plate of toast onto the dining room table and sat beside his father. "Apparently they got the call yesterday and didn't have time to tell anyone."

"We'll be taking the bus to Port Isaac to meet them," Victor said. "You're coming with us."

Jack fumbled his fork. It clattered noisily on his plate. "Why do *I* have to go?"

"With Ethan here, your grandfather will pay the college tuition for both of you. It'll be good for you to see how much it's changed." He sipped his coffee and turned to look through the glass doors, in the direction of the distant city.

Jack knew what his father meant: he needed to get accustomed to being around crowds. Just thinking about it made him squirm. He crossed his arms and leaned back in his chair, following his father's gaze across the fields. "How long are we staying?"

"We'll see how it goes," Emily said. "Maybe you and Ethan will stay in Fairview until school starts."

- - - - -

After dinner, Jack lay on his bed, brooding over the news while staring at a map of Cirrus pinned to the sloped ceiling.

College had always been a distant concept, even though both his parents had engineering degrees and his grandfather was a respected scientist. Now that the famous Holden Marke was involved, Jack knew he'd be under pressure to go along with their plans. He'd have only a year to change their minds.

His phone chimed.

<Can we talk?> The Caller ID was Sarah Rogers. By *talk*, she meant video.

Jack sat up, subconsciously smoothing his pillow-tousled hair before allowing his camera to connect. "Sure, what's up?"

"Not much." She was calling from her bedroom. The room behind her had changed over the years—toys had been replaced by sketches, replaced by piles of scattered clothing, replaced again by watercolors—but Sarah looked the same. At least that's how it seemed to him. If he pictured her in the past, he saw her as she was now: pretty, confident, and always smiling. "Sometimes it's just easier than texting."

"I agree. My cousin called today. He's on his way to Cirrus."

"You don't look happy. Aren't you and Ethan close?"

"Sort of." Jack tried to appear casual. "But we've never actually met. What if we can't stand each other in person?"

Sarah laughed gently. "I'm sure it'll be fine." She paused, then adjusted her phone so she was out of the frame. "You've spent enough time online that you probably know everything about each other."

He wasn't sure how to respond. This was one of those moments where he felt he needed to say something, but was worried that whatever he said would come out wrong. As with Ethan, he'd never met Sarah in person, though they'd spent thousands of hours together online. They'd also discussed their after-graduation plans for years, and these always centered on Caerton.

"It's not just Ethan," he said when Sarah reappeared. "Our grandfather will pay our tuition if we go to college together in Port Isaac."

A worried expression passed over her face. "That sounds great."

Jack shifted uncomfortably. "But I already had plans for Caerton."

Sarah nodded but said nothing.

"Maybe I can convince him to loan me the tuition money, instead. That would cover half the franchise fee to start my own business. Of course, I'd be in debt to the corporation for another decade, but at least I'd be working."

"Will he go for that?"

That was a good question. Jack had never met his grandfather, hadn't even spoken on the phone with him in years. That wasn't because Holden wasn't involved with the family, but—as a teenager—Jack spent a lot more time with friends than family.

"I'm going to have to show him that I can do the job on my own. But since he lives on Earth, I'll have to convince my parents first. I have an idea."

Later that night, shortly before he fell asleep, Jack heard the mysterious drone leaving town, its unrepaired rotor still singing a warning tune.

Chapter 4

Doctor Holden Marke was well past retirement age but still actively involved with Seattle-based Naef Dynamics. The company provided an uncommon service—testing of portal crystals—and he was the foremost expert. These days, he normally worked from home and only came to the lab for meetings or when a problem required his expertise.

Field Instability, he thought as he drove into the empty parking lot of an unimpressive three-story structure in the city's industrial section. *That's not possible. Not anymore.* His intern had reported the warning in a text message sent after midnight.

He'd seen that error himself, thousands of times. But that was thirty years ago, when he was trying to build an ultra-stable portal. Only when he finally succeeded did he realize how dangerous it could be if misused. He'd destroyed his prototypes and buried his research.

Could someone on my staff be experimenting with the same concept? Right under my nose?

It wasn't yet seven a.m. when Holden entered the building, but it was already eighty degrees outside and would top one hundred for the nineteenth day in a row. He hurried through the empty lobby—the business was closed on Saturdays. He passed by the unoccupied reception desk, climbed the vacant stairwell, opened the laboratory door, and froze. All the lights were on, revealing fifteen workstations arranged in a neat grid in the center of the white-walled room. He wasn't alone.

"Sorry, Doctor Marke," Garett said. "Is that in your way?" The intern's electric bicycle leaned against the wall near the entrance. "I can move it."

"It's fine. I just wasn't expecting you here on the weekend." Holden had dressed in faded jeans and running shoes, but Garett was wearing the same casual slacks and dress shoes he wore throughout the week. "Have you been here all night?"

Garett brushed a hand through his unwashed hair. "No,

the baby has been crying through the night the entire week. I slept through half of Friday, so I came back to catch up on my journal. Is there anything I can help you with?"

"The circuit board you messaged me about. Where is it?"

"I'll get it for you." Garett headed for the Archive, a shielded room that housed thousands of portal testing rigs on a dozen twenty-foot-long racks.

As Naef Dynamic's senior employee, Holden could have taken a private office on the second floor but preferred to immerse himself in the daily activity of the workshop. He sat at his tidy desk in the corner to review the sensor logs, skipping directly to the section on radioactivity. *All normal.*

Not only that, the last log entry for the testing platform was for an air filter change, more than a year ago. He leaned back in his chair and relaxed; the error had not been caused by someone trying to pass a radioactive substance through a portal.

His relief was short-lived though. The data in the other sections made no sense.

The sensors had recorded a huge temperature spike on the wormhole's outbound side, but not the inbound one. And the rig was part of an efficiency study that passed only a low-power laser.

Nothing in this configuration can produce that much heat.

Garett returned, carrying a book-sized transparent container, "When I opened the case, I thought I smelled smoke, or possibly gas, but it faded quickly. Later, when I checked the crystals, they weren't cracked or discolored; they were just gone." He set the case on the table next to the microscope.

"Thank you." Holden rolled his chair to the inspection station and withdrew the circuit board from the container. He pushed it into the microscope's receiver, then leaned forward to look through the binocular eyepiece. Seconds passed while the machine's twin probes focused on the mounting rings for a pair of artificial gems—the anchor points for the wormhole.

"Is it okay if I ask questions while you work?" Garett asked. "I've got to meet with my thesis advisor. There's an evaluation form she wants me to fill in."

"Yes, go ahead." He twisted the controls and zoomed in on the empty rings.

"How long have you been with Naef Dynamics?"

Holden didn't look up. "Oh, it's been twenty-four, twenty-five years." The inbound ring appeared normal, but a thin layer of black soot coated the outbound one. *Strange.* He checked again. The edge of the burn—a sharply defined line—covered just one side of the ring.

"Why did you leave the university?"

"She wants to know that?"

"That's for me, actually. I'm trying to decide what to do next year."

Holden sat up. "You could apply for a job here. Your work this summer has been exemplary."

"Thanks. Don't get me wrong, it's been an honor working here—working for you—but I'd like to move into research. I was just wondering why you gave it up."

"I didn't quit research entirely. Naef has been very accommodating." He nodded toward the twenty-foot window that divided the lab. "The Archive wouldn't exist without their support."

"But …" Garett made an apologetic gesture with upturned hands. "Excuse me for saying so, that's because it's you. You were already famous. Your innovations made it possible to mass produce crystals. You could have gone to any university in the world and continued your research."

Research. Everything came together on that single word.

To create a wormhole, a pair of crystals had to be identical, down to the number and arrangement of individual atoms. Years before learning how to mass produce them, Holden had tried entangling multiple pairs to create a single portal with many inputs and one output. But the resultant wormholes were unstable and collapsed immediately, so he dropped that study soon after publishing.

Now, he faced an undeniable reality—something had come *out* of this wormhole without having first gone *into* it.

That explained the instability too. The failure didn't

happen here. No one on his staff was involved. It could have started with any crystal in that production lot. Someone had succeeded where he had failed—a boon for science.

But have they discovered my other research along the way?

"I'm sorry," Garett said after the extended silence, "that was too personal."

"No, not at all. You've brought up a very good point. I could have continued at the university but …" He recalled why he'd gone along with certain projects when he was Garett's age. "But one must consider the motives of whoever is funding the research. There was a great deal of pressure on me to focus on specific technologies. Naef gave me the freedom to pursue my own goals."

"If you could do it all over again, would you do anything different?"

Holden glanced at the silver photo frame on his desk. "I would spend more time with my family."

Garett followed his gaze. "They're going to Cirrus, aren't they?"

The digital frame was cycling through newly received photos. Holden hadn't seen the latest set: a dozen snapshots of his son, Nathan, his step-daughter, Grace, and their son, Ethan, as they experimented with simulators at the New Mexico spaceport.

"They're leaving today, as a matter of fact." He ejected the testing board from the microscope and dropped it into its clear case. "Whatever you decide, make sure your family comes first. I've worked far too many late nights apart from mine. Weekends too."

"I think I understand." Garett reached for the transparent container. "Can I put that away for you?"

Holden drew the case back. "No, thank you. I'll take care of it."

He waited until Garett walked away, then pressed his thumb to the corner of the frame to view the private folder. A single new image had been uploaded: another family, on another world. The boy, Jack, was Ethan's age and bore a strong resemblance to his father, Victor. His mother, Emily, like Nathan, resembled Holden's wife, an Okanogan woman who'd passed away years before her grandchildren were born.

Holden gazed wistfully at the scene for a full minute before releasing the frame. Then he selected a calibration board from a shelf under the microscope. He swapped it with the damaged one in the case, then dropped the whole assembly into the recycling bin, to ensure no one investigated further. Eventually, one of his assistants would install a new set of crystals and re-use the device.

He returned to his desk and entered the damaged board's identity code into the search engine, then slipped it into a drawer. The computer produced a page of details: the missing crystals predated mass-production and had been grown for fuel delivery.

Naef Dynamics gave him the opportunity to keep up with current developments in his field. He knew where the research was happening and who the major players were. Also, the existence of his Archive wasn't widely known. That gave him a slight advantage over whoever had destroyed the crystals—they wouldn't know that he knew. That disparity wouldn't last long though. He'd have only a short time to find answers.

The computer also displayed the name of the company that had ordered the crystals: OTH (Over the Horizon) Fuels.

Holden had a starting point.

Chapter 5

Saturday – Three Days to Newton

Jack ran his fingers across the length of the metal blade, trying to decide if the rough spot was a scratch or just dirt.

His worksite that Saturday afternoon was on the shady south slope of a pine-covered hill sixty miles west of Fairview and five miles from the nearest road. His workbench was a folding platform mounted to the truck's side, and the drone he was repairing had crashed several days ago after the wind blew it into the trees.

He glanced at the cracked fuselage. *More like someone flew it directly into a tree at high speed.* The damage to the plastic shell was minor, but two of the aircraft's rotors had snapped. He'd already replaced those and was examining a third when his text alert sounded.

<Hey, watch this.> A message from Chase appeared next to his Surfer Dude avatar.

This is not going to end well, Jack thought as he joined the chat room.

Chase's video—recorded from a helmet-mounted camera—began with him sitting on his bike at the top of a steep mound of compacted earth.

He pushed off. The ground rushed up at the camera. There was a jolt as he hit the base of the next ramp, a glimpse of blue sky above, and then he was airborne. He kept the view centered on his landing zone as he performed a tailwhip. It looked like it would be clean, but he landed short, digging his front wheel into the loose soil at the top of the pile. He went down with a sound somewhere between a cough and bark.

The motion blurred as he tumbled in the dirt. When he finally stopped, several pairs of feet ran up to the camera, now lying sideways at ground level. Someone asked, "You okay?" Chase's strained voice replied, "I'm good." The video ended.

<Ouch.> A string of text appeared. *<Did you break anything?>* This was a response from Sarah. Her avatar winced.

<Nah, just bent a few spokes.>
<I meant bones, actually.>
<Oh, yeah. My arm. I totally broke that.>

<Are you serious?> This line was from Jada. She changed her avatar regularly, and today it was a seated golden buddha. Its stunned expression was way out of character.

Chase's image appeared, his forearm and wrist in a blue cast. As always, he wore a goofy smile. He also had a wide scrape on his chin, which improved the appearance of the wispy goatee he was trying to grow. *<It's okay, I can still ride.>*

Jada's avatar rolled its eyes. An additional Face Palm emoji slid past.

Jack frowned and double-checked his phone's settings. He normally set its emotion detector to block reactions his friends might be offended by, but Jada believed a text conversation should be unfiltered. He'd received *eye-roll* and *not-amused* emojis from her many times.

He pressed and held Chase's avatar—the gesture to send a private message. "You don't want Jada upset at you again." His words appeared on his screen as he spoke. "She might not help you with your assignments if your arm hasn't healed." A yellow triangle with an exclamation mark popped up in the suggestion box. Jack nodded his approval; the Caution emoji joined the text.

<It's okay. You know she can't resist me.> A Sunglasses emoji glided into place. Not surprisingly, Chase had replied publicly and his words went to everyone in the group.

<Resist you?> Jada's unfiltered emoji showed her irritation. *<What's that supposed to mean, Jack?>*

Chase's avatar laughed silently. *<You're busted.>*

"Thanks. *Now* you remember to send a private message." He lifted his finger and spoke. "I only told Chase he'd better be nice to you. He's always asking for your help anyway, and he might need more of it in September."

His diplomacy seemed to have calmed Jada; her next emoji was neutral. Jack thought the discussion would get back on track until she added the taunt: *<He's not getting my help at all if they split up our classes.>*

Jack had never met Jada in person either. She and Sarah lived five hundred miles away in Caerton—the largest city in the sector—while he and Chase were the only two students in their grade in Fairview. They attended class through a video connection, but the school board was considering merging all small-town schools into a separate division.

<*I don't really have to worry about that,*> Chase replied, <*considering the world's gonna end soon.*>

A flurry of new emoji followed this remark: Mad Scientists, aliens, mushroom clouds, and of course, Sir Isaac Newton.

End-of-the-world prophecies had been around for thousands of years. The current one was credited to Newton, one of history's most famous scientists. Virtually everyone knew of the prophecy, although the details changed depending on who you heard it from. Chase had already given several versions of the tale. The one thing everyone knew was that, decades ago, a group of people known as *Travellers*—who could supposedly *remember* the future, move objects with their minds, and control other peoples' thoughts—unanimously agreed the world would end this month.

Jada's avatar closed its eyes and shook its head.

<*What?*> Chase sent. <*The corporations know all about it. That's why more people have come to Cirrus in the last few months than in the past decade. They want to get as much money off Earth as they can before the end. They've even risking sending people through portals again.*>

<*What good is money if the world ends?*> Jada asked.

<*I said they know about it. I didn't say they were smart.*>

<*People are coming now because Cirrus is stable,*> Sarah texted. <*We're not just growing crops for Earth anymore. This was all started decades ago.*>

<*No, they're going to cut Cirrus off and pretend it was destroyed. Then they're—*>

Jack missed the rest of Chase's story because his phone buzzed to indicate a private text from Sarah: <*Does he really believe those stories?*>

"No. He just likes to see what reaction they get. I normally let him carry on. He always has an answer—a ridiculous one—for any argument."

<He sent me and Jada a link to a website on Earth that claims Cirrus isn't real.>

"Yeah, I've heard that one before. It's because we orbit on opposite sides of the Sun and none of us will ever see the other through a telescope."

<Last month, he said the corporations are reading and controlling people's minds through their phones.>

"Well, he doesn't seem concerned about that now." Chase's phone was peppering his part of the ongoing conversation with additional emojis, emphasizing key parts of his theory. "But that's the thing about conspiracy theories; there's always a bit of truth. Our phone's sensors are useful for emojis and avatars, but true mind-reading is a long way off."

Chase finished his rant and signed off, saying he had to run errands for his mother. Jack also logged off, leaving the girls to chat with each other; he wanted to focus on the repair. This drone was large and expensive, designed to carry heavy loads. At high speed, a deep enough scratch might turn into a crack and result in the loss of the aircraft—something he didn't want to be responsible for.

He scrubbed harder with his thumb at the rough spot. The metal warmed under the friction and the defect faded away.

Got it, he thought, relieved. He didn't have a third blade of the right size and was worried he'd have to take the drone back to the shop to print a replacement. At just two weeks into his plan for proving his ability to handle any repair, he couldn't risk a setback.

He gripped the ends of the propeller and flexed it slowly, watching how light reflected off its curves, feeling the way it resisted. His parents owned a machine for testing rotors, but he'd discovered that his intuitive sense for mechanics extended to detecting hairline cracks as well. They used to double-check his work until they found the device always agreed with Jack and that he did it much faster.

He reassembled the machine and launched it, paying attention to the noise it made as it climbed and then sped south on its programmed course. It was still in sight when his phone rang. Sarah was calling him direct.

Jack activated his camera. "Hi. I thought you'd be back at work by now."

"I've got a few minutes left on my break. I just remembered you're going to meet your cousin tomorrow. How are you feeling about th—? Where are you? I hear birds."

"A couple of hours west of Fairview. A forestry drone crashed on the side of a hill. I convinced Dad to let me ride out and fix it."

"Lucky you. I wish I could get out of the city sometimes."

"I'll walk up top to give you a better view." He started climbing through the damp grass with the phone's camera pointed ahead. A cool breeze ruffled his hair. "You'd like it here. It's peaceful. Isolated."

"I think isolation is more your thing."

He was quiet for several steps. "Yeah. Maybe."

"Sorry, I didn't mean your phobia. Just that *I* wouldn't be comfortable so far from civilization."

"It's okay. I know what you meant."

"But you're coping better, aren't you?"

"I am. It's … I don't know." His thoughts were still on whether working in a larger city was the right move. He stopped and swiped the screen to select the front camera. "Do you ever feel like Caerton is too big?"

"Maybe. But it's … No, I want to study ecology. The university here is the only place I can do that, and Caerton will always be where the major decisions are made."

Jack nodded and continued climbing. He reached the top of the rise and entered a clearing with a view through the sparse trees.

He swapped cameras again and panned across miles of flat grassland. "What do you think?"

Sarah grinned as she studied the image. "I'm jealous. I'd show you my workplace, but right now it's just a blank wall. What's that?"

Jack had been scanning the landscape when a bright flash

flooded the screen. "I see it too." He steadied the phone for a better shot of a mile-wide round basin formed by a scattering of mounds in the shape of a horseshoe. Reflected sunlight shone from a point at the bottom of the hill.

"Another crashed drone?" Sarah asked as he zoomed in on the nearest of several clearings.

"Can't tell. Hold on, I'll check the database." He lowered the phone and swiped through the records. "Nothing. It's either new or very old."

"Isn't it strange to find two crashes so close together?"

"Not really. There are tens of thousands of drones in this sector. But now that I've spotted it, I can't just leave garbage lying in the woods." He examined the hillsides. "I'm gonna walk down. It'll be quicker than going back for the truck. How's your job going?"

"Really well. I'm working with Penny this week. She's got a new project starting at the aviary and I get to help." As Jack made his way down the hill, Sarah described the job in detail and what her role would be. "I'll be doing field work with her on the weekends for the next year."

"You earn university credits for that, right?"

She shrugged. "Yeah, but I'm taking Advanced Placement courses this semester, so it won't make much difference."

"Whoa," Jack said when he reached the base of the hill.

"What's wrong?"

"This." He panned the camera around the football field-sized clearing.

Four gray crates, eight feet long, were stacked in two piles under the trees at the foot of the hill. A larger white container, mostly shattered, lay at the end of a shallow furrow a short distance away. Beyond that, connected to the damaged crate by a thick cable, was a machine unlike any he'd had seen before.

"What *is* that?" Sarah asked.

"It's a drone. But it's *huge*."

Jack approached cautiously. Tipped over on its side, the aircraft was taller than him, with a full rotor-span of over twelve feet. It was completely black, without any markings. All four rotors were mounted on stubby wings that could rotate to provide additional lift at high speed.

"It looks military." A cluster of pods on each side reminded him of weapons systems he'd seen in photos.

"You should get out of there."

He moved closer, examining the rotors. "Yeah, in a minute." He spotted a chip on the leading edge of a blade over his head. "I know this one."

"You've seen it before?"

"No, but I heard it." The damage wouldn't be enough to bring the aircraft down, but it would cause a vibration—a vibration that would interfere with sensors. "It flew into Fairview a few days ago. I think it landed at Hank's shop."

"Who's Hank?"

"He's the one I always call 'Mister Big'. He imports almost all the machine parts that come from Earth into Fairview. But some people say he's a smuggler. He lied about this drone."

"What's in the box?"

Jack walked over to the smashed crate. "Tools. Construction equipment." He pointed the camera into the jumble for Sarah.

"I don't see any writing. What are they building?"

"Don't know. But something's missing. All of this is in the shadow of the trees. There's nothing here that would have caused the reflection we saw."

He stepped back and surveyed the scene. The parts strewn across the meadow told a clear story. Without a ground-based landing system to guide it, the damaged drone had set its cargo down while still moving sideways. That sudden stop had tipped the heavy crate over and yanked the drone, tilting it into the trees. The aircraft had taken significant damage. The owner would have to replace two body panels, the flapping hinge, the two rotors that hit the ground, plus the chipped one that had caused the crash. But the scattered bits were black and non-reflective. Jack moved farther into the clearing and spotted a shiny metal sphere in a shallow pit. He crouched beside it, pointing the camera.

"It looks like a chrome bowling ball," Sarah said.

Jack clipped his phone to his belt and tried to pick up the sphere. "It's heavy. It must be solid metal."

"What are you doing? Leave it there."

"I'll put it back. I just want to know what it is."

He hefted it over to the nearest stack of crates. Each box was roughly three feet deep but only two feet tall, making a convenient table to set the sphere on. Like the drone, it had no markings. The only features on its smooth surface were a shallow groove that went all the way around the middle, and an H-shaped slot.

"It looks as if it comes apart. This is some sort of keyhole." He unclipped his phone and positioned it over the slot for a close-up photo. "There's a red light flashing inside."

"You really should put it back."

"I will." Jack turned his attention to the second stack of crates. "I just want to know what they're building out here." Each container had a single latch holding the lid in place. He shuffled over, unhooked the cover, and aimed his camera at the handle. "Don't you want to see?"

"Yes, all right. But then you should—"

He flipped up the lid with an exaggerated "Ta-daaah."

"Jack, *get out of there*."

He froze. His phone's flashlight had switched on as soon as he opened the sheltered crate, revealing a neatly stacked pile of assault rifles.

"This isn't right." Jack prodded one of the weapons to see if it was real. "There's not supposed to be guns on Cirr—" He froze again when branches broke. People laughed in the distance. "Someone's coming."

Chapter 6

Sarah had been in a hallway when Jack opened the crate. Despite the video's poor quality, she'd seen enough. She ducked into an empty office where she could speak in an urgent whisper. "Jack, you have to go."

"I'm going, I'm going."

The scene on her phone blurred as he dropped the crate's cover and ran, heading for the hill.

"The sphere," she half-shouted. "They'll know—"

Jack cursed and dashed back to the first container. He shoved the metal ball and ran away again. The sphere rolled to the front of the lid, wobbled on the raised edge, then turned and drifted to the rear of the crate. It tumbled off, landing in tall weeds, hidden from view.

"It fell—" she started to warn him, but he'd apparently seen the same thing. He stopped running. Sarah heard voices in the background. "No, keep going. I hear them too."

The image jerked as he moved into the denser woods covering the hill. Fading voices and distant laughter accompanied the shaky video while he climbed. Sarah didn't speak again until flashes of brightly lit grass marked the thinner forest at the summit.

"Are they following you?"

He didn't answer. She waited as he rushed down to the truck, gathered his tools, tossed them into the cargo box, then drove away. The scene bounced wildly as the vehicle trundled through the forest. Finally, after a few more minutes, he started laughing.

"It isn't funny." Her fear vanished as he kept laughing. "Seriously. They had guns."

"It's not that." Jack set his phone on the dashboard so she could see his face. It didn't make her feel better that he was still grinning. "I was worried my parents wouldn't let me take the truck if I couldn't fix the drone outside the workshop. I was just imagining their reaction if I told them what really happened."

"So, what are you going to tell them?"

He seemed perplexed. "Nothing."

"Who are you going to tell?"

"No one. I've learned my lesson; I'll stay away from anything like that in the future."

"But you said yourself—there aren't supposed to be guns on Cirrus."

"Don't tell anyone, okay? It'll get back to my parents and they won't let me work out of town. Then I can't prove I can run a business on my own. It's not a big deal. There's probably a good reason for them being out there."

Sarah wasn't about to acknowledge that Jack was right, but knew he was normally very cautious. He wouldn't have gone to the site if he hadn't expected a crash to clean up. She reluctantly agreed not to tell.

"I have to go now," she said as footsteps approached the office door. "Jada's coming in to fill her volunteer hours for graduation. Call me when you get to Fairview."

- - - - -

Sarah reached the parking lot just as Jada was securing her bike in the rack with dozens of others.

At five-foot-two, Jada might go unnoticed in a crowd except for the dozen brightly colored tattoos that graced her arms and calves. She also had three piercings in each ear and a shiny gold stud on the side of her nose. Her bike, with its custom snakeskin paint job, was another expression of her individuality.

"Ça va?" Jada asked. In Caerton—a city as multicultural as New York or Toronto—most people spoke a little of several languages besides English. Jada was fluent in her parents' native tongues: Hindi and French. She'd also taught Sarah how to swear in both. "What are we doing this afternoon?"

Sarah desperately wanted to tell Jada what Jack had found. "I'm supposed to show you how to clean the owl cages, but I have to do something first." She would keep her promise not to report Jack's discovery, but that didn't mean she couldn't investigate on her own.

She led Jada into the conservation building, to a room

where half a dozen workstations faced an array of large screens on three walls—like a war room. A glass display cabinet in the center of the windowless room held a collection of winged, wheeled, and crawling drones ranging in size from a beetle to a hawk. This department was a stop on the visitor tour, and the machines were examples of the aviary's survey equipment.

"Take a seat," she said, then sat beside Jada at a workstation.

Jada spun in her chair, gazing at the diverse scenes on the wall-mounted displays. "What's all this?" The images were recorded by drones—aerial views, videos captured from an inch above the ground, or crawling through grass, or floating on a pond.

"We program our surveys here." Sarah switched the larger central display to a map of the sector. She pressed a button, creating a blizzard of yellow dots that obliterated the map. The only uncovered areas were the rim walls and parts of the Wayward Sea, which filled the center of the fourteen-hundred-mile-wide rectangle. "Whoops. That's not right."

"Are you sure you know what you're doing?"

"Penny only showed me how to do this last week. I was trying to display all the drones, but there are too many. I have to pick a smaller area."

Jada was watching an adjacent monitor on which tall grass lurched in sporadic waves. "The videos are really jerky."

"No one watches them. They only record one frame per second unless they're repositioning." As she said this, a butterfly entered the scene, alighting on a nearby twig. The computer displayed genus and species information in a pop-up box above the insect. "See. The AI's accuracy rate is almost a hundred percent."

"Can you view any drone in the sector?" Jada asked as Sarah wrestled with the controls.

"If I knew the drone's ID, I could enter it directly. Otherwise I have to do this." She used the mouse to draw a rectangle on the screen. That zone—with only a few hundred dots—swelled to fit the entire display. She clicked a yellow drone icon. The view from its camera popped up on an adjacent screen. "Why?"

"We could send one to buzz Chase."

Sarah laughed. "We don't actually fly them in real-time. We set points on the map and let the AI fly or crawl them to that spot."

"Can't you make them follow a target?"

"Yes." She knew Jada was still talking about Chase. "But we're not doing that, either."

"Fine." Jada slumped in her chair. "What are you doing?"

"I'm following … I have to survey an area west of Fairview." She cleared the drone layer to start over with a fresh map. "It should only take a few minutes."

Jack had texted last night to say he was safely home, just over two hours after he left the site. *That could be fifty or a hundred miles.* He'd said *west*, but probably didn't mean *due* west. Still, that was a large area to search. However, he'd shared the view from the point of the tallest hill and the horseshoe-shape stood out in her memory.

She drew a rectangle covering the entire area between Fairview and the sea. Penny had shown her how to access a topographical map, and she remembered the hilltop as being at least four hundred feet above the surrounding plain. That narrowed the search zone considerably. The land west of Fairview was generally flat, and the Spine had not been visible from his viewpoint. That eliminated the few clusters of hills in the map's northern half. She zoomed in on a likely grouping to the southwest and found the right spot on the first try.

The horseshoe outline was distinctive on the terrain map, but less so when she selected an aerial view. She was certain that Jack had approached from the south slope, so that gave her an even better idea of where the site was. She zoomed in on the basin, set the asset filter to flying drones only, then switched to the survey view to see how many were in the area.

Not a single one.

She zoomed out. There were roughly two dozen drone icons scattered across the miles of hills around the basin, but nothing in the mile-wide depression.

Jada was watching, so Sarah explained what she was doing as she worked.

"This is the area I want to search … I mean, survey. There are no flying drones there now, so I'm going to pick one that's nearby." She clicked an icon on the side of the hill where Jack had parked. The screen showed its identification number. "All I have to do is drag it to a new position."

She released the icon in a band of trees that separated two of the basin's clearings. It jumped back to its starting position. A warning popped up on her screen.

Jada read the message aloud. "Invalid selection." The entire basin was outlined in orange.

That's strange. It's as if the area is off-limits. She tried again, this time dropping the icon on the hill outside the orange zone. On a different monitor, the drone lifted off and slalomed through the trees in real time. *Okay, that makes sense.* If someone was building out there, they wouldn't want a survey drone interfering with their work.

A dotted line on the main screen depicted the drone's intended flight path. "That worked," Jada said.

"Yeah. Now I'm going to set waypoints, so it moves around for a different view." She placed markers around the basin.

"How long will it watch for?" The dotted line grew as Sarah added new destinations.

"Two weeks." *Oh, right. That won't work.* "But Penny said I can change that." She continued circling the basin until the computer flashed another warning. "Huh. It will only let me set twenty-six waypoints. I wonder why."

"You said they watch for two weeks. Maybe twenty-six is the schedule for an entire year."

"Maybe. Penny said something about that, but I don't remember what. I'm going to set the end date for tomorrow and see what happens." She entered the date and the computer accepted it without warning. "That should work."

"Now what's it doing?" Jada pointed at the central display. Dozens of dotted lines were converging on the basin.

"Oh, no." Sarah frantically tapped at the controls. "I

remember what Penny said. If I set a date of less than two weeks, the computer divides the job among other drones. I didn't send just one, I sent the entire cluster."

"Is that bad?"

Sarah paused. *Maybe this is a good thing.* She'd have twenty-six different viewpoints. In only a day, she'd know what was happening. She allowed the cluster to continue, studying the screens as the drones approached their targets in real-time. The first hovered near a branch fourteen feet off the ground, then eased itself onto a bare section where it would have a decent view. Within minutes, the remaining drones had settled on branches of their own. Their rotating cameras began transmitting one-frame-per-second updates.

Four of the monitors flanking the central display were cycling through the videos, and one camera was rotating toward a clearing. Sarah didn't know what it would find there, but thought it better that Jada not see. "We should go now."

"Hold on." Jada pointed to a motion-detect alert. "What's that?" A falcon—light-brown with a black-streaked breast—had landed in the same tree as a drone. She read part of the pop-up display out loud. "Falco Tinnunculus. Female. Banded."

"It's a kestrel. They're common in that area. But we both have other jobs to do."

"Hold on, there's another one." A second alert was flashing.

Jada had no intention of leaving before seeing the next event, so Sarah switched the main display to the alerting drone and blanked the others.

There was no bird in that shot, but the intermittent images were jumpy, as if the tree was shaking. Then a dark blur filled the screen. The next four images were of spinning ground and tree trunk, with the silhouette of a man swinging a thick branch. Two more images of cloudy sky followed before the man stepped into view again. Sarah saw him clearly before his boot blocked the camera.

The signal died.

After a moment of stunned silence, Jada said, "Uh, I'm

gonna go with: Homo Sapiens. Male. Angry. Was he wearing a uniform?"

"Yes." Sarah recognized the uniform as the same one her mother wore. "That was a CorpSec officer."

Chapter 7

Sunday – Two Days to Newton

As a theorist, Simon rarely worked alongside the two specialists who built the equipment he designed. But this project was different. He'd been there at every step, closely monitoring the construction of each new component.

"This is just a power-up test," he reminded the technicians as they finished calibrating the device. "To confirm that the numbers match with theory on a larger scale." He gave them two thumbs-up.

Simon was the sort of man who spoke with his hands, qualifying every sentence with a matching gesture. At thirty years old, he was tending toward pudgy, but could fill twice as much space as others with his flailing arms. He was unaware that his assistants had repainted the yellow caution lines around the robotic workstations to add a few more inches of clearance.

"We won't go over ninety percent." He chopped the air at eye-level. "I'm not expecting visible effects and certainly no damage."

One of the techs arched an eyebrow.

Simon noticed the subtle expression. "This isn't like last time. That fire was intentional. It was … it was just a bit bigger than I expected. And it cut months off the development schedule."

The second tech lowered her gaze to focus on the equipment.

Simon shook his head and returned to his own work. The two were experts in their fields but didn't fully understand the theory behind the resonator. There were only a handful of people in the entire world who did. The fuel module experiment had been necessary—simulations couldn't provide all the data—and it validated years of work in only a few minutes.

"Look. All of this …" He swept his arm past the scattered

equipment. "Is temporary. No one got hurt—" The first tech flinched as Simon's bare fingers narrowly missed an exposed twelve-hundred-amp coupling. "And there was no real damage. And Pieter's promised to make things right. What we're doing now will revolutionize communications."

After the fires, his biggest concern was that Pieter would stop the project entirely. He'd been surprised, and relieved, when Pieter moved his team into luxury apartments at the Everett campus. Not only could he focus on his work, but there would be no more in-person meetings in Seattle. Simon viewed his boss as friendly, brilliant, and compelling—but also terrifying.

Which one of us suggested the experiment with the fuel pumps? He remembered explaining the concept, but had meant to ask for funds to construct another testing rig. The live experiment was simpler and quicker, but also bold and risky—*so unlike me*—and Pieter had jumped on it, commending him and promising to take care of things. Simon had left that meeting unsure whose idea they'd agreed on.

And that wasn't the only time he'd experienced strangeness around Pieter, whose persuasiveness was legendary. He swore he'd once seen a pen leap into Pieter's hand from the surface of his desk, but then convinced himself he'd imagined it under the stress of the testing schedule.

Today's test was much larger than the earlier one— millions of crystals. He'd chosen a grouping of portals that were in use on both Earth and Cirrus, a set where the exact number wasn't important. He double-checked his settings as a high-pitched vibration filled the air. "Ready?"

Both technicians nodded.

Simon placed his hand over the keyboard. "We'll start at fifty percent." He took a deep breath but couldn't prevent a smile from forming as he pressed the key. In his mind, he was making history.

The lights flickered.

His smile vanished. "Uh oh."

Pieter would not be happy.

Chapter 8

As the bus approached Port Isaac, Jack couldn't decide whether he was more nervous about meeting his cousin or going into the city—it had changed so much since his visit a year before. Then, with fewer than ten thousand residents, it hadn't been too different from his hometown. Now, with soaring towers that housed half a million recent immigrants, it resembled a brightly colored set of child's building blocks at the foot of an irregular staircase.

Like all major cities on the space station, Port Isaac's corporate owners had built it near one of the ninety-six spaceports. But the Wayward Sea met the rim mountains in a way that created both a natural harbor and a backdrop that was stunning even for Cirrus. Jack leaned against the window, craning his neck. A fresh layer of snow frosted the trees crowding the lip of the half-mile vertical wall that loomed over the city.

<Call me.> Sarah's message appeared on his phone as the bus descended a ramp to the underground mass transit corridor.

Being a Sunday, the bus Jack and his family were riding was only half full. He was the youngest person onboard by two decades and had taken the last row at the back for himself. Most of the adults were on the upper viewing level, leaving him enough space to converse freely without being overheard.

"Hi. What's up?" He could see blue sky behind her head. "Aren't you working today?"

"I needed a break."

He didn't need an emotion detector to know Sarah was upset—she wouldn't normally take a walk in the middle of her shift. And it wasn't hard to guess what was bothering her.

She lowered her voice. "I can't stop thinking about what you found yesterday. You really should tell someone. We can do it anonymously."

Jack glanced at the stairs to the viewing deck. "Then

everyone will know about it and my parents won't let me out of town. Let's wait. It won't be as big of a deal once school starts. There are only a few weeks left in the break and I've got to convince them to loan me the money. We'll send a tip to the police in September."

"Fine," Sarah said, although she sounded anything but.

"Uh oh. We're pulling into the station. I should get ready."

"Just relax. It won't be that bad. I'll call you later."

Jack steadied his nerves as the bus parked. The platform was relatively quiet, but he expected worse to come. He waited until the other passengers disembarked, then followed his parents to the escalator. Hundreds of voices echoed from the glossy tiles covering the sloped passage, increasing in volume as they neared the ground level.

Here it comes.

There were so many people, so many voices. The forty-foot ceiling and soaring arches did nothing to lessen the confinement he felt as he threaded through the shifting crowds, a step behind his parents. He struggled to ignore the noise and focus on his goal: the bright rectangles of sunlight that marked the exit.

A dense knot of pedestrians crossed in front of his family, forcing them to wait. Most walkers were on their phones, paying little attention to their surroundings, but it felt to Jack like they were speaking directly to him or talking about him. All their anger, suspicion, expectations, and laughter were directed at him. He became lightheaded, felt a tightness in his throat—a full-blown panic attack was only moments away. He darted around his father and sprinted for the glass doors.

Another blockade of people approached the entrance from the outside bus stop. He was going to be caught in the middle of the group. He needed an escape. *Let me out.*

The lights flickered.

And then, a tiny miracle. As if by magic, the glass panel he was rushing toward swung open, letting him hurtle through and dodge the crowd without slowing.

Directly across from the station, a park offered sanctuary. He dashed across the street, scrambled up a short knoll, and flopped onto the cold grass under a maple tree.

I can beat this. He took several deep, calming breaths. *I just need more time.*

Victor and Emily spotted him as they exited the building. They ambled toward him at a leisurely pace, then sat on a bench next to the sidewalk. He appreciated that they no longer fussed over him, but left him to unwind on his own.

Demophobia. Jack tumbled the word in his thoughts. He'd been given a diagnosis but no cure. *Why can't I be as comfortable around people as machines?* That was easy; electrical and mechanical devices were orderly and predictable—they just seemed to cooperate with him. Even random events like the power surge that had triggered the exit door's proximity sensor always worked in his favor. In contrast, people were noisy and impulsive.

He turned his head and touched his chin to his shoulder, trying to loosen neck muscles already cramping from the tension. This was the first step in the meditation exercise his therapist had taught him. The practice had yet to prevent an anxiety attack, but it helped him recover more quickly.

Ethan's train would arrive within the hour. Jack closed his eyes and sought to clear his mind of crowds, business plans, and assault rifles hidden in the forest.

- - - - -

Jada tossed her mop and pail into the cupboard. "I am so sick of cleaning bird cages."

"That's what I did my first summer," Sarah said. "Now I get more interesting jobs every year."

"I'll be working in my parent's restaurant next summer. And probably for the rest of my life."

"You could apply for a job here."

"Hey, I'm not complaining; I enjoy working there. Eventually, I'll take over the place and set my own hours. What will you be doing? Still counting dead birds?"

"That's not quite what I do. C'mon, I'll show you. There are tour groups on the weekends, but we've got time before they pass through my section."

She led Jada into a room on the conservation building's

first floor. Two large cages, connected by a smaller enclosure in the middle, filled one side of the room. Hundreds of colorful birds fluttered inside each cage.

"This is where we band the birds. It's done robotically but someone has to supervise, to make sure they aren't injured." She pointed to a complicated arrangement of spindly robotic arms in the smaller compartment. "They're moved into the second cage after the leg bands are attached. You'll get to see it in action if you wait for the tour." She crossed the room and touched a button on the pedestal-mounted survey console. "And this is where I check the mortality data."

"Which means …?"

"Just watch."

A waist-high sloped conveyor belt—like a smaller version of an airport baggage carousel—began rolling across the recessed wall behind a large monitor. From an opening on the right, a series of rectangular boards approached, carried by the conveyor, until the first one stopped behind the console. A wall-mounted paddle above the belt flipped down, covering the board. Then the monitor lit up with a grid of thousands of red dots.

"What do the red lights mean?" Jada asked.

"Leg bands are basically antennas attached to wormholes. This machine listens for GPS signals through portals on these index boards. If the bird is moving, its location is triangulated and the light turns green."

The display changed as she said this. There were now only hundreds of red pixels. After another ten-second listening cycle, there were fewer than ten. The paddle flipped up after the fourth round and a robotic arm flitted over the board.

Jada leaned over for a closer look. "Now what's happening?" The crystals themselves were smaller than a grain of sand, but a grid of indentations etched into the board corresponded with the dots on the monitor.

"The computer replaces crystals for birds it knows are dead. If it's not sure, it flags the data for me to review."

"So, your job *is* counting dead birds."

"Not really. The data shows whether a colony is thriving

and identifies breeding grounds. But there are millions of banded birds in this sector and hundreds will die naturally each day. This is just housekeeping."

She tapped the screen to display more detailed information. "Species, age, habitat, release date, and so on, along with a map of the bird's movements. This one hasn't moved for a couple days. It's at coordinates I recognize, so it's probably dead."

"Why does being in that spot mean it's dead?"

"I've noticed there are dozens of places across the sector where the bands accumulate. My guess is they're being dragged there by scavengers."

"See, this is not what I call an interesting job. This is what I call morbid."

Sarah shrugged. "It has to be done." She pressed a button. The robotic arm removed the crystal for that bird, and the conveyor shuffled the next index board into place.

"Aren't you worried about working in front of the machine?"

"What do you mean?"

"I don't know. Radiation, maybe? There's like tens of thousands of wormholes on that board."

"Some people get vertigo around dynamic portals, but these are static. Besides, the water crystal in your phone is a lot bigger, and you put that right against your head." The door from the hallway opened. "Anyway, the tour group is here."

Jada moved to the front to watch the banding demo. Sarah stayed at the back of the now crowded room to avoid being elbowed. From that vantage point, she noticed someone in the group who didn't seem interested in the demonstration.

The tall, well-dressed man was studying the people, not the birds. He stood at the group's edge where he could see everyone at once. As the guide spoke, he glanced more and more frequently at his expensive-looking gold watch. He was so engrossed in checking the time that he didn't notice a uniformed man enter behind him.

Sarah's pulse quickened. *The CorpSec officer who smashed the drone.*

The officer scanned the crowd as he moved into the room. His eyes passed over her without stopping before he took up a position with a view of the tour guide.

What's he doing here?

She slunk back, hiding herself partially behind the console, until she pressed right up against an index board on the conveyor. She searched for Jada, but her friend was hidden by a wall of taller visitors.

This is no coincidence, Sarah thought as she spied from the corner of her eye. *He's here because of the drone.*

The officer had quit scrutinizing the crowd. He seemed bored, waiting for the demonstration to end. The tall man, however, had changed his behavior. He'd stopped observing people entirely and was staring only at his watch. Ten seconds passed. He looked up abruptly.

The lights flickered.

Someone in the group yelped when they went out completely. Many of the caged birds squawked in unison. There were no windows in the room, so it was totally dark for several seconds.

Sarah staggered a half step under a sudden wave of vertigo as the light returned. She was behind the group and no one saw her stumble—except for the well-dressed man.

He was staring directly at her. Their eyes met. She felt—

"Oops, sorry," a woman said after jostling Sarah. "I didn't see you behind me."

"That's all right." Sarah stepped aside and looked for the man, but couldn't find him. The officer had also left the room.

"Sorry about that, folks." The guide waved to get everyone's attention. "I don't know what caused the lights to go out, but follow me and we'll continue the tour outside."

Jada wove her way through the group to rejoin Sarah. Then they both shuffled along with the crowd to the hallway and waited silently until the room cleared.

"That was cool," Jada said. "It's like a giant spider. As soon as a bird landed anywhere, the robot grabbed it and—"

"Did you …" Sarah considered the sense of familiarity

she'd experienced. "Did you feel anything when the lights went out?"

"Like what?"

She glanced through the open door at the index board she'd been leaning against. She'd never hear the end of it from Jada if she admitted feeling something while near the equipment. "Nothing. It's not important." She checked her pockets.

"What's wrong?"

"My phone. It's gone. Somebody stole it."

"Someone from the tour group? Where are you going?"

Sarah was already running to the exit. She shouted over her shoulder, "To get my phone back. I know who took it."

"Shouldn't we call Security?"

"No time." She ran after the group.

Jada caught up with her in the parking lot where another tour group was gathering. "Do you see them?"

Instead of answering, Sarah sprinted around the group and headed for the dense stand of hemlock trees on the far side of the pavement. Jada followed as she ran onto a stone-patterned footpath that snaked along a stream to a grassy clearing. Two paths exited the sheltered glade, but Sarah didn't even consider those. She strode directly to a picnic table that overlooked the water. Something shiny sat on the near corner.

"What is that?" Jada asked as she came up behind her.

Sarah picked it up. "I'm not sure." The object was a blocky, H-shaped piece of metal with a ring—too small for a finger—mounted on one side. Tiny, circular metal pads, set in a plastic substrate, studded the other face. "It seems really familiar."

Jada crossed her arms. "I don't like this. It feels like we're being watched."

A raft of ducks chattered noisily among the tall grasses lining the stream, and other birds sang in the trees. Sunlight filtered through the branches above, but nothing else disturbed the secluded clearing.

"It's okay, he's gone." Sarah pocketed the strange object. "For now."

"How can you be so sure? And how do you know it was a man who stole your phone?"

"I … Do you ever get the feeling you've done the same thing before? Like déjà vu?"

"I think I'd remember chasing a thief. Let's go back and call Security."

The tour guide was talking with the CorpSec officer as Sarah and Jada crossed the parking lot. He recognized the girls and pointed them out.

"That's the guy who stomped on your drone," Jada whispered.

"He was watching the banding demo too. He knows the drone came from here."

"So what? You were just doing your job." Jada gave her a suspicious glance. "Weren't you?"

The officer met them in the middle of the parking lot.

"Can I help you?" Sarah asked.

He raised a clear bag filled with pieces of drone. "Is this one of yours?"

Sarah peered at the bag. She knew what it was, of course, but he'd smashed it so completely that it no longer resembled a drone. "I'm sorry, I don't recognize it. You'll have to ask my supervisor."

"Then I'll need to check your records for yesterday's survey operations."

Jada shouldered ahead of Sarah. "It's Sunday. Come back tomorrow."

He placed his hands on his hips and glowered down at Jada. "I'm not asking."

Jada stepped closer and stared up at him, mimicking his posture and forcing him to bend his neck farther. "Neither am I."

The officer—who towered over Jada—held his position for a few seconds longer before stepping back. "Fine," he said with a grin. Not a pleasant one. "I'll see *you* in the morning."

"Not if I—" Jada began, but Sarah jerked her arm and spun her away.

"I am *so* fired," she said as they hurried indoors.

"Don't worry. You're not the one he's gonna complain about. And I don't really work here, remember? I only need ten more hours for my graduation quota. I can get those anywhere. And you've got bigger things to worry about. You need to report your phone as stolen before someone uses it."

Jada was right, she had bigger concerns. But they weren't just for the phone or what Penny might say tomorrow morning. If CorpSec was looking for her, they might also be searching for Jack.

Chapter 9

Ethan Marke had only a few moments to enjoy the view before his walking companions joined him. He leaned against the brushed aluminum atop the gallery railing, at the front of the cabin where the image on the main screen was close to what he would see if it were a window instead.

Cirrus filled the entire screen—an awe-inspiring sight. He could see a patchwork of forests, deserts, seas, islands, and grasslands through its transparent roof. Unlike smaller stations whose centrifugal force pinned everything to the inner surface, the world-sized ring rotated just once per day and used gravity generators to realign the natural force from its substantial mass. Cirrus' inner surface was an ice-covered ocean and its habitable zone wrapped around its outward-face. The same stars crossed the night skies of both Earth and Cirrus, six months apart.

A bright dot at the center of the ring—a single pixel on the sixteen-foot-wide screen—flared and drifted to one side.

Another ship, he realized. *And another thousand passengers.* Soon, his own identical vessel would also change course and head for one of ninety-six spaceports.

"Hi, Ethan," Tyler and Maria said in unison.

"Hey, guys." Ethan stepped away from the viewing gallery and onto the walking track. For reasons he couldn't guess, the two kids had taken to following him around since the first day.

"Could you see the Spine yet?" Tyler asked.

"Just. Go back and have a look."

If Tyler heard, he chose not to return to the gallery. "Did you know it goes all the way around Cirrus? Even under the seas? The islands are really mountain peaks."

Ethan glanced at a smaller viewscreen set into the wall above the spongy track. A dark, sinuous line—Cirrus' most famous natural-*ish* feature—split the world in two. The world-spanning mountain range was one of the few geographic features he knew of. Probably because it had resulted from a mistake on a colossal scale.

Even though they were much younger than him, he didn't really mind Tyler and Maria tagging along. He'd learned a lot from them over the past week—they both knew more about Cirrus than he did. Something else he learned early into the trip was that space travel was mind-numbingly boring. He was glad for the diversion they provided.

"Do you want to play a game?" Maria asked.

"Sure." Ethan touched his fingers to his temples. "*Psychic Tag. You're it.*"

Tyler laughed but Maria pouted—she already knew the point of that game was to play nothing at all.

"Where are you going to live?" Tyler asked.

"Nowhere. I'm buying a motorcycle and driving around the entire station before I go back to Earth."

"Whoa." His eyes widened. "Really?"

"Sure, why not?" Ethan wondered if he'd been as gullible at that age. He knew it was unlikely he'd ever return to Earth. Even those who worked as cabin crew on the liners and freighters wouldn't return, after having spent months training for a job they would do just once.

"That's more than seventeen thousand miles," Tyler said. "How long's that gonna take?"

"A few months, I guess."

Ethan decided he wouldn't be surprised if Tyler replied with exactly how many miles he'd have to travel each day, and what his best route was—this kid had all the numbers. He'd already informed Ethan that the ring had a surface area of fourteen million square miles. With only a third of that being water, and all of it being equatorial, Cirrus boasted half as much arable land as Earth. Ethan reasoned that his younger companion had been expecting to relocate to Cirrus for most of his life and studied every aspect of it.

This world would also be Ethan's new home, although not one of his own choosing. A transparent wall separated the walking track from the rest of the cabin. They were just passing his empty seat in the section reserved for *unaccompanied minors*.

"I'm going to be living in Port Isaac," Tyler said.

Ethan decided not to share that this would be his new home too.

"I'm moving to Camp 17," Maria said, "but I'm not allowed to talk about it. My mom is a genetist … geneterist … she makes dragons." Only then did she seem to remember this was something she wasn't supposed to mention. She covered her mouth with her hand.

"I think you guys are playing too many fantasy games."

"They're not real dragons. Dad just calls them that. They're a kind of lizard built to make sure the mice don't take over. Mom says they eat one thing until they're all gone and then they starve to death."

"That's, uh …" He didn't know how to respond. It seemed she was describing a genetically engineered animal. However, considering she was only ten-years-old, he doubted there was much accuracy in her account. Still, there were a lot of strange rumors about Cirrus.

"How will you get over the sector walls on a motorbike?" Tyler asked.

"Gravity is lower at the top, isn't it? You remember how tall they are, don't you?"

"Four miles." Tyler welcomed any opportunity to show off his knowledge of Cirrus, which was great for Ethan because the only thing he knew about the eight-hundred-mile-long mountainous berms was that they divided the ring into twelve sectors and had something to do with weather control. "That's the same as the train tunnels in the rim walls. That means gravity is … one-half-gee." Apparently, he also knew the rate at which Cirrus' artificial gravity decayed.

"There you go. It'll be easier the higher I climb."

"But you get less traction in lower gravity."

"Have you ever ridden a motorbike?"

"No."

"There you go."

"But—"

Ethan felt a change in the apparent gravity, as if he rode a large elevator.

"What's happening?" Maria asked.

Tyler rushed to the gallery railing. "We're changing direction."

Until now, the ship had been flying straight toward the ring's center. Tyler had described the reason for this with the misplaced enthusiasm only an eleven-year-old could. If the ship's thrusters failed, the vessel would sail harmlessly through the ring and off into space—forever.

The overhead speakers instructed everyone to take their seats. Tyler and Maria practically sprinted to theirs. Ethan remained at the viewing platform.

A man in uniform approached—the first officer he'd seen on the entire trip. "Quite the view, isn't it?"

"Yeah, it is. I guess you want me to get to my seat."

The officer placed a firm hand on his shoulder. "We've got time. I'm Captain Howse, by the way."

"Ethan." He extended his hand and Captain Howse shook it.

"Traveling alone, Mr. Marke?"

His stomach knotted. "Uh, yeah."

"It's been a quiet flight. Especially the first two days."

He said nothing. The bullies he'd subdued at the start of the trip had slept through the first two days.

They both focused on the main screen, but Ethan watched the officer from the corner of his eye. Howse was the embodiment of every cruise ship stereotype, right down to his immaculate navy-blue uniform and perfectly trimmed beard. He stood at ease before the railing, watching Cirrus grow larger.

Captain Howse nodded to the screen as an arc of ice and fog swung into view. "This is my favorite part. We always approach from the summer-side, then loop through the ring to dock on the winter side. Do you know why that is?"

"I heard it was in case the engines fail, to prevent the ship from puncturing the roof."

The captain chuckled. "It's a good story, but only partially true. The asteroid defense system would gently push us aside if our flight path ever crossed the roof. This approach is faster—saves time."

"What would happen if an asteroid hit the roof? Isn't it only held up by air pressure?"

"The roof would seal itself, but there would be short-term weather changes." Captain Howse turned to face Ethan. "Every action has a reaction, Mr. Marke."

"Am I in trouble?"

Howse bobbled his head. "That depends."

"On what?"

"If I were returning to Earth, I'd be inviting you to join me. Accessing a person's medical record is a serious breach of privacy."

"You're not going back?"

He hesitated. "Two weeks' shore leave. An *abundance of caution*, they call it. That means I'd have to arrange for detention. I'm the law on this vessel. I make the final decision. Why did you do it?"

"Those guys were being jerks. They would have hurt someone."

"Leaving Earth is a life-changing event, especially for people your age. Not everyone handles it so well. Their behavior was inappropriate but you could have just reported it. Why are *you* coming to Cirrus?"

A lump formed in Ethan's throat. He couldn't dodge the direct question.

"This wasn't supposed to happen for another year—I thought I'd be finished with school. It would have been my choice then, but my parents' jobs got transferred early. We only had a day's notice. We couldn't even get seats on the same ship."

"You had other plans?"

"Not really. But Cirrus is a backwater. It's nothing but farms. A collection of melted asteroids."

"Is it?"

Ethan knew it wasn't true. Cirrus was by far the largest of the space stations, and Port Isaac would soon be indistinguishable from any modern city on Earth. He'd eventually have as many options there as anywhere else. "I didn't get to choose."

"Would you have stayed if you had the choice?"

He'd had been avoiding that question for years. "I don't know."

Captain Howse patted Ethan's shoulder. "Welcome to Cirrus, Mr. Marke." He walked away.

Ethan returned to his seat as the ship completed its loop and rose to the top of the eight-mile-tall rim wall. All eyes were on the nearest video screens, and the view reminded him just how incredible the artificial world was.

From a distance, the transparent roof had seemed as insubstantial as a soap bubble. At its base, it was as thick as the metal wall itself: three hundred feet, but Tyler had explained that it thinned out as it extended over the landscape. Somewhere below was Port Isaac, protected from cold vacuum and harsh radiation by a barrier that was only two feet thick.

The screen dimmed as the ship dropped into a darkened slot in the rim wall. Whether he liked it or not, Ethan would be home in less than an hour.

Chapter 10

Pieter was one point behind when his driver—a large man with close-cropped hair and neck tattoos visible above his black suit jacket—tapped on the squash court's transparent window. He acknowledged the signal with a nod.

Marcus, twenty years his junior and the club champion, was a master of the low, fast serve. Ordinarily, Pieter would have welcomed the challenge and played fair, but the interruption meant Danny was on his way to the office with news.

As soon as the younger man hit the tiny yellow ball, Pieter willed a small amount of downward force against it. Instead of hitting the wall an inch above the service line as intended, the ball struck the line's mid-point.

Pieter caught it and stepped into the left service box. "Bad luck."

Marcus, having apparently committed his first foul in months, frowned and moved toward his own box.

With another subtle push, Pieter's forehand serve drove the ball along the right-side wall where it dipped unnaturally a fraction of a second before Marcus could intercept it.

Marcus ground his teeth as the errant ball rolled to Pieter. "I'm off my game today."

"You still have a chance." Pieter smiled and placed a foot inside the right service box, positioning himself for a backhand serve.

Marcus smirked, expecting an easy volley.

But for the winning point, Pieter let the ball bounce naturally from the wall and arc directly toward the champion. Countless hours of muscle-memory guided Marcus's arm for the return—one that would have connected if the ball hadn't sped up and climbed instead of dropping.

Momentarily unaware he'd missed, Marcus' shoes squeaked loudly on the varnished floor as he pounced on the T, preparing for a rally that would never come. By the time he turned around, Pieter was already leaving.

- - - - -

As he left the club, a gang of freelance reporters approached. A balding man, whose head was already speckled with sweat in the late-morning heat, shouted, "Mr. Reynard."

Angel, Pieter's driver, surged up the last three steps to the sidewalk to intercept him.

Pieter waved dismissively. "Don't bother." He'd encountered the journalist several times. That was the price of finally taking his place on the world stage. "He's harmless."

Nevertheless, Angel placed himself in front of the group and raised an arm to make it clear they would not pass. The reporter who'd shouted, emboldened by his camera-wielding colleagues, stopped inches from Angel's chest and stared up into his face.

"Hey, it's a free country. I want to ask your boss about Newton's Prophecy." He leaned to look around Angel's massive shoulder.

Pieter continued walking to his air-conditioned limousine, eager to both escape the heat and learn what Danny had found. "My views on the subject are well known."

"Haven't you heard? The world ends in two days."

"Superstitious nonsense."

"But—"

He silenced the reporter with a raised hand. "My apologies. Mr. Gilvray, isn't it? I'm quite busy this morning—I'm traveling to Brussels. We could discuss it there if you'd care to join me? We'll be back by lunch." He held a straight face as the reported quailed.

"I … I don't have my passport."

Angel snorted and turned his back on the man to open the door.

Pieter ducked into the car. *They always back down.*

He had no intention of traveling to Europe today, but could safely avoid an interview when the reporter realized he'd have to pass through a portal to get it. A man like Gilvray might stand up to Angel in a public place, but he wouldn't risk his life or sanity for a story.

- - - - -

Seated at his desk, Pieter flipped through Danny's hundred-page printed report, taking in only the headings and the dozens of photos. Danny wasn't his real name, of course. Pieter knew this but didn't care. How Danny unearthed the report's data was something else he didn't care about. "Who are we looking for?"

"Page fifty-seven."

He stopped on the correct page. "Doctor Holden Marke?" He didn't need to ask Danny if he was sure. Danny was exceptional at collecting information. His name did not appear on company records or banking transactions, even though he accounted for a significant portion of Special Projects' budget. He had connections through a broad network of criminal gangs and smugglers. He was a dangerous man, and exceptional at that too.

"We tracked the missing crystals to Naef Dynamics. OTH Fuels sent several pairs there for testing."

"Destructive testing. Why weren't they destroyed?"

"Some were, but Marke kept a set for his personal project—the *Archive*."

Pieter recognized the name, of course. Simon had used one of Holden's theories to create his device. He skipped ahead to the photos of the Archive. A dozen six-foot-tall racks filled the rectangular room. Each supported five shelves of portal testers. "There must be thousands of them."

"Nearly twelve-thousand pairs."

Twelve-thousand. His own collection—a set of virtually every crystal used on Cirrus, plus a carefully chosen selection from Earth—was only a few hundred pairs and had taken years to assemble.

"Get these photos to Simon. Maybe this has something to do with today's test and his *spill-over* problem." On the drive to his office, Pieter had learned about the power fluctuations. "And tell him to have the backup resonator ready for tomorrow's test. I have a new use for it."

"Marke's been collecting for decades. He seems to have his own agenda."

"He'll know about the refinery experiment by now. Where

is he?"

"He's been at his home in Newcastle all week. What do you want done with him?"

"Nothing yet. Keep an eye on him and see what he does about it." He examined a photo of Holden that included his wife, a Native American woman. The caption indicated that she had died more than twenty years ago. "Who's next?"

"Carl Prior."

He compared the photo—at least twenty years out of date—to the one of Holden. "A brother?"

"Half-brother, I think."

"You're not sure?" He gave Danny the piercing glare he reserved for employees when they delivered bad news. Danny didn't flinch.

"There's no solid connection between the two. Their mothers had the same name, but I haven't determined if it was the same woman. Carl has been living in Caerton for almost eighteen years."

Pieter skimmed Carl's profile. There was little of interest other than he had paid the retirement fee for his residence on Cirrus after his university lease expired. That wasn't unusual—many thousands of people had each paid millions for the privilege of staying on Cirrus without being sponsored by a corporation. Their money was always welcome. "Why is he important?"

"He's not. But his daughter might be."

"How so?"

"The story goes that Carl and his partner, Émile, adopted an Armenian orphan and named her Emily. After the girl finished university, Carl took a research position on Cirrus. Émile was to join him the following year, but died before that. Emily, who had some field experience, applied to fill the vacancy as Carl's assistant."

"And you're saying she was accepted."

"The AI passed her."

"So what's the problem?"

Danny reached over and flipped the page to reveal two photos: one labelled 'Emily Prior', and the other 'Nathan

Marke'—Holden's son.

Pieter bolted upright in surprise; the AI had missed something a human inspector wouldn't have. Emily, supposedly Armenian, was clearly of Native American descent, as was Nathan. The chance of this being coincidence was slim. "How did they pull this off?"

"I can't prove it's the same woman. But if it is, perhaps they found a sympathetic ear in the immigration department. Or maybe there was confusion with the names Émile and Emily. Either way, she moved to Cirrus fifteen years ago, married Victor Scatter, and took his last name."

"So, it's Emily *Scatter* we're hunting, and she's really Holden's daughter, not Carl's." He considered the implications of a substitution made decades ago. If Emily Prior never existed, who else on Danny's list might be nothing more than a false data trail? "We need to know more. Where are the Scatters now?"

"Fairview."

"We already have an anti-personnel drone there. Have it ready to fly."

Danny hesitated. "It's standing by, but I'll send contractors as well. If they deliberately hid the family connection, they might expect to be watched."

"Tell me about Holden's son."

"Nathan Marke is emigrating to Cirrus, today, with his wife, Grace, and son, Ethan. They'll be settling in Port Isaac."

"Today? That's no coincidence."

"Their application was registered years ago."

"But you suspect they're all one family, don't you? When were their seats assigned?"

For the first time, Danny had to check his own notes. "The same day as the refinery test." He was silent as he made the connections. "I'll send a team to Port Isaac to meet them."

"If all this is true, then someone planned this a long time ago." Pieter leaned back in his chair. "An impressively long time ago." His voice held admiration, but also menace, like a fighter stepping into a boxing ring with a smaller opponent.

"Any more family?"

"The Scatters have a son, Jack. There are no photos of him."

"Jack." Pieter sat up abruptly, his confident façade unexpectedly shaken. "Jack Scatter. He's the one. What do we know about him?"

"He's just a kid. The only thing remarkable about him is that he's an original Cirran, born a year after his parents arrived."

"But he's the one we have to watch." Pieter stood. "Come with me."

While Danny would work to confirm the tenuous link between Holden Marke and Carl Prior, Pieter was already convinced. He crossed his office to a blank section of an interior wall. A wave of his hand caused a door-sized panel to slide open, revealing a windowless room, half the size of a squash court but as brightly lit.

"Leave your phone," he reminded Danny.

Danny dropped his phone in the usual tray and followed. He pressed a button on the inner wall to slide the door shut. Despite being a foot thick, the metal panel glided silently into its locked position. The sealed chamber was now as silent and secure as a bank vault.

Not only was all outside sound blocked, the floor itself—an immense block of concrete and steel riding on inertial dampers—eliminated external vibrations. The only object in the room was a vertically mounted ring set partially into the floor. The black ring's thickness—eight-inches—was a good indicator of how much current the frame could draw.

"Caerton," Pieter said.

The frame's address carousel—a multi-chambered cylinder—ejected a pencil-like cartridge, spun half a turn, and inserted another. A world away, an identical frame was doing the same thing.

On the floor below, sophisticated computers and powerful generators sprang into action. Thousands of amps coursed through the ring, causing a familiar hum. His ears registered a change in air pressure as a door materialized in the opposite wall. A green light glowed at the frame's apex to indicate the wormhole was stable. He stepped through without hesitation. Danny followed.

Visually, nothing revealed that they'd traveled one-hundred eighty-six million miles. The portal chamber on Cirrus matched the one on Earth, except the door was on a different wall. But the mind always knew when it traversed a wormhole. Without fail, every person who used a portal experienced déjà vu on their first trip. For most, it was a slight disorientation that diminished with each passage. For a small number, the feeling was profound. Those who experienced the phenomenon most strongly—Travellers— believed it connected their consciousness across time, allowing them to *remember* things from their own future. Pieter Reynard was such a man.

He'd been *travelling* since infancy and trusted the intuitive knowledge he gained. He couldn't foresee every detail—he wouldn't have come up with Jack's name on his own—but right now he knew for certain that Jack Scatter was the one person who could interfere with his plans.

"Do you get any insights at all from these trips?" Pieter asked. "It would save so much time."

"I'll do surveillance my own way."

If Danny felt fear, he refused to let it show. In fact, Pieter had never seen Danny display any emotion, ever. He often wondered if it was due to rigorous training or the man's ability to see a half-second into the future—a limited version of the *Traveller Effect*. Regardless, Pieter had come to rely on him, even if he didn't completely trust him.

The portal shut down as the opposite door opened, and he stepped into an office nearly identical to the one in Seattle. It boasted the same exotic hardwoods, ergonomic furniture, and fourteen-foot floor-to-ceiling windows.

It even had the same water feature wall next to the portal chamber, with a bond more profound than just its appearance. In Seattle, the ice-cold water flowing over slabs of Van Gogh granite came directly from the Oort Cloud mine. After draining into a second array of portals at the base of the wall, that same water poured in a sheet from the top of the stones on Cirrus. For Pieter, the subtle, multimillion-dollar connection between the three worlds exemplified his corporate and personal style.

Other than the wall and other artwork, the big difference was its elevation. From the one-hundred-fiftieth-floor penthouse, he had a commanding view of the entire city.

Danny selected a phone from a slot near the door, made a brief call to dispatch watchers to Port Isaac, then said, "If the Marke family contacts Carl Prior or the Scatter family, we'll know for certain that Emily Scatter used to be Emily Marke."

"Be prepared to pick up Jack Scatter too."

Danny sent a text message, and Pieter sat at his computer to research Jack Scatter. The data trail he followed revealed little. There was nothing to attract unwanted attention, except for the lack of photos. That wasn't unusual—not everyone posted photos of themselves. Yet, as he dug, he found nothing useful.

Jack's social media page contained photos of friends, but none of himself. That oddity caused him to expand his search. He was surprised to find that the friends' pages mentioned Jack but didn't have photos of him.

Someone has removed them. Unless he's been extremely cautious his entire life.

As he probed, a second pattern emerged: connections that ended abruptly, fragmented conversations, ambiguous references. Someone else was missing too.

Whoever it is, they've deleted their entire profile recently. Very recently.

Someone like Danny could remain invisible forever, but this was different. The missing person was active in their social circle, female, and probably the same age as Jack. *She can't stay hidden for long.* Pieter knew he just had to wait until someone in her network noticed and commented. That would reveal her identity.

He created a placeholder icon to represent the missing profile, then retrieved photos of each member of the two families. With the images arranged on the same screen, he considered what he knew and what remained hidden. There were too many coincidences, too many points where a single missing link obscured the entire path. He dragged the empty placeholder to the center of the screen.

"I believe we have found another Traveller."

Chapter 11

Victor pointed to the arrivals board above the station's main doors. "Here he comes."

Jack drew a calming breath and exhaled deeply; Ethan's train had just entered the station's lowest level. He moved closer to his parents, but stayed behind the park bench to keep some distance from the crowds. Shortly, the doors opened and hundreds of people streamed from the lavish, Beaux arts-inspired building.

His cousin had recently reached the six-foot mark, but those extra inches made the person stepping onto the sunlit sidewalk seem older than Jack expected. In reality, they were only a few months apart, and he'd have recognized Ethan's slicked-back, medium-length black hair and carefree smile anywhere.

Ethan tugged his collar to cover his neck against the cold—his light jacket wasn't suitable for a Port Isaac winter. Like most other arrivals, he was carrying a single backpack that contained all he would ever bring from Earth.

Emily waved her arms. "Ethan. Over here." She leaned toward Victor. "He looks exactly like Nathan did at that age."

Ethan heard his name and crossed the street, ignoring traffic, which was almost entirely pedestrians and bicycles.

Emily seized her nephew in a hug. Victor shook his hand. He and Jack exchanged silent nods. All around, a similar scene played out between people who hadn't seen each other in many years or—like Jack and his cousin—had never met in person.

Victor checked the arrivals board again. "Your parents are landing in four hours. We'll wait for them at your apartment. It's only a short walk."

"How was the trip?" Jack asked, struggling to make conversation.

"Long. I've got cool pictures though." He glanced at Jack's parents walking ahead, deep in their own discussion, then passed his phone over. He leaned closer and said quietly,

"Check this out. The entire trip is under constant acceleration or deceleration, but we had about ten minutes of zero-gee at the mid-point."

In the video, Ethan appeared to hang his phone in mid-air, then tuck himself into a ball floating at chest height. Using the seat backs to push off from, he rotated his athletic frame through three complete mid-air rolls in the aisle.

Jack laughed and handed back the phone. "Did you take any flak for that?"

He shrugged and his smile faded. "The flight attendant gave me a dirty look. I think he was just jealous."

Despite his flippant remark, Jack got the sense that his cousin wasn't in a good mood—and he had an idea why. Fairview was a small town, and he often felt confined there. Port Isaac was much larger, but still tiny compared to Seattle. He guessed Ethan was feeling the same way about Port Isaac as he did about Fairview.

Less than a block from Ethan's building, his parents' text alerts sounded at the same time. They were still facing away, but he noticed a falter in his mother's step and sensed her alarm as she turned to face him.

"Jack …" Emily's calm manner seemed forced. "You and Ethan can go to Fairview this afternoon—I know you want to get ready for your trip. Your father and I are staying here tonight, to help Grace and Nathan get settled. We'll join you tomorrow."

"Is something wrong?" He was certain that his mother was hiding something but couldn't work out what part of the statement was false; they'd already discussed the possibility of staying the night before leaving Fairview.

Victor glanced at his phone. "It's nothing important. But the late bus is usually full, so you two should head for the station now to make sure you get seats on the early one. There's no reason to bring your luggage upstairs."

Ethan accepted the change of plans without question, even though they were only a few steps from the entrance to his building. "C'mon, Jack. Let's go."

Jack realized that his father was covering for him,

suggesting they might miss the bus when he knew Jack would be more comfortable in a less-crowded one. He waved to his parents and followed Ethan. As he turned, he noticed two vehicles—black vans with blacked-out windows in the rear and CorpSec logos on their sides—parked across the street. There was nothing unusual about the vehicles themselves except that the two men inside each appeared to be watching Ethan's building.

- - - - -

Danny rode Pieter's private elevator to the basement and entered the arcade.

At twenty-five-hundred-feet, Pieter's needle-like building was the tallest in Caerton, but not the largest. Some, broader at the base, contained thousands of apartments, or a mix of business and residential suites. However, every tower in the city had an arcade, a cavernous underground bay that was part warehouse, part market, and part factory. Virtually any product needed by the thousands of tenants above could be sourced or 3D-printed there, then delivered by conveyor to their floor's central locker.

As it was nearing the lunch hour, the central market was frantic with hundreds of vendors preparing meals for their regular clients. Danny, ignoring the tempting aromas and the chaos of a dozen different languages, took a table at a café that catered solely to the arcade's workers. Two men and two women at the next table recognized him, stood and bowed respectfully, then hurried away without finishing their drinks.

He turned his chair to put the wall at his back so he could see anybody watching him. Satisfied that no one passing would be in range long enough to hear anything important, he made a phone call.

"Where is Jack Scatter?"

"The family left town this morning," Hank said.

"Where?"

"We think they went to Port Isaac."

"You didn't follow them with the Enforcer?"

"It's … No, sorry. But they got on the Port Isaac bus. They should be there by now."

"Where is the drone?"

"It's at ... You sent a message that CorpSec might be searching for the Scatter kid. His family's shop is right across the street. I couldn't take the chance that they'd find it in a door-to-door search."

"*Fool.* Do you think you avoid arrest through your own cunning? I own Fairview's corporate security. Where is it?" Danny heard labored breathing as the obese man struggled to maintain his composure.

"On its way to the camp."

"Redirect it to Port Isaac."

Hank paused. "It's, uh, carrying a cargo."

Danny sighed. "How long before it gets there?"

"Soon, but, there's a problem. One of its rotors has a crack. But it's okay. I was thinking ahead and sent spare parts out there yesterday, just in case. My guys will replace the blade and have it ready to fly in an hour. Two at the most."

He did a quick mental calculation. "You are a lucky man, Hank. The rest of the family doesn't arrive for four hours. If you fail me again, you will not be so lucky."

"There's, um, another problem. One of my guys called. There are more of those little drones—maybe dozens of them—hiding in the trees around the site."

"The same as the first?"

"Could be. He says they're tiny. Fist-sized and camouflaged. What do we do?"

"Surveys drones." Danny dismissed the number as a paranoid exaggeration. "Catch one and send me a photo. What about the safe?"

"We found it. It wasn't buried, after all. Someone moved it. Someone was at the site."

Danny disconnected without responding. Pieter might not have foreseen how Jack Scatter fit into the picture, but Danny now suspected who had been there and moved the safe. He made another call.

In Port Isaac, one of the vans parked next to Ethan's building drove away.

- - - - -

Jack forgot about the corporate security van as soon as he started walking; there was still much to see in the city that was new to him. Fairview's architecture was diverse, but Port Isaac's was eclectic. They strolled past buildings that could have been transported from Paris, Tokyo, or Moscow, as well as delicate forms that could only have risen on Cirrus, which would never suffer earthquakes or hurricanes. Ethan was impressed by the newly built stadium directly across the street from his own building. He'd be able to watch games from his balcony when the domed roof was open.

Wherever possible, Jack cut through parks or chose quieter streets as he led Ethan to the bus station. He hoped his cousin didn't notice he was avoiding crowds. He'd already told him about his phobia—as he'd told Sarah and a few other close friends—but hadn't conveyed the full extent of his anxiety. Until this morning, he hadn't really known how severe the problem was.

His friends were supportive and understanding, and sharing made it easier for him to cope. But for now, Ethan was feeling the stress of moving to a new world and didn't need additional concerns.

At the station, Jack found that their timing couldn't have been better. With the next major arrival still hours away, the underground complex was as quiet as it would ever be. After purchasing tickets, they descended two flights to the bus and cargo level. They claimed a pair of seats at the very back of the bus, minutes before it left the station.

Jack stood aside to let his cousin pass. "Take the window seat."

"Why?"

"Trust me."

The half-empty bus emerged into bright sunlight near the thousands of tall greenhouses that grew most of the city's food. There, Ethan got his first real view of the rim mountains over the roofs of the glass-walled buildings. He started to speak, but then grinned and stared at the cliffs.

The mountains began as six-mile-tall, thirty-mile-thick belts of partially molten rock, held up and confined against the metal wall by gravity generators. When the engineers switched off the field, the rock flowed and tumbled, creating a diverse landscape of steep cliffs hugging the outer wall, then rolling foothills and—far inland—broad, level plains.

"They're taller than Mount Everest," Jack said. "In most places, the mountain is only a few miles thick. But something went wrong here and it cooled too quickly. Instead of flowing toward the middle of Cirrus, the whole thing held together and only the outer edge collapsed to make these steps."

"Has anyone ever climbed them?"

"Not that I've heard of." He'd seen Ethan's videos of himself climbing near Leavenworth. Those crags were impressive, but trivial compared to even the shortest vertical pitch on the rim wall. "Are you making plans?"

Ethan shrugged, but then smiled and kept watching the scenery until the bus turned northeast to follow the coast. Only a few boats trawled in the distance on the calm sea. On the other side of the road, orchards climbed a gentle slope. Hawk-sized drones zoomed above the trees, scaring away the birds. Higher up, larger, faster drones moved to and from the city, their purpose unclear.

"I haven't seen a single person outside the city," Ethan said. "Is everything here done by drone?"

"Not everything. A lot more than on Earth though."

"How many drones does your parents' company have?"

"Most of our work is preventive maintenance—replacing parts *before* they wear out—so we only have a few larger ones to recover other crashed drones."

"Does that happen a lot?"

"All the time. The ones used for planting seedlings get blown into trees or tangled in weeds. Sometimes they get chewed on by animals if they stay on the ground too long."

Ethan laughed. "So, you send a big drone to rescue a little drone. What happens if the big drones crash? Are there even bigger drones? Do you ever get them flying back to your shop with animals still chewing on them?"

"Believe it or not, that happens. We had a squirrel come back this spring. Mostly, the recovery drone does simple repairs in the field. Sometimes we send a truck to go pick them up, especially if they're in the middle of a dense forest. Which reminds me, I found something really strange yesterday." He described the crash scene and the mysterious sphere, but left out the part about the weapons; he still didn't want that story to get back to his parents.

"I don't know about the sphere, but I've seen H-shaped electronic keys. Maybe it was some kind of safe. But why use a drone to deliver the machinery? Why not set up a portal?"

"An unshielded portal large enough to send those crates could be detected from a hundred miles away. I wonder what it's all doing out there."

"What were you doing out there? I thought you said the recovery truck was self-driving."

"The drone was miles off course, on the side of a hill in the trees. The truck takes forever to work in those conditions. My parents have started letting me drive it on my own."

"You're allowed to drive a truck?"

"Not on paved roads."

"They just raised the driving age in Seattle again. It's twenty-one now. The only place I've ever driven is a video game." Ethan reclined his seat. "What's this trip you're supposed to be getting ready for?"

"I've got a job driving a fertilizer truck for the next week, spreading manure in developing ecosystems. The guys who own that contract have family arriving in Port Nelson and want to spend time with them. Dad suggested I ask if you want to come along. You're not sensitive to dynamic portals, are you?"

"I'm not, but Mom is. She'll be having a miserable trip. How about you?"

"I've never actually been near a full-size wormhole, but I'm sure they'd affect me because I can feel something from the smaller ones. It's nothing like the fluttering and nausea other people describe, just a bit of pressure. Kind of like a cold draft."

He showed Ethan a map on his phone—a circuitous route through dozens of isolated forests.

"The truck has a three-inch dynamic portal connected to a pump and a hose. So even if you were sensitive, you'd be able to keep some distance from it."

Ethan wrinkled his nose. "I don't want to spend my vacation on the poop-truck."

"It won't be that bad. We'd have masks for the smell. The job is mostly driving around and avoiding getting stuck. The AI has problems where there are no roads. It'll be more like a camping trip."

"Hmm, maybe. This is the first year I can remember that we haven't gone camping."

"It might be your only chance to see more of Cirrus for a while. We've got seaside resorts, ski resorts, and nature resorts, but you have to stay inside the fences. Some areas are too fragile to let people wander around on their own. Plus, it's normally a two-man team and there's a second hose. You'll get paid for it."

"Yeah? That's a bonus. Okay, I'll go with you."

"And then you get to see what we do with Earth's main export."

Ethan laughed. "And you're welcome for that, by the way." It was common knowledge that the fertilizer used on Cirrus was transported by portal from Earth. Cirrus shipped food to Earth—Earth sent back manure.

"I doubt you had much to do with it; it's mostly from cattle. But you're right, we don't produce hardly any of it on our own—there aren't that many cows here yet. Which also means it'll be a long time before you get a real hamburger."

"You can't get a hamburger on Cirrus?" He expressed mock outrage, but Jack sensed actual disappointment.

"Not beef. There's rabbit. Or cricket."

"Ewww."

Chapter 12

Jada swiped her phone briskly. "You don't exist."

Sarah leaned over, trying to read the screen upside-down. "Is that good?"

"Well, it means that whoever took your phone isn't using it to pretend to be you. But even your name has disappeared from my contact list." She scrolled through her social media pages. "I can't find your profile anywhere. It's like you've been erased."

"Is that normal when you report your phone as stolen?"

"It could be. I don't think it happens very often."

"Well, there's nothing I can do about it today; the stores close early on Sundays. I won't be able to get a new one until the morning. Can I borrow yours?"

"You should have gone there yourself," Jada said.

"What? Where?"

"Port Isaac. You're calling Jack, right? Don't pretend you haven't thought about it; it's only an hour by train."

"Oh. Yeah. But he's meeting his cousin for the first time. Jack wouldn't want me there."

"Are you crazy?" Jada shook her head but handed over her phone.

- - - - -

Jack was discussing Seattle's restaurants with Ethan when a text arrived. He'd been feeling a certain amount of jealousy— Fairview had few options for dining out. While cooking wasn't something he was interested in, trying different types of cuisine was. Besides opening his own repair shop, he also had ambitions of visiting Earth someday. Restaurants were high on his list of things to see there.

<Are you alone? This is Sarah.>

He might have been confused that Sarah was messaging him from Jada's phone, except he was more alarmed by the number of emoji quivering behind her text. She was scared.

He typed, *<I'm with Ethan. What's wrong? Why are you on Jada's phone?>*

There was a delay before her emoji-less reply arrived. She'd turned off Jada's emotion detector.

<*Mine was stolen. Call when you're alone.*>

He'd never wanted to have a video call more badly, but couldn't speak freely with Ethan in the next seat. His own detector would have been streaming emojis if it had been enabled. What was happening in Caerton?

<*Can you send me a photo of the sphere?*>

What does that have to do with anything? He typed, <*Sure, why?*>

<*I couldn't see it clearly while you were moving. It seemed familiar.*>

He found the photo. Without thinking, he automatically sent it to Sarah's phone, not Jada's.

<*Did your cousin arrive?*> The curious emoji slinking after the text showed that Jada had taken her phone back.

Jack replied aloud. "Yeah. We're on our way to Fairview right now."

"Is that Sarah?" Ethan asked.

"Yeah. Well, her and Jada."

<*Send selfie.*>

"Shuffle over." Jack held his phone out so that both he and Ethan fit in the frame. "Jada wants a picture."

Ethan seized him in a headlock, then said through gritted teeth, "I'm ready. Take the shot."

Jack repositioned the phone and snapped the photo, feigning a choking expression. He sent the image with the text: <*Getting along better than expected.*>

"Do you have a picture of her?" Ethan asked while Jack waited for a response.

"Uh, yeah. I'm sure I've got one." He scrolled through his photos, surprised to see how many there were; he'd never thought about it before.

Ethan grabbed the phone, laughing. "*How old is this?*" He flipped it over and inspected it from all sides. "It's an antique."

Jack chuckled. "Yeah, it's one of Dad's that he brought from Earth. He gave it to me when I was five, and it's the only one I've ever had. It's tough too. I dropped a wrench on the screen and it didn't leave a mark. And unlike your phone, which only has cloud storage, this one has sixteen terabytes of memory." He reached over and swiped the screen. "That's Sarah."

"Hey, she's cute. And you've never met her?"

"I haven't been to Caerton since I was five or six. And there's only ever been forty-nine students in our grade in the entire sector. Most of us have never met. *What?*"

Ethan had been silently mouthing 'excuses, excuses' as Jack spoke. "I'm just surprised. You've been talking about her for years."

Jack knew what he was getting at but was too preoccupied wondering what Sarah was upset about. He was happy to change the subject when another text arrived. "Jada says your ship was one of the last to leave Earth. Did you know that?"

"Apparently, there were threats made against the ships. I met our captain before we docked. He says they're just being cautious."

Ethan hesitated when he mentioned the captain. Jack guessed the meeting had something to do with Ethan's time in the server room, but wasn't in the mood to explore. Instead, he checked the news feeds for more information.

"This site says that not only have they suspended passenger service, they've stopped the empty vessels from returning to Earth for the past two weeks. Freighters, too. That means almost every ship that can travel between Earth and Cirrus is docked in one of the spaceports."

"I'm sure everything will be back to normal by Wednesday." Ethan opened a video file that echoed his statement, saying flights were expected to resume once Newton's prophecy had passed without incident.

Despite the pundits' remarks and Ethan's dismissal, Jack experienced his very first moment of uncertainty. It had been easy to ignore Chase's views on the subject, or to pretend to agree and add his own absurd ideas as the mood suited him. But the decision to ground the ships was a clear sign that someone with a lot of power and money had real concerns.

End of the World was a vague and overused expression. He

had no fears that anything remotely similar would happen, but this newly formed doubt hovered at the edge of his awareness like a distant memory.

Ethan stood. "I'm going up to the viewing deck."

Jack waggled his phone. "I'll join you in a minute." Ethan smiled knowingly.

<Can I talk to Sarah?> Jack waited for the emoji-free reply before sending: *<What's happened?>*

<I messed up. I sent drones to the site. Lots. Too many.>

<Did anyone see them?>

<Can't talk now.>

- - - - -

From a distance, Fairview resembled a lumpy pyramid. Its buildings rose ever higher in broken bands centered on a forty-story tower, which had a domed observation deck at its summit.

The other passengers, preparing to disembark, had moved to the lower deck, allowing Ethan to take the front seat. The bulky towers rising from an otherwise featureless plain kept him riveted to the view through the panoramic window, but Jack was still distracted. *Could someone trace the drones to Sarah?*

"You're not very talkative," Ethan said as the bus pulled into town.

"Uh, just tired." That much was true. He couldn't tell Ethan he suspected his mother had lied in Port Isaac, or that he was worried about what Sarah had done, but he'd had the recurring dream again last night and not slept well after. The dream had ended the same way two nights in a row—the sound of running had been unmistakable.

He waited until everyone else got off the bus at the above-ground station. "Our house is on the south side of town," he said as he stepped onto the empty platform. "It's a ten-minute walk."

It was early evening, and many people strolled along the street.

"Why do I get the feeling everyone is staring at me?" Ethan asked.

"What? Oh. I don't know what small towns are like on

Earth, but a new face will stand out here. Especially one of our age. Virtually everyone is younger than us or like a hundred years older. Also, if any of them have young kids, chances are I've babysat for them."

"Ah, that's right. You're one of the original aliens."

Jack was feeling more relaxed now that he was in his hometown. He laughed. "Remember, to me, *you're* the alien. I suppose even my parents are aliens."

"Aren't they all?"

"At least I wasn't one of the very first born here. Those guys still get followed around and interviewed every year."

"I guess I can put up with a bit of attention. I'll pretend they're looking at my flashy clothes."

"Well, your clothes aren't much different from what everyone else is wearing. Except for your shoes. You could see those from space."

Some townsfolk *were* staring at Ethan, but Jack was more surprised to see a CorpSec van parked directly across the street from the bus station. "That's really weird," he said quietly.

"They're not weird, they're just brightly colored."

"Not your shoes. That vehicle."

"What's strange about a police van?"

"Well, they're not *police* in the same sense they are on Earth. And it's not strange that they're here. What's weird is that it was parked across from your apartment in Port Isaac."

"Don't they all look alike?"

"I guess. But I'm sure those are also the same men in it."

They continued walking. Before he rounded the corner, Jack glanced behind, but the vehicle remained parked opposite the station. Ten minutes later they crossed a tree-lined street and arrived at his place, in the middle of a block of eight two-story, stuccoed townhouses.

The first thing Ethan said when they got inside was, "Do you have anything to eat?"

"There's leftover pizza in the fridge. You're welcome to whatever you can find."

Jack moved to the front window and peered through the

blinds. Something about the CorpSec van had unsettled him. *Why do I feel like we're being watched?* However, there was nothing unusual on the street, so he dismissed the idea. He went to the opposite side of the house and opened the patio door.

Ethan joined him outside. "Wow, you really are on the edge of town." To their left, blocks of matching townhouses extended in a straight line for more than a mile. On the right, one of the four roads into Fairview interrupted an identical row. "It's like an island."

The entire town had been built on a raised platform of earth. Hundreds of thousands of acres of canola spread in front of them across a level plain. The top of the grain was well below the backyard, creating the impression they stood on the shore of a yellow-green lake.

Ethan pointed south, to a collection of industrial-looking concrete structures squatting in the distance, at the end of the tree-lined road that descended into the field. "What are those buildings?"

"Workshops and storage yards for the farm machinery. Our shop is down there too. The big drones are pretty noisy, so it has to be outside of town." Jack went to the kitchen to make himself a sandwich. "I'll take you on a tour. Maybe there's something interesting going on at the town hall."

- - - - -

The sun had already set by the time they left the house. Jack led Ethan through a series of well-lit but mostly empty parks.

"So, what do you do for fun here?" Ethan asked.

"Yeah … Fairview isn't really known for fun. Mostly, everyone here just works."

"Don't the farming machines do that?"

"Sure, but there's more to it than field work. The farmers have to meet a quota if they want their contracts renewed, so there's always fights over weather control, and bidding wars for newly terraformed land."

As they got closer to downtown, they encountered more pedestrians and cyclists. Jack greeted several people as they walked. Soon, they arrived at the town hall.

Like most buildings on Cirrus, the building had been printed using a concrete-like material. However, the facade was patterned to resemble wood and brick, in a style that wouldn't have appeared out of place in a small town in North America. In front of the steps that led up to a set of white doors, a placard described the agenda for tonight's meeting.

Ethan read the notice and summarized, "They want to move the moon?" His expression suggested he thought he'd misread the sign.

Jack laughed. "Yeah, I've heard their arguments already. They're actually kind of funny. Basically, it's about helping nocturnal creatures that evolved to rely on the cycles of Earth's moon."

"That sounds … I don't know, crazy."

"It is. But remember, the *Eye* is hollow and doesn't orbit Cirrus." He pointed at the bright sphere rising in the east. "It's trapped in one spot opposite the sun. That means it's always a full moon here, except for twice a year. There's one group of scientists who have a plan for constantly changing the distance and another group who want to orbit several smaller moons. You want to go in and listen for a while?"

"I'll pass."

"I know what you mean. It's not computers or artificial intelligence. Fairview's all about ecology."

"I have other interests. But … multiple, fake moons?"

"Why not? Those stars are fake."

Ethan looked straight up. It wasn't completely dark yet, but the sky over Fairview already held many points of light, much brighter than natural stars.

"Only above the cities," Jack continued. "Those lights are embedded in the roof. You'll notice there are few streetlights here, but they say it's always as bright as a full moon on Earth."

Ethan held out his hand to create a vague shadow on a nearby bench. "What's wrong with streetlights?"

Jack could only shrug at this.

They carried on through the town and were in the middle of another park when Jack's phone beeped. He checked the screen, hoping Sarah was calling. Instead, there was a message from his mother.

"That's strange. Mom never leaves voicemail. She always texts."

"Not like my mom, then. She calls for everything."

Jack pressed the playback icon and heard Ethan's mother's frantic voice. "Get out of the house. Go to your grandfather's apartment in Caerton. We'll wait for you there. Turn off your phones. They're tracking you. *Turn off your phones NOW.*"

Chapter 13

Danny sat in a dimly lit, windowless room, surrounded by monitors. A console-mounted joystick allowed manual control of a dozen drones, but for the moment he let the hummingbird-sized aircraft fly through Port Isaac on their own. While the AI scanned pedestrians on the sidewalks far below, he read the new message on his phone.

<All aircraft were tasked Saturday afternoon from the aviary.>

After his contractors captured the first drone, Danny had forwarded the photo of its remains to a woman he knew only as 'Eyes'. She claimed to have access to thousands of secure drones across the sector and had identified it as being based out of Caerton.

With that information, he'd sent someone to investigate. But since then, the workers at the basin's camp and construction site had found twenty more tiny spies. He'd given their identification numbers to Eyes, hoping she could hack the aviary's servers and see how long they'd been watching.

He typed, *<Wipe the data.>*

<Done. Would you like continuous monitoring of the remaining drones on that server? Standard fees apply.>

Before he could reply to negotiate price, a tone sounded from the console to signal that his drones had reached their destination. He focused on the larger central screen—a view from a helmet-mounted camera. "Move in," he said.

"Understood," a hushed voice replied through a speaker embedded in the console.

Danny glanced at the image on a side panel: a ninety-story tower seen from high over the stadium in Port Isaac. A section of the building went dark as he watched.

The action unfolded on the main screen, beginning with a jerky, night-vision run down a darkened hallway. A brief pause at a closed door followed. There was a loud thump, then a lurching view of the spartan interior of a tiny apartment.

"Clear," the voice behind the camera said.

"Clear," a second voice called from another room.

"Sir, the place is empty."

Danny switched screens, slapped his hand on the camera control pad, and zoomed in on the windows. The display showed only his two operatives as one brushed the curtains aside. "*Find them.*" He angled the camera toward the street.

A light flashed on the console—a traffic control warning.

"Unidentified Drone Operator," a slightly mechanical female voice purred from the main speaker, "your aircraft is on a flight level reserved for emergency services. Please descend to Public Air Corridor Seven immediately."

Danny glanced at the screen. He was certain he'd selected Level Seven, but the display showed '8'. He twisted the control column, dropping the drone sharply, then swiped the camera pad again to zoom in on the main doors.

"Unidentified Drone Operator," the honeyed voice repeated, "your aircraft—"

"*I'm already at Seven.*" But the warning was for the drone on the building's north side.

Swearing loudly, he punched a key to swap displays, and forced the second drone to the lower level. He tried to return to the original screen, but two more warning lights flashed for his attention. He checked the screens for the tower's east and south faces. The number '8' was prominently displayed in the corner of each. By the time he finished moving the aircraft and resetting the camera, four people—the Scatters and the Markes—were running onto the sidewalk at the west entrance.

"Unidentified Drone Operator, your aircraft is—"

"*What are you talking about?*"

In a rare moment of indecision, Danny hesitated. He'd been at the correct height all along. Too late, he pulled back on the stick just as a large cargo drone bore down on his much smaller craft.

The picture spun wildly. Before the screen went black, he recognized a number painted on the building's corner: 6. He'd been tricked into moving the drones into the high-speed delivery corridor.

His fingers flashed over the control panel as he fought to

save the other drones around the tower, but each image shattered chaotically and vanished. He didn't even try to protect the half dozen spies scattered at key points above the city—he'd been outmaneuvered. In seconds, a series of programmed collisions destroyed all but two of his aircraft.

"Thank you," the voice crooned, "for making air-safety a priority."

Chapter 14

Detective Priya Singh paused in the middle of her workout to answer her phone.

"Davis," she groaned. "It's my week off. In fact, the week hasn't even begun. I only got back to Earth a few hours ago."

"Yeah, sorry. But I got a message addressed to you, and I can't make sense of it. You'd have done the same thing if I was off."

"Without a second thought. Did you drive my car?"

"What? No. I rolled it back a foot. No one drove your *baby*."

The exercise room was one half of a two-car garage. A matte-black, seventy-fifth anniversary Mustang convertible— Priya's first car—shared the other side with Davis' motorcycles. He'd added a third to his collection and needed more room.

"What's the message?" she asked.

"It's an anonymous tip regarding an arson. Actually, a bunch of arsons."

"I'm not working an arson case."

"None of us are. But it's addressed to you, so I thought you should see it."

"I didn't hear about any fires before I left. When did this happen?"

"Weeks ago. But that's not the confusing part. They weren't even here. They're all Earth-side. In Australia, Brazil, Oman, France, Finland, and one in Seattle."

"That doesn't make sense. Why send it to me? Can't we turn it over to the locals?"

"Your name's on it. You decide."

"Okay, send me a copy."

Her phone chimed to alert her that it had received the file. She skimmed it, noting dates and times, as well as names of cities she'd never heard of. *This isn't going to be as simple as I hoped.* She decided to finish her five miles on the treadmill first.

To escape the heatwave, she'd moved a monitor downstairs into the garage. She told it to open local news sites for the cities mentioned in the letter.

Sydney's news services had no mention of a fire, but the air charter company had made the headlines—one of their floatplanes had gone missing over the ocean. The date of the disappearance was the day after the alleged fire.

There was a reference to a fire at a hangar in Finland, except it had already been written off as an accident. The burned aircraft was in for scheduled maintenance, and the local fire department blamed the incident on faulty wiring.

The story was the same for the other cities—minor fires at companies linked to the aviation industry.

This isn't a lot to go on, especially as there's nothing to suggest criminal activity.

Priya finished her run, then switched to the sparring dummy. Despite being only five-foot-three, she had no difficulty delivering powerful kicks to the dummy's head. With her years of martial arts training, she could easily take down an opponent twice her size.

After her workout, she went upstairs and turned on music—loud. She didn't have to worry about roommates. Although she shared the space with Davis and Katherine— the third detective in her unit—a three-week rotation meant they rarely crossed paths on Earth.

She considered the letter again. *There's got to be a simpler way.* She called Davis back. "I don't want to go into the office today. Can you check if there's another Detective Singh?"

"Just a second." Priya heard him typing before he spoke again. "There is, but *his* first name is different. Also, the letter wasn't sent electronically. Katherine found it left at our office door."

"On paper? Did anyone see him?"

"Might have been dropped by a micro-drone. But that still means whoever it was knows where you work."

"Right. Can you check the central database, then? Find out if the arsons were reported to another police force?"

Davis worked through the list with her, but they drew a

blank.

"There's two more names on the list that aren't companies," she said. "Who's Pieter Reynard?"

"You're kidding, right? You don't know?"

"Am I supposed to?"

"How could you not? Late fifties. Belgian. *Owns half the city*. Sound familiar?"

"A little. How about Holden Marke?"

Davis typed. "He's not in our system."

"I just noticed something. If I take time zones into account, every fire happened at the same time. I'll try Little Brother."

"You sure? Remember …" He mimicked their Chief's voice. "*'It's a tool. It's not evidence'.*"

Priya laughed. "Oh, don't quote that at me. I've heard it too often. And it's not like I can fly off to France. I'll talk to you later."

She went to her desk and connected her phone to the larger monitor. She wasn't familiar with Cherbourg, but France was a country that embraced Little Brother. She logged into DAIGON and saw the ubiquitous warning: *Your activities on this site will be recorded in the public logs. Do you agree to the following terms and conditions?*

"Not a chance." She clicked *Yes* without reading.

She'd suffered through countless meetings about the network of public cameras that covered virtually every city in Europe. The department's opinion was that DAIGON shouldn't be relied on. As far as she was concerned, Little Brother was incorruptible.

The courts took a different view. To begin with, DAIGON wasn't owned by anyone, was free to use, and the raw data was scattered around the world across an unknown number of nodes. Even though governments, militaries, and private corporations used the same technology, images collected by the Distributed Artificial Intelligence system were not admissible in court.

She found a camera overlooking the small French airport and set the time to a few minutes before the alleged arson.

Nothing was happening, so she fast-forwarded until two firetrucks raced into the picture.

Both trucks stopped near a hangar barely visible at the screen's edge. The firefighters emerged, but she saw no urgency in their actions. Several entered the building while another wandered around the outside. Ten minutes later they left without having used so much as a portable fire extinguisher.

Priya pondered her next move. While there was no sign of an actual crime, somebody had gone to a lot of trouble to link several isolated events. She searched the internet for the two names on the list that were not companies. The computer returned a multitude of results for each.

Doctor Marke was something of a celebrity in the science world. There were thousands of links to scientific papers and lectures under his name. Priya scanned their titles, but most went over her head.

She was disappointed to find no reference to a fire in connection with him or the company he worked for. Had there been, she could have handed the note over to the Seattle police.

As Davis had reminded her, Pieter owned half the city of Caerton. He'd inherited a portfolio of transportation companies, then found himself in the right place at the right time to turn his family's significant fortune into an immense one. On Earth, he was just one more multi-billionaire out of thousands who'd built the space station. On Cirrus, he ranked as a major player, though he kept a low profile. Besides sharing Caerton, he had sole-ownership of several smaller communities along with vast tracts of land and resources.

Priya read through the list of Reynard's assets. *Fairview. I've seen that name recently.* She called Davis again. "Remind me why Fairview was mentioned in a briefing last month."

He typed for a minute before answering. "Why do you remember a single reference to a small town but don't know who Pieter Reynard is?"

"There's no reason for me to recognize him if he isn't involved in anything illegal."

"Well, other than a report from Customs and Immigration regarding undocumented travel, his file is clean. His Chief of Security is a different story."

"That's Danny Kou, right?"

"Yeah, and that's the reference to Fairview. He's never been charged, but Kou has ties to a range of criminal organizations. One of them's linked to a company in Fairview. Suspected of smuggling."

"That doesn't explain why Reynard's name is on the list. We're missing something. When did those travel violations happen?"

"There's a cluster. Let's see. Yeah, right around the time of your fires."

"They're not *my* fires yet."

She thanked Davis for saving her a trip into the office and ended the call, but couldn't shake the feeling she'd missed something. *Is someone trying to draw attention to Danny Kou?* That seemed unlikely. Whatever the tipster's motive, the fires were the focus.

On a hunch, she searched the internet for other fires on that night. The computer rewarded her with hundreds of images of the same scene. At the time minor fires had sprouted around the world, an inferno destroyed a pumping station in Louisiana. The damage estimate was in the millions of dollars. All that remained was the heat-blistered company logo on the fence, with the words: Over the Horizon.

I've seen that name before too. She returned to Little Brother and replayed the airport video. As the firetrucks were leaving, another vehicle was entering through the main gate. She paused the video and zoomed in on the blue and green lettering on its door. *OTH Fuels.*

Priya sighed, knowing she'd be following this through to the very end now. She even understood the underlying psychology. Whoever sent the letter had deliberately omitted the big fire, had let her find the connection on her own and convince herself that there was more to the story.

As a police detective seconded to the UN's off-world policing division, her real employer was the Washington State

Patrol. Each of the crimes—if they were crimes at all—was beyond her jurisdiction, but she needed more information before she could take action.

She considered the last name on the list. *Doctor Marke.* The address given was for his home, outside Seattle.

One of the first things Priya liked to do on her days off was take her car out for a long drive, enjoying the wind in her hair as the hydrogen-fueled Mustang thundered out of tight corners. The car was older than her and boasted one of the last internal combustion engines Ford made. It lacked the refinements of modern vehicles but was a thrill to drive. She checked the weather forecast for the morning: sunny skies.

I'd prefer the Olympic Peninsula Loop, but an hour of cruising on the I-5 is better than nothing.

Chapter 15

Ethan's reaction to his mother's panicked message was swift, confident, and entirely the opposite of what she asked. He pulled out his own phone with the intent of calling his parents.

"Wait." Jack pushed his arm down. "She said to turn off your phone. Who's tracking you?"

"I don't know. I'm calling to find out."

"That's exactly what she said not to do."

Ethan hesitated with his thumb over the dial icon. "Why did she call me from your mom's phone? And what did she mean by 'go to grandfather's'? He's in Washington. It's Uncle Carl who lives in Caerton."

Jack replayed the message at higher volume. "She definitely said *grandfather*."

"She also said turn off your *phones*, not *phone*."

"Why would she want me to turn off *my* phone?" He tucked it into his back pocket. *What if Sarah calls?*

"I've never met Uncle Carl. I don't even know what he looks like. I think the message was meant for both of us, and you're supposed to tell me how to get to his place."

Jack knew that phones could be tracked, but he'd never known anyone who'd switched theirs off. For any reason. Ever. He withdrew it again and brushed the screen several times, delaying. "Why is someone tracking you?"

"It was *your* mom's number. Maybe they're tracking *you*."

Jack thought of Sarah's warning about the drones she'd sent to the basin. But then he recalled his mother's strange behavior before they left Port Isaac—she'd been evasive about Ethan's parents. *That message was definitely intended for Ethan. But if someone's tracking his phone, they might be watching mine too.* He hovered his thumb over the power button. When Ethan shut his phone off, so did Jack.

"Now what?" Ethan asked.

"Let's go back to the house and see if we can contact them some other way. Maybe from the neighbors."

"She said to get *out* of the house."

"*Well, I don't know what else to do.*" Jack hadn't meant to shout. He lowered his voice and walked to the street. "We'll just be careful."

"Let's take the bus to Port Isaac."

Jack kept walking. "The next one won't be until morning."

They were still in the park closest to his house when a CorpSec van passed at high speed. By the time they reached the sidewalk, it had stopped in front of the townhouse.

"Why are the police at your house? Let's get them to find out what's happening." Ethan started running.

"Wait." Jack grabbed his arm and pulled him off the sidewalk. "These aren't police like you have on Earth." He pulled Ethan farther from the street. "They work for the corporations."

As he watched, a second van coming from the opposite direction stopped beside the first. Two men got out of each vehicle and marched to the house.

Jack edged into the cover of the bushes, pulling Ethan with him. "The second car is local. I recognize the officers. The other two aren't even wearing uniforms and I'm sure they're the ones I saw in Port Isaac." *Which means they saw me leaving with Ethan and knew where to look for him.*

The uniformed officers watched the street while the others filed around the block of townhouses, gazing through the windows. When they reappeared, they held a brief discussion on the sidewalk, then the pair in plain clothes strode to the house. Only a few seconds later, the door opened and both men rushed in while the uniformed officers waited outside.

"Didn't you lock the door?" Ethan asked.

"I did. How'd they get inside so quickly?"

The men returned less than a minute later. They spoke to the other officers briefly, then all four got in their vehicles and drove away.

"Now what?" Ethan asked.

"We'll wait a few minutes and sneak into the house."

"And do what? What if they come back? What if they're watching the house?"

"Fine. We'll go to Caerton."

"Won't they be watching the bus in the morning?"

"Yeah." Jack looked up and down the street. "We have to leave tonight. Let's go to the shop."

He dashed across the street to the access road that led to the workshops. The widely spaced trees on either side of the road offered little cover, but he didn't expect anyone to be watching from the fields. There were no streetlights on this stretch either, but they ran the entire length anyway.

"Are we allowed to be here?" Ethan asked as they approached the cluster of two dozen darkened buildings. The narrow road passed through the middle of the group before disappearing into the fields. "I hear machinery ahead. What if someone calls security?"

"Don't worry about it. I'm here every day. Our shop is near the end of the street."

They sped past the open bays of the largest building, where harvesters and other farming vehicles hung in sturdy maintenance frames. There were no human operators at this hour—robots were handling the routine work. A track-mounted arc welder underneath a six-wheeled tractor illuminated them briefly. They hurried to get out of the light.

Jack's building was an unremarkable, two-story structure with a single window and a door facing the street. The door unlocked automatically for him. Ethan followed him inside but scanned the windows and alleys across the street before closing the door.

The family's workshop was Jack's favorite place in the entire town, and he felt a measure of comfort and safety once he locked the door. He passed through the front office to enter the warehouse. Some of the drones stored there were the size of birds, others were almost six feet across. There were also shelves of spare parts and accessories. A variety of drones—whole and disassembled—rested in maintenance jigs on the workbenches on the other side of the room.

He pointed to a pile of nylon bags. "Put all that in the recovery truck in the loading bay."

"What is it?"

"The camping gear for the fertilizer trip. There's a second sleeping bag for you. There's also a box of food over there, on top of the fridge." He signed on to a terminal on the workbench and set to work at the keyboard.

Ethan carried the pile into the loading bay, then stopped for a moment, confused. "This is the *truck* you've been talking about? You know, where I come from, that word means something very different."

"Yeah, that's Dave."

"Dave?"

"Drone Assist Vehicle. DAVe."

The recovery truck was an open-sided All-Terrain-Vehicle, slightly larger than the compact, four-wheeled, off-roaders popular on Earth. This one had two seats, a cargo bed, and a robotic arm attached to the rear. Countless scratches accumulated from years of crawling through forests had discolored its plastic body panels. Once white, Dave was now lightly camouflaged in streaks of browns and greens.

Ethan finished loading the gear and rejoined Jack at the workbench. "What are you doing now?"

"There are half a dozen crashed drones waiting to be picked up in our zone. I'm programming Dave to go after a couple of them."

"How does that help us get to Uncle Carl's?"

Jack tapped the screen. "This crash site is a third of the way to Caerton. We'll ride along that far and figure it out from there. If anyone checks, it'll look like Dave's driving by itself."

He finished on the computer and Dave woke up. Lights on the dash showed it was running diagnostics. Ethan moved to take the passenger seat.

"No, wait." Jack held up a hand. "We can't ride it yet. It'll follow the path on the north side of the field—right past our house. If there's someone there, we'll be spotted for sure. We'll have to cut across the field and catch it."

"Catch it? You mean jump on it while it's moving? How fast will it be going?"

"Faster than I can run. But if we get ahead of it, it'll stop to avoid us." He brought up an aerial map of Fairview for

Ethan's benefit. He'd spent years exploring the area around the town and its adjoining lake and knew every path and shortcut for miles. "We're here. Dave will go north first, then follow the walking path along the houses before it turns south. We'll go straight across here. It'll be going faster than us, but it has to go four times as far."

Ethan studied the map for a few more seconds. "Okay, got it."

Jack switched off the building's lights, then powered down the computers so it would look like no one had been there.

"As soon as I open the door, we run. That'll give us a bit of a lead. Ready?"

Ethan nodded. Jack pressed a button on the truck's dashboard. The bay door slid upwards.

"*Go.*" He ducked under the door and headed south at a dead run, then turned at the last building to plunge into the field. Ethan was right behind him.

"You're sure it'll stop for us?" Ethan puffed.

"It won't run us over if that's what you mean."

"Then why didn't one of us go ahead to stop it and wait for the other?"

Jack said nothing for a few paces then shouted—angry at himself, not Ethan, "That would have been an excellent suggestion a few minutes ago."

They continued in relative silence on a narrow path through the waist-high canola. The soft earth muffled the pounding of their feet.

Ahead, the ground rose at the field's edge to match the elevation of the town. The workshop sat lower than this and Dave had begun its journey even lower, at the same grade as the field. To reach this spot, it would have to climb a short slope at the field's north-east corner. Jack scrambled up the bank and flopped on the shoulder of the dirt track.

"Did we make it?" Ethan gasped, searching for the truck.

"It must have stopped. Maybe someone was out walking in front of the house. It's only just coming around the corner now." Jack pointed toward the town. "We've got a minute to spare."

In the distance, Dave's front bumper marker lights were coming into view as it swung onto the track. Ethan exhaled loudly and joined Jack on the higher ground. "That wasn't too bad, but I'd have preferred to walk."

"I'm not sure we had the time." Jack pointed across the field. "Look."

A black van crept slowly through the alley between the workshop and the neighboring building. Its headlights illuminated a swath of grain as it approached the field. The reflected light was bright enough to reveal two men seated inside.

Anticipating Ethan's concern, he added, "Don't worry, they can't see us. Not unless they turn off their lights."

Which is exactly what they did.

The boys froze, then looked at each other and relaxed because it was now so dark they couldn't see each other clearly; it would be impossible for anyone else to spot them at this distance. The men got out of their van and trooped to the rear of the building. One reached down to try the sliding garage door while the other checked the personnel door beside it.

Jack stood. "We've got to get ready to catch our—" He stiffened, cursed, turned and ran. "*Run.*"

Ethan joined Jack in a panicked dash. "What's happening?"

"Dave will turn on its headlights if it senses an obstacle. They'll see the lights. There's a bend in the road up ahead. We can get in when it slows down."

The gravel path was smooth and level, but Dave was moving faster than either of them could run. Jack was rapidly running out of breath. The noise from Ethan's feet increased as he sprinted to catch up, but the crunch of gravel under Dave's tires was almost as loud.

With only seconds to spare, Jack veered sharply left into the trees and leaped into the weeds. "Get off the road. *Not there.*"

Ethan had caught up. But following a fraction of a second too late, he ended up on the outside of the curve where Dave's forward-looking sensors would sweep over him.

"Don't move," Jack hissed.

Ethan held his breath.

The truck slowed. Turned.

Flashing lights illuminated Ethan's hiding spot as Dave stopped directly in front of him.

Jack swore and jumped onto the path, reaching for the door handle. "*Get in.*"

Ethan, temporarily blinded, stumbled to the side of the truck, gripped its roof rack, and hauled himself over the door panel. He landed heavily in his seat as Jack shut off the autopilot and all the lights, even those on the dashboard. "Why aren't we moving?"

"Just wait." Jack shifted in his seat, trying for a better viewing angle. "I don't think they saw us."

The road passed at an angle through a line of trees separating two fields. The undergrowth blocked much of the view, but he could still see the maintenance buildings. The CorpSec vehicle was parked there, but with no sign of its occupants.

"Where do you think they went?" Ethan asked, trying to slow his breathing.

"I'm not sure. Maybe they—" An intense light flared through the window of the workshop's back door. A second later, a booming sound wave swept past, creating a dull thump in Jack's chest. "*They blew up our workshop.*"

"No, look." Beams of light played across the window from the inside. "Flashlights. I think it was just a stun grenade."

"*Just* a stun grenade." Jack fumbled the dashboard controls with shaky hands. "Let's get out of here."

He pressed the accelerator. Ethan was still watching as someone opened the workshop's door from the inside. A thin cloud of white smoke drifted out.

Jack drove in manual mode so Dave's marker lights wouldn't turn on. There was barely enough reflected light from the clouds to make out the road, so it was another ten minutes of slow driving before he felt confident that no one would see them. He re-engaged the autopilot and Dave accelerated to its normal cruising speed.

With little visual reference, it felt as if the truck sped along much faster than it did. There was a lake not far below, on the left. However, it was too dark to see the water's surface. The pale weeds lining the shore blurred past at an uncertain distance until the dusty road curved southward into another field. The farther they got from town, the darker it became.

"How far—" Ethan said. He hadn't spoken since they started driving. Dave's electric motor was nearly silent, and they traveled on a soft dirt track; his voice had sounded like a shout. He started again, quietly. "How far do we go tonight before stopping?"

"I don't think we should stop. Dave can drive itself through the night. By morning we should be at least a hundred miles away."

They continued in silence for a long time. Eventually, Jack asked, "Do you think they're following your family from Earth?"

"*No.*"

"Were your parents ever in trouble with the police?"

"I could ask you the same thing, you know. It was *your* mother's phone they called from, and the cops were at *your* house. Maybe they're following your parents."

Jack had no answer to that. He wanted to call Sarah. *But what if Ethan's right? Would that connect her to me and put her in danger?* Aunt Grace had made the call, so she and Uncle Nathan *must* be involved. But the mood in Port Isaac had been anxious; his own parents must know something too. *Are they protecting Ethan's parents?*

Dave navigated southeast, twisting through many small oases of trees. They were much closer to the middle of Cirrus than to the southern rim, so the night wasn't as cold as it had been in Port Isaac. However, it soon became cool enough that Jack had to dig his sleeping bag out of the cargo box.

Much later, Dave rolled onto a long, smooth stretch of road. Exhausted, the boys reclined their seats and fell asleep.

Chapter 16

Monday – One Day to Newton

"Was it necessary to burn down the warehouse?" Pieter asked.

One of the large screens on the wall of his Seattle office was tuned to a local news station and showed the early morning commuter traffic. The second displayed live aerial footage of the charred, smoking shell of a building on the outskirts of Fairview. A concrete block wall wavered, then collapsed inwards under the pressure of a water jet directed from a truck on the street.

"Hank had become … careless," Danny said. "An armed drone in a warehouse would have raised questions. And we still need access to the Scatter's workshop across the street."

Pieter silently conceded that Danny was right; the fire and the ongoing cleanup were an effective cover. And immediate termination of the smuggler's contract was an appropriate response for not having the Enforcer on standby.

He stalked to his desk. "Careless is not the word I would use." The loss of the anti-personnel drone had wiped out much of his surveillance capability in the sector's southern half. "But at least we know for certain that the Scatter and Marke families are related." *But why did they hide the family connection?* "Where is Doctor Marke now?"

"He's still at his home."

"He's been seen there?"

"We followed him there yesterday. He hasn't left."

Something's wrong. "Check. Send someone in."

Danny said nothing but started typing on his phone.

"Have our guests been delivered to Caerton?" Pieter knew the Scatters and Markes had been captured in Port Isaac last night.

"They'll be in the city in three hours."

"Has anyone found their phones yet?"

"Emily's is still missing."

"Pull her history. Find out if she contacted Jack."

"I already tried. She doesn't have a local account. None of them do."

"They've been on Cirrus for almost two decades and still use an Earth-based network?" Pieter's jaw clenched. "There's definitely another Traveller playing the game."

"The girl whose profile is missing?"

"No. Whoever she is, she can't possibly have access to a large portal. But she's involved. Somehow. The real Traveller is protecting her."

Danny's text alert sounded. "He's gone."

Pieter's intuition had told him Holden was missing even before Danny spoke. The disappearance was the latest in a string of failures: the boys had escaped last night, their current location was unknown, their parents had evaded capture for hours, and the identity of Jack's friend was still veiled. *Too many coincidences.*

"We need to identify the other Traveller," Pieter said. "Soon." The task would be daunting, and he'd need more clues, but there was other business to take care of first. He told the office AI to call Simon in Everett. "I want good news," he said as Simon's image appeared on the screen.

"It's great news. Doctor Marke's design is ingenious. I only need a minor change to our connectors to have the backup resonator ready by tomorrow morning. And I merged it with one of our own to be sure it works."

"Has the final test begun?"

"Yes. I'll be heading to Cirrus to oversee it as soon as I'm done here."

Pieter disconnected and addressed Danny. "And the identification of the correct portals? That will also be done in time?"

"I've persuaded one of Marke's assistants to help."

Pieter grinned at the use of the term 'persuaded', in appreciation for Danny's success rate, not whatever action was behind it. Pieter wasn't sadistic; he didn't take pleasure in violence, but he didn't care about it either. "Is he reliable?"

"He's been married less than a year and they have a

newborn. I've given him incentive to cooperate."

"Good. But there's a more pressing problem. Where are the boys?"

"They didn't return home during the night. We're watching the bus station and stopping every transport truck and grain carrier. They must still be in Fairview."

"No." Pieter shook his head. "They've left town. Even if they had to walk."

- - - - -

Jack and Ethan weren't walking, although they almost wished they were.

"I feel as tired as you look," Jack said.

Ethan rubbed his eyes. "Every time Dave crossed a slope, I dreamed I was falling and woke up."

Five-point harnesses had let them sleep in their seats, but Dave kept a steady pace over uneven ground. Overall, they'd each gotten no more than three hours of sleep and awoken at dawn in a grove of poplar trees. Dave's robotic arm was reaching for a drone that had attempted to land in tall weeds. One propeller had snagged, jerking the machine to the side where it crashed into a tree.

Ethan threw his sleeping bag into the cargo box. "How long do we have?"

"Replacing a prop is a standard repair. I could do it in minutes. It'll take Dave half an hour."

The drone had ended up on its side against the tree. Jack could have tipped the aircraft over to speed up the repair but was in no hurry to start driving. The three-jointed arm maneuvered to a grapple point and eased the craft down.

Ethan stood on the opposite side of the truck but wasn't watching Dave. Instead, he was holding his phone, staring at the black screen. When he noticed Jack watching him, he dropped it into his pocket. "I need to take a walk." He stomped into the trees.

What we really need is to borrow someone else's phone. Jack wanted to call Sarah, to be sure she was safe. He wanted to call *anyone*, to find out what was going on, but Aunt Grace's message was clear.

He fetched food from the camping supplies, then reached automatically for his phone for water.

I didn't bring water. Fresh drinking water from a phone's portal was something everyone took for granted, but that service wasn't available without power. Fortunately, a stream ran nearby. *We're going to have to fill up before we leave.*

After eating, he searched the cargo box and found a couple of plastic jars. He also found Dave's spare power cell, a stubby white cylinder with a red lightning bolt printed on it. The blinking LED showed it was connected to a power source at the shop. A light on that device would turn on if he drew electricity from the remote.

If I knew Morse code, I could signal someone. Except the only person I could contact would be someone in the workshop, and they might be hunting us.

Jack slumped on the grass, leaned against the truck, and reflected on the events of the last twenty-four hours. Ethan had been irritable even before they left Port Isaac, perhaps from the stress of a long trip. They'd had disagreements over the years, but solving those was as simple as going offline for a few days. Here, not knowing how long it would take to get to Caerton, nor even how they'd do that, he had few options to give Ethan enough space to cool down on his own.

The early morning sun on his face was welcome in the cool air, and the calm setting was a sharp contrast to the fear and anxiety of the previous night. He still held the power cell and found himself staring at the light as it blinked hypnotically. He soon fell asleep.

- - - - -

Sarah arrived at the aviary shortly after dawn. Her shift didn't start until eight, but the conservation building would be empty at this hour. She could review videos in private before going downtown for a new phone.

The aviary did not have strict security. Her pass card allowed her into every room on the main floor other than personal offices. She returned to the survey department and queued up footage from the basin. Only one of the cameras was still working, but most of the others had been recording through Sunday morning.

She tapped a map icon for a survey drone near the weapon-filled container. The view was uphill, so she spun the control knob to fast-forward until the camera pointed into the basin, shortly before noon. That gave her a clear view of the large drone and the men trying to repair it.

Jack would have shaken his head in disbelief, Sarah thought. *These guys don't have a clue what they're doing.* Parts were strewn around the aircraft. For some reason, the men fixing it had removed all the rotors, not just the ones Jack said were damaged.

But the camera the CorpSec officer smashed was on the other side of the basin. What's there that they don't want anyone to see?

She selected that drone and set the time to shortly before it was discovered. As the camera panned the clearing, it had recorded a group of workers erecting a camouflaged tent, large enough to shelter fifty people. Scattered around the site were more piles of fabric and poles, enough for dozens of tents.

Someone spoke from the doorway behind Sarah. "Not what you expected, is it?"

She gasped and pushed herself away from the desk to face the entrance. The man who had watched her during the banding demonstration was leaning casually against the doorframe. "Who are you? You don't work here."

"No. I don't." He seemed unconcerned about trespassing.

As with the first time Sarah saw the stranger, he was well-dressed and wearing a gold watch. He was about her mother's age, good-looking, athletic, with impeccably trimmed short hair. She edged around the room to put some distance between them. "What do you want?"

"We need your help." The man saw her discomfort. He sauntered farther into the room, placing the display case full of drones between them, and leaving her a clear path to the door. He then sat in one of the office chairs, leaned back, and propped his feet up on a second chair.

Sarah saw that she could leave whenever she wanted but said, "You stole my phone."

He juggled his hands, weighing her words. "Borrowed it." He grinned.

"Why?"

"To protect you."

"From what?"

He shook his head.

She crossed her arms defiantly. "Why do you need my help?"

"Because your friend needs ours." He dropped his feet to the floor and held out a slip of paper with a long alphanumeric string written on it.

Sarah couldn't read it from across the room, but recognized the pattern of numbers and letters. "It's a drone ID."

He rolled his chair away from the scheduling console to leave her plenty of space.

She had a clear pathway around the right side of the display case to reach either the exit or the computer. If the man had done anything other than smirk when she met his eyes, she'd have right then, but his overly confident expression was infuriating. She stepped around the left side, directly past him, snatched the paper from his hand, and entered the ID into the console.

The image zoomed away from the basin until the sector's entire southeast quarter filled the screen. The crosshairs slid past Fairview, then plunged like a meteor to an isolated spot on the opposite side of Jack's hometown.

A panoramic view of a forest appeared, spun once, then settled on a utility truck just visible through the branches.

She touched the controls to set a new position for the drone, next to the truck. The one-frame-per-second video shifted into real-time as the aircraft lifted off. It glided smoothly through the forest, stopping in front of a sleeping figure leaning against the vehicle.

- - - - -

Jack's dreams reflected his circumstances: worried, cut off from family and friends, uncertain about Ethan. After a troubling vision of his parents being abducted, he imagined his cousin watching him from the woods, picking up a large branch, and leaping over a bush. He woke as birds scattered. Ethan was charging toward him, wielding a three-foot-long branch like a baseball bat.

"*Stop.*" He rolled away as Ethan swung.

"*Got you.*"

Jack scrambled to his feet, searching for something to defend himself with. But Ethan ran past and swung the branch again, hammering the ground. "*What are you doing?*"

Ethan stomped on something fluttering in the tall grass. "Didn't you hear it? It was right in front of your face."

"I fell asleep." Jack approached cautiously. The remains of a tiny aircraft littered the ground, mixed with splinters and bark. "It's a survey drone."

"Where did it come from?"

Jack gestured broadly. "They're all over the place. They move around, counting animals and insects."

Ethan ground it into the soil with his heel. "Was it looking for us?"

"I doubt it. They're slow. And there are far too many of them for anyone to watch all the video." He flipped the sparrow-sized drone over with his foot to inspect the ruined camera. "Someone will eventually check up on this one, but that might take days."

Ethan dropped the branch and slumped against the truck. "We should call our parents." He said this as if he wanted to convince himself. "Maybe they've already sorted it out. If we don't turn our phones on, we'll never know."

"I've been thinking about that. If they could, they'd have checked the shop and noticed that Dave is missing. Dad could have tracked it on the shop computers and sent us a message through the dashboard. He could have even re-programmed it to come home."

"They can track us?"

"Yes, and I know what you're thinking. Anybody who can access our computers can track Dave. But they've got to get into the application first."

"That won't take long. I could open that file in a few

minutes."

"Sure, but the men following us last night didn't look like hackers." Jack instantly regretted his choice of words; he hadn't meant to imply that Ethan was a hacker. Ethan's parents were computer security experts, and he'd been teaching himself their trade for years. "They were just thugs. They'll bring in someone who knows what they're doing: a professional. Also, if they knew where we were going, they'd have had someone waiting here, or at least sent a proper drone."

"That doesn't prove they don't know. They might be waiting to see what we do next. Can they track us if we disable the autopilot?"

"No, the navigation module sends our position data. And I know what you're going to say. If we switch it off, they can't track us, but then they'll know for sure that we're here. Right now, they can see where Dave is, but for all they know we're still hiding in Fairview."

Ethan considered this for a while before asking, "Are all nav modules the same? Can you swap them between the truck and the drone?"

"Yeah, they're interchangeable."

"Then we just have to swap the modules and send the drone back to Fairview. If they're tracking us, they'll see the drone. It'll look like we're on our way there. Will that work?"

Jack shook his head. "No, that's … Wait, that's brilliant. No one's going to look at anything but the ID. But there's one thing I need to do first." He changed the dashboard display to show the diagnostics Dave was running on the drone. He pointed to a line on the scrolling list. "Tell me when it gets to here." Then he got a screwdriver from his toolkit and removed a panel on the drone's fuselage.

Ethan watched the display. "Just about. One more line. And … now."

Jack pulled a cartridge from the drone. The diagnostic panel flashed red.

"Why did you do that?"

"We can't change Dave's programming without letting

them know we're here. That means we have to use the second drone, the one that crashed closer to Caerton. But I don't know why it crashed—it might be too badly broken to fly. We'll have to take this one with us. I'll finish the repairs myself."

With the first drone appearing more seriously damaged, the robotic arm prepared it for transport. While they repacked their gear, the arm secured the drone on the overhead rack. The entire operation took only a few minutes. Then Dave retreated from the forest on the same path it had used to find the crash site.

Jack checked the map as they rolled onto the dirt track. "We'll be at the second drone in about six hours. That gives me plenty of time to replace a prop, but I'll wait until we're on smoother roads. For now, I'm going back to sleep."

He wrapped himself in his sleeping back, relieved that their ordeal was nearly over. Even Ethan seemed optimistic. They only had to avoid getting caught for the next six hours and they could go wherever they wanted.

Chapter 17

The image on the scheduling console froze but Sarah still recognized Jack through the digital noise. And the foot in the colorful sneaker must belong to Ethan.

"What happened?" She struggled with the controls, trying to restart the video. "Is he okay?"

"Probably just tired." The man appeared as unconcerned with Jack's situation as he was with being in the aviary outside of public hours. "They're a long way from home."

"Why hasn't he called?" *And how did end up hundreds of miles from Fairview?* "What do you want?"

"Like I said, we need your help."

"I'm not doing anything until you tell me what's going on. And who is *we*?"

The man kept his distance but leaned forward. "You were only trying to help your friend. But the drones you sent have attracted a certain amount of attention." He flipped his hand over to reveal a portal-chipped access card with the aviary's logo. "I can wipe the video and any data that connects you to it. After that, we'll do our best to hide you, but it's only a matter of time before they find you. And Jack."

"Who are *they*? What do you mean, hide me? Is that why Jada can't find my profile?"

He sat back and shrugged.

"Why shouldn't I call security? Or CorpSec?"

"You could, but that won't help your friend. As for CorpSec … you could have called them Saturday."

Sarah knew exactly why she hadn't called; CorpSec was already involved.

"What do you want me to do? I'm only a student. I don't have access to systems outside the survey department."

"This has nothing to do with your work. Do you have the key?"

"What key?"

"The one I left for you in the park. Do you still have it?"

Somehow, Sarah knew the blocky object had to be a key.

"It's in my locker."

He inserted his access card into a slot in the console. "I have work to do. Go get the key and meet me in the parking lot."

Don't, her instincts said. But if the man had wanted to harm her, he could have done it any time—they were the only ones in the building. Also, there were cameras everywhere. And he knew where Jack was.

"What's your name?"

"Terrance." He turned and started typing. "I'll be outside in ten minutes."

- - - - -

Sarah spotted Terrance on the far side of the parking lot. He walked away, letting her follow at whatever distance she was comfortable with. She stayed ten yards behind as he overtook slower walkers who strolled along the stream, an offshoot of the large river that flowed through Caerton. The area was also popular with cyclists and—even at this hour— they encountered early morning commuters on the wide, paved trail.

Terrance stopped at a bend in the path, pretending to tie his shoe while checking for observers. "*Quickly.*" He leaped off the pavement.

She followed into the dense brush before anyone saw, then noticed cut branches on the ground. Although it seemed thick, the remaining foliage was thin and springy, and easily pushed aside. *Someone's planned for a fast exit.*

They'd gone about a hundred yards when Terrance stopped. He crouched and motioned for her to do the same. Somewhere ahead, tires crunched through loose gravel.

He started walking again, more slowly, when the noise passed, then stopped at a tall chain link fence that marked the edge of the forest. Inside the fence, the dog-sized wheeled drone that patrolled the property was scooting around the corner of a two-story, windowless building.

"We're at the reservoir," Sarah said when she got her first view of the complex. A half mile of domed tanks squatted in neat rows beyond a second fence.

"Actually, this is UV Mobile, Armenau's ultraviolet filtration facility." He kneeled beside a tree and searched in the weeds until he found a plastic jar hidden there. He unscrewed the top, withdrew two pairs of gloves, and handed the smaller pair to Sarah. "Put these on."

She accepted the gloves but didn't put them on. "What for?"

"UV Mobile is the source for drinking water for every mobile phone in this sector. Naturally, security is tight."

"Yeah, no doubt. Why are we here?"

"The thing I want you to steal is inside."

"*You didn't say anything about stealing.*"

"Would you have come?"

"Of course not. And now I'm leaving."

"Wait." Terrance pulled a phone from his jacket and offered it to her. "You have a message."

Sarah recognized the phone as her own. She took it and checked the screen. "It's from Jack. But it was sent yesterday."

Terrance pressed an icon on his phone. Sarah's chimed and vibrated as additional messages from Jack, Jada, and others finally connected to her restored profile. Then it rang, displaying an unknown-caller icon.

"Answer it."

She accepted the call uneasily. "Hello?"

"Good morning, Miss Rogers." The pleasant voice was that of a much older man. "How are you?"

"Who is this?"

"It's best that you don't know—for now. You have no reason to trust me, but I mean you no harm. Please look at the picture your friend sent."

Sarah opened Jack's first message and saw the attached photo. "That's the sphere he found on Saturday."

"Do you have the key?"

She fished the object out of her pocket but had already guessed what she would find. She double-tapped the image to zoom in on the slot. The key matched the shape of the opening exactly. But much more than that, Terrance had left it at the aviary long before Jack sent the photo.

"You knew Jack was going to find the sphere. You knew he'd send me a photo. You're a Traveller." The elderly man chuckled. "Your goon said you want me to steal something." Terrance grinned at the word 'goon'. Sarah glared at him. "Why?"

The man on the phone said, "To prevent something terrible from happening."

"To Jack?"

"Not just him. Many people may be hurt."

"If you know what's going to happen, why don't you do something about it?"

"I am."

Sarah understood he meant her. She appraised Terrance; he certainly looked like a more-capable thief than she was. "Why does it have to be me?"

"I can't tell you that. But you *can* walk away—that is your choice. However, it will turn out better for everyone if you help."

Every instinct warned her to leave and call for help. But CorpSec was already involved, and they weren't on her side. "Will I get caught?"

"A Traveller's memories are not perfect. But no, there's little chance you will be discovered today. There's no one inside."

Sarah turned to Terrance. "You said it's very secure."

"It is." He pulled a phone from the plastic jar. "That's what this is for."

"It looks like a normal phone. What does it do? Hack the cameras? Use a magnetic pulse to destroy them?"

"Well, no. It's a phone. You use it to call my, um, associate, in the security office and he disables the system."

"If you have someone working for you on the inside, why doesn't he get whatever you're after? Or why not you?"

Terrance shook his head again.

Sarah's patience with that response was wearing thin "Fine. Let's do this."

He handed her a plastic card—which she put in her pocket—and told her to wear her phone's earbud and put the gloves on. "The fence rail is etched with a nanopattern that will tear your skin."

"*Are you kidding me?*"

"No." He looked at her as if this was obvious. "Dial the number and hang up after one ring." He pointed at the door. "Then watch the access panel. Don't touch the fence until the light turns green."

"Why not?"

Terrance gave her the look again. "It would be bad."

Sarah shook her head but put on the gloves and flexed her fingers. The material was thick but allowed enough range of motion to use the phone, which had only a single, unnamed entry on its contact list.

"You'll only have thirty seconds to climb over and get inside."

She made the call, then pocketed the phone and moved ahead of Terrance. There was only a single door on this side of the steel-clad building, with a green and blue logo painted on it. She had a clear view of the red light on the door's keypad. After nearly two minutes, the light changed.

Terrance said, "Go."

She sprinted for the fence, leaped, and caught the eight-foot top rail. Her gloves stuck unnaturally to the metal, almost as if the rail bit into the fabric.

Terrance spoke just loud enough for her to hear. "Don't let your skin touch the metal."

I know that.

With one foot planted in the fence fabric, she was able to swing the other over without touching the rail. The gloves protected her hands as she rotated and repositioned to lower herself to the ground.

"Run," Terrance called.

Like I need to be told.

She sprinted for the door. The light on its access panel was still green. She yanked the handle. A high-pitched annoying squeal confronted her. She ducked inside without bothering to see what she was rushing into.

Ceiling lights turned on automatically, revealing a tall,

narrow room with shelves against the outer wall. The inner wall was a grid of square metal panels with latches at the corners. The irritating sound was coming from behind the numbered panels, and the air smelled of hot plastic.

A metallic click startled her away from the door. She'd beaten the time limit by almost ten seconds and the door had just locked itself.

"You're in the maintenance room," the old man said through the earbud.

"What's the noise?"

"It's not so different from your counting workstation at the aviary. On the other side of those panels are the drinking water portals for every phone in this sector. I imagine you're hearing the sound of high-pressure water being forced through millions of portals."

"I think I'm *feeling* that sound. And it's hot. Does anybody actually work in here?"

"Only when they absolutely have to; we won't be disturbed. Let's get to work, shall we? You're looking for a sphere like the one your friend showed you."

Sarah moved farther into the sweltering room, past shelves cluttered with sections of pipe, valves, and assorted tools. She found nothing that resembled the sphere, but there was a plastic shipping crate on the last of a series of work tables that divided the room. A note tacked to the side of the container read: 'contaminated materials - hold for pickup'. She lifted a flap to peer inside.

"I've got it." She tipped the box and rolled the metal ball onto the table.

"Do you see the keyhole?"

She removed her gloves and dropped them on the table. Then she dug the key out of her pocket and pushed it into the slot at the top of the sphere. A perfect fit.

"Nothing's happening," she said.

"Wait a moment."

The sphere clicked. Then its top half rotated a few degrees and rose on four metal posts, leaving enough space for fingers.

"Careful," he said. "You mustn't jostle the safe until the halves are completely separated."

Sarah slipped her fingers into the gap. The hemispherical shell was heavy, but something inside kept the two pieces in line as she lifted. When she'd raised it four inches, she felt it clear the guides. She tipped the shell over and set it on the table next to the bottom half.

The sphere's interior—a cubic void within a complex arrangement of gears and blades—was not what she expected. Jack might have been able to work out exactly what it was meant for, but to her it seemed the mechanism was designed to destroy its contents: an unmarked plastic cube.

"Open the container," the man said.

She gripped the cube. Its cover came off easily. Inside, a pack of playing cards rested in a rectangular slot. A cluster of styluses—like the one for drawing on her phone—stood upright in a grid of holes.

"Terrance gave you a card. Find the matching one in the deck and replace it."

Sarah opened the pack. They weren't playing cards. They were secure access cards—portal-chipped to an authentication server on Earth. She recognized the logo on several as the symbol for Caerton's corporate security. *What have I done?*

"We have little time, Miss Rogers. Did you find it?"

She examined the card Terrance had given her. The logo wasn't CorpSec but seemed familiar. "What are you going to do with this?"

"The question you should be asking is what the person who brought those cards to Cirrus intended to do with them."

He was right. The cards would give the holder access to a secure building; she had to decide who that someone was going to be. She couldn't guess how Terrance would use it, but at least it wasn't for a CorpSec building.

She found the correct card and put in her pocket. "Okay, I've swapped it."

"How are you holding up?"

"The noise is getting to me—it's making me dizzy. Is there a way to make it stop?"

"We're almost done. Please wait, I'll be right back."

Sarah stewed over her situation. Here she was, breaking into private property to steal for a man she'd just met, to help a friend she'd never met, guided by another man she would never meet. *Jack had better appreciate this.*

While she waited, Sarah scanned the rest of the deck. Briefly, she thought she'd found a card for UV Mobile, but it turned out to be for the neighboring reservoir. The two logos shared the same color scheme and even the same font. *Would the reservoir card open the door here?* On impulse, she slipped that card into her pocket and replaced the deck.

The man returned to the phone. "Now I want you to replace one of the cartridges."

"Terrance didn't give me a cartridge."

"It's your phone's stylus. We couldn't risk losing it."

She ejected the stylus from her phone. There was something wrong with it. She'd used it thousands of times, but now the texture was different—less worn.

"Miss Rogers? Did you hear me?"

Sarah was having difficulty concentrating. She swayed under the same vertigo she'd felt Saturday in the aviary. "Sorry, what?"

"Do you remember the number I gave you earlier?"

"Number?"

"Yes. Try to remember."

The vertigo was getting worse. So was the heat. She was sweating and just wanted to get out of the hot, noisy room. *You didn't give me a number.* "E2," she snapped as she wiped her forehead.

"Excellent. That's the one that will shed light on our common problem. Replace the cartridge at E2."

Numbers from zero to nine on one side of the grid, and letters from A to J on another, identified the cartridges. She found the slot corresponding to E2, removed that cartridge, and inserted it into her phone.

"Now put the sphere back together."

Sarah replaced the cube's cover, then flipped the top shell over and aligned it carefully over the lower guide posts. That's when she realized she hadn't put the replacement cartridge in the cube. And she shouldn't have wiped her brow.

She tried shifting her grip to lift the shell, but it was heavy and her damp fingers were slippery. It dropped heavily onto the four metal posts, leaving a narrow gap between the halves.

Uh oh.

She held her breath. For about a second, nothing happened. Then the pins snapped into the sphere's lower half and the top cover settled with a dull clap. A light in the H-shaped slot flashed. The top shell rotated a few degrees and the sphere vibrated softly.

"Is the safe locked?" the man asked.

The sphere made grinding noises.

"*Oh, yeah.* It's locked."

"Then it's time to go. Make the call."

She set the plastic shipping crate over the sphere, slipped the extra cartridge into her pocket, then hurried to the door while pulling out Terrance's phone. After dialing the number, she listened for one ring and hung up.

The light seemed to take forever to change. The moment it flashed green, she slammed the door open and ran for the fence. She'd taken only two steps when she realized she'd left the gloves behind.

"Where are you going?" Terrance shouted as she turned around.

Sarah dashed across the room. The squeal seemed louder than before. The vertigo hadn't quite resolved, causing her to slip on the concrete floor. She crashed into a table before grabbing the gloves, then sprinted to the exit.

The cooler air outside was instantly refreshing. The vertigo passed as she ran for the fence while pulling on the gloves. As before, she leaped and grabbed the top rail in one smooth motion.

Terrance rushed to the fence. "Jump." He reached up for her.

She vaulted the rail and slammed into him, knocking him backwards. Together they rolled off the gravel margin. When Sarah looked back at the door, the light on the panel was red.

Chapter 18

"I'm sorry, Doctor Marke," Priya said. "There's nothing I can do if you don't file a missing person report."

"I don't know for sure that they're missing. But there's far more at stake here, Detective. Are you aware that Over the Horizon Fuels is a division of Armenau Industries, owned by Pieter Reynard?"

The statement caught her off guard. That was the missing connection. She'd come to Holden's house hoping to learn why his and Pieter Reynard's names were on the arson list. Instead, he assumed she knew something about his family and why he hadn't been able to reach them since last night.

Holden himself was almost exactly as she imagined he would be. Internet photos depicted a man in his mid-seventies, clean-shaven, with thinning white hair, and wearing bifocals. His house confirmed that he'd been a widower for many years—floor-to-ceiling bookshelves, dark wood paneling, and dark leather furniture in the living room brought to mind an English gentleman's club. What she hadn't expected was his Bermuda shorts and bold Hawaiian shirt. And that he knew about Pieter Reynard.

"As I said, I'm investigating a report of a suspicious fire. What is your involvement with OTH Fuels and how does it involve your son?"

Holden offered a slip of paper. "I received this after Nathan called to say they were warned to leave Port Isaac."

Priya recognized the note as the same one she got from Davis. "Who sent it?"

"I don't know. It was slipped under my door."

"At your home or office?"

Holden hesitated. "At my home."

"And why do you think there's a connection to Armenau?"

"When you first asked, I answered truthfully—there was no fire."

"But?"

"Two weeks ago, at the time of the fires, my testing

equipment detected a … *problem*, with one of a batch of crystals that had been grown for fuel delivery. Each company named in the letter used a crystal from the same batch. Over the Horizon was their provider, and Armenau Industries owns OTH."

"This isn't a lot to go on. A less trusting officer would suggest you wrote this note yourself, had it sent to Cirrus and delivered to my office. This could implicate you in the fires. If I look into your cargo manifests, will I find one for a shipment to Cirrus?"

"No. You won't."

"You're seem very sure of that."

Holden appeared to weigh an important decision. "Does Customs and Immigration still do spot checks?"

"Believe it or not, even though every registered frame has a flux monitor, they still send a wormhole-sensitive person to compare their experience with reported use."

"Has Armenau failed any checks recently?"

Priya hesitated, wondering how much information she should share. "Yes, his personal portal at his office in Seattle. Why does that—you seem relieved."

"I have something to show you."

- - - - -

Holden's proof was simple, unmistakable, and terrifying.

Priya had a lot of experience with portals. Her job required regular travel between offices in Olympia and Caerton. She also transported criminals to trial on Earth that way, if they passed the mandatory psych-assessment. She didn't enjoy portal-travel but wasn't concerned about safety; the department's frame had a long and stable track record. As for the detainees; well, if they didn't want to risk being cut in half by a field collapse, then they shouldn't have committed a crime.

Holden had passed through the portal first, to demonstrate its safety, then allowed her to follow. The passage was flawless. There was none of the usual irritation, disorientation, or unpleasant sensations. She understood at once that this technology could revolutionize travel.

But then he did something unthinkable. He picked up a container filled with a glowing compound and reached for the portal.

"*Stop*," she shouted when she realized what he was about to do.

Before she could move, he extended his arm through the wormhole.

It should have collapsed. Holden should have lost those fingers that wrapped around the container's leading edge. None of that happened.

"You can pass radioactive materials through it?"

"Yes. *Any* element. In any quantity."

And there was more. Priya wasn't sensitive to the vertigo large portals caused, but Holden used a flux meter to prove his device created no disturbance at all.

"As remarkable as all this is …" She inspected the frame carefully, looking for some difference between it and the ones she was used to. "I still don't see what it has to do with Armenau or your family going missing on Cirrus."

"This technology could be a nightmare in terrorist hands, but it's not the one I'm concerned about. Pieter may be building something else. Can you track down one of his employees if they travel between Earth and Cirrus?"

"I've got a contact in Customs and Immigration. Why?"

"Since the fires, my equipment has recorded a series of unusual events involving an increasing number of portals. I've spent the last few weeks investigating Armenau and have learned that a bright young man named Simon Pedlar is working there. He may be duplicating my early research."

"You've created an ultra-stable portal that can transport a nuclear bomb anywhere in the world, or be used by criminals to smuggle anything without being tracked. And Pieter Reynard might be using your research to build one for himself, but that's not what worries you?"

"I don't believe he's managed to build a similar portal. If he had, he wouldn't fail a spot check."

"Then what is Simon building for him?"

"I'm not sure. But it could be something much worse."

Chapter 19

Pieter was still in his Seattle office when he received a text alert from Cirrus: <*We've located Jack.*>

He raised an open palm to his desktop screen. "Sorry to cut you short, James. Something has come up that requires my personal attention. Can we pick this up tomorrow?"

"How about this afternoon? You *are* coming back to Cirrus, aren't you?" For a tense moment, Pieter wondered what his business partner knew of the events that had unfolded in the last day, until James added, "Join me for nine holes after the scrum?"

Of course, the press conference.

James Gutierrez controlled all public and business communications in the sector: internet, phones, and entertainment. Together, they owned the city of Caerton and millions of acres of surrounding cropland. Both were scheduled to meet the press at City Hall this afternoon—a show of confidence on the eve of Newton's prophecy.

Pieter forced a convincing smile. "Yes, of course. But you'll have already stolen the show by then. Isn't your own performance at noon?"

James shrugged off the subtle taunt, smoothing his silver-gray mustache. Unlike Pieter, who'd shunned the press until recently, he enjoyed being seen in public, especially with celebrities. "True, but we don't want our investors nervous, do we? A casual round of golf will go a long way to restoring morale."

I'll be glad when this pretense is over. If things went well, he'd not only maintain investor confidence, but gain the power and respect he'd been striving for. "I'll be there. Tee-off without me if I'm late." He planned to be late.

Pieter performed well under pressure, which was a good thing because this day would provide a lot of it. Simon had already started the final equipment test, one that would run into the evening. He'd bring almost every portal crystal on Cirrus to within a fraction of a percent of merging into a single wormhole. There were risks—the smaller-scale tests had only proven the method to work with thousands of crystals, not millions—but no other way to test the resonators.

Danny had received the same message about Jack and entered Pieter's office as soon as he disconnected. "They left town last night on a drone recovery vehicle. We're tracking it now."

"Show me," Pieter said, as both an order to Danny and a directive to the office AI to accept commands from him.

Danny instructed the computer to project a map of the sector's eastern third onto the wall. Caerton and its surrounding lands dominated the upper-right corner, above his head. Port Isaac lay in the lower-left near the floor, and Fairview was at hip level, roughly three-hundred miles north. A jagged red line overlaid the map, tracing a route that led southeast from Fairview, turned north to cross the highway, then backtracked to the Scatter's workshop.

"The vehicle is following a programmed course. It stopped here …" He touched a point on the red line near his knee. "And picked up a drone four hours ago. It then joined a major trunk road heading north. They're here now." He tapped another spot south of the highway.

"Where are they headed?"

"The program will take them to a second crash site in this forest, north of the highway." He highlighted a large zone halfway between the two larger cities. "But we plan to stop them at the crossroad. I've got a car coming out of Fairview that should get there in two hours."

"Why not cut their power and pick them up where they are?"

"Not until we have eyes on them. I've already got drones in the air, but we have no way of tracking them if they escape into the forests."

"Could they have already done that?"

"They'd have to walk a hundred miles in any direction." Danny's map gained more lines—drone flight paths running search patterns to surrounding communities.

Pieter realized too late that reading the map had been a

mistake. He normally relied on intuition to guide him, but the map presented too many data points, too many facts, too many absolutes. These clouded his vision. While only a few were aware of his ability to remember the future, he was careful not to let anyone, especially Danny, discover the relatively simple way of defeating the talent.

"Do you want to re-task an Enforcer from Caerton instead?" Danny added another flight path to show how a larger, armed drone could make the intercept before the car.

"No, I want those for crowd control." After losing the one stationed in Fairview, Pieter had only four left. Two patrolled his estate north of the city twenty-four hours a day, and he wanted the others covering the public event in downtown Caerton. "How did you locate them?"

Danny displayed a blurry image on the wall. "We had already hacked the survey drones in case we found a photo for facial recognition. This image is from the first crash site."

An all-terrain-vehicle occupied most of the shot, but there were also two people in the frame. A foot wearing a brightly colored sneaker was all that was visible of one. Pieter's intuition told him the other was Jack.

Had he been one to give praise, he'd have acknowledged that Danny had thought of everything. "Keep me informed. I want you on Cirrus to oversee preparations for the press conference." The annoyance he'd felt during his meeting with James was still growing. "I'll be there in an hour."

Danny said nothing, but followed Pieter to the hidden portal room. He dropped his phone into the tray as the chamber opened.

"Caerton," Pieter said from the doorway. He let Danny enter on his own and slide the door shut.

He meant to return to his desk. Something made him pause—a fleeting moment of doubt. He was still too agitated to let his talent to provide clarification, and the feeling passed without a revelation. Instead, he waited until he sensed the flux from the portal, confirming Danny had made the passage.

- - - - -

Danny left Pieter's office in Caerton but didn't head

directly to City Hall. He returned to the arcade across the street where he could speak freely.

The survey drone photo had not been entirely his work. His contractors had hacked that system but had no way to review the countless hours of footage. They'd gotten lucky by concentrating on unusual events: power failures, navigation errors, crashes. Someone else had directed the drone to find Jack. That—together with the deliberate spying on the camp—proved they were watching his activities. They'd seen the weapons and weren't bothering to hide it.

Pieter had dismissed the idea of the girl being the unknown Traveller. Danny agreed, but she still presented the best option for finding the real one. However, she was one person in a city of a million. He'd need more eyes. He made another phone call.

Chapter 20

Jack never did get back to sleep. There were few paved roads on Cirrus and the track from the poplar grove was far too rough. Eventually, Dave turned north onto one of the hard-packed gravel roads that grain carriers traveled between the fields and mills.

Hours after loading the drone, Jack maneuvered himself into the cargo bed underneath the damaged aircraft. He'd replaced propellers hundreds of times, although never from below. Only after getting into position did he realize he couldn't see well enough—he'd have to do the repair by touch alone.

A muted beep from the dashboard was the only warning Dave gave before it braked and swerved off the road. Jack was trying to cope with the strong wind and was caught off guard. He dropped his tools and tumbled headfirst into the driver's seat.

"Why are we stopping?" Ethan scanned the sky. "Have they found us?"

Jack struggled to pull himself up. A huge, bright green vehicle was approaching. "It's okay, it's just a harvester. This is a *grain road*—it has the right-of-way here."

The giant machine was taking up the entire road and not slowing at all. Dave stopped in a designated pullout, giving Jack time to gather his tools and pop his head through the roof rack to make a final adjustment.

The driverless grain harvester turned out to be the leader of a convoy. Dave automatically rejoined the road as soon as the last farm vehicle passed.

"That's another thing the nav modules do." Jack flipped on the windshield wipers to clear the dust. "They coordinate passing. That way the roads only have to be one lane wide."

- - - - -

Over the next couple of hours, the cousins encountered more unmanned farm machinery. Some were bulky harvesters; others were large grain carriers towing one or two trailers.

Typically, Dave pulled over to wait, but would occasionally speed up minutes before meeting a larger vehicle, timing its arrival at the pull-outs to swing past without stopping. Once, they found themselves gaining on a wide harvester only to have it unexpectedly veer away, revealing a carrier bearing down on them on the single-lane road.

Ethan ducked involuntarily as Dave followed the harvester to safety with only a second to spare. "Does it always have to be so close?"

"They'd leave more room if we registered as passengers. But I didn't think we wanted to do that."

Eventually, a paved surface replaced the gravel road. "There's something going on ahead." Ethan craned his neck for a better view. "Looks like a traffic jam."

"On Cirrus? Not likely." Jack checked the map. "We should be crossing the highway. I don't understand why traffic is stopped."

The road ahead expanded to three lanes. Vehicles were still approaching in the oncoming one, but a long line of idle tractor-trailers blocked the left-turn lane. Dave slipped into the remaining lane, eased up to the intersection, then stopped.

Ethan flipped through screens on the navigation console. "The GPS says there's a traffic accident."

"Where?"

"Here."

"Here?" The intersection was clear.

"As in, *right here*."

Jack leaned forward to see around the carrier stopped on his left. A single harvester was approaching from that side— the road to Fairview—but no vehicles were turning onto the highway to go that way. "It must be farther—"

Without warning, a transporter hauling two trailers shot through the intersection from the right, peppering Ethan and his side of the truck with loose gravel. The tractor-trailer combo brushed past the oncoming harvester at high speed before veering sharply into its lane. Its front wheels found solid grip and screamed as they slid sideways, spinning the tractor around. The trailers immediately jackknifed and rolled over, carrying the mayhem farther along the highway. A cloud of dust and grain ballooned into the sky.

The dust settled in an unnatural calm. No vehicles moved. Nobody rushed to the scene. Even the birds were silent.

Ethan broke the silence with a nervous question. "Was there anyone inside?"

"There … It was empty. I saw inside as it turned. But there was a black van parked on the shoulder down there."

"Did it get hit?"

"I'm not sure." The cloud was spreading out. Jack could make out the underside of the tractor, much closer than he expected. "No, it's okay. It was at least a hundred yards farther down the road."

"Why did it crash? And why did the GPS say there was an accident before it happened?"

"The carrier must have been out of control. The AI would have stopped traffic to let it pass."

They waited in silence until the vehicles across the road began moving again.

"What are they doing?" Ethan asked as a grain carrier pulled its two trailers onto the road to Fairview, even though it couldn't pass the wreckage. The carrier on Dave's left crawled onto the highway too, further blocking the road.

"It doesn't look like we could get to Fairview even if we wanted to," Jack said.

"What should we do? Take the highway to Caerton? We could be there tonight."

"You still want to go on the highway after seeing *that*? It's too risky. And Dave isn't licensed for the highways; we'd have to switch to manual and wouldn't have the nav module for passing. We're better off on the grain roads."

Dave's navigation module decided for them and drove straight across the intersection.

- - - - -

Few vehicles shared the narrower road as they left the ordered cropland behind them. Otherwise, they encountered only small herds of deer in the undeveloped forests, marshes, moors, and hills. Hours later, the Spine came into view at a fork in the road. The fastest route to Caerton now followed the wider road to the left, over a pass, but Dave's programmed course split to the right, taking the lesser road into the trees.

"This is the largest forest in this sector," Jack said. "It's over seventy miles across. Our drone is near the middle."

Ethan studied the GPS map. "We'll have a lot of options once we ditch the nav module. This path looks like the fastest." He tapped one that exited the woods on the eastern border and ran northeast along the base of the Spine. "We'd have to cross the highway eventually, but then there's another road that runs parallel to the sector wall."

"I'm thinking we take a less obvious one." Jack touched the screen, lighting a path that left the forest at its northern tip. "If they somehow know where we're going, we should stay off the main roads."

"What about this one?" Ethan traced a route that led to another town in the south, identified by only a number. "We could go there and get on a bus."

"That town is actually restricted. They do genetic modifications on animals there."

"And they need to close off the whole town? I heard a story about genetically engineered predators. Is it dangerous?"

"I don't know much about the work they do there, but most plants and animals on Cirrus are modified to some degree. Even the soil here is engineered."

"How do you engineer dirt?"

"On Cirrus, that comment would get you kicked out of the room. Apparently, there are thousands of different soils and none of them are dirt. You'd have to ask Sarah about that though. She knows a lot more about stuff like that than I do."

Jack highlighted his original choice. "This one here doesn't go to any towns at all, it goes over the Spine at its narrowest point and eventually meets up with a grain road."

"Okay, it's got more forests anyway. We'll need those for cover." Ethan zoomed the map to look for details. "The pass goes between two mountains: the Vault and the Mirror."

- - - - -

When Dave was about a mile from the drone's flagged position, it slowed to a crawl, left the path, and began picking its way through the trees. Ethan got out and Jack joined him to walk behind at a leisurely pace.

Ethan yawned and stretched. "It feels so good to be not sitting down. I've hardly moved in the past week. I'd prefer to risk my sanity traveling through a portal than do that again."

"What was it like? Leaving Earth, I mean."

Ethan didn't respond right away, long enough for Jack to realize the question could be taken two ways. He'd meant leaving physically, traveling in space.

"Kinda sucks to leave my friends behind," he finally said. "But I guess that would have happened anyway. Even if I'd gone to university in Washington, most of the guys I hung with were planning to go out of state. And we moved around a lot since I was a kid, so it's not so different from that. Although I don't think I'd have been chased through a forest if I stayed."

"Are you kidding? That fake GPS hotel listing you set up had people driving twenty miles into the woods."

"Actually, I created a whole lakeside resort." Ethan held his head high. "One of my hotels had a five-star rating for a while."

"*Lakeside?* It was *literally* a bag of old cell phones hanging from a tree by a beaver pond."

"Meh, I was young and foolish then."

"Wasn't that last year?"

"A lot has happened in that year."

"And didn't you hack your school's computers to give your friends fake academic awards?"

Ethan waved dismissively. "That wasn't a hack. That was data-entry. The school gave me that job."

"What did your friend Kevin get? Wasn't it something like *Award for Excellence in Video Gaming?*"

"Hey, he was *really* good at that."

"And what about the *Award for the Most Awards?*"

"I might have gotten carried away."

- - - - -

Dave eventually reached the remote spot where the second drone was. It turned out not to have crashed at all. Instead, its boring tool—used for taking core samples—had jammed in a tree trunk. Jack let the robotic arm free the drone. Anyone checking the logs would still not know for sure that he and Ethan were riding along.

The forest around the site was a triumph of genetic engineering. Less than three decades old, it had a well-developed canopy more than eighty feet above the fertile ground. As soon as the robot finished its task, the drone lifted off. Jack lost sight of it within seconds. He heard it buzzing back and forth, climbing through the trees, then the sound faded as it rose into the open sky.

"Time to memorize the map," Jack said as he returned to the truck. "We won't have one soon."

"The first part looks easy." Ethan traced a thin line. "We just go north. Once we're on the other side of the Spine, we follow the small river downstream and then the big one upstream all the way to Caerton. What about the Spine, though? Can Dave handle it?"

"We'll worry about that when we get there. For now, let's get ready to release the other drone."

Jack disconnected the clamps securing the aircraft to the cargo rack while Ethan removed the cover to Dave's computer. The plan was to replace the drone's navigation module as soon as Dave returned to the road—they didn't want to risk someone seeing an autonomous vehicle stopped for no reason.

Dave labored for twenty minutes over rough ground to reach the road. Jack hit the brakes as soon as the wheels touched the dirt track. Ethan yanked the module from the truck's control box and thrust it into the drone. At once, the drone powered up and lifted off. It accelerated smoothly, following the road to Fairview exactly as if it were driving.

"How long before it gets there?" Ethan asked.

"If we're lucky, it'll be almost five hours. If they think we're coming back, they'd try to catch us outside of town. So, maybe only four hours, or three. Maybe less?"

Without a navigation module, Dave was invisible to anyone trying to track it. But without a GPS, Jack had to find the correct route by memory. He pressed the accelerator and drove deeper into the forest.

Chapter 21

Why me?

That question had been running through Sarah's thoughts all morning as she paced the banding room in forty-second intervals. She barely glanced at the screen before filing the GPS data and requesting the next set of index boards.

Why did I have to be the one to go over the fence? Terrance had a man on the inside. Why didn't he get the card? Why didn't Terrance do it himself?

She considered her options. The man who discovered her drone at the basin had been wearing a CorpSec jacket. Who could she trust? Call the police? And tell them what? That she'd broken into a secure warehouse and stolen—. Her hand drifted to her pocket, touching the stylus she was supposed to have put in the sphere. What *had* she taken? It didn't matter now; she'd given Terrance the card and the other stylus, but destroyed the rest of the evidence, ground it into powder.

And why had the older man insisted he'd told her a number? She'd been eager to leave and picked the combination at random, but he'd acted as if E2 was correct.

With no solid answers, she left the conservation building and headed to the parking lot. She stopped and stared at the path to the reservoir. *There's still the phone.* Terrance had returned it to the jar behind the tree, saying his accomplice would retrieve it later. *All I have to do is show the police how it opens the door and let them track down that person. And then what?* She'd have to tell the police where Jack was. Was that safe? *What if the point was only to stop me from calling the police?* She was lost so deep in thought she didn't notice Jada approaching from the bus stop.

"Are you ready?" Jada asked.

"Huh? For what?"

"It's my last day here. You told me we'd do something special."

"Oh, right. Sorry."

"You seem upset. Is there another tour today?" Jada

grinned. "Should I hide my phone?"

"Ha-ha, funny." Sarah had forgotten her promise, but decided she could really use a distraction. "Our falcons are finally out of quarantine. You can help feed them. We'll take a shortcut through the wetland."

The aviary was huge, with more than five hundred acres under a two-hundred-foot-high netting. They wandered past dozens of enclosures housing hundreds of species in various habitats. The wetland was the largest zone, but the area under the nets enclosed only a small part of it—thousands of acres of marsh continued to the south.

"How did it go with your boss and the CorpSec guy? Did you get in trouble?"

"Huh?" With all that had happened that morning, Sarah had forgotten about the visit. "No, actually. He never came back."

"He wouldn't dare." Jada held herself a little taller and began to strut.

Sarah laughed. "You're right, I owe you."

"True. You can repay me by painting a snake head on my new helmet."

"I've never painted a snake before."

"I've seen your work. You're the best artist I know."

"I might be the only artist you know. But I'll give it a try."

"There are ducks here." Jada stopped walking at the midpoint of a short bridge. "Why are they breeding ducks? Weren't those released years ago?"

"There are a lot of different types of ducks. Sometimes a colony only survives a few years and we have to start over again. Half of all attempts fail completely." Sarah rested her elbows on the railing and gazed across the wetland at a group of large birds wading in shallow waters. "Those are Great Blue Herons. They're extinct on Earth now. These are the only ones that exist anywhere."

Thirty of the long-legged birds waded around tufts of tall sedge, searching for small fish and crustaceans. One chose that moment to stretch its wings. Jada had never seen a bird so large before. Its wings—six-feet across—stretched considerably wider than she was tall.

While Jada watched the herons, Sarah watched her reaction. She was pleased to see it was similar to her own first experience.

"We get so few opportunities for close encounters with nature," Sarah said. "I wish more people were interested in the animals we share this world with. Maybe Earth wouldn't be in such a sorry state if everyone spent some time with them."

Jada watched the birds for a few more minutes. "I still want to see the falcons. Is that okay?"

"It's fine. Everybody wants to see the raptors, especially at feeding time. The herons are special to me because I started working here the day the last one died on Earth. We're saving whole species on Cirrus, not individual birds."

She led Jada to the conservation building, to an area across the hall from the banding room. Several dozen large cages lined the walls. Most were empty.

"Is that all there are?" Jada asked. A half dozen of the tawny predators occupied separate cages.

"We don't breed them here. These were found sick or injured. If we can't rehabilitate and release them, they'll be sent to Port Isaac."

As she fed the falcons, Jada noticed Sarah's concerned expression when her phone beeped. "Is something wrong? Is your new phone causing problems?"

"It's actually my original phone, and it's working fine. That was a message from Penny."

"You don't look happy. Is it about the CorpSec guy?"

"No, she sends me links to environmental news on Earth. It's just that I haven't heard from Jack. I sent him a couple of texts this morning. But he's probably just busy. His cousin arrived from Earth yesterday."

"Ooh, where's he from? We've had new people coming into the restaurant every day this month. Yesterday there was a group from Hawaii. They had pictures of the beaches."

"We have beaches here too."

"The beaches are different on Earth." Jada's tone

suggested this was something everyone knew.

"That doesn't mean they're better. We've still only terraformed half of Cirrus. Eventually, people in Hawaii may become jealous of our beaches."

"That might take decades, maybe hundreds of years. Earth has those things right now. What good is it if we can't leave the cities?"

"That'll change. Soon. Most environments are stable now. I heard they intend to release ten thousand species of plants and animals next year. And Earth isn't doing very well at preserving what they've got. Here, watch the video Penny just sent." She tapped an icon.

"This is Samantha Coleridge reporting from the banks of the River Avon, where the West Midlands Psychiatrist Association's annual Shakespeare Festival has been cancelled due to unseasonal flooding."

"People on Earth are nuts," Sarah said, watching a group of bearded men in Elizabethan garb standing on a water-surrounded mound as their beer tent floated away. She checked the time. "And we've got to get back to work. Let's go out through the banding room."

As she passed the console, Sarah prepared the survey computer to run a test cycle so the mortality data would be ready for review when she returned. Jada made another comment about the dangers of working near radio waves and portals.

Sarah was about to reply when her phone beeped again. "It's not him. I'm getting worried."

"I wouldn't worry too much. Jack's … well, he's Jack, isn't he? He's not gonna go out and do something stupid like Chase would." Jada's phone beeped. "And speaking of …" Jada scrolled through Chase's message. "He's sent another stupid doomsday video. He says there was a big accident involving hundreds of vehicles near Fairview."

"*Let me see.*" Sarah grabbed at Jada's phone but she'd already started the video.

Aerial footage showed wreckage strewn across the highway for a hundred yards. Long lines of farm machinery waited on both sides of the mess. A work crew was cutting trees to let traffic get around the twisted carrier.

"That's Chase for you," Jada said. "There *are* hundreds of vehicles there, but only a single grain carrier flipped over."

The video then showed a representative of the Traffic Control Authority making a statement to reporters.

"Was it a terrorist act?" a reporter asked.

"I can't comment at this time. But we're asking the two young men who were at the scene to come forward as potential witnesses."

Sarah didn't catch the rest of the interview because she had fixated on the logo on the wall behind the woman. It was the same design as on the access card she'd swapped at the reservoir.

Traffic Control. Terrance did this.

All her frustrations boiled over. She slammed her hand on the console, accidentally starting the machine. "What is *wrong* with people?" The first index board slid into place. "It's going to take a hundred years to repair Earth's climate. Cirrus was supposed to give us time to do that. The work we're doing here is as important to Earth's future as it is to ours. We already have dozens of species here that have gone extinct on Earth. And it's not just birds. Other cities have reptiles and amphibians that haven't been seen there in decades."

"*Whoa.* I know you're passionate about your job. But that's intense, even for you."

"Sorry, it's just ..." Sarah leaned back against the console. "Cirrus belongs to the people of Earth as much as it does to us. There'll be a billion people moving here in the next decade, but they shouldn't bring their problems with them. We don't need ..." She gestured at Jada's phone. "We don't need crap like this."

"It was an accident. These things happen."

Sarah took a deep breath and exhaled slowly. "Maybe it wasn't an accident."

"Oh ... It was near Fairview, wasn't it? This is about Jack. You think he and Ethan are the two they're looking for? Don't worry about him. He's Mr. Reliable, Mr. Common-Sense. Even if the crash was deliberate, he's far too cautious to be involved."

Yeah, I'm the one who did something stupid. Jack had been impulsive, but he wouldn't have gone to the basin in the first place if he hadn't thought there was a mess to clean up. *It was my mistake. And now I can't go to the police without involving him.*

"Still …" Sarah slipped her phone into her pocket. "It's not like him to be out of touch for so long."

"If you had the other half of his phone's portal, you could tell—" A chorus of agitated tweets interrupted Jada. Every bird in the cage on the right side of the room was darting around, jumping from perch to perch or flapping about chaotically. The non-banded birds in the neighboring enclosure were acting normally. The ceiling light panels buzzed and brightened. "What's going on?"

"I … I don't know." Sarah felt a growing disorientation, similar to the vertigo she'd experienced before her phone went missing. She stared at the index board on the conveyor. Neither she nor the board was moving, but its pitted surface seemed to her like a deep well she was tipping into.

"Why are all the pixels red?"

"What?" Sarah pushed herself from the console. Every dot on the monitor had turned red. She waited through several cycles. There was no change. "Something's wrong. I'd better get Penny." She'd taken only a single step when the banded birds abruptly went silent. The lights returned to normal and the monitor displayed only a single red pixel.

"That was weird," Jada said. "What happened?"

"I don't know, but it's over now." Even her light-headedness had passed the moment things returned to normal. "Sorry, what were you saying about Jack?"

"I was only joking. You said you could locate any bird by listening to the GPS signal. I was suggesting you use it to find out where Jack went."

"I'm sure he'll tell me when he gets here tomorrow."

Recovery from her surprise, Jada blurted, "*Jack's coming here*? You're finally getting together? When?"

"He … I … I'm not sure. I think he told me he'll be here in the morning." *Did Terrance say Jack was coming to Caerton?*

Confused, she changed the subject. "I should get back to work. I'll walk out with you. We'll stop by the owl cages on our way."

As she walked away from the console, Sarah wasn't even sure she'd spoken to Jack at all. The memory had already faded like a dream upon waking.

Chapter 22

The forest was cool and damp. Dave's electric motor made less noise than its tires did, snapping through the brush covering the road. And there was a lot of that.

The route Jack and Ethan had agreed on forked several times as it headed deeper into the woods. It was obviously the least used—parts of it were almost completely overgrown. Jack drove as fast as he dared, but it still took two hours to reach the forest's northern edge, where they stopped to scan the skies.

"Do you see anything?" Jack asked.

"No," Ethan said, "but a high-flying drone will spot us long before we see it anyway." He focused on the ordered rows of an orchard across five miles of shortgrass prairie. "I say we just go for it."

"You're right." Jack twisted his hands into the padded steering wheel. "We need to stay where a drone might mistake Dave for a farm vehicle." He slammed his foot to the floor and sped away from the forest.

The drive became harrowing. Dry, loose gravel provided poor traction as he sped for the protection of the trees. More than once he nearly lost control while cornering.

Ethan cinched his harness tighter.

"Mind if I drive?" he asked warily when they finally stopped in the middle of the grove.

Even though he'd admitted to having only ever driven a simulator, Jack agreed to let him take over. Within minutes it became clear that he had a knack for driving—more precisely, for driving fast. The road narrowed and twisted as the ground rose and fell through the highlands, but he reached speeds equal to what Jack had achieved on the grain roads.

Jack cinched his harness tighter.

"I just thought of something." Ethan grinned impishly as he drifted into a corner. "The drone's going all the way back to Fairview at eye-level."

Jack erupted into laughter, having conjured an image of a

drone flying in traffic. "It has to pass through a couple of intersections before it gets to the shop. It'll stop at red lights." Ethan started laughing too.

- - - - -

By mid-afternoon, they reached the base of the Spine. They'd seen many drones as they dashed between orchards and vineyards, but all were engaged in farming tasks such as planting or scaring birds. The road turned east, rising steeply into a broken and tortured landscape.

The Spine was a chaotic place—not made for easy driving—and wasn't supposed to be made at all. When the molten mass of the rim mountain slumped, it pushed the cooler, partially hardened inland crust ahead of it. Instead of slowing as planned to create a trough-like depression for a central sea, the viscous material collided with its counterpart advancing from the opposite side, forming mountains again. The cousins had to find their way over or around four-mile-tall jagged peaks that resulted from a misplaced decimal point.

"This road doesn't look like it's been used in years," Jack said as Dave climbed. He caught glimpses of plains and forests far below through breaks in the trees. "I'm surprised it was on the map at all."

Ethan slammed on the brakes after rounding a sharp bend. "Was this on the map?"

On the left, the mountain rose vertically. Ahead, a narrow ledge traversed a curved wall above a sheer drop on the right. Without so much as a weed along its two-hundred-foot length, the stone shelf seemed to merge into a shaft so smooth it could have been gouged by a gigantic claw.

Jack leaned over his door. "There was nothing about suicide, if that's what you mean." Broken slabs of gray stone covered the floor of a gorge hundreds of feet below.

"Is this even a road?"

"Yeah, I can see it continuing into the trees on the far side."

Ethan got out and approached cautiously. He stamped his foot on the bare stone, proving only that the narrow ledge could support the weight of an impulsive teenager. "Maybe we should walk."

"We've got another four hundred miles, and we'd have to carry all our food and water." Jack could see to the horizon through the break in the trees. They'd already climbed a mile above sea level, and the GPS had pictured the pass as being another mile higher. "We need Dave."

"We need to be alive to drive it."

"The road wouldn't have been mapped if it wasn't safe. And the surface doesn't look natural. I'm sure it was cut."

Ethan shook his head.

"Okay." Jack inched onto the ledge. "We'll walk across first and use the winch to tow the truck after us."

"It's too narrow. And it curves inward. The winch will just drag Dave over the edge."

Ethan was right—one of them would have to steer. "Then one of us will sit on the hood and turn the wheel through the window. There's a rope in the cargo box. We can tie it to trees on each side to make a safety line. Then we'll make harnesses. If Dave goes over, we'll still be attached to the rope."

"*That's a horrible plan.*" Ethan grinned. "Who gets to sit on the hood?"

"*Gets to?* Don't you mean *has to?*"

"Can I turn on my phone for a selfie?"

"No."

Ethan pretended to be disappointed. "Fine, I'll do it anyway."

The rope was long enough to span the ledge, but the winch cable was not. After much discussion and experimentation, they decided it would be too difficult to drive the truck from the outside. So they unbolted part of the roof rack, and Ethan—harnessed to the safety rope—drove while Jack trudged ahead, pulling the steel cable as it unspooled.

He was wearing a backpack with their food in it. Ethan carried nothing, not even his jacket, to be sure he wouldn't snag on anything if he had to leap from a falling truck. If they lost Dave, the only item they'd have from the cargo was the spare power cell, and only because Jack had forgotten it in his pocket.

"Almost there," Jack called.

A loud whine made him look back just as Dave jerked and sideswiped the rock wall, rebounding to stop with half its rear tire folded over the shelf's edge.

Ethan seized the safety line. "What was that?"

Dave's daytime running lights were unusually bright. "Power surge. Are you okay?"

He put his hands back on the steering wheel. "Yeah, I'm good."

The lights faded to normal and Jack was about to resume walking when—with a sharp pop—a football-size stone flake spun out from under the rear tire and plummeted into the gorge.

Ethan heard the noise. He grabbed the rope again and pulled himself out of his seat. Dave rolled backwards and tipped as its rear wheel settled into the cavity.

"Stop," Jack yelled. A high-pitched tone sounded from the power cell in his pocket. The truck steadied. "Keep your foot on the brake. There's a hole behind the wheel."

Ethan stomped on the pedal. "*Do something.*"

Dave was in a precarious position. If it rolled back even an inch farther, its center of mass would shift toward the unsupported rear wheel. There would be no stopping it from slipping off the ledge.

Jack spotted a sturdy-looking branch on the closest tree—a pine with a trunk more than a foot in diameter. He began twirling the winch cable, letting it slide from his grip in an ever-widening circle. After only a few rotations, he was struggling to hold on as the metal hook swooped above and below the ledge.

Another loud pop. "*Do it now,*" Ethan shouted.

Jack released the cable. "C'mon, c'mon," he pleaded as the weighted end arced toward the forest. The power cell emitted another shrill tone.

The hook dropped over the branch a moment before the line went taut, then recoiled at the perfect angle to wrap around the limb several times.

He pulled the cable to make sure it was solid. "Start the

BROKEN SKY

winch." *Why is it doing that?* The power cell had started pulsing, but he couldn't tear his eyes away from Dave to check on it.

Ethan hit the switch and the motor took up the slack. The tree bent, snapped loudly, and leaned sharply toward the truck. He released the brake slowly. Dave held its position.

"Just a bit longer," Jack pleaded. The cable had wrapped at the limb's strongest point, near to the trunk, but the branch was only a few inches thick. The noise from the power cell was constant now.

Dave shifted. It rolled forward half an inch. Another inch. The tree groaned and bent farther. Jack tensed.

Crack. He yelped at the sound—loud as a gunshot—from his pocket.

Dave lurched backwards, but then stopped and rolled ahead. The tree would bend no farther.

Ethan scrambled onto the hood and steered the truck so close to the wall that its tires left black smudges on the rock. Then, bent awkwardly over the windshield, he began laughing—from relief—as he guided his harness along the rope while steering. Jack regretted that they couldn't use their phones. With his butt in the air, Ethan's selfie would not have been the machismo-look he'd been hoping for.

With his cousin safe, Jack withdrew the spare power cell from his pocket. Its connection light was out and fragments of crystal spilled from the contact port. *What happened?* He'd seen—and heard—crystals fail before, but only under extreme load, never when idle. *The power surge?* That didn't make sense because the cell wasn't connected to anything. There was no power flowing to be affected by a surge.

Later, as they were reassembling the roof rack, Ethan said, "That was an impressive throw. It was almost like magic the way the cable wrapped around that branch."

"Well, if you hadn't been so quick on the brakes, we might've lost Dave before I had a chance."

"Oh? That wasn't me. Dave stopped rolling before I hit the pedal. Does it have some sort of safety feature to keep it from rolling backwards?"

"Um, maybe." Jack was too baffled by the unexpected

142

failure of the power cell to recall what his parents might have told him about the truck. "But I'm not going back to find out."

- - - - -

The road trended ever higher, mostly on the exposed face of the mountains. But Ethan also guided Dave through confined canyons with sides so steep that even the mountain goats avoided them. By late afternoon there was little evidence they followed a man-made trail at all. They traversed spurs where they picked their route based on what appeared the least treacherous. Only once did the road fork. Jack chose left, to continue climbing.

"I think we're near the summit," he said. "If we're still on the right path, there should be a creek ahead. I need water."

"What makes you think we're at the top?"

"It had been getting cooler as we climbed, but now it's warmer. It's summer on the northern side of the Spine. Also, we're going north instead of east. We should be on the Vault."

The forest they entered was so dense Jack couldn't tell how far it extended. Fortunately, a clear path cut through the trees, so he knew they were still going the right way. "There it is." The creek cut across the road in a narrow, gravel-filled trench.

Ethan pulled Dave well off the path to hide it under the trees. "I'm hungry."

"You're always hungry. But I'm sort of hungry now too."

He kneeled by the creek to refill his water bottle while Ethan unloaded the cargo box and put together a simple meal. They had just settled into their seats when all the dashboard lights went out.

Ethan started pushing buttons. "What happened?"

Jack tried the key. No response. "They disconnected the power." He flipped open the maintenance panel and extracted a thumb-sized metal cylinder. Its LED was dark. "The source for the power cell is in the workshop. They were waiting for us there."

Ethan jumped out and began pacing. "So, what do we do now? Do we give up, or go on foot?" He kicked a low branch off a nearby tree, then picked it up and hurled it into the woods. "We should call our parents and find out for sure what's happening."

"No, let's think this through. We just have to figure out a different way to get there." Jack removed a pair of binoculars from the cargo box and started walking. "I need a minute."

He followed the creek downstream to a steep drop-off and peered over the edge into a narrow basin saddled between the Vault and the Mirror. After an initial near-vertical drop of sixty feet, the water tumbled another fifteen-hundred feet over the Vault's sharp corners and angles.

Trees on either side of the creek blocked his view of anything but the forest below, but a tall outcropping of bare rock towered on his right. He found a safe route to the top and sat facing the Mirror's relatively smooth face. Beyond that, the Spine continued to the horizon.

The sun had already slipped behind the Vault, leaving him in deep shadow. The Mirror's upper half was still brilliantly lit, but the reflected sunlight gave him no warmth.

Maybe I should let Ethan call his parents. To find out what's really going on.

He was certain that his own parents were not in trouble with CorpSec, and being in trouble with the real police seemed even less likely. Some people mistrusted the corporations and their security forces, but he'd always heard that these issues revolved around money. After all, most corporations on Cirrus had moved their operations from Earth to avoid taxes. Being an off-world company was the easiest way to avoid contributing to their home nation's guaranteed income fund.

Would Ethan even know if his parents were involved in something illegal? And why had they taken different vessels to Cirrus? How had they gotten seats so quickly? Grace was an expert in computer security. So was Nathan, but he also had experience with artificial intelligence systems. Could they have planned this?

He tried putting these suspicions behind him and turned his attention to the north, the direction they needed to go. The Spine descended more steeply on that side, and the forest

continued in patches down the slope and through the narrow
foothills. After that, the fields and isolated forests faded into
the distance. Beyond that was Caerton.

At least it's downhill from here, Jack thought, anticipating the
long walk ahead.

He leaned that direction and considered the creek that
spilled into the forested saddle below. It hid among the trees
in the basin but its path was obvious—the foliage was darker
where there was more water.

On a larger scale, similar lines of heavy growth extended
from glaciers in the Spine out into the northern plains. There,
another feature caught his attention. His pulse quickened. He
lifted the binoculars and focused on a large coniferous forest.
Under magnification, the trees surrounded a round lake. The
lake itself featured a round, tree-covered island.

Jack jumped to his feet. The crag he stood upon wasn't as
tall as the surrounding trees, but he was high enough to see
that the ground was flat for much farther than it appeared
from the road. He'd thought they were crossing the face of
the mountain through another forested stretch, but the trail
actually cut across the base of a deep, hanging valley.

He climbed down as fast as he could, stumbling at the
bottom and landing in a roll. Without a pause, he sprang to
his feet and sprinted back to the truck.

Ethan was eating, although not with much enthusiasm. He
heard Jack running. "What's wrong?"

Jack yelled, "Follow me," as he ran past.

Ethan jumped from his seat. "Have they found us?"

"It's not that. I'm just looking."

"For what?"

"I'll know when I find it."

Jack weaved through the trees with Ethan following. He
vaulted an egg-shaped boulder, then turned sideways to
squeeze through a crack in another that was large as a bus.
Soon, he reached the far edge of the woods, where the valley
narrowed and the forest gave way to bare stone. A tumble of
large boulders blocked his view, but the brightness above
suggested a wider space beyond. The stream flowed from the

top of the rocks. He started climbing.

"What are you looking for?" Ethan asked when he caught up. "Have you been here before?"

"Yes. I mean, no. I'm not sure."

Jack reached the top where a large slab formed a shallow, overhanging shelter. There was an opening underneath—the mouth of a cave. A few trees had found decent soil among the rocks, and one stood directly in front of the overhang. Its trunk had grown wide enough that the cave entrance wasn't visible at all from the base of the rock pile. He crouched facing the opening and hesitated for only a moment before crawling through.

Ethan climbed the pile to join him. "You sure that's safe? Some of these rocks look like they've fallen recently."

"It's here." Jack sounded like he didn't believe it himself.

"What?"

"This." He crawled out wearing an enormous grin, holding what appeared to be a standard power cell. It was grimy and discolored but otherwise matched the one from the truck, right down to the red lightning bolt.

And its connection light was blinking.

Chapter 23

Press conferences can be productive, tedious, confrontational, or anything in between. The one Pieter had just suffered through was a mixed bag. James went on at length, reassuring the crowd with his too-white teeth and nonchalant smile. Pieter tried to keep it brief, dismissing Newton's Prophecy as fearmongering.

Unfortunately, there had been a major traffic accident on the highway involving a grain carrier. The cause was still under investigation but the timing could not have been worse. Pieter was hardly surprised when a reporter told him the transporter was one of Armenau's vehicles—it was turning into that kind of day.

He'd arrived on Cirrus that morning, hoping to be free by noon to oversee the final test. That didn't happen. Instead, James had arranged meetings with high-value investors and politicians—meetings Pieter had to attend in case he needed their support in coming days. As a result, he was out of the loop on the most recent developments.

At three o'clock, he instructed his driver to take him to the city's reservoir. Danny was already waiting there in an underground chamber.

Pieter surveyed the converted water tank as he entered. On one side, racks of portal testers and supercomputers matched those in Doctor Marke's Archive. Next to them was the resonator—the original. He was pleased to see that the second device was already disassembled and ready for transport to Earth.

Danny didn't wait for Pieter to ask the obvious question. "We haven't caught them yet. But we know where they went."

Pieter already knew some of the details. The boys had left town the night before, having hitched a ride on a self-guided vehicle. The plan to catch them this morning had failed miserably. "What went wrong?"

Danny sent a video to Pieter's phone. "The intercept team was waiting at the crossroad. They saw the front wheels of a transport turn and lock. It slid across the highway and rolled over."

"An autonomous unit? Turned on its own in the middle of the road?"

Danny started the video, recorded by one of his contractors. A harvester passed by the parked CorpSec vehicle just as Jack's truck pulled up to the intersection. Seconds later, an oncoming grain carrier swerved into its lane and flipped over. A gritty yellow wave flowed along the road and covered the van in several inches of grain.

"It completely blocked both lanes, forcing us to detour to a single-lane road. That's when the TCA got spooked and my crew was caught in the middle of a convoy."

Pieter scanned the news on his phone. The Traffic Control Authority—fearing a terrorist act on the eve of Newton's Prophecy—had cut the maximum speed of all self-driving transporters in the sector.

Danny continued. "It took two hours to get back to the main road. They'd already got into the forest, where they swapped the vehicle's transponder and sent a drone to Fairview in their place." He brought up a map on a nearby workstation.

Pieter examined the grouping of irregular shapes on the screen. "What are these zones?"

"The outer loop shows how far they could have gone before we cut the power. The smaller ones are where we're concentrating our search."

Pieter silently conceded that the boys' plan had been clever. However, they couldn't possibly have engineered the crash, and it had been much too effective to be coincidental. That the carrier was one of his own fleet seemed like a deliberate taunt. Someone else was responsible—another Traveller. *How much do they know?*

He had an additional concern—one he couldn't even begin to address. The afternoon's resonance test had had an unexpected outcome, far beyond a simple power surge. He had *felt* it. And if he sensed it, then other Travellers did too.

There were also rumors of animals acting strangely all over

Cirrus. Some were comparing this to stories of dogs barking before an earthquake and linked the event with the prophecy. Fortunately, he could ignore that and let others discredit those reports as fear-mongering. In truth, he had little choice in the matter; the test had been a success as far as the equipment was concerned. Not only was there no turning back, his plans had reached the stage where timing was critical.

Danny gestured at the lines drawn on the western side of the forest. "We're think they're headed for Port Isaac, but avoiding the main roads. We'd cover a lot more ground if you'd dispatch Enforcers."

Pieter turned away from the monitor as new data appeared on the map. He tapped an icon on his phone. A much simpler diagram showed the positions of the anti-personnel drones that patrolled his estate or shadowed him on Cirrus. At that moment, an Enforcer hovered high above the reservoir.

He'd refused Danny's earlier request, though he understand his head of security needed freedom to work effectively. Now, his intuition told him Jack would play a crucial role in the plan's success. Danny had become too aggressive recently, but the high-speed drones might swing the balance in his favor. "Two," he finally decided. "No munitions."

Danny tapped an instruction into his phone. "If they're on foot, we'll have them by morning."

Pieter reconsidered the map, which showed a range of variables, including the possibility they'd been picked up in another vehicle. "And if they're not?" However, even as he asked, he knew the boys were on their own. Someone had blocked traffic to give them time to escape; whoever was helping them was working remotely.

Danny answered the question anyway. "We're checking all transporters in the area and stopping all other traffic."

This act was highly illegal. Luckily, the TCA's own actions and worries over terrorism meant Pieter could avoid complications for a while. And he only needed one more day.

"The closest settlement is Granton." Danny tapped the town's marker. "Their CorpSec is part of the Ballard co-op—

we don't have anyone on the inside. If that's where they're headed, they'll still be hours away on foot. They might connect with Ballard and ask them to call the police."

"No. Corporate politics isn't something people their age are interested in. Every town would be the same to them. They had an opportunity to contact local security last night. They didn't. That can only mean someone told them where to go." And having said it, Pieter knew it was true. "They were told to go somewhere."

"Where?"

"Let's find out."

The circular chamber they stood in had no interior walls. A steel ladder, in the exact center of the room, led to a hatch in the domed ceiling, thirty feet above. The ladder continued through an opening in the floor. An open-cage style elevator ran next to it. Danny opened the door for Pieter and followed him into the cage.

The lower level was completely different. Ten rooms ringed the chamber, creating a smaller, circular space centered on the ladder. They'd been printed using the weather-resistant concrete blend normally used for exterior walls, and had the appearance of being constructed hastily, choosing function over form.

Metal doors, each with an access panel beside it, secured each room. Danny waved his card over a sensor to unlock a door, then slid it open for Pieter.

"Good day to you all," Pieter greeted the four people in the cell. "Mrs. Scatter, where is your son going?"

Chapter 24

Ethan took the power cell from Jack's open hand. "What was that doing in there? Did you leave it there?"

"I … It's really hard to explain. Yeah, I think I left it here a long time ago. Except it wasn't me. I'm not sure."

"What? When? That makes no sense at all."

"Sorry. I don't understand it myself." He could see suspicion in Ethan's face; he was having the same doubts that Jack had about him. "Trust me for now. If I knew how it got there, I'd tell you."

Ethan didn't look happy, but accepted that he wasn't going to get a better answer. "Is it compatible with the truck? It looks old."

"Dave is older than I am. There's only ever been one factory in this sector that makes small cars. Every model uses the same motor. It'll work."

"Then let's get out of here." Ethan clambered down the rocks.

Jack stayed on top, examining his surroundings. *This must be the same place.*

In his dream, the cave was exposed, not hidden behind trees. Of course, the trees he remembered were only saplings, but the creek was in the same spot. So, there were differences, and yet too many similarities to ignore. Everything about the place seemed so very familiar.

Beyond the wall was a pond he'd never paid much attention to in his dream. It wasn't broad—perhaps a hundred feet across—but he got the feeling it was very deep. He edged closer, peering into the clear water. The suspicion became a certainty. Just like how he knew what part was broken inside a machine; the pond was much deeper than it was wide.

Ethan was waiting at the bottom of the slope. "Are you coming?"

"Yeah … I'll be right there."

Was the dream a distant memory? he wondered as he climbed down. *As far as I know, I've never been here before. And if it's a memory, who was the man who led me to the cave?* Jack was certain it was someone he knew, someone he trusted. *There's no way that finding the power cell exactly when I need it is a coincidence.*

Ethan was cleaning the cell as he walked. "This has been here a long time. Why would someone leave a working power cell out here? And why is it still connected? And where is it powered from?"

"I really don't know." As Jack followed, the feeling of familiarity faded the farther he got from the cave. He stopped and retreated a few paces. The sensation increased.

"Where are you going now?"

Jack stopped. "It's nothing. I'm just trying to remember something." He joined Ethan and the sensation faded again, as if he'd passed through an invisible curtain.

He decided to keep it to himself; there was enough tension between them already. He didn't want to say something to make Ethan think he was hallucinating, even though he was certain that the feeling came from this place, not himself.

Ethan opened the service panel and removed the dead cell. "Wait. As soon as we plug this in, someone's going to be paying for the power. What happens when they see a connection that's been disconnected for … what? Years? Suddenly come back to life?"

"I know for sure it's not connected to our meter, so we don't have to worry about someone in our shop seeing it. But you're right. There's a chance someone, somewhere, will notice."

"Should we wait until after business hours, so whoever owns the other end is gone for the day?"

"We have no way of knowing where the source is. It may already be night there. It might even be on Earth. We need to get as far from here as possible. It won't take them long to figure out what we did and how far we could have gone before they cut the power. We'll have to risk it."

Ethan connected the cell. Dave's lights came on.

"Don't shut off. Don't shut off," Jack wished aloud.

After a full minute, the lights were still on. Ethan shrugged. "Okay, let's go." He hopped into the driver's seat.

For the next two hours, Ethan drove as fast as he safely could, for the path down to the foothills was rough and unpredictable. As it had been on the way up, in some places the route was nothing more than bare rock. He followed what he thought was the easiest path, hoping to find the real road on the far side. There wasn't much cover on the mountain's north slope either, and they didn't stop to check for drones until they were into the rolling hills.

Jack held up his hand. "Quiet. Listen."

Ethan had been about to pull away from the shelter of a willow grove. He stopped the truck and whispered, "I don't hear anything."

A distant buzz intensified into a loud, rhythmic thumping. Jack instinctively ducked as a large black drone passed overhead at high speed. He leaned out of the truck, trying to identify the aircraft as the noise receded. "That was close."

Ethan twisted in his seat. "I can't see it, but it sounded way bigger than the farming drones we've seen so far. Do you think it was looking for us?"

"Maybe. I don't understand why it was so low though. If it was searching for us, it's got to be easier from higher up."

"Maybe they can detect a portal from that height—like a scanner at an airport. Or maybe they're hoping to catch us by surprise."

"I guess so. There's no way we could have hid in time if we were in the open." *Or maybe they don't want to be seen, themselves.*

Ethan checked the position of the sun, orienting himself. "That drone was coming from the north. If someone were driving from Caerton, how long would it take them to get here by ground?"

"If they used the highway? Four or five hours."

"How long until dark?"

Jack considered the darkening sky, the familiar way red, orange, and yellow refracted through the roof. "We might have an hour before we'll need headlights."

"We shouldn't leave until then, in case there are more drones. But then we should be safe to drive for a couple of hours." Jack agreed and Ethan turned the truck back into the willows, driving a hundred yards before he was satisfied that no one could see them from the road. "Here comes another one." He switched off Dave's power.

After the drone passed, Jack said, "That one's going fast too. I think it means they're not looking for us here. We must be far outside their search area."

- - - - -

It never got completely dark anywhere on Cirrus, except at the spring and fall equinoxes when the ring eclipsed the Eye. When they finally left their shelter, there was just enough moonlight to pick out the track in open areas without headlights. Driving through the forests was another matter entirely, and they made poor progress.

Several miles into the trees, they crossed a bridge over a wide river. Jack spotted a narrow trail on the opposite side, running east, parallel to the water. A tall strip of weeds between the tire tracks showed it wasn't well-used.

"I know where that goes." He was thinking of the lake he'd seen earlier. "It should be a dead-end. We need to get off the road for the night and it's as good a place as any."

Ethan drove carefully for another fifteen minutes to reach the lake. He stopped a few yards above a rocky shoreline that stretched fifty feet to the water. Narrow tracks led away from the road, following the shore in both directions.

Jack pointed left. "Let's take that one. It looks like it goes into the trees. We'll need to be under cover before we stop for the night."

Ethan turned left and drove toward a wall of large boulders that extended from the forest into the water. With nothing between them and the lake on the right, moonlight lit the track well enough for him to drive at a jogging pace. He slowed at the barrier and swung back into the woods.

A voice boomed from the darkness. "*Stop*."

Chapter 25

Ethan slammed on the brakes, spraying twin arcs of loose gravel ahead of Dave. The two men standing on the road jumped aside to avoid being struck. Although it was too dark to see faces, one man was huge, easily a foot taller than the other, and powerfully built. He was the one who had shouted.

"Who's there?" the second man barked.

Jack and Ethan—caught completely by surprise—said nothing.

The taller man fumbled with a flashlight. A moment later, he shone a light on the truck and stepped closer. "Who are you?"

"Uh, I'm Ethan. This is, Jack?" His voice pitched at the end of the sentence, sounding like a plea for help, not an answer.

After a long silence, the second man said, "It can't be them. Can it?"

The first sighed heavily. "You'd better come with us. Leave your headlights off." He turned around, dimmed his flashlight, and walked away.

"We can outrun them," Ethan whispered.

Jack glanced around, then leaned over. "There's no place to turn around."

"The forest? On foot?"

"They've got flashlights. We'd be running blind."

The men stopped a few paces farther along the road, waiting for Ethan to follow.

"Follow them for now," Jack said, "but keep looking for another road."

"Who are they?" Ethan drove ahead, keeping a safe distance from the men. "Why does it sound like they recognized us?"

"Well they're not CorpSec. They'd have us in handcuffs by now."

"I don't recall seeing a town on the map around here."

"There wasn't. But remember what I told you about the

construction equipment I found. I've heard stories about people who smuggled themselves onto Cirrus and are living off the land. They're not supposed to be out here."

The track ended at another rocky shoreline. Sand, it seemed, was something this lake did not have. The terrain was rough, but Ethan could still drive over it. At the far side, the tall man pointed to an opening in the trees. "Park under there. Beside my truck."

Ethan whispered, "Those are *not* trucks."

Jack followed his gaze. Several compact all-terrain-vehicles—similar to Dave—sheltered under a rough canopy assembled from cut branches and fallen logs. Beyond the shelter was a dense forest of pine and spruce.

As Ethan crept past, the taller man said, "I'll take them to Niels. He'll want to see them for himself. You can tell the others and let them decide what to do."

The second man turned on his own flashlight, dimmed it to create just enough light to avoid obstacles, then trudged uphill, deeper into the trees.

Jack was wondering who Niels was when Ethan whispered, "Get ready to run."

"He said there are others. If they live out here, they'll know these woods."

"It's now or never."

"Wait. I have an idea." Jack studied the parking shelter as Ethan drove the final yards. "When I say so, start the winch."

He hopped out and leaned on a wooden post. The structure swayed. It wasn't much—not even an inch—but he sensed which connections were the weakest and knew exactly how much weight they'd bear. He ran to the front bumper, slapped the quick-release lever, and drew out enough cable to wrap around the driftwood beam above his head. "*Hit it.*"

Ethan started the winch, grabbed Jack's backpack, and jumped from the truck as the nose lifted.

"*Hey,*" the tall man shouted. "What are you doing?" His deep voice carried more surprise than anger.

Ethan edged toward the rear of the shelter while leaning into the truck to hold the winch button. Dave's front wheels rose six inches off the ground. The wooden beam creaked.

"That's enough." Jack shoved harder. "Help me push." The support post cracked loudly.

The shelter had only been designed to hide the vehicles. With Ethan's added weight behind the post, it quickly failed to do even that.

"*Stop that,*" the tall man yelled as the structure tilted. He sounded more concerned than upset.

"Let's go," Ethan shouted.

Jack followed Ethan up an incline. Branches slashed and stung his hands and face, but he kept his footing on the rough terrain.

The canopy crashed to the ground. "*Get back here,*" the tall man bellowed. Now he sounded angry.

Ethan cursed after bouncing off a tree. "I can't see a thing."

"Back to the shore." Jack veered toward the lake, where the light was brighter. "We need the moonlight."

Other voices joined the deeper one. Someone opened a door, spilling a rectangle of light into the forest, but the cousins had already gained thirty yards.

Ethan reached the stony shoreline first. He crouched next to a tree, waiting for Jack.

"Boats," he said when Jack joined him. They'd exited the forest next to a jetty made of piled stones. A single tree at the end of the short quay provided cover for a half-dozen skiffs and canoes.

Jack ran to the first vessel. "This one has a motor." He found the safety switch and raised the propeller shaft out of the water. The prop spun silently when he twisted the throttle.

"They've all got motors," Ethan said as he untied a second boat and shoved it away from shore.

While Jack piloted around the jetty, Ethan released the remaining boats. Several people were running toward them, shouting. He leaped into Jack's boat as the tall man stepped onto the quay. Jack gunned the motor and steered for the center of the lake.

Eventually, the commotion on the shore faded. The

trolling motor gave their skiff a top speed of less than ten miles per hour, but Jack wasn't concerned because all the boats Ethan freed had the same motor.

They'd been cruising for ten minutes and weren't much more than halfway to the opposite shore when Ethan said, "We have to decide where we're going."

"Yeah. I saw this place from the Spine. That's an island ahead of us. We can hide there for a while and then cross to the west side of the lake. We should end up a few miles from the grain road."

"And then what? Will a grain carrier stop for us the way Dave did?"

"It … I don't know. It should. We'll worry about that when we get there."

As the boat neared the island, Jack felt calm, much more than the situation called for. They'd been chased by CorpSec from Fairview and were now fleeing an unknown group with only a ten-minute head start. There was little to be calm about, but the lake felt so familiar, just like the cave on the Vault.

He turned the boat to follow the shoreline at a distance of fifty yards. "We need somewhere sheltered, where we can hide the boat from anyone passing by."

Ethan pointed to a gap in the trees. "That looks like it could be a bay."

Jack released the throttle and let the boat idle toward the island. He wondered if it was smart to take the first shelter they found, but the sense of calm overshadowed his concern.

"Perfect," Ethan said as Jack piloted them into the cove. Steep walls surrounded the hundred-yard-wide natural harbor, but trees grew right down to the waterline, creating many places to hide the boat. "We'll have to climb out, but no one would think we'd stop here."

They beached the boat at the bay's far end, then dragged it out of the water and behind a tree.

Ethan hopped up to the foot of the rocky slope. "That doesn't look too hard."

Jack assessed the wall. It was no more than sixty feet tall and free of trees and shrubs. The moonlight revealed many possible routes up the near vertical face. "I agree. As long as there are no loose stones, we should be safe."

Ethan led the pitch, picking his way up the jumbled slope in the growing moonlight. His arm span was a couple of inches greater than Jack's, but Jack didn't have much trouble keeping up. Still, they had to be careful of their footing and it took fifteen minutes to reach the summit.

Ethan scrambled through the final obstacle: a short chimney that flared at the top. He slipped several times on mossy stones before finally mantling his way over the ledge.

Having seen the spots that gave Ethan trouble, Jack had less difficulty through the chimney and rolled onto the cool grass above only seconds later. Then he looked back and saw there was a much easier route to the top that followed the bay's natural curve. That path began farther away and was considerably longer, but had many flat surfaces along the way. They were regularly spaced and free of trees, almost like … *Uh, oh. Steps.*

He spun around as Ethan stumbled across the grass and collapsed onto a rustic wooden bench in front of a grassy knoll. Ethan didn't seem to notice the incongruity but was just glad to have finished the climb.

Before Jack could warn him, two men approached the bench, one from each side. They were both breathing heavily, as if they'd been running.

The tall man leaned over, placing his hands above his knees, and drew several deep breaths. When he finally looked up with a pained expression, he said, "Don't do that again."

- - - - -

"Niels …" The tall man opened the door without knocking. "I've brought guests."

"Yes, I know. Please, come in."

Neither Jack nor Ethan had considered trying to escape again, even after the tall man's companion left the three of them alone outside the cabin hidden in the trees. Heavy curtains covered the windows facing the path, revealing only dim outlines against darker walls—the building would be invisible to drones any time of day or night.

Jack stepped into the brightly lit room. it wasn't at all what he expected. The interior layout was one large space with a kitchen—filled with modern appliances—a dining area, a living room, and a small office. Open doors led to the single bedroom and a bathroom. A rubber mat lay in front of a painted steel door on the far side of the cabin. It had been a hot summer day and was still warm outside, but the house was comfortably air-conditioned.

The walls were sparsely decorated with framed photos. From a distance, he couldn't see much detail. But unlike the photos in his home, there were no children pictured, only small groups of adults.

He finally noticed the cabin's occupant, a slightly built, much older man seated at a massive dining table with twelve matching chairs.

"Would you like something to drink?" Niels asked. A pitcher of ice water waited at the near end of the table.

The large man glowered at the four glasses; one for each of them. "You know I hate it when you do that." Then he faced Jack and Ethan. "I swear he's got cameras hidden all over this sector."

Niels laughed. "There will be time to question my talents later. But first …" He frowned at the tall man, but there was enough amusement in his expression to show he was teasing. "You didn't introduce yourself, did you?"

A brief scowl, directed at Niels, crossed his face. "No," he growled. "Sorry. My name is Anders. Niels, this is Ethan and Jack. Is that correct?"

"Yes, sir," Jack confirmed. In the cabin's light, Jack got his first clear look at Anders. The man was … *old*, much older than he'd sounded in the dark. Probably in his seventies. Jack would have felt a twinge of regret at having led the senior citizen on a chase, except the man's height was intimidating— he was nearly seven feet tall.

Niels gestured to the table. "Please, sit down. The others will be here shortly with food." This earned him another glare from Anders.

"I'll go down and help them carry it up."

"Don't worry about him," Niels said when Anders left. "He's been upset with me for a few days now."

"Why?" Ethan asked.

"He's worried I might be right."

"About what?"

"About everything." Niels' tone hinted that he was neither boasting nor exaggerating.

"You're a Traveller, aren't you?" Jack blushed, not knowing if he'd offended Niels with the question or the name. Travellers were strongly associated with Newton's prophecy, a subject some considered absurd.

Niels saw his embarrassment. "It's all right. That is one of the names they call us. Though I haven't left this island in more than twenty years."

He must be in his nineties. That made Niels possibly the only person Jack had ever met who was born in the twentieth century. He was clean-shaven, had wispy gray hair, and was well-dressed. He may not have left the island in a long time, but his clothes had come from Earth recently. Then Jack noticed the table the man sat at—easily the largest piece of wooden furniture he'd ever seen. "This is real wood, isn't it?"

Ethan rubbed his hand over the lacquered surface and looked at Jack strangely. "Yeah. Obviously."

Jack glanced around the cabin again. "Log walls." He faced Ethan. "Nothing on Cirrus is made of wood. It's still illegal to cut down trees."

Niels saw Ethan's face drop. "Don't worry, you haven't fallen in with a den of thieves. You'll see when you meet the rest of our group. They all came to Cirrus legally and are only secretive because they want to build a fishing lodge."

This only prompted Ethan to look confused.

Niels continued. "As with harvesting trees, fishing is not permitted. However, my friends have been working on this project for many years. They've done the science and are certain that this river system can support a sustainable commercial fishery. They're getting ready to present their case to the corporation and ask for a license."

"Excuse me, sir," Jack said. "Anders acted like you knew

we were coming. Did you?"

"Yes, though I learned it so long ago I've already forgotten the details. I remember that one of you came from Earth recently. I know you are cousins and that you're traveling to Caerton. I also know you need help—someone is trying to stop you."

"Who?" Ethan asked.

"Do you know about our parents?" Jack asked. "Where they are? If they're safe?"

"No, sorry." Niels seemed genuinely disappointed—the same way Jack felt. They'd been running for more than a day with no clue if they were doing the right thing. "But we can ask Little Brother." He got up and shuffled to the back of the room where a modern computer sat on an antique writing desk. "Where were they when you last heard from them?"

"It was just after seven pm," Ethan said. "We'd passed the community hall in Fairview, right after the debate started. They should have been at our new apartment." He gave as much of the address as he remembered.

Niels brought up a map of Port Isaac and chose a camera overlooking a park from a tower in the neighboring block. He set the time for exactly seven.

Ethan pointed at the left edge of the screen. "That's our building. But why is the power out?" His apartment was somewhere in the band of ten darkened floors separating the tower's upper and lower halves.

They watched in silence. Ethan's new home was in a section of the city not yet fully occupied, and there wasn't much traffic.

"That's them," Ethan exclaimed. Four people dashed onto the sidewalk, illuminated by the lights above the main entrance. "Can you zoom in or follow them?"

"He can't do that." Jack knew his cousin had little experience with Little Brother in Washington. "If he tries to track them, the AI will see what he's doing and flag it in the public reports."

"Can you see if they made it to Caerton?"

"The AI is smarter than that," Niels said. "Even if we were

to split the task between multiple devices over several hours, the system will recognize that the same people are being watched. Unless your use is registered—such as a parent keeping an eye on children walking to school—it will report a violation."

"If we found them in Caerton," Jack said, "that might tell whoever is chasing them where they went."

The camera captured enough detail to identify the boys' parents escaping around a corner. It also recorded the two men who followed them from the building less than a minute later, dressed in CorpSec uniforms. They stopped outside the main doors, looked around, and appeared to argue before running in the opposite direction.

"Well," Ethan said, "at least we know they got away."

"I'm sorry I can't do more," Niels said, "but I cannot attract attention to myself. At least not until after tomorrow."

"Why?" Jack asked. "What happens tomorrow?"

Anders' deep voice rumbled from the doorway. "Haven't you heard? Tomorrow is the end of the world."

Chapter 26

Detective Singh waited next to her car outside Armenau's research center in Everett. She'd called in a favor from a friend in Customs and Immigration and learned Simon was returning to Earth that evening. The sun was setting when he emerged from the three-story parking garage, carrying a worn-out leather file satchel and a disposable coffee cup.

"Simon Pedlar." Priya didn't phrase this as a question. She flashed her ID.

Simon faltered, nearly dropping his coffee. "Yes." He glanced over his shoulder at the door to Armenau's multi-level parking structure.

She followed his gaze. *Why is he looking at the security camera?* "Is there a place we can talk?" She'd spotted a café earlier, mid-way along the neighboring block. It had a sidewalk patio. "The coffee shop?"

Simon nodded and turned that direction without waiting for her. He kept his head down, angled away from the camera as he walked. "What's this about?"

"I have some questions about the fire at Over the Horizon's pumping station in Louisiana." She'd already decided to act as if it was a foregone conclusion that Armenau was responsible for the fires. "I'm sure you're aware that several of OTH's clients have made claims resulting from the fire. They're alleging negligence, but I've reviewed the file and it looks like an unfortunate accident to me. So, if you cooperate, we can wrap this up tonight. Everyone will get their payouts and go on their way."

He relaxed visibly. "Yes, of course. I'll be glad to help."

She chose an outdoor table partially sheltered by a trellis draped with climbing roses. The waiter brought a menu and Simon ordered an overpriced latte. Priya asked for black tea.

"You'll have to excuse me." She tipped a thick stack of papers from her bag. "I don't understand the technology very well, so I'll be referring to my notes."

The pile was mostly junk. The only important ones were

the few with Holden's name displayed prominently in the header.

Priya watched Simon's reaction as she revealed the first one. The paper's title made no sense to her, but his response was unmistakable. His body tensed. This was the paper where Holden developed his theory for merging wormholes, something he promised to explain more fully if Simon reacted to it.

"Why don't you start by telling me about the work you do for Armenau."

"There's not a lot I'd be allowed to say."

"Keep it in general terms, then. The insurance company is saying OTH knew of a fault in the equipment. Do you care to comment on that?"

"Oh, I don't know if I can help you at all then. Armenau only purchased OTH last year. Anything related to the original equipment's design is before my time. And we only starting growing our own portal crystals three years ago."

"But you're their lead researcher and the one who understands the technology best. If the insurance company takes this to court, you'll be on the stand. Convince me the fire wasn't due to a design flaw."

"All right." He considered Priya's stack of documents. "There's nothing different about the portal crystals we create compared to anyone else. My own research is mostly about efficiency."

While he spoke, Priya flipped through the papers, exposing the titles printed in large, bold type. She pretended to be searching for one in particular, but was evaluating his responses as the names went by.

She felt more energized than she had in a long time, as if the day's events had sharpened her senses, made her more aware. She'd even experienced mild déjà vu after passing through Holden's portal that afternoon, something she hadn't felt in years. Simon's unease decreased with every new paper, but she still caught the telltale flickers of recognition in his face and body whenever Holden's name came up.

Eventually, she arrived at the one she worried about the

most. The title meant nothing to her, but Holden assured her it contained a phrase Simon would understand. If he reacted, then he was working toward an ultra-stable wormhole, one that could pass radioactive material.

Simon didn't appear to notice. Priya left the page exposed longer than most, to be sure he saw the heading, but the words had no effect on him.

She didn't want to stop with the big one, in case it created suspicion. She flipped through a few more, ones Holden said weren't important, mostly related to production methods. Unexpectedly, he perked up.

"Oh, I see you've got Varley's works. See, that's much closer to what I'm interested in." His excitement seemed genuine as he opened his case and pulled out his own, shorter stack of papers. "I'm working on a special project now, but then I'll focus on optimizing production efficiency. You probably don't know how wasteful current methods are— over forty percent of finished crystals have imperfections and are discarded. I'm hoping to get that down to twenty percent within five years."

As he spoke about his work, his passion became evident. He flipped through his own pages, which consisted almost entirely of diagrams and equations. He gestured across the formulas, explaining them to Priya as if she were a colleague and understood every word.

She listened attentively and got a sense of the man's character. She found him likable, a bit on the nervous side, and didn't believe he was involved in anything illegal—at least not willingly. The longer he spoke, the more relaxed he became. He even made a few nerdy jokes, at which she genuinely laughed.

He paused unexpectedly after turning up a single sheet that stood out from the rest. Instead of diagrams, Priya saw columns of numbers. After scanning the document briefly, he shuffled it to the bottom of the pile.

"Well, that's all I need for now." Priya gathered her papers. "As far as I'm concerned, the fires were an accident. I'll be telling the insurance company there was no negligence." She picked up the menu, fanned her face with it, and flashed a smile. "Could you get me a glass of water, please?"

"Certainly." Even though the sun had set, the temperature was still in the nineties. He stood and walked inside.

Priya had her phone ready. She had no idea what was on the page Simon hid, but knew that Holden needed to see it. As soon as he stepped indoors, she flipped the stack, snapped a photo, then set the papers down exactly as they were.

She sat back and reflected on the interview. Her instincts told her Simon had no criminal intent, but they also warned that he knew more than he let on. She got the feeling he was a man who knew he was in too deep, and wondered if he'd sent the arson tips himself as a way to escape. She was trying to think of how to get him to open up when a movement up the street caused her to glance that direction.

Danny Kou was getting out of a black car at the end of the block.

Priya spun slowly in her chair, stood, and glided away without looking back. She sidestepped into the parking spot in front of a plumber's van, then moved to a position where she could see through its tinted windows. Danny was facing away, talking to the car's driver, but glanced her direction as she watched.

Seconds later, Simon came out of the café carrying two glasses of water. Puzzled by not finding Priya, he looked around and recognized Danny, who had returned to his conversation.

He turned away quickly and returned to the table, where he fumbled and spilled the water before sweeping his papers into his ragged case in a single motion. That done, he poured the rest of his coffee into his disposable cup, then walked toward Danny.

He knows what sort of man Danny is. Why else would he pretend he'd just stopped for coffee? But what's he hiding? His meeting with me? The document?

Priya thought about Holden's missing son and daughter as Simon walked away. It was unlikely Pieter had told him anything about the abductions, but she couldn't shake the feeling he knew more. The déjà vu she'd felt earlier in the day seemed to linger—*He's more important than he seems. We'll be meeting again.*

Chapter 27

As the nine guests followed Anders into the modest cabin, each took a long look at Jack and Ethan before greeting Niels. Jack couldn't be certain what they were thinking, but—as with their initial encounter with Anders—it was apparent that he and his cousin had been expected.

Niels' friends were much younger than him, but still in their sixties or seventies. They introduced themselves and asked polite questions: had the boys really found the lake without a map, had Ethan really only arrived on Cirrus yesterday, how had they avoided CorpSec for a whole day; and other questions that revealed Niels had predicted their arrival.

"Enough questions," the woman introduced as Natalya finally said. "These boys are hungry." She was a tall woman, taller even than Ethan, and spoke with a heavy Russian accent. She was also Anders' wife. As soon as she started setting the table, the others joined in as if she'd ordered them to.

The group had brought plenty of food to the island— something Jack and his cousin appreciated, and also plenty of beer—something Anders and a few of the others appreciated more. The conversations grew louder and more animated through dinner.

Jack learned about Niels' friends and life on Cirrus in the decade before his parents arrived. The first wave of workers did not live on the station full time. Most had adult children and even grandchildren on Earth. All the group members were now retired or semi-retired and had incredible stories— and probably a few lies—to tell about themselves and each other. Jack was sure these stories had been told many times before, but got the feeling the storytellers were glad to have a new audience for them.

"How long have you lived on Cirrus?" Jack asked Anders.

Suresh, a dignified-looking gentleman with a thick salt-and-pepper beard, laughed. "Don't believe a word he says."

Henri, a mechanic with meaty, weathered hands like Jack's father, slapped the table. "He not only has the body of a troll, but an ego just as large."

Aziza, who reminded Jack of his school principal, cautioned Henri, "Don't make these young men think poorly of us." She grinned, then nodded toward Anders. "Let the giant speak."

Anders laughed, and Jack understood the teasing had been in good humor. From what he'd seen so far, Anders was modest and quiet-spoken—for someone with a chest as large as a bear's. He answered Jack's question, but it was his friends who really told his tale.

Jack had assumed from Anders' physique that he'd been a construction worker, a miner, or worked another profession where his size would be an asset. He was surprised to learn Anders taught microbiology at the university in Reykjavik before coming to Cirrus thirty-two years ago.

Suresh and Henri pieced together the story of how he and another scientist had hiked on the inner, ice-covered surface of Cirrus. They described how Anders' colleague had fallen into a crevasse and broken his leg while trying to drill through the ice to sample the water below. Anders carried the injured man several miles, enduring the inner surface's crushing two-gee gravity, to a spot stable enough for a rescue craft to land. Natalya had piloted that ship, and that was how the two met.

"How did you get there if it wasn't safe to land a ship?" Ethan asked.

"This was before the roof was fully grown. We went over the rim wall and skied down the outside." Anders spoke casually, as if the feat were trivial.

"You jumped off the top of an eight-mile-tall wall and landed on skis?"

"It's not as difficult as you might think. The wall has gravity generators. After the initial free-fall, the apparent slope is very gentle. By the time we reached the base, we had to switch to snowshoes."

Jack studied the other guests' expressions but none seemed to doubt Anders' tale.

He continued. "It was quite beautiful. There is atmosphere on the ring's inner surface. When the solar wind is strong, it strips some air away and causes it to interact with the magnetic field. You can sometimes see an aurora through the roof in the summer, if you're close to the rim. On the outside of the wall, though …" He gazed at the ceiling with a rapt expression, reliving the event. "The colors are brilliant. It was like walking through a rainbow."

Natalya had her own story and wasn't as shy as Anders about telling it. She boasted of beating Suresh in a race around the entire circumference of the ring. She'd been a pilot, ferrying workers to high-elevation construction sites, and Suresh worked as an engineer on the train tunnels in the rim wall. Shortly after the completion of the magnetic levitation tracks, they each constructed their own vehicles—little more than thrusters with seats attached—and sped through the airless corridors at speeds far beyond what they were designed for. Natalya won the race, keeping her average speed above three-thousand miles per hour for over five hours.

Later in the evening, as cooler air flowed through the open window on the building's tree-sheltered side, Jack found himself alone in conversation with Anders. He was about to ask a question when someone else entered the cabin. Anders watched the man as he went straight to Niels and whispered in his ear. Niels appeared to thank him. Then the new arrival spoke to the room at large. "Sorry I'm late. Traffic has been held up all day." He grinned as if he'd told a joke.

"That's Terrance," Anders said, and didn't take his eyes off the man as he moved through the cabin, greeting the other guests.

Terrance sauntered over to them and offered his hand. "Hello, Jack. I'm glad to see you got through the mess on the highway."

"We saw the accident but missed the traffic jam. Do you know what happened? Was anybody hurt?"

"No, it was a self-driving vehicle, nothing serious. A minor programming error … apparently. Please excuse me, I want to say hello to your cousin too."

Programming error? Jack smiled politely to hide a cluster of worrisome thoughts: *Was Terrance involved? Had the error been accidental? And if not, was it meant to help or hinder them?*

Anders watched with the same careful expression as Terrance wandered away. When he saw the concerned look on Jack's face, he misunderstood, thinking Jack had noticed his own reaction. "Don't worry about him. He may look like a scoundrel, but Niels trusts him completely."

"You don't?"

Anders considered for a moment. "I wouldn't go that far. I just sometimes wonder what he gets up to. He was on the island this morning but left in a hurry. Niels frequently asks him to run errands. He seems to have a lot of connections."

Jack wouldn't have described the man's appearance as untrustworthy. However, Terrance and Anders could not have been more different. Anders looked like he'd be at home in the forest wearing a plaid shirt and swinging an axe. Terrance wore expensive, imported clothes. He was decades younger than the rest of Niels' friends, and Jack had also seen a flash of gold on both his wrists when they shook hands.

Anders continued. "He worked with post-melt bombardment team in the final stages of Cirrus' construction. They used huge, unstable portals for breaking up asteroids to extract the valuable metals. Terrance's job was diverting the rocky materials to Cirrus-bound wormholes. The mining company fired him when they caught him trying to spell his name in gigantic letters under one of the sector walls. No one knows for sure how far he got, but I heard he'd completed a one-mile-tall 'T' made of nickel."

Jack muffled a laugh. "That can't be true."

"It wasn't just him. There were rumors that others created deposits of gold, silver, and other metals, in locations known only to themselves."

"You said earlier that it might be the end of the world. Do you believe that?" The story had been in the news increasingly as the predicted date approached. Jack hadn't given it much thought then, and not at all since leaving Fairview. But here was a scientist and scholar who seemed to have at least some regard for the story.

Instead of answering the question, Anders asked his own.

"What do you know about the date? For the supposed end of the world?"

"Not much, except it was picked by Isaac Newton."

Anders shook his head. "Newton never picked a date, only a range of years. And the first one passed decades ago. Tomorrow's date was set by the Travellers. Do you know why?"

"Not really."

"Real Travellers claim to remember things that will happen before their next trip through a portal, or from any future trip, including their final one. Back when using portals was more common, many noticed there was a limit to how far they could see. Logically, this meant they never traveled past that point in time. There might be many reasons for this. An obvious one is that the Traveller dies after the last date they remember. So, it became common for them to retire from whatever service they worked for, refusing to travel when they could no longer see the future."

"But isn't that what they call a self-fulfilling prophecy?" Ethan seated himself next to Jack with another plate of desserts. "If they refuse to travel, then they can't see the future. And if they can't see the future, they refuse to travel."

"Exactly. My guess is it's easier to accept retirement over the alternative." Anders sat quietly for a moment. His jovial mood faded and he spoke softly. "Niels described this night more than a decade ago. It's the last one he remembers."

"Does he think he's going to … die?" Jack asked.

It took Anders a moment to respond. "No. No, I don't think he does." Then more forcefully; "And neither do I."

"Hold on," Ethan said. "For this to be the last night he remembers, he'd need to use a portal again. But there's nothing here."

"You're right, but Niels is … he's different. He won't say how he knows, and I can't imagine him ever leaving his island again."

"It's a nice spot." Jack looked to the lake through the cabin's only uncovered window, the one sheltered under the trees. "It's so peaceful here."

"When I say his island, I mean *his* island. He owns it. Had it specially created for him. Apparently, Terrance had some part in that."

"He owns the entire island?" Jack had only a rough idea of what that would cost. It would be an astronomical number.

"He bought it with what he made on the lotteries."

"He could predict lottery numbers?" Ethan asked. "I didn't think Traveller's memories were so precise."

Anders' cheery mood returned; this was a story he enjoyed telling. "They're not. They're more like the ancient Oracles—the answer you get depends on the question you ask. But like I said, Niels is different. He didn't win *a* lottery; he won *all* the lotteries.

"Instead of playing the numbers he knew would win, he signed up subscribers and gave them a set of numbers that contained only a few winners. That way they won only a bit more than they bet. Word got around quickly, but he only accepted a few subscribers each week and never played all the correct numbers himself. Most subscribers didn't share the information he gave them—that would spread the winnings too thinly. Then, when he had enough interest, he took *every* subscriber, hundreds of millions of them from all around the world, and gave them the correct numbers, for *every* lottery."

As Anders spoke, Jack couldn't help but think the odds of finding a power cell in a cave exactly when needed must be on par with picking winning lottery numbers. Someone had predicted the event, but the man in the dream wasn't Niels.

"I don't understand," Ethan said. "Wouldn't sharing the numbers mean that everyone won, but got almost nothing?"

"Everyone except Niels. He made … well, nobody really knows. His subscribers generally won less than a dollar—which most never bothered to collect—so the lottery corporations were happy. Some people complained, but he'd done nothing illegal—they paid for the numbers and he provided them. From start to finish, the whole thing took nine weeks, and he did it in a way where no one ever found out who he was. Some people thought of him as a folk hero. If he knew the numbers, that meant someone else did too and the average person never had a fair chance."

"But you know it was him?"

"He told us the story a few years ago. I never really believed him, until tonight, until you two showed up." He shook his head and stood up to walk away. "And I don't believe in this end-of-the-world crap either. But something's going to happen. Something big."

Chapter 28

E2.

Of everything that had happened that day, that ID bothered Sarah the most. She fidgeted with her phone's stylus, which was actually the cartridge she'd taken from the slot labelled E2.

He never gave me that number. I made it up. So why was it so important?

She recalled the old man's parting words after insisting that Terrance call his boss before she handed over the access card. "All your questions will be answered tomorrow."

What if that's too late?

She pushed the E2 cartridge back into her phone. Maybe she'd have to wait a day for his answers, but there was one mystery she could solve on her own. *Did Terrance cause the crash near Fairview?*

Sarah logged on to Little Brother and selected a camera on the north side of the reservoir—a mile-wide complex between the aviary and the city. After they'd split up, she went south, returning to work, while Terrance had wandered north.

Little Brother wouldn't let her track the man wherever he went, but if she knew when he passed one spot, she could guess when he'd arrive at another, such as the Transit Authority's offices. Of course, that's something Little Brother knew to the microsecond, so she'd have only one chance to confirm Terrance's destination without alerting him.

Her chosen camera—mounted on the roof of a six-story apartment block—overlooked the intersection at the complex's northwest corner. To the east, she had a clear view of the pedestrian path's exit from the forest and the reservoir's main entrance on the boulevard beyond. To the south, the road ran parallel to the forest, interrupted by just two T-intersections. The first led to the reservoir's warehouse at its southern edge, the second to UV Mobile.

She set the time to just after they'd parted ways and watched the sidewalk along the forest, in case Terrance crossed that street mid-block. However, after a few minutes, he crossed the boulevard and continued north along the stream between blocks of apartments.

An hour, Sarah guessed. That's how long it would take to walk downtown. But if he took a bus, he could have reached the Authority's headquarters in minutes. *Do I watch that building for an entire hour, or jump ahead?* If she picked a time too close to his arrival, the AI might flag her second sighting right away. But if Terrance wandered into a scene she'd been watching for an hour, it should only monitor her following searches for a third instance.

As she pondered, a CorpSec vehicle moved into the frame and stopped at the intersection.

That's him. Sarah recognized the driver as the officer who'd shown up at the aviary. *Was he following me?*

The van turned south. Her pulse quickened, thinking they'd nearly been caught. But instead of continuing to where she and Terrance had been only minutes earlier, it turned at the first intersection. The rooftop camera couldn't see the driveway through the forest, but had an interrupted view of the reservoir warehouse through gaps in the treetops. The van showed up thirty seconds later as a black smudge stopping in front of a white roll shutter door.

That's no coincidence. Even if the officer hadn't come to UV Mobile, he was somehow connected to both the reservoir and the basin.

From her back pocket, Sarah drew the second access card she'd removed from the deck. Terrance had almost certainly used his at the Transit Authority. Did she dare use hers to enter the reservoir? *What can I hope to gain? Is it safe?*

She'd tried calling Jack after getting her phone back, but he never answered or returned her calls. If her guess was right, he was somewhere between the Spine and Fairview, with Ethan. What he was doing out there, she didn't know.

But CorpSec had found her and they'd eventually find him, if they hadn't already. She changed her clothes, thrust the card into her pocket, and jogged down the stairs.

"Mom," Sarah shouted from the bottom of the stairwell.

"I'm going out to meet Jada. I'll be home by ten."

She didn't wait for her mother's reply, or for her to ask why she was wearing black jeans and a black hoodie at night, but darted out the back door to the bike racks. Using her bike's electric motor, she was soon at the outskirts of Caerton, whizzing along the winding path through the forest.

She paused at the head of the driveway. The parking lot—what she could see of it—was empty. She tightened the string on her hoodie, wheeled her bike onto the single-lane road, and hurried to the gate a hundred yards ahead.

A level patch of ground ten yards before the gate provided easy access to a spot sheltered from both the road and cameras inside the warehouse compound. She moved her bike into deep shadow and waited. The white bay door she'd seen in the video was shut, as was the smaller personnel door beside it. No light shone through the few windows facing the road. After several minutes of no activity, she approached the chain link fence.

The fence's top rail looked identical to the one she'd climbed with Terrance's gloves. Looking around, she spotted fallen branches she could use to get over it, but then she'd be trapped on the other side. Her only option was the access card. If that didn't work, her investigation was over.

Cautiously, she approached the mesh gate and held the card inches from the reader. *Last chance.*

She was so engrossed in worry that she didn't notice the small black patrol vehicle creeping silently along the fence until it stopped on the lawn next to the gate.

Sarah froze and swore silently. Like an electronic guard dog, the wheeled drone waited to see what she would do next.

If I leave, it'll report me. If the card doesn't work, it'll report me. If I … There were no other choices. She slid the card into the reader's slot. The lock clicked and the access panel's light turned green. The patrol drone didn't move. She swore again and prepared to run.

With only a slight buzz, the wheeled sentry rolled across the lawn, bumped over the curb, bounced onto the driveway, and continued to the grass on the other side.

Sarah released the breath she hadn't realized she'd been holding, then pushed the gate open and dashed across the parking lot.

The personnel door's access panel was the same as the one on the gate. Its light turned green the moment she inserted the card. She pulled the door open a crack. There were no lights on, so she entered slowly. As soon as she stepped inside, ceiling panels illuminated the front half of the building, which was roughly half the size of a soccer field.

The back of the warehouse, and both sides of the front half, were obscured behind rows of tall steel shelving filled with plastic pipes of various diameters. She closed the door and paused next to an empty loading zone large enough to park a semi-trailer. Surrounding that, hundreds of large plastic crates had been stacked in neat piles.

After listening for a moment, she snuck deeper inside, checking the passages between the stacks as she went. The containers were of different sizes, so the alleys weren't straight, but formed a maze that prevented her from seeing more than thirty feet.

As she advanced, Sarah noticed that the gaps between the crates and shelves formed a T-intersection at the end of the loading zone. She focused on the opposite branch of the T as she crept along the final stack. Down that passage, a grimy yellow forklift was parked in front of a thick, three-foot-wide ring, set vertically into the concrete floor.

A portal. This was the reservoir's shipping department, where they'd receive parts from other cities. Maybe even from Earth.

Sarah bobbed her head around the corner of the crate she had her back to. The passage behind her continued uninterrupted to the building's far side. *There's got to be an office in here somewhere.* She sidled away from the crate. *Most likely closer to the portal.*

She'd taken just two steps when men's voices echoed from the rear of the warehouse. The lights in that section turned on. With lightning-fast reflexes, she turned and dashed to the exit. But then the rolling bay door's motor engaged and the steel shutter began to rise.

Panicking now, she stumbled into the nearest passage between crates and scurried into the maze. She crouched on the floor at a safe distance, cupping her mouth in her hands to muffle her rapid breaths. *Trapped.* A vehicle rolled into the loading zone. Bits of gravel wedged in its tires made a rhythmic click on the concrete floor. *Trapped. Trapped. Trapped. Trapped.*

Evening air—scented by jasmine blooming in the adjacent forest—flooded into the warehouse and spread through the alleys, cooling both the floor and Sarah's nerves. She couldn't leave, but she hadn't been seen. *All I have to do is stay out of sight.* Thinking more clearly now, she turned her phone's ringer off. Then she took a deep breath and slunk forward, hoping to find a spot where she could see without being seen.

The larger crates were not stacked directly on top of each other, but had pallets in between to allow a forklift to pick them up. Without stepping into an alley with a direct line of sight, she moved close enough to find a view of the portal through aligned pallets.

"Evenin', Astrid," the older of two men greeted a woman in blue coveralls. "You're early."

"Hey, Vince." Astrid crouched on the balls of her feet and gazed through the wormhole, which the younger man had opened. A pair of long gray crates sat on a pallet in a brightly lit room on the other side. "It looks like they're ready for us."

"That they are," Vince said. "But we've still got a few minutes. Shut it down, Adam. We don't want to trigger an alert with Customs."

The younger man touched a button on the portal frame, closing the wormhole. Although Sarah was hiding forty feet away, she still saw a slender rod pop up from the control panel.

"Ugh." Vince rubbed his balding head. "I need coffee before we start. I'll even reheat the tar young Adam here brewed this morning."

"It wasn't that bad," Adam protested as Vince walked away.

The senior warehouse worker looked over his shoulder before stepping into an aisle between shelves. "Did you taste it?"

"I don't drink coffee, but it smelled fine. And I only make it because you added it to my job description."

Sarah didn't hear the rest of the conversation, which was punctuated by laughter, because the three workers had moved too far away. She stood and padded back to the loading bay. An empty white van, parked inside, must have been where the woman had come from. Behind it, the tall bay door was wide open, offering a clear view of the compound's open gate.

I should go. After all, she'd discovered a new connection between the guns and the reservoir, and the old man had promised she'd learn everything she needed to know tomorrow. *But who decides what I need to know?* And there was something familiar about the rod Adam ejected.

 Certain that the workers were far away, Sarah darted to the portal. She peered into the transparent cylinder on top of the control panel. The ejected rod was one of a dozen held there. Each was finger-length and slender, the diameter of her phone's stylus. The one positioned above the frame's inlet was a different color, though—matte black, like her stylus.

She removed the pencil-shaped cartridge from her phone and compared it to the rods in the container. Except for the length, it was an almost exact match.

What are the chances this is coincidence? She ran her finger along the cartridge's length and felt an invisible seam at its midpoint. *None at all.*

With a firm twist, Sarah unscrewed the tip of the stylus, revealing the same needle-like point as on the twelve rods.

Large portals were not an everyday feature of her life, but she understood the principles. There would be a tiny crystal embedded in the tip of each cartridge, and those would enable this frame to create a wormhole to one with a matching crystal. The black cartridge poised over the frame's address chamber was a direct link to the guns.

This is the evidence I need.

Sarah examined the cartridge holder and discovered how

to detach its cover. She carefully removed the black cartridge and screwed on the cap from her own stylus, then slipped it into her pocket.

As she leaned over the frame for a better angle to work from, bright lights flooded the loading bay. Another vehicle was driving into the warehouse.

Still holding the E2 cartridge, she slapped the transparent cover closed and fled into the maze. The vehicle's timing couldn't have been better. As she moved, Sarah heard the three workers returning from their coffee run.

"It's almost nine," Vince said as Sarah crouched against a crate. "Fire up that ring and let them know we're ready."

"Hey," a new voice shouted. "Do you always receive shipments from Earth at night?"

Sarah perked up. She didn't recognize the woman's voice, but the tone was unmistakable. *A police officer.*

"Let me see your shipping manifests," the officer snapped.

Okay, maybe not police, but Customs. She crawled across an aisle to find a better viewpoint. *That's just as good; they outrank CorpSec.*

"I … We …" Adam, pale and shaky, trembled in front of the portal, looking between the uniformed woman and his co-workers. Vince stood defiantly with his arms crossed.

The woman strode directly to Adam and barked at him. "I sent three smugglers to Earth last week. You'll be joining them if your paperwork doesn't hold up."

Finally, an officer I can trust. She could reveal everything and keep herself and Jack safe. She stood and started walking from the shadows.

Vince doubled over in laughter. Adam looked as if he was about to faint until the women laughed too.

Vince slapped Adam on the back. "Tonight's delivery is on the books. And it'll match to less than a pound."

Sarah's shoe squeaked as she dropped to the floor. She tensed, but no one except her had seemed to hear it.

"Where's the address cartridge?" Astrid asked. "Did you remove it?"

Adam, only partially recovered from the prank, replied

nervously. "I … I only ejected it. It should still be in the carousel."

Sarah moved quickly. While everyone was occupied by the portal frame, she'd escape through the open bay door. Turning a corner, she recognized the smooth concrete of the loading zone behind a black van. She sprinted. And ran straight into a burly CorpSec officer.

Despite his bulk, the man reacted with the speed of a snake. He slammed Sarah face-first into the wall of crates, knocking the wind out of her. Before she could react, he flipped a jacket over her head, grasped her right hand in his, and used his left to lock her in a Half Nelson.

"I've caught a thief," he shouted. Sarah struggled uselessly as he marched her back to the portal. "He's a scrawny one."

"The address cartridge is missing," Adam said. "He must have taken it."

The officer pushed Sarah against a wall of crates and held her with his knee in her back. He pried open her hand and snagged the E2 cartridge. "Got it."

"What do we do with him?" Astrid's voice pitched higher. "Did he see our faces? Can he identify us?"

"Thirty seconds," Adam said. "If we don't start transferring the cargo on time, Customs will be suspicious. We can't risk an audit."

"Open it," the customs officer said. "We'll push him through and let Earth deal with him. Or maybe the portal will scramble his head and save us the trouble."

Not through the portal. Sarah gripped a corner of the crate, preparing to fight. She'd heard stories of people who'd traveled through low-power cargo portals—the trip rarely ended well.

"That'll create a difference in mass," Vince said.

"Write it up as a return of defective parts. I'll sign off on it."

Sarah couldn't see the lights dim when the wormhole opened, but she heard the building's air conditioning system struggle with the brownout.

"Hey, that's not our—" Adam began.

Multiple voices erupted in panic.

"It's going to over—"

"Shut it down."

"Cover your—"

An intense squeal assaulted her senses before the collapsing wormhole yielded a thunderous bang and a light so intense she saw it through the jacket. The men and women around her screamed. The officer holding Sarah staggered and released her. She whipped the covering off her head. The officers and warehouse workers were writhing on the floor.

A sulfurous, metallic-smelling cloud of thin smoke drifted toward the bay door, and that's where Sarah went too. Her ears were ringing, but she heard the CorpSec officer yell, "Stop him."

"I can't see a thing," Vince wailed.

In seconds, Sarah was running through the open gate. She mounted her bike, engaged its electric motor, and was halfway to the paved forest trail before risking a glance over her shoulder. The officers were stumbling to their van. With a wind at her back, she heard shouted commands right up until she turned the corner.

"You've only got minutes to clean this up."

Despite her near-panic, Sarah realized what he meant. *That was a big field collapse. Customs will be coming to investigate.*

She began peddling to exceed her bike motor's top speed. A loud screech of tires on pavement and light sweeping through the trees told her they'd correctly guessed she was heading into the city.

Sarah frequently cycled to work and could maintain a steady pace for miles, but the panicked sprint was taking its toll. She was running out of breath as she passed a trail-side sign warning of traffic ahead. With a loud rumble, the unseen van overtook her on the parallel street.

An amber light, marking the crosswalk, flashed atop a steel post fifty feet ahead. Sarah stood on her pedals and pumped furiously. Another squeal told of the van's slide through the intersection.

She erupted from the woods and shot into the street,

missing the black van by inches as it lurched onto the sidewalk to block the path. Partially blinded by headlights, she barely avoided the concrete bollard that prevented vehicles from entering the pedestrian walkway. The driver, seeing her escape, gunned the engine to race around the block.

Cameras. Sarah tucked her head to her chin as she sped along the well-lit corridor between twin apartment complexes. With only a phone call, the pursuing officers could have CorpSec looking for someone matching her description.

No, wait. Cameras. CorpSec could watch the street in real-time, but Little Brother wouldn't track her without a court order. And whoever these officers were, she doubted they'd call for backup anyway.

Instead of turning west mid-block and taking a pedestrian path home, Sarah sprinted north. She could already see the colorful tents of an open-air market hosted in a park two blocks ahead. All she had to do was mill through the crowd until she'd passed so many cameras that there was no chance of trailing her discreetly.

She rolled into the park and dismounted, joining hundreds of other pedestrians on the promenade. After ten minutes of wandering, she sheltered under a vendor's tent, unzipped her hoodie and shook out her shoulder-length hair. That wouldn't fool Little Brother, of course, but human observers would be looking for a boy.

After another ten minutes, she strolled to the north side of the park, leaned her bike against an elm tree, and watched the street. A single CorpSec van made several slow passes around the block, but never stopped. Eventually, the driver gave up and drove deeper into the city.

Sarah mounted her bike and started for home with mixed feelings. She'd failed to get the answers she wanted and had uncovered a new mystery. Still, the old man had been right about one thing: E2 had shed a lot of light on the problem.

Chapter 29

Tuesday – 24 Hours to Newton

The party at the cabin had continued past midnight. Though each of Niels' friends were older than his parents, Jack felt completely at ease and accepted. Having grown up in a town where almost everyone was decades older, he generally preferred the company of adults. Ethan, a natural extrovert, was comfortable in any gathering.

It wasn't until the end of the evening that Jack had realized he'd felt no anxiety, despite being in a large group. They'd behaved more like a family than friends or colleagues, though smaller, close-knit groups had troubled him before.

There had been good-natured arguments and even some teasing, but no one ever took offense. The only time there arose the slightest hint of trouble was when Terrance answered a text message. This earned him a glare from several of the others, prompting Terrance to apologize directly to Niels. Apparently, Niels did not allow phones on his island retreat.

When things finally wound down, Niels had decided the boys should stay on Icarus Island—the others' residences on the far shore were only temporary buildings. In fact, the only reason all of them had come on the same night was because of his prediction from long ago.

- - - - -

It may have been the relief of learning that his parents had gotten away from whoever was chasing them, or the aftereffects of the party, or just being tired from lack of sleep and too much time on the road; whatever the reason, Jack fell into the deepest slumber he'd had in months.

As always, he knew when he entered a lucid dream, one he had some control over. This one began with him outside of Niels' cabin; he recognized the front door. An owl hooted in the distance, causing him to look skyward, toward the brightening clouds.

And then he was flying.

Jack smiled, in both his real and imagined states. This was his favorite type of lucid dream. He knew from experience that he could choose his destination if he was careful to avoid sudden moves.

Don't try to take over, he reminded himself. *Share control with my subconscious. That's the trick.*

He let the dream follow its own course initially, spiraling upwards. He soon gained enough height to see more of the island and started paying attention to details. In a flight dream, he usually flew closer to whatever caught his interest. Upslope from the cabin, a clearing in the trees held a vegetable garden.

What's he growing, Jack wondered, then found himself swooping low and fast over the tidy rows.

The conscious part of his mind understood the logic of having a garden in this spot, given the difficulty of crossing the lake. He wouldn't be surprised if there really was one there. In Fairview, his lucid dreams matched up exactly with the fields and forests he knew so well from years of exploration.

He noticed the shoreline and zoomed that direction, overshooting and eventually making his way across the lake. *Where's Dave? Maybe it will blink its lights.* He circled a rocky beach but saw nothing below. *Of course not, it's too dark. The only features I'll recognize are the sheltered bay and the rock wall below the wooden bench.*

That subtle thought caused him to swing around and head back to the island. The cove emerged from the darkness. He flew over the cliff and searched for where he knew the cabin should be at the end of a short path. The building was exactly as he'd seen it last evening, well hidden in the forest.

He slalomed between trees, making his way to the cabin and landing on a branch, which tapped against the window. *Landing? I've been dreaming the role of a bird.*

In previous dreams of flying, he'd always assumed what he saw came from an imagined human perspective. But what startled him awake wasn't the dream's novelty, but when he peered through the window and recognized himself sleeping on the cabin floor.

- - - - -

Jack sat up and faced the window, catching a blur of motion as a small gray owl flew away. He hesitated, momentarily stunned by the preposterous coincidence. Then he chuckled quietly to himself, reasoning that he'd heard the branch scratching the glass, and blended it into his dream.

Shortly after, Niels came to wake them. They'd decided to leave as early as possible, to stay ahead of searchers. While waiting for Anders and his boat, Jack discovered that what he thought was the cabin's back door, opened to a workshop. The machine-filled room was as large as the rest of the building and as modern as any he'd ever seen. It was also *drafty*, in the way he sensed the wormhole distortion that made others nauseous.

Ethan looked over the collection of high-tech equipment. "What's all this? It looks like you could build nanobots here."

"Yes, I can." Once again, Niels' reply didn't sound boastful, even though this was a complicated task. "But I do little of that now. Mostly I'm working on this." He handed Ethan a device that resembled a flashlight. "Point it at that cup and press the button."

The cup slid erratically toward Ethan. "*It's a tractor beam.*"

"That's right. It's like asteroid defense jets at the top of the rim walls, except it pulls instead of pushes. Oh, don't worry about that," Niels said when the cup tipped over, spilling the last few drops. "It takes practice."

"I thought those jets pushed objects with a stream of dark energy." Jack said. "Does that mean you've figured out what the energy is?"

"No more than anyone else," Niels said as Ethan experimented with the beam projector, tipping the cup over several times. "It's like the early days of electricity; we know the energy field is an integral part of wormholes, but we don't know if it's dark energy, dark matter, or something else. That doesn't mean we can't use it though. Cirrus might not exist without it."

"Yeah, we learned about dark matter and why the tunnels

are unnecessary in Physics this year."

"Tunnels?" Ethan asked. "Dark matter?"

"Our classes are different from yours—we spend a lot of time on Cirrus' ecosystem. There are tunnels connecting the seas in each sector to the ocean under the ring's inner ice cap. The valves inside were intended to fine-tune Cirrus' rotation by balancing the seas. But the gravity generators caused a sphere of dark matter to accumulate in the void in the middle of the station, which makes it more stable than it should be. So the valves only control the tides now."

"Does that mean you could take a sub between sectors?"

"They pass through the crust. You'd be crushed."

Ethan passed the projector to Jack to play with. When Jack used it, he felt a connection between it and the cup, similar to the pull of a magnet. Niels explained how to balance the beam between pushing and pulling. Soon, Jack was guiding the cup in a smooth figure-eight across the table.

Ethan crouched to get his eyes level with the tabletop. "How are you making it float?"

"What?" The cup jerked when Jack released the button. "No, it was still sliding."

Ethan appeared skeptical. "I'm sure it was floating." He looked to Niels for confirmation but the man only said, "You seem to have a natural talent for it."

Jack was aware that Niels had been watching carefully, and got the feeling Niels knew he'd be able to use the device effortlessly. The stories from last night left him thinking there was still much that Niels knew but hadn't told anyone. He wanted to ask more questions, but Anders arrived just then to take them across the lake.

As Ethan slung Jack's backpack onto his shoulder, he remembered he hadn't received an answer to his question last night. "Do you know who's chasing us?"

Niels hesitated before answering. "You'll be reunited with your family in Caerton soon. Your grandfather can tell you a lot more about that."

Ethan followed Anders from the cabin but Jack lingered.

"There's …" Jack glanced at the door to make sure Ethan

was out of hearing range. "There's someone else—"

"She'll be fine." Niels grinned. "I may not remember everything clearly, but this one I'm certain of."

- - - - -

Encouraged by Niels' confidence that Sarah was safe, Jack was actually looking forward to continuing the journey. It wasn't until they'd left the island that he realized Niels had referred to Uncle Charles as their grandfather. And so had Aunt Grace. He was wondering about this when the sense of familiarity he'd been feeling since yesterday faded.

As Anders piloted the boat across the lake, Jack became certain that he hadn't imagined it—they were at the same distance where he'd felt it yesterday. Just like the cave, he knew he'd never been here before either. *Does Niels feel the same sense of connection? Is that why hasn't left the island in twenty years?*

"Sir," Jack said. "Last night you said Niels had the island specially created for him."

"That's right. Had it blasted out with an asteroid." Anders watched for their reaction and got the response he expected.

"*What?*" Ethan exclaimed. "That's insane."

Jack understood now why the lake was perfectly round. He knew from school that Cirrus' crust was less than two miles thick and partially constructed from asteroids and comets. "I don't remember reading anything about that in history class."

"They covered it up. Some say it was a miscalculation, that the asteroid was denser than expected. I'm not so sure."

"It was deliberate?" Ethan asked.

"The impact was planned, but the crater went much deeper than predicted, right down to the core. It even affected the gravity generators in the area—snapped some of the lines."

"Why plan to hit it with something so big at all?"

"Cirrus will never have earthquakes. There were a lot of cliffs in the rim that were even taller than they are now. The shock wave traveled around the ring seven times and caused thousands of slides. So, the mountains are safer now, more settled because of the impact. And Niels got his island. The lake is deeper than expected, that's all."

- - - - -

If Jack still had doubts about Niels' friends, they'd have evaporated soon after reaching the shore. He passed a collection of single-room shacks on the hike to the now-restored car shelter. They'd been built mostly from branches, tarps, and warped plastic panels. These people were clearly not part of the group hiding weapons and tools outside of Fairview. The huts had been invisible last night, and he guessed the trees would hide them from passing drones in daytime too.

Ethan grabbed the handlebars of a motorcycle leaning against the shelter and tilted it, testing its balance. "This wasn't here last night."

"It's Terrance's," Anders said, as if it were obvious who the powerful machine belonged to.

"Can we look at your GPS for a few minutes?" Jack asked.

"Sure." Anders led them to his truck. "I'm sorry I can't let you borrow it. I've got to travel on the highways tomorrow." He left them to study the map.

"It looks like we have to follow the rivers." Ethan swiped and tapped the screen. "There's a service road on the north side of the forest that will take us there. All the other roads are controlled. You ready to go?"

"Just a minute. I want to check something."

Jack scrolled the map to the intersection east of Fairview. A yellow triangle indicated a traffic advisory—the crash site was still being cleaned up. He was about to get out of Anders' vehicle when another thought occurred to him. He swiped over to the Vault.

"What are you looking for?"

"It's not there." Jack tapped the screen. "The route we drove through the Spine. Look."

Ethan took over. He zoomed and panned but found nothing. "What does that mean? We both saw it yesterday."

"I'm not sure." Jack glanced at the group of people chatting by the shacks. "But I don't think we're getting the whole story."

Anders returned and described for them a shorter route out of the forest, one too insignificant to show up on the map. Ethan would need to drive slower, but it would save them an hour of backtracking.

Ethan shook Anders' hand. "It was a pleasure meeting you."

Jack extended his hand and added, "I hope we'll meet again. Did you say you're not leaving until tomorrow?"

"Yeah," Anders said gruffly. "I'll stay another night and keep the old man company." He grinned. "Someone has to make sure he doesn't build himself a portal and skip town again."

Chapter 30

Danny arrived in Caerton before dawn. But instead of traveling by train to Port Isaac as instructed by Pieter—to search for Jack—he stayed in the city. He made his way to the noisy workshop at the back of UV Mobile.

As per his orders, the shipping crate had been left on a table. He lifted it to expose the sphere and inserted an H-shaped key. The safe's upper shell rose on four metal pistons. A thin cloud of bluish dust—all that remained of his cargo from Earth—spread from the gap.

He roared and hurled the sphere, then overturned the table, smashing it into a tall rack. A section of steel pipe wobbled on the top shelf, then rolled for the edge.

The girl.

The drones had been a deliberate taunt, he thought. Whoever this Traveller was, they wanted him to find the electronic spies at the camp. It would have been simple to delete the footage of the destruction of the drone that had found Jack, but they'd left that too. It had all been too easy—someone was leading him to the girl. She couldn't possibly be the one behind the scheme, but someone wanted him to think so.

He had less than a day to find the answers, and few options. *She's connected somehow. And if they want me to find her, then that's what I'll do.*

The heavy chunk of pipe rolled silently off the shelf and plummeted toward Danny's head. He couldn't see as far into the future as Pieter could, but his talent was more precise. He stepped aside from the deadly projectile with half a second to spare and left the room without looking back.

- - - - -

After so much time driving, Jack's seat was as painfully familiar as it was comfortably restrictive. Like the all-terrain-vehicle itself, Dave's seats had been designed for rough roads. That meant there were no lumps, angles, or pinch-points for Ethan to complain about. That didn't stop him though.

"If we follow the rivers to approach Caerton from the west, how long will that take?"

Jack guessed. "Eight hours at least."

"But if we use the grain roads, we should get there in three, right?"

"Not without a transponder. The roads here are the same as the others—one lane wide and the distance between pullouts is much too long. But we don't have to rush; our parents got away. They're safe."

"I know. I'm just sick of driving."

"I'll take over."

"Not that sick."

- - - - -

The aviary was a noisy place at dawn. Thousands of birds flitted and splashed, chorused and chittered through their morning meals. Danny strode the net-covered boardwalk that cut through the heart of the complex, paused briefly at a chain link gate to extract a slim, powered crowbar from his jacket pocket, then broke the lock and entered the administration building unnoticed.

He found the records office. The only staff working at this hour were outdoors—he wouldn't be disturbed. His contractors had already hacked and searched their server and determined that no regular staff member fit the girl's profile. Pieter had already worked out that she was Jack's age, but all the regular employees were over thirty. That meant she was a volunteer. Unpaid. *An intern.* Danny opened a folder on the Human Resources Manager's workstation and found the file easily.

Tracking an unknown person was difficult. Now that he had an ID, the job would be much easier. He texted a name to Eyes: *<Sarah Rogers.>*

Danny checked the time. He still had to put in an appearance in Port Isaac to satisfy Pieter.

An hour there by train, an hour to take care of business, and an hour back.

He'd thought about ignoring Pieter's order, but that would leave traces. With less than twenty-four hours to go, now was not the time to take chances. He left the aviary and headed for the train station.

- - - - -

The sun was only just coming over the horizon when Ethan drove out of the trees. The transition was abrupt; one moment they were driving past a pitch-black crag Anders said marked the edge of the thick forest, the next they were bumping through a field of tall grass. Drones had planted the forest decades ago, resulting in long, perfectly straight borders. There were only a few smaller trees in the field, naturally seeded by the wind or animals.

Ethan stopped Dave at the end of the dirt track, near a three-way intersection. The grain road traveled east; their route went north. "Last chance."

Jack shook his head. "It'll be safest to head north and follow the river. We can take breaks if we need to. Either they think we're stuck without power, in which case they'll be searching for us on the other side of the Spine; or they think we got a ride with someone, and we could be anywhere in the sector."

Ethan pointed down the road, where a cloud of dust was rising in the south. "I hope those are just farm vehicles."

"I'm sure they are."

"Then I'll wait until they turn. I don't want to be caught in front of a convoy if it goes straight through for some reason."

A minute later, a pair of grain carriers slowed for the intersection and turned east. Both cabs were empty. The giant vehicles sped up the grain road, raising another dust cloud.

"Okay," Jack said, "let's go."

Ethan shot out of the field, straight across the intersection, into the churning haze.

"*Wait, where are you going?* You were supposed to go north." This was no time for one of Ethan's stunts, Jack thought as he clutched the grab handle mounted below the roof rack.

"Look." Ethan pointed south again.

A hundred feet above the road, a large black drone with stubby wings was approaching. The wings were set in their vertical position—for slow flight or hovering—instead of horizontal for high-speed pursuit. Jack couldn't see it clearly through the dust, but the aircraft was the same size as the one he'd seen at the basin.

"That's no farming drone," Ethan shouted.

Jack spun in his seat, scanning for cover. "We need to get back to the forest." The closest trees were too sparse.

"It's too far. I have a plan." The carriers had a lead, but Dave could accelerate faster. Ethan swerved alongside the second vehicle.

"Getting us killed is not a good plan." Jack gripped the handle tighter.

"We're going to hide in plain sight."

The road ahead narrowed to a single lane. It would be a tight race. Jack swiveled to watch the drone. *Is anyone watching the video in real time?* The moving grain haulers would certainly trigger an alert. "It's almost to the intersection."

Only yards before the second lane ended, Ethan swerved violently in between the carriers, enveloping Dave in a cloud of dust. "Is it following us?" He was too busy concentrating on the distance to the lead vehicle to look around.

"I can't see anything. The dust is too thick."

"Wait a second." Ethan sped up again. He drew to within two feet of the carrier, in a pocket of clear air.

Jack glanced ahead. "If that brakes, we're done for."

"I'll worry about that. Where's the drone?"

A few seconds passed before Jack spotted the drone through the churning dust. It was continuing north, following the service road that bordered the forest.

"We're safe." Jack faced the lead grain carrier again. Its high tailgate loomed twelve feet above them. "Or maybe not."

- - - - -

Over the next two hours, Ethan shadowed a variety of northbound vehicles. As Dave had done, he frequently braked and swerved into pullouts to avoid oncoming traffic. Eventually, they stopped behind a line of semis waiting at an intersection.

"Don't follow." Jack pointed to a bridge on a side road. "I remember that river from the map. Turn right."

Ethan reclined his seat and drove with only one hand on the wheel. "I'm beat. I didn't know driving would be so hard."

"For future reference, that's not how you're supposed to do it." Jack shook his hands to relieve the fatigue caused by repeatedly gripping the dashboard. "But it saved us at least five hours. Caerton's on the other side of this forest."

The cousins traded places for the final stretch. They encountered other vehicles in the woods, mostly small two-seaters like their own. After two days on dirt tracks and gravel roads, theirs was easily the dirtiest vehicle around. They were themselves almost as dusty. Jack gave a friendly wave whenever he passed another car, and no one paid them further attention.

Emerging from the forest, they found themselves on the outskirts of Caerton, on the lip of a crescent-shaped plateau that bordered the northern half of the city. Their viewpoint overlooked rows of vertical farming greenhouses. The structures were identical to those in Port Isaac, except there were many more of them.

Caerton was also much farther inland than Port Isaac. The rim mountains were too far away to see, but they still influenced the local environment. Between the city and the rim, an enormous lake collected fresh water that melted from the glaciers. The river that drained the lake cut a steep ravine through the plateau and ran through the city itself, east of the downtown core.

"Where does Uncle Carl live?" Ethan asked.

Jack pointed to the cluster of massive towers in the city's center, many of which were over a thousand feet tall. "Right downtown, within walking distance of the train station."

"Finally. We're only about ten miles away."

"The building we're looking for is called the Magnolia, but I don't know the address. We'll have to find the station and work our way out from there."

"That doesn't sound difficult."

"It's not." Then Jack slumped in his seat. "But I just remembered; Dave doesn't have a permit for Caerton. And I don't have a driver's license anyway."

"I thought you said you had one. Isn't the age lower here?"

"It is. And I've got an off-road permit now. But you still have to be nineteen to drive in the cities."

"What about buses?"

"I don't know if we can use our IDs safely. CorpSec might be able to track them."

Ethan considered the distant towers. "So, we walk?"

"We can drive to the end of the greenhouses. That'll save us an hour."

Jack drove to where the paved roads started once again, then pulled over and parked on the grass next to one of the tall, glass-walled structures. "This is as far as we can go."

Once past the greenhouses, Caerton resembled Fairview in that its buildings grew taller toward the center. They'd begin their journey walking through miles of brownstones and four-story apartment blocks, and end up navigating canyons of glass, concrete, and steel. But they'd gone just half a block when Jack stopped.

"What's wrong?" Ethan asked.

"I know where we are."

"About two hours from downtown?" Ethan trudged on.

"No, this is where Sarah lives." A large park and soccer field separated the greenhouses from a cluster of townhouses. "Let's cut through here. I think I can find her street."

"Any chance her parents have a car?"

"Not likely. But we can at least get a map and not waste time getting lost."

Jack remembered the street name. He soon found the correct address and recognized the building—a three-story structure with dormer windows on its steeply sloped roof. Sarah's room occupied the top floor of a narrow unit in the center of the block. He walked to the door and rang the bell.

Ethan waited behind Jack, glancing nervously at the street. A few seconds later, a woman in a CorpSec officer's uniform opened the door.

"Jack Scatter." She'd seemed surprised, but now smiled. "I was wondering when we'd meet."

Chapter 31

"Come in, Jack." The uniformed woman stepped back and opened the door wider.

Jack was about to turn and run, fearing CorpSec had finally caught them, when the woman added, "You're at the right house. I'm Sarah's mother. I recognize you from the photos on her phone." She'd misread his expression as confusion.

"Who is it, Mom?" Sarah stepped into view from the stairwell, then stopped in surprise when she saw Jack.

"You didn't tell me you were expecting friends from out of town."

"Uh …" If Jack had been able to look away from the woman, he might have noticed Sarah blushing. "We came on *really* short notice."

Ethan was also trying not to stare at her uniform. "Actually, we're just passing through. We're, uh, working for our uncle's company outside of town. He dropped us off at the worksite this morning, then we found we had left our ID and phones at his apartment. We're staying at his place."

"Oh." Sarah brightened. "Where does he live?"

Jack was grateful for Ethan's quick thinking. "His building is called the Magnolia."

"I know it. It's right in the center of town. Jada's family runs the restaurant on the roof. You can borrow my phone."

"Thanks." Jack relaxed, believing Mrs. Rogers only recognized him from one of Sarah's photos, but he still had to come up with a convincing story. "The rest of the crew has gone farther out of town. They won't be back until tonight." He slapped his shirt sleeve, raising a cloud of dust. "Can we borrow a bus pass?"

"Sorry, boys," Mrs. Rogers said. "You'll need your IDs." Her voice held a tone of authority, as if she was used to explaining the rules. Her phone beeped just then and she tapped the screen. "And I've got to get to work." She gestured with her phone. "The shuttle will be by in one minute. You can't even ride that without ID."

"I can borrow bikes from the neighbors," Sarah said. "I'll ride downtown with you."

Mrs. Rogers looked the boys over carefully. "Well … all right." Jack guessed they either seemed trustworthy enough or she didn't want them tracking dirt through her house. Her phoned beeped again. "Thirty seconds. I've got to go. Be home by dinner."

Exactly thirty seconds after the tone, a long, open-sided vehicle stopped in front of the house. Mrs. Rogers slid into a seat on the neighborhood shuttle, which would take her to a bus stop where a larger bus would carry her downtown.

"Jack." Sarah pulled his arm. "We need to talk about—"

He cut her off, knowing she wanted to discuss the weapons. "This is my cousin, Ethan."

"Ah, right." She smiled. "Hi, Ethan. Come in. I'll call the neighbors. Wait here." She then practically ran from the room and up the stairs.

Jack glanced at his surroundings. The slender townhouse's ground floor contained only the compact kitchen and dining room, and adjoining living room. There were many photos on the living room's shelves and walls. Some depicted a much younger Sarah with a man he guessed must be her father. Most showed only Sarah and her mother.

Only then did Jack realize he'd finally met one of his best friends in person for the first time. Unlike meeting his cousin—something that created mixed emotions—meeting Sarah felt completely natural, as if he'd done it a thousand times. He hadn't even considered *not* coming to her for help when he recognized where he was. What he didn't realize was that he was still staring at the empty doorway.

"Jack." Ethan had to punch his shoulder to get his attention. "What's going on?" he whispered. "Why didn't she arrest us? Does she know everyone Sarah goes to school with? Why does everyone know more about what's happening than we do?"

"Calm down. I don't know. Maybe they're not looking for us anymore, or not looking here. Port Isaac's CorpSec isn't the same as Caerton's. She might just work in a different department."

"Or maybe she went to get backup."

"Relax. We'll be at Uncle Carl's place soon."

Sarah returned. She'd completely changed her outfit in the brief time she was out of the room. "The twins down the street will lend us their bikes. Mine's around back. I'll meet you outside."

Ethan kept looking at the windows to see if anyone was watching as they waited on the sidewalk. "Was there anyone else home? Does her father work for CorpSec too?"

"Her parents separated a long time ago, and she doesn't have a brother or sister. Stop worrying," Jack said, as much to himself as to Ethan. "We'll be safe soon."

Sarah rode out to the street from a breezeway that passed through the block of townhouses. "Follow me." She rode ahead and met a younger boy pushing a bike in each hand. By the time Jack and Ethan caught up, she was telling him they would have the bikes back in the afternoon.

"What work are you doing for your uncle?" Sarah asked as she led them farther into the city. "How long are you staying?"

"We're …" Jack was uncomfortable lying to Sarah, but couldn't tell her CorpSec had just chased them all the way from Fairview because of something Ethan's parents may have done on Earth. "It's sort of a family project. I don't know how long we'll be here. Hopefully for a day or two." His last comment was genuine. Although he didn't know what was happening, he wished he could stay awhile.

"I hope so." She toggled her bike's turn signal. "We'll take the freeway from here."

"We're going on the freeway?" Ethan hovered his hand over the brake lever.

Jack had ridden in Port Isaac and knew what to expect. "On Cirrus, a freeway is for bikes, not cars."

Sarah rode past the bus stop and veered onto a ramp that descended under the street. "Keep to the right. The eastbound tunnel takes us all the way downtown."

Ethan marveled at the tunnels. They were bright and clean,

as wide as the street above, and as tall as Sarah's three-story townhouse. Pedestrians traveled on elevated walkways suspended below the ceiling. Bicycles used the floor or the ramps crossing below the pedestrian level. He followed Jack into the wide center lane and was caught by surprise when his bike sped up on its own.

"Sorry," Jack said, "I forgot. Your speed is controlled when you enter the center lane. You can't go less than fifteen, but you can go faster if you want to pedal."

Ethan grinned and sprinted ahead, pedaling furiously.

Jack moved into position beside Sarah. "Sorry about cutting you off earlier, but I never told Ethan the whole story about the basin."

"That's what I wanted to talk to you about. I accidentally sent a flock of drones there. Someone saw them and—"

Ethan cut into the empty right lane and locked his brakes, causing his bike to slide sideways and leave a black stripe on the floor. Laughing, he swerved back into the center lane and lurched ahead to rejoin Jack and Sarah. "This is a blast. I don't think I ever want to drive a car again."

- - - - -

Shortly before they'd entered the tunnel, a tiny black drone, smaller than a butterfly, approached the Rogers' townhouse. The craft's operator, a woman known as 'Eyes', spotted the cousins waiting at the front door. She didn't recognize them, but decided to follow when they moved away. When the girl joined them, the surveillance software alerted her that it had found a match. She switched the craft to tracking mode.

The discreet spy struggled against the wind to follow the girl and her companions to the freeway. Clever as the software was, it still lost track of its quarry when the expected group of three cyclists vanished. Eyes assumed control and realized that the group had split apart. In the calmer air of the tunnel, she pushed the aircraft to close within fifty yards. That was near enough to read the freeway pass number printed on the girl's bike. She switched the tracker to automatic. It wouldn't be fooled again. She picked up her phone and sent a message to the man who was returning to Caerton on the next train.

<I found the girl.>

- - - - -

More riders joined the flow of bike traffic, forcing Ethan to keep to the posted speed limit, which soon dropped to ten. If that wasn't enough to tell a visitor they'd reached the downtown core, then the coffee shops on every corner were an obvious sign.

Jack was feeling uneasy among the increasing crowds until Sarah turned off the freeway and led him to the correct address with a final turn onto a cross street. They deposited their bikes in the Magnolia's underground parking lot.

When the elevator arrived, doors opened on both sides. Jack counted silently as seven people entered from the opposite side and three from his.

An elderly woman held her hand out to prevent the door from closing. "Going up?"

"Yes, ma'am." But Jack hesitated. His stomach churned and his heart raced with the memory of the train station.

Sarah pulled his sleeve. "Maybe we should take the stairs. I know you don't want to get dirt from your work clothes on anybody."

He stepped back and allowed the elevator doors to close. "Thanks," he whispered as they detoured to the stairs.

"What floor does Uncle Carl live on?" Ethan asked.

Sarah looked at him quizzically. "I thought you stayed here last night."

"Uh, yeah. I wasn't paying attention though." He mouthed a silent 'sorry' when she looked away.

"He's on the fifty-second level," Jack said, "but we're not going to walk all the way up. The commercial levels only take up the first five floors."

At the first residential level, Jack reached for the door access panel. *Oh, no. It doesn't matter what floor Uncle Carl lives on. If my handprint doesn't work, I'll have to tell Sarah the truth. And then I'll have to tell Ethan everything too.* Fortunately, the lock clicked when he placed his hand against the scanner. He pushed through into the secure hallway and headed for the elevator.

The Magnolia's apartments had two floors, like Jack's townhouse. So, when the elevator opened at level fifty-two, he entered a bright, open atrium where real trees—Magnolias and Japanese Maples—grew in an ornamental garden. At each end of the garden, which ran the entire length of the building, floor-to-ceiling glass provided natural light and impressive views over the city.

"This is nice." Sarah brushed a hand over the flowers growing in the raised bed. "Does your uncle's apartment face the garden?" A dozen doors lined each side of the rectangular atrium. Above, tree branches blossomed inches away from the second-floor windows.

"No, he's in an outside row." Jack led the way to a corridor that passed through a break in one of the inner rows. There were no names on the doors, but he remembered that his uncle's unit was right at the end of the connecting passageway. He knocked on the door and waited. There was no reply.

"Should we …?" Ethan inclined his head toward the handle.

Jack hesitated. The building's AI apparently still had his handprint on file. That was enough to gain access to the hallway and elevator, but what about Uncle Carl's door? He'd to have to tell Sarah the truth soon. Would he and his uncle recognize each other after all these years? Would Carl even recognize Ethan at all from photos? He didn't know if his parents were going to be inside or what message they had left. He prepared himself for an uncomfortable conversation, but felt a click when he clutched the door handle.

"Uncle Carl?" Jack called as he opened the door. "Mom? Dad?" The place was quiet. "I don't think he's home. We can go in and wait for him though."

"I hope he won't mind if I raid his fridge," Ethan said when he saw that nobody was there. "We haven't had anything to eat for hours."

"Did he go to your job site?" Sarah asked.

"He's semi-retired now," Jack said. "I'll check upstairs, in case he's sleeping."

Compared to Jack's home, Carl's place was tiny. However,

the living room was open to the second-floor ceiling and the entire outside wall was a floor-to-ceiling window, making the room seem bright and spacious. The compact kitchen fit entirely under the master bedroom on one side, while the opposite wall had built-in shelves with hundreds of books. It even featured a rolling ladder for reaching the upper levels.

"No one home," Jack confirmed from the balcony.

"Are those real books?" Sarah drifted to one of the tall bookshelves flanking the electric fireplace.

He joined her downstairs and leafed through a random book. "Yeah, they're real."

It had been a decade since he last visited. He'd always taken the books for granted. Now that he thought about it, there weren't many old-style paper books on Cirrus. Even children's coloring books were normally plastic sheets of electronic paper.

Sarah flipped carefully through a leather-bound hardcover. "Can you imagine how much it cost to bring them here?"

"I'm not sure about the books, but I remember that." He pointed to the square painting hanging above the fireplace. "I heard it was an original and it's very expensive."

She wrinkled her nose at the impressionistic landscape, but Jack found he couldn't stop staring at it. It was the one thing in the apartment he had a very clear memory of.

"What's in here?" She was in full explore mode and had opened the door to a room underneath the second bedroom.

"That's his office." Jack followed her into the windowless room. "He used to work as a geologist. I think he likes to keep up with current research."

"I found your phones." She gestured to a pair of phones on the desk next to the door.

Jack picked up the phone with the blue case—identical to the one in his pocket—and touched the screen. He recognized the logo of the same Earth-based provider he used. He flipped over the green case. That one bore the trademark for Aetherton, one of Cirrus' largest carriers.

Before he could respond, Ethan entered, eating a sandwich. "That doesn't look like it has much to do with geology." He pointed out the equipment on the workbench behind the desk.

Happy for the reprieve, Jack set the phones down and said, "Yeah, the microscope makes sense for a geologist, but that's a signal generator. Here's an oscilloscope. This is all for electronics." He leaned over to see what was under the table. "Ethan. *Look*."

"What? *Oh*." Ethan recognized the red lightning bolt on the white cube Jack had found.

Sarah came over too. "What is it?"

"It's a power supply for a remote cell." Jack crouched to inspect it more closely. It was the same style as the one in Fairview that powered Dave. "And it's got an active connection."

She had no way to know what that meant, but Jack was certain that he knew what the supply connected to.

Someone spoke behind them. "It seems I have some explaining to do."

They spun to face the man in the doorway. Jack, surprised yet pleased, exclaimed, "Uncle Carl?" But at that same moment Ethan, perplexed, said, "Grandpa?"

Chapter 32

Ethan was right, Jack realized. Although he'd initially been confused by the resemblance, the man standing in the doorway was his grandfather, not his uncle.

"Why are you on Cirrus?" Ethan asked. "*How* are you on Cirrus?"

"Apparently, I have quite *a lot* of explaining to do. But first … your parents. We think they're being held here, in the city."

"No, they got away. We saw them on video."

"I'm sorry, Ethan. Your father called to say they'd been warned to leave the apartment, but I haven't heard from them since."

"Why were they arrested?"

"Not arrested, taken." The elderly man noticed Sarah's alarmed expression but continued anyway. "We believe they're being held by Armenau's corporate security." He stepped aside to introduce a woman Jack hadn't noticed in the living room. "This is Detective Singh. She may know where they are."

"Hello." The officer gave the briefest of smiles before her stern expression returned. She wore no uniform, only street clothes and a light jacket bearing the logo of the United Nations Off-World Police. However, even if she hadn't been wearing the jacket, her confident manner suggested a police or military background.

"So, you can force them to release our parents?" Jack asked.

"It's not that simple. Corporations' private security may detain suspects before handing them over to us for—"

"But you're UN." Jack didn't care that he'd interrupted. "Aren't you in charge?"

The detective's expression hardened. "There's no official record of their detention. That limits what we can do. We suspect Pieter Reynard—the head of Armenau Corporation—is behind their abduction."

"Why?" Ethan asked.

She hesitated, appearing wary of providing too much information. "We're still putting the pieces together. It's possible this is something that goes beyond a simple kidnapping."

A tense moment followed this remark. Jack didn't think the kidnapping of his family was a simple matter. The detective seemed to understand that she'd chosen her words poorly.

"I'm sorry," she continued, "but we've decided not to make a move until we know more. Reynard's men were spotted leaving Port Isaac around the time your parents disappeared. We believe they're perfectly safe. Reynard has offices downtown and his corporation owns half the city; there are many places he could hold them."

The green phone on the desk—the one from Earth—rang. Priya picked it up as if she knew the call was for her. She listened for a moment, her jaw clenching. "Holden, they're coming."

"Who's coming?" Ethan asked.

Priya flipped the phone around to display video from a camera in the building's lobby. A group of five men dressed in black, carrying heavy duffle bags, were stepping into the elevator.

"Jack," Sarah began, "I'm sorry, they're—" But at the same time, he said to her, "They're after me and Ethan because of something his parents did on—"

"*Hey*," Ethan said, "you don't know that."

"No," Sarah said. "I was trying to tell you. They're following me. And maybe you, because of what we—"

"Actually," Holden said, "they're looking for me."

"Wait." Ethan shoved Jack's shoulder, forcing Jack to face him. "All this time you thought they were chasing *me*? It sounds like I'm the only one they're *not* chasing."

Priya raised her hands. "*Stop*. It doesn't matter who they're after. I'm responsible for the safety of all of you now."

Holden stared at Sarah for a few seconds, as if troubled by a challenging math problem. He faced the detective. "She'll be safer on the other side."

"All right." Priya dropped the phone on the desk. "Let's move."

Holden spoke cheerfully as he stepped from the office. "Come along, everyone."

Jack followed but Sarah hesitated, looking to him for an explanation. Realizing that he was the only person she knew, he was wondering how to reassure her when the detective beckoned her forward.

"It's okay." Priya's features softened. "The men who abducted your friends' parents are on their way upstairs. We're just going someplace safe for a while. You'll be coming right back here."

With little knowledge of the situation, and only a short time to decide, Sarah chose to trust the officer.

Instead of going to the front door as expected, Holden went to the ladder, which rested directly in front of the fireplace, even though none of them had moved it earlier. He touched a spot on the painting's Art Deco frame, peered at it closely, and seemed satisfied with whatever he found there. Then he pushed the ladder, but only the top half rolled away.

He gestured toward the lower half, which seemed locked into place against the mantle. "Jack, would you like to go first?" He pressed another spot on the frame. The painting flickered before vanishing to reveal a room on the other side of the wall.

Jack heard a puff of air waft through the opening and felt a mild pressure on his eardrums. He climbed the first steps and put his hand where the painting had been. His fingers passed right through. It was no illusion—there really was a passage to another room. *The neighboring apartment? Uncle Carl must be leasing that one too. But why the difference in air pressure?*

"Grab the top of the frame and pull yourself through," Holden said.

Jack poked his head through the opening. A ladder identical to the one he was standing on leaned against the mantle in the other room. He reached up, found a solid handhold on the frame's edge, then pulled himself through without difficulty.

There was something odd about the second apartment, although Jack couldn't put his finger on it. It wasn't the wealth of polished wood, antique furnishings, or thick carpeting, nor the passageway through a frame above a fireplace flanked by bookshelves that bothered him. *Why didn't he just build a secret door behind the shelves?*

"It's best if I come through next," Holden called as Jack stepped off the ladder. "I may need your help."

While waiting, Jack decided the alignment of the bookshelves was off. But he didn't have time to figure out why because Holden—having passed one leg through the opening—straddled the frame's edge and struggled to get his other leg through. Although he had a solid grip, he was more than seventy years old. Jack instinctively moved to a position where he could catch his grandfather should he slip.

Ethan followed easily, gawking around the room in confusion.

Sarah was next, ducking through with no problem at all. But then she stood still on the ladder with a bewildered expression.

Holden offered his hand for support. "Perhaps you should have a seat until the feeling passes."

"Woah," she whispered as he led her to the couch. She sat, continuing to gaze around uncertainly.

"I'll be right there," Priya said. "It looks like it will need a few minutes to recharge."

"I know this place." Sarah had regained her voice. "I've been here before."

"You have?" Jack asked. "Whose apartment is this?"

"I don't know about Sarah." Ethan strode across the room. "But I *have* been here before. Many times." He pulled the curtains apart.

The first thing Jack noticed was that the sun had gone behind the clouds. In the other apartment, the sunlight shining into the living room had been dazzling. Here, the light on the trees beyond the window was gloomy.

Trees? Is this window open to the atrium? Then he remembered that another block of apartments stood between them and the central garden. They were on the fifty-second floor—there shouldn't be trees outside.

Ethan exclaimed, "We're back on Earth."

Chapter 33

"Welcome to Earth, Sarah," Holden said. "And no, you haven't been here before, but Ethan has. This is my home in Washington. What you are experiencing is the déjà vu that accompanies a passage through a portal. It can be especially strong on one's first trip."

"A portal? The painting is a portal?" Jack was so surprised that he failed to notice he hadn't experienced anything unusual at all.

"Yes, and quite a clever one, I think. I designed it myself."

Ethan had already wandered onto the deck overlooking the backyard. Jack joined him there and inhaled deeply, noting how different the air smelled. "It's so hot." He shaded his eyes as the sun emerged from the clouds. "It never gets this hot on Cirrus."

"This isn't bad," Ethan said. "It was a hundred and ten when I left." He paused and looked around. "Or maybe it was raining. I'm not sure anymore. I think I'm feeling the déjà vu from the portal."

They were high on a hill in Newcastle with a view of a golf course through a gap in the trees. There was no denying they were on Earth. Ethan was taking it all in stride, but then he'd been here only weeks ago.

"Dusty," Ethan exclaimed, starting down the stairs two seconds before a dog trotted around the corner of the house and began barking happily. "Jack, this is my dog. Well, I guess she's Grandpa's now. We couldn't afford to bring her."

Dusty was overjoyed to see Ethan after the long absence and jumped all over him. When Jack reached the yard, the golden retriever greeted him the same way. For Jack, being jumped on by a dog was a real treat. There were few dogs on Cirrus, considering how expensive it was to bring even a suitcase.

Dusty heard voices inside the house and dashed up the stairs, followed by Ethan. By the time Jack got there, Sarah and the dog had already discovered each other. Dusty was enjoying a belly rub.

"That was too close." Priya stepped off the ladder and pressed a spot on the frame. With a flicker, the open passage vanished, replaced by a painting identical to the one on Cirrus. She crossed the room and spun the monitor on Holden's desk. The screen showed a view of the apartment on Cirrus. The angle suggested the camera was hidden inside the painting's frame.

As they watched, four large men, weapons drawn, burst into the living room. Two ran upstairs while the others rushed into the rooms on the lower floor. A fifth man entered, walking. He glanced around the empty living room, then pulled out a thumb-sized scanner and moved deliberately toward the fireplace.

"The portal," Jack whispered. "He's going to find us."

Holden spoke normally. "Don't worry, I've taken precautions."

The fifth man was Korean, late thirties, and clearly the group's leader. He was solidly built but slimmer than his companions. The others had put on body armor after leaving the lobby, but he wore an expensive business suit with no tie, which only made him appear more menacing. He glanced briefly in the camera's direction before moving out of sight, scanning the bookshelves.

Priya opened a desk drawer, pulled out a black phone with the UN logo on the back, and put it in her pocket. Seeing this, Holden said to the others, "I'm sorry, I should have warned you. I'm afraid your phones will no longer work. It's not possible for portal crystals to remain entangled when they pass through another wormhole."

Jack was getting used to being without, but Sarah regarded her now useless phone with obvious disappointment. Then she pointed at the monitor.

"Those are the men from the reservoir."

"Where?" Priya asked.

"You remember. That's where you think Jack's parents are being held."

"*I* know the reservoir. It's one of the places we're putting under surveillance. But what do *you* know about it?"

"Now I'm confused," Jack said. "Do you two know each other?"

"Well, this is unexpected," Holden said, "but not unheard of. In theory, when one travels through a portal, one's consciousness is connected across multiple points in time. It's called the Traveller Effect. Some people remember things they will experience before they make the return trip. Apparently, between now and when she returns to Cirrus, Sarah will hear Detective Singh discuss the reservoir."

"Hold on," Ethan said. "Isn't that a paradox? Sure, they're going to talk about it *now*. Because Sarah brought it up first."

"It is complicated. However, if she hadn't said it first, it's likely the detective and I would have discussed the search for your parents. The reservoir would have been mentioned."

"Does this mean I'm psychic now?" Sarah dashed to the window for her first view of Earth. "Will everything I remember come true?"

"More importantly," Jack said, "does that mean that's where our parents really are?"

"No," Holden said to Sarah. "There is no such thing as a *psychic* in the sense that someone can accurately predict the future. Anyone who tells you they can is either lying or deluded."

"But what about Travellers?"

"Some honestly believe they can see the future. But the trouble is that the part of the brain that interprets these memory fragments is the same one that enables us to visualize the things we imagine. In other words, anyone who *tries* to look into the future can never be sure if what they see is a memory or their own imagination."

"But," Ethan said, "Sarah remembered a conversation with someone she'd never met before, about a real place."

"Have you been to the reservoir before?" Holden asked.

"Um, yes." Sarah's cheeks reddened. "But that … you think it's a coincidence?"

"Hmm. The Traveller Effect has been proven for the first trip only. But this seems quite specific. There's a fair chance this is a true memory and not imagination."

"That car." She pointed to Priya's convertible in the driveway. "I remember driving that car. Does that mean I get to drive it now?"

"And *that*," Priya said, "is imagination." She smiled to show Sarah she wasn't mocking, only that she understood the confusion.

In that moment, Jack saw that the detective was a lot younger than he'd first assumed. Back in the apartment, when she was wearing her *game face*, her manner gave the impression she was older. Now that the situation had calmed, he guessed she was still in her twenties. She was also several inches shorter than Sarah. None of this changed his perception of her being in charge though. She watched the men in the apartment with a ready confidence that made him think she'd jump through the portal without hesitation if that were necessary.

Ethan pointed to the monitor. "He's back." The fifth man had moved into view and was staring directly at the camera.

Jack shivered involuntarily, sensing the stranger was incredibly dangerous. The man reached up and the image swung away, then stopped, facing a shelf full of books. "He's found the safe in the wall."

"Are you remembering things too?" Sarah asked.

"No. At least I don't think so." It only just occurred to Jack that he hadn't experienced the same déjà vu his friends had. "Something about the bookcases was wrong. Now I see they're inset into the wall, the same as the fireplace. But the fireplace is fake and the wall above it is even with the front of the shelves." He knocked on the wood paneling, producing a hollow sound. "That means there's an empty space behind the painting."

Holden swung the frame from the wall, revealing a hidden safe. "You've always had a keen, mechanical mind, Jack." The painting's back panel was solid metal, an integral part of the portal frame itself.

"What's in the safe?"

"It's to throw them off, isn't it?" Ethan said. "You're

hiding the portal in plain sight. If someone tried to steal what they thought was a valuable painting, they'd find the safe. They'd assume anything inside was even more valuable."

"Exactly. There's an industrial-grade portal crystal in each safe. They have flaws that make them noisy to scanners."

Until now, the men searching the apartment had worked silently, communicating using hand signals. Now that they were sure the place was empty, they spoke freely. In Newcastle, Jack heard Danny speak his and Ethan's names.

Sarah seemed unfazed when he also mentioned her, but Jack was confused. If it had been him and Ethan, that would have made sense. If it had been him and Sarah, that would have made sense too. *But all three of us?*

"Who are they?" Ethan asked. "Is one of them Reynard?"

"No," Priya said, "those are his personal guards. The man leading them is Danny Kou. If he's on Cirrus now, it means Reynard is most likely there too. He's known to use his own private portals to visit Cirrus and his other offices around the world."

Reynard and Kou. Those names seemed familiar to Jack, although he couldn't remember where he might have heard them before.

Holden interrupted his thoughts. "I expect you both have many questions. Why don't you go change first. Ethan, your clothes are in the spare room. Jack, I'm sure something of Ethan's will fit you."

Jack brushed his shirt, creating a cloud of dust. He'd forgotten how dirty they were.

Priya motioned to Sarah. "And I have some questions for you. Come with me and we'll see what else you remember."

- - - - -

By the time Jack and Ethan finished cleaning up, Holden had laid out breakfast for them.

"I've asked Detective Singh to give us some privacy. Most of what I have to say is a family matter, though there are a few things she won't want me to tell you. I'm sure you have questions about your parents. But first, Jack, I believe you want to know why you didn't experience déjà vu when you went through the portal."

"It's because I've been here before, haven't I?"

"Yes, many times. In fact, you and Ethan used to play in the yard together."

"*What?*" Ethan nearly spit out his toast. "When?"

"Oh, you wouldn't remember. You were only three years old the last time you met. And that leads to the next big question–why I was in Carl's apartment."

Jack was barely aware of what Holden was saying. It made sense now—not just why he hadn't experienced déjà vu, but why the painting in the apartment was so familiar, and how he and Ethan maintained such a close friendship through only a video connection. He spent much more time on-line with classmates he'd never met in person, but Ethan was more like a brother than a friend.

"Carl is, or was, my half-brother. When I'm on Cirrus, I pretend to be him."

"Why do pretend …" Jack started to form the obvious question, but then realized he'd been confused not by the similarity between the two men—the man he remembered as Uncle Carl a decade ago had in fact been Holden. "Did I ever meet Uncle Carl?"

"Yes, but you were very young. As for why; years ago, your parents, *both* of your parents, got caught up in dangerous events. It wasn't their fault, but what they did angered some very powerful people."

"It was Armenau, wasn't it?" Ethan asked.

Holden hesitated. "Yes. Your father used to work there."

"He did? What happened?"

Holden delayed for even longer. "All I'll tell you is that Nathan's part was never fully revealed, and only Emily and Victor had to go into hiding."

Jack didn't know how to respond to this. Like Ethan and virtually every teenager before them, he assumed their parents had no life before they were born.

Holden continued. "After you came along, Jack, your parents decided they couldn't live that kind of life with a child. Carl had already applied for a research permit. He knew someone who could change the records to show that Emily was *his* daughter, not mine. That made it possible for her to move to Cirrus without being detected. Other than our mother, who died when we were young, there wasn't anything to link Carl and me. And the difference in our last names hid even that connection."

Ethan had some experience with digital security through his parents' work and his own studies. "That should've been impossible, even before these things were controlled by AIs. He must have had some serious connections. How long did he live on Cirrus?"

"Oh, not long, only a few years. He never even wanted to go there. He took the other half of the portal on a freighter and returned right away. I used the portal to visit Cirrus and pretended to be him. Even though he was eight years older, we share some resemblance. Also, his neighbors had never met him and had no reason to think I was not him. As a geologist, his frequent absences could be explained by having to spend so much time in the field."

"What happened to him?" Jack asked.

"I wish I knew. I don't know where he is or even if he's still alive."

The three of them were silent for a while—this was a difficult memory for Holden.

Eventually, Ethan broke the silence. "I have a question. Why did I have to take a shuttle to Cirrus instead of using your portal?"

Holden laughed. "Mainly because you wouldn't be able to live in the open if you hadn't moved there legally. This entire subterfuge has been for Jack's benefit."

"My benefit? What do you mean?"

"You already know that children were not allowed on Cirrus, but you might not know it was common for women to hide their pregnancies to avoid being sent back to Earth. After Emily and Victor emigrated, Carl and I brought you back and forth until they moved to Fairview, where they pretended you were large for your age. You were born on Earth."

Ethan grinned. "Jack, you're not a Cirran. You're one of

us. Congratulations."

"Thanks. I guess."

"He's also older than you. Jack, your real birthday is actually next month."

Ethan chuckled. "Too bad you're still not old enough to drive."

"There's something else you should know. As a means of travel, dynamic portals were no more dangerous than driving a car—accidents happen. They were banned because of what they can do to the mind. Everyone who travels by portal experiences déjà vu at least once. Some experience depression, obsessive-compulsive disorder, or hallucinations. Carl was prone to bouts of depression before he ever used the portal. I believe this got worse with each trip. Eventually, he disappeared."

Ethan coughed and spoke with his mouth full. "We used the portal. Will something happen to us?"

"It's unlikely at your age. Negative effects happened only to very young travelers or to those with a pre-existing condition." He spoke directly to Jack. "Few had ever travelled as infants in the decades before you were born, and their own difficulties didn't show up until they were in their teens. As soon as we learned of that, we stopped bringing you here. We've been watching you closely ever since and have no concerns. Also, I'm confident that this type of portal is less likely to cause problems."

"What's different about it?" Despite his grandfather's certainty that his early travels caused no lasting harm, Jack couldn't help but worry about hallucinations—his experience on the Vault had seemed very real.

"Do you understand how wormholes are created?" Holden pushed his plate aside and went to the living room.

Jack stood and followed. He was familiar with the basics: large cargo portals used crystals as initiators only, to create a dynamic field; in a smaller static portal, the wormhole developed entirely within the crystal. "Sure. Field effect portals, like yours, can transport a lot of mass but use way more energy. Static portals are more stable, but there's a limit to how much mass they can transfer."

Ethan joined them in the living room. "And the crystals are made of artificial gemstones. So, they're usually only a fraction of an inch across."

Holden stopped in front of the painting. "Well, this one doesn't use the field effect, and …" He tapped the smooth pane covering the canvas. "That's not glass."

The boys gawked at the clear panel, realizing they were looking at what was easily the largest diamond in the world.

Chapter 34

Ethan was awestruck by size of the crystal hanging over Holden's mantle. "That's a diamond?"

"Mostly," Holden said. "All portal crystals require additional elements, and those atoms must be arranged in a specific pattern, so it's a composite. However, the wormhole is very stable. It's unlikely you felt any physical effects at all when you came through."

Jack was impressed by the gem's size too, and had to agree he'd felt nothing during the passage, but wanted to continue the conversation about his parents.

"You said our parents upset some powerful people. Was one of them this Reynard person Detective Singh mentioned? Is that why he kidnapped them? Is that why they're chasing us?"

"No, this was before he took over. I'm not entirely sure what he wants with any of you. It may have to do with what I learned recently. Come with me. I have something to show you."

Holden led them downstairs, where Ethan thumped on a thick metal door at the bottom of the steps. "It's for shielding. I've been down here before. It's seriously impressive."

Jack had a reasonable knowledge of electronics and computers, but Holden's basement was fascinating. He could only identify half the tools in the workshop: a compact super-computer in one corner, several high-resolution 3-D printing machines, a centrifuge, and a lot of testing equipment.

There were also portal crystals of various shapes and sizes scattered on shelves around the room: dime-sized discs mounted in conventional ring frames, colorful marbles held in c-clamps, cubes, prisms, octahedrons, and more. Jack didn't need to touch the gems to experience the formless pressure he normally felt from them. Maybe it was because of the shielding, or perhaps the number and variety enhanced the effect. Whatever the cause, compared to Niels' workshop, which had felt drafty, this room was alive with currents.

It also smelled strongly of tea. At least a dozen empty mugs were scattered on shelves, tables, and other flat surfaces. He recalled a story his parents had told about his grandfather's fondness for tea and talent for identifying which country it came from with a single sip.

Holden picked up a transparent book-sized box. "This is a crystal testing platform." He scrutinized the complex circuit board inside, as if there was something he didn't understand. "What you need to know is that none of the crystals I monitor have failed under normal circumstances. Not ever. Certainly, there have been failures caused by a fault in the field shaping circuit, but never a failure of the crystals that wasn't deliberate. This pair was not only destroyed, they were completely disintegrated—reduced to dust."

"What could do that?" Jack asked. "Aren't diamonds indestructible?"

"Not all portal crystals are made of diamond and even diamonds can be damaged. You could shatter one with only a hammer if you struck it right. However, there would be fragments left behind. Whatever did this affected the entire crystal. And not just this pair. Every crystal."

"What do you mean by *every* crystal?"

"Every one in this batch. They're cloned in large quantities, millions of identical crystals at a time. But the conditions vary constantly, so each batch will be slightly different, if only by a few atoms. It takes six months to grow a crystal, and it's such a difficult process that only half can be paired. The rest are discarded or recycled.

"I believe Pieter has built a device which causes every crystal in the same lot to oscillate together, to achieve a resonance. I also think he knows I've learned of this—he's almost certainly working from one of my own papers. I removed this from my Archive …" Holden picked up the box again. "To keep anyone else from discovering it. It seems he's found out anyway."

"But why would he want to destroy portals?"

"I'm not certain it was intentional. The purpose of my research was to combine multiple portals into a single wormhole–an academic goal, not a practical one. If the destruction was deliberate, then perhaps he intends to hold them for ransom. So many industries rely on these now that he could hold any corporation hostage."

"Wouldn't they just arrest him? He's the owner of one of the largest corporations on Cirrus. He can't exactly hide."

"I don't believe he plans to do it in a way where he can be identified. If this is all true, I'm the only one who could *prove* he's behind it. He may be doing this to force *me* to remain silent."

Ethan had been examining objects on the workbench while listening. He picked up a slender, glass-like rod. There were hundreds of them, in a variety of colors and sizes. "What are these?"

"They may be the next generation of portal crystals." Holden picked up a thicker blue rod. "A cylinder is the perfect shape. The data and power crystals in your phones were grown as discs, essentially cylinders less than a hundred molecules thick. But a longer cylinder has a larger volume and therefore a larger matrix. The amount of mass or energy it can pass without overloading is proportional to its volume."

Ethan spun the rod between his fingers. "So, who makes these?"

"Right now, only me. These are the only ones that exist."

"Oh." He put it down gently—even a conventional crystal array cost more than an average person earned in a month. The tiny water dispensers in phones were affordable only because they were composed of hundreds of smaller crystals.

Holden laughed. "It's all right, they're fairly durable. Let me show you."

He inserted the rod into a cutting machine and entered a number on its keypad. The apparatus whirred while shifting the rod into position, then emitted a sharp snap. A thin translucent disc dropped into a caddy on the cutter's opposite end.

Ethan leaned over to examine the paper-thin, dime-sized disc. "So, you can make them any size you want."

"That's right. That slice is thousands of times thicker than the crystals in your phone."

Holden opened a box and selected a gold coin, about the size of a quarter. He placed it into a second machine, transferred the newly cut disc to an adjacent slot, and pressed a button. After a few seconds of buzzing, the coin dropped into a tray. He passed it to Jack. "The crystal must be bonded to a rigid surface so it doesn't break."

Jack tilted the disc, causing light to refract from its surface. It wasn't a coin, of course, but a *coin portal*. The machine had embedded the crystal disc so that it looked like a gem inset in a gold coin.

"I've never seen a coin portal with a single crystal this big. And they're never round, either. They're usually an array of smaller hexagonal crystals." He offered it to Ethan.

Ethan flipped the coin. It had a printed circuit etched on the back. "Is this real gold?"

"It's only plating, for corrosion resistance," Holden said. "Otherwise, it's not much different from what you find in a power coupling."

"That's something else I don't understand," Jack said. "The power cell we found in the cave. That's connected to the source in your office on Cirrus, right?"

"As part of our subterfuge, my brother was required to submit research papers. To do that, he needed firsthand experience. He told me he cached the cell somewhere in the Spine as a spare, in case of a breakdown. After he disappeared, I could never bring myself to disconnect it. I suppose I've always hoped he's still out there."

Jack shifted uncomfortably in his chair. "I've been dreaming about that cave for years. In the dream, there's also a man. I never get to see his face, but I get the feeling that I know him. Maybe I was remembering an actual time when Uncle Carl took me there?"

Holden sat quietly for a minute, deep in thought. "When you were a child, my brother brought you here quite often. For a while, he even carried the portal frame in his truck. And he enjoyed spending time in the mountains. In some ways he was like you; he preferred being alone. But I don't think he would have taken you into the Spine. Perhaps he told you stories of the place and his description lodged in your memories."

Jack decided not to mention the strange feelings he'd experienced on the Vault and again at the island. He was sure there was more to it than just a memory; the sensation seemed to radiate from those places. And he didn't *prefer* being alone. Sometimes it was easier that way.

"Is it possible he knew we'd need the power cell there?" Ethan asked. "He used the portal too. Could he have been a Traveller?"

"That would have been an extraordinary accomplishment, knowing the exact place all those years ahead. If my brother ever had visions of the future, he never shared them with me. It's most likely a coincidence. After all, he had reasons to be in the Spine."

Having recently met Niels and learned about the lotteries, Jack wondered if Traveller's memories were better than what his grandfather knew. But instead of mentioning Niels, he asked, "What reasons?"

"I found documents on his computer after he disappeared. It seems he'd taken an interest in Cirrus' artificial gravity field, which is made of billions of strings of focusing cells deep in the crust. It was inevitable that some would snap during construction. The loose ends were eventually buried, but engineers speculated that there are places where the lines lay close to the surface, forming loops or spirals. I believe that's what Carl was searching for."

Jack recalled Anders had mentioned something about broken lines under the island. "Why?"

"All I know is someone was paying him to locate these places. The documents don't say why or who he was working for."

"Grandpa? Do you have a picture of your brother?"

"I have only a few." Holden began opening folders on his workstation. "It was a challenge ensuring no one—including the both of you—ever found a photo that properly identified him. We decided it was best to avoid having our pictures taken at all."

He found the file and swiveled the monitor. Like Holden in years past, one of the men in the photo was tall and thin. They definitely weren't twins, but they were similar enough to confuse someone who met them only occasionally.

Jack guessed from Carl's appearance that the photo was taken at least thirty years ago. He examined the rest of the image for clues to its age and was surprised to recognize the man standing beside his uncle. He was about to say something when Ethan exclaimed, "Jack, look. That's Niels."

"Niels?" Holden asked. "You met this man? Are you sure that's his name?"

"Well …" Jack thought about the story of how Niels left Earth after making a fortune. "I don't know if that's his *real* name, but it's definitely the same man from the island. Do you know him?"

"I did." Holden studied the photo and smiled at the memory. "It was a long time ago. I met him when he ran Armenau's research center."

Ethan looked as if he'd been betrayed by a friend. "Niels is working with Reynard?"

"No, that's unlikely. He was a partner with Pieter's father, long before Pieter took over. They never got along. But Niels had a partnership or controlling interest in a lot of different companies. Even I used to work for him. I didn't know he'd found his way to Cirrus."

"You worked for Niels?"

"He was an absolute genius. He had degrees in math, engineering, and physics, and a gift for recognizing which avenues of research were most likely to bear fruit. One of his companies funded the research for the method I developed for mass-producing portal crystals."

"He's a Traveller," Jack said. "He knew we were coming to the island."

Holden was dumbstruck.

Jack was certain that he knew what his grandfather was thinking; Niels had been pulling strings on Earth and Cirrus for a very long time. "Do you think he was the one who hired

Uncle Carl?"

"Niels was instrumental in the creation of Cirrus. His greatest talent had always been finding and organizing the people who could bring the necessary technology to life, myself included. Without him, it may have taken decades longer to complete the station. So, yes, he may have had a reason to look for those lines."

"He showed us a working tractor beam." Ethan described the device.

"Really? Well, that *is* impressive. Hmm. I can guess how it might work, but controlling the beam would be a challenge. Somehow it must sense the mass of objects it interacts with. Otherwise, it wouldn't be much different from a gravity cell, able to act only in a straight line on whatever is in its path."

Holden's expression was like that of a child talking about a new toy he wanted. Jack understood it completely; he felt much the same when it came to machines. Holden was still speculating when they heard muffled footsteps upstairs.

"It sounds like the detective has returned with your friend. We should go hear what they've discovered."

Chapter 35

Priya was smiling when she led Sarah into the living room—the interview had obviously gone well.

"We've made progress. But I need to make some calls now. It'll be hours before we decide what to do next. Sarah wants to see more of Earth. Why don't you three take a walk? Just don't leave the neighborhood."

Sarah sprang to the door. "Let's go."

Ethan headed for the hallway closet. "I'll get Dusty's leash and a tennis ball for her to chase."

"That's a leash?" Jack said. "It looks more like a game controller."

"This is just the remote. The motivator is in her collar … which you'd know if you had dogs on Cirrus. It's the opposite of an emotion detector. It stimulates the part of her brain that creates happiness. If she gets too far away, the signal fades. Basically, she *wants* to stay near."

When they caught up to Sarah, she was standing on the front lawn, staring at the world around her in awe. Like Jack, one of the first things she noticed was how different everything smelled.

She breathed deeply. "What *is* that?"

Ethan sniffed. "Um, diesel, I think."

"Not that, the flowers." She spotted the neighbor's garden along the sidewalk and ran to it. "There's so many types. I've only ever seen some of these in the conservatory." She gazed up the street, which was teeming with flower beds. "Let's go this direction. Priya says there's a park over there."

"Priya?" Jack asked. "Is that Detective Singh's name?"

"She's amazing. Did you know she has her third-level black belt?"

"We don't know anything about her," Ethan said. "We just met her. How do girls exchange so much personal information in so little time?"

Sarah laughed and told them about Priya as they walked—how she'd been born in London but immigrated to New York as a child, that she studied anthropology in university but ended up joining the New York Police Department, then became a detective and moved to Washington for an opportunity to join the UN's off-world police division.

"She's much nicer than she lets on. On Cirrus, she was only worried about our safety."

"You've only been gone half an hour." Jack was also surprised at how much Sarah had learned. "Wasn't she supposed to be asking you questions?"

"I told her everything she needs to know. She'll be sending us back to Cirrus this afternoon."

"*Send* us back? I was thinking she wouldn't *let* us *go* until they've sorted things out. I thought we might be here for days."

"Things are going to happen quickly now." She glanced around. "There are so many trees here. I can't see what's beyond. Let's get to higher ground so we can see farther."

One of the most striking differences Jack observed as they walked was the number of single-family houses—there were few of those on Cirrus. And there were cars; lots of cars. On the quiet cul-de-sac where Holden lived, parked cars lined the entire street. When they crossed a busy road, he was amazed to see four lanes of bumper-to-bumper traffic.

"I think I've seen more private vehicles in the last three blocks than exist on all of Cirrus."

Ethan, having always lived in cities, was accustomed to the traffic. He answered indifferently, "Everyone drives their own car here."

Jack didn't have the same appreciation for cars Ethan did. And despite the claim about everyone driving, there were a lot of buses. Also, few private vehicles had steering wheels— most people never actually *drove* their cars after their initial training.

A tall pickup truck, old and rusted, with over-sized tires, passed them. Sarah covered her ears when its youthful driver tromped on the accelerator. Its gas-powered engine thundered as it shot away.

"See that?" Ethan pointed at the speeding vehicle. "*That's* a truck."

Sarah looked at Jack quizzically. He smiled and shook his head, indicating it was better not to ask.

Even Dusty seemed unbothered by the noise and constant movement. At intersections, she knew to wait until Ethan started walking. A button on her leash could create a brief spike of happiness to reinforce positive behavior, but this was unnecessary as she was already well-trained.

They passed a golf course with a view of the metropolis over the open fairways. Seattle's distinctive skyline mirrored the contour of the Olympic mountains, which were barely visible through the haze. That's when Jack felt the full impact of where he was. He was really on Earth. He was walking on a different world. Sure, it was a much hotter world than he was used to, and kind of stinky, and the haze over the city was distinctly brown, but it was full of wonders that didn't exist on Cirrus. He'd even seen a thin plume of volcanic ash rising from Mount Rainier, something that could never happen on an artificial world.

He stopped abruptly. "I want to go to a restaurant."

"Now who's always hungry?" Ethan said. "We just ate breakfast."

"I don't mean now, but before we go home. I want to try something we don't have on Cirrus."

"I'm up for that. But right now, I need something to drink. There's a convenience store down the hill."

"We don't have phones anymore," Sarah said. "How will we pay?"

"It's okay, we still use debit cards on Earth. Some places even take cash."

When they entered the store, Jack and Sarah were as awestruck by the display of junk food as they were by their first view of Earth.

Jack gawked at the shelves. "I've never heard of half of these brands. We don't have this much selection back home."

The clerk behind the counter overheard him and gave him a strange look.

"Um, they're from Canada," Ethan said. The clerk nodded

as if this explained everything. Jack apologized for the disturbance to bolster Ethan's story. Sarah rolled her eyes at both of them. Ethan paid for their snacks and they continued their walk to the park.

"Detective Singh said not to leave the neighborhood," Jack said. "Do you know where we are?"

Ethan reached automatically for his phone, then his shoulders drooped when he remembered he'd left the useless device at the house. "Wait a minute." He squinted at the miniature display on the dog's controller, turned himself around and pointed. "The park's that way." Then he slumped again. "Right now, Dusty is better connected than we are. I've never been without my phone before."

"And I had just got mine back," Sarah said.

"What happened to your phone anyway?" Jack asked.

"Someone stole it. A guy with a gold watch. Terrance. I think he's a friend of Niels."

"How do you know about Niels?" Ethan asked. "We haven't had a chance to tell you yet."

She shrugged. "I just remember."

"That's so freaky," Jack said. "But why would Terrance do that?"

"Well," Ethan said, "he *is* a hacker."

"He told you that?"

"No. But we were talking at the party and there're things he knows that only a hacker would."

"But why would one of Niels' friends steal Sarah's phone?"

"He said it was to keep me safe," Sarah said.

"From what?" Ethan asked.

Sarah stopped walking. "Jack, we have to tell him."

Jack sighed. "Yeah, I guess it doesn't matter anymore."

He told Ethan what he'd found outside Fairview, and Sarah filled in the new details about CorpSec and the warehouse. Then Jack and Ethan relayed the full story of their escape from Fairview.

"So," Ethan said as they reached the park, "Pieter Reynard is chasing you and me because of what Grandpa found, and someone else is chasing you and Sarah because of what you found?"

Jack nodded.

"Then it really is your fault, after all."

Jack flung Dusty's tennis ball at Ethan's head, but he ducked it easily, laughing. Dusty ran after the ball.

"Why is Detective Singh sending us to Cirrus?" Jack wondered aloud. "Won't we just have to keep running?"

"Well, I can't stay here," Sarah said. "If I don't come home on time, my mother will call me, see that my phone's not working, and report me missing. If that happens, there's an automatic alert filed with the police. Priya doesn't want to get officially involved until they've found your parents."

"And they can also use it as an excuse to arrest us," Ethan said. "You were seen with us. They might say we kidnapped you."

"So," Jack said, "we have to go to Cirrus to be seen by Little Brother? Then what do you and I do once Sarah leaves? Do we come back here?"

"There's not much we can do on Cirrus anyway." Ethan seemed to accept they'd have to do whatever the detective told them to. "Did she say when they're going to the reservoir?"

"She doesn't have enough information yet. Oh, she did say that Reynard might be a Traveller too."

Jack wasn't surprised at all. It was as if, as soon as Sarah said it, he knew it must be true. In the past two days, Travellers had been elevated in his mind from myth to fact. "Detective Singh said he uses his own portals frequently. I wonder if his future memories are as accurate as Niels'. How will the police catch him if he knows what they're going to do?"

"But Travellers don't know everything," Sarah realized. "It's like your grandfather said—I wouldn't know for sure if I had just imagined Niels' name if you hadn't confirmed it. And he wouldn't know me if I hadn't reacted to the portals."

"What do you mean?"

"I've felt déjà vu before, when I was standing next to a lot of portals at the aviary. Terrance didn't know who he was looking for. If I hadn't nearly fallen over, he wouldn't have found me."

"But don't you have to pass *through* a portal to feel déjà vu?" Ethan asked.

"It wasn't *exactly* the same as when we came here; it passed more quickly. But there were *thousands* of portals on that board. Maybe the same thing happens if you're too close."

"That sort of makes sense," Jack said. "I didn't experience déjà vu either, but I've always felt something around portals. I assumed it was like the worm-sickness others feel. But maybe it's part of the Traveller Effect. Do you feel anything like that?"

Sarah shook her head.

"What do you feel?" Ethan asked.

"Hand me Dusty's leash." Jack rubbed his thumb over the controller. He went back and forth over a particular spot on the case until he was sure he'd located the portal crystal underneath. "It's like forcing two magnets together." He returned the leash. "Kind of like what we felt using Niels' tractor beam."

"I didn't feel anything then, either."

"No? I thought it was obvious. We could ask Grandpa if distance makes a difference, but then we'd have to tell Detective Singh about Sarah breaking into the reservoir. Would that help or just get her into trouble?"

Sarah winced. "There's nothing we can do until this afternoon anyway. Let's not think about it for a while. Look, there's a soccer ball someone left behind."

Despite the heat, Jack's mood improved as they played. It felt good to be with friends and not worry about who might be chasing them.

"C'mon, Jack," Ethan said when it was his turn in goal. "You're not even trying."

Jack wasn't holding back, but Ethan was unbeatable, blocking every attempt with ease. "Do you play on a team?"

"No, but you're telegraphing. I can tell exactly where you're going to kick it."

Jack made sure not to look at the side of the net he was

aiming for, but Ethan moved as if he'd shouted directions.

After failing a dozen more attempts, he said, "I've had enough. It's too hot." He kicked the ball over to some younger kids, then returned to the shaded table.

At another table a short distance away, a woman received a phone call and reacted with shock. Then a group of girls lying on the grass nearby sat up and began texting with worried expressions. Soon, there were more phones ringing or beeping around the park.

Ethan noticed the spreading alarm. "Something's happening. What a time to be without a phone."

The woman nearest them called to her children with a note of panic in her voice. "It's time to go."

"Excuse me," Sarah said. "What's wrong?"

The woman began hustling her children from the park. "There's been an attack."

Jack was on his feet instantly and running down the hill. Ethan and Sarah raced right behind him.

Chapter 36

"I need you all to return to Cirrus," Priya said.

"Sounds like a good idea to me," Jack said. "Have you seen what's happening?"

"I've been a little busy."

Jack, Sarah, and Ethan had been watching news on the large monitor in Holden's living room. Reports of an attack on the United States Navy were flooding the internet. The latest feed was a cellphone video of a frigate running aground on the coast of Japan.

"No one seems to know what happened," Jack said. "Some reports say it was a chemical attack by a terrorist group or doomsday cult, or even a hoax." He switched the monitor to television-mode for a local update on the large crowds gathering in downtown Seattle. "And they're planning end-of-the-world parties and protests everywhere. People on Earth are nuts."

"Some are," Priya agreed, "but that has nothing to do with why I want you back in Caerton. Pieter's men might start watching the house. If they see you or Ethan here, they'll learn about your grandfather's portal. We want them to think you're in the Magnolia, in a different apartment."

"What if Pieter's goons are still there?" Ethan asked.

"They're at the reservoir right now." She flipped her tablet over to show a video of Danny Kou walking with another man through the glass doors of an office building. "My partner, Davis, saw them."

The second person in the image seemed familiar to Jack. He was much taller than Danny, well-dressed, fit, and clean-shaven. "That's Pieter Reynard, isn't it?"

"Yes," said Priya and Sarah at the same time.

Embarrassed, Sarah sat back in her chair and allowed Priya to continue. Jack had also been certain the man was Reynard, but had guessed from the video's context. He wondered if Sarah had worked it out that way or experienced another memory.

"You three will leave the Magnolia together and stay on the surface streets where you'll be safe. Go with Sarah as far as the theater on Third Avenue. She'll go home by herself and you two will return here. Pieter's men may be watching the building, but *we* will be watching them. If it's not safe, Davis will stop you at the elevators and take you to our office. He won't be wearing a uniform, but he'll identify himself. If he lets you pass, take the elevator to the roof, then the stairs down to the apartment."

"But what about Sarah?" Ethan asked. "They can't search the whole building for us. Wouldn't it be easier for them to kidnap her too and make her tell them where we are?"

"I would never tell." Sarah sounded offended. "I—"

"It's okay," Priya interrupted. "I already thought of that. I used Little Brother to track you all leaving her house. Twice. If anyone else tries to track her, it'll block them, create an alert, and notify her mother. I also asked Davis to use our facial recognition software to see if the AI could identify her."

"And?" Sarah asked.

"You've been very smart. He couldn't get a match. Most people your age aren't that careful."

"That wasn't me. My phone was …. it crashed. All my photos disappeared."

Priya was silent for a moment. "We'll look into that when we have time. But even if they manage to identify you, your mother is a CorpSec officer. They can't touch you without risking her including the whole department and thereby involving us."

With the plan agreed upon, Holden taught them how to use the portal. He showed them a series of five squares within the wooden frame's geometric border. At first glance, the shapes appeared to be inlays of different types of wood.

"These squares …" He touched one, causing them to shift from varied browns to a uniform tan. "Tell you how much charge is stored. There must be one bar for every person who will pass through. There are marks in the same spot on the opposite frame, but they may not match—it takes less energy to transport mass from Cirrus to here."

"Why is that?" Ethan asked. "Why should there be a difference?"

"You cannot cheat the universe. Cirrus has an *apparent* normal gravity at the surface, but it's much less massive and that's what counts. Think of the solar system as a mountain. The portal allows you to make a short climb out of Cirrus' gravity, then a long slide down to Earth. Going the other direction requires a lot more energy."

Priya confirmed through the video link that the apartment was empty before she opened the wormhole. Sarah went first and expressed her disappointment at not experiencing déjà vu again.

Holden stopped Jack before he passed through the frame. "Take these and put them in my office, please." He handed over a large bundle of rods, along with the coin portal he'd made earlier.

"Aren't these your new portal crystals? Won't they be ruined like the ones in our phones?"

"No, they'll eventually be broken into segments and entangled by another process."

Ethan was the last to go through the wormhole.

"Remember," Priya said, "if you see anyone following you, don't panic. They won't touch you while you're in a public place. Just get back to the Magnolia. And stay away from the reservoir. I'm serious."

"Don't worry." Ethan grinned. "I know better than to argue with a third-level black belt." Seeing her confused look, he added, "It's okay, Sarah told me." He pressed the hidden switch and closed the portal.

- - - - -

"I didn't tell her that," Priya said. "We have bigger problems."

"What do you mean?"

"I have some experience with Travellers. As part of my training, I debriefed officers who were trying out for the intelligence branches. I met a few who had an actual first-time connection, like Sarah did, but none experienced valid memories beyond their first trip."

"And you think Sarah is remembering things from future passages? That she's a *real* Traveller?"

"It was a difficult interview—she's a bright girl. As I asked questions, she jumped ahead a lot, making connections. But it was always with things she could have learned from Jack or Ethan. I also asked her about you, to work out what she might have known beforehand. She told me there's a room at the reservoir similar to your lab. In hindsight, the things she remembered—which I suspect might be true—have a common thread: me. She thought I told her about the reservoir, and that I described your lab. And she seems to have told Ethan about my black belt. The reservoir and the black belt are things I could still tell her about. But ..."

Holden continued her train of thought. "You've never been to my lab."

"Exactly."

"Well then. We should go downtown so you can see it for yourself."

- - - - -

"We're not going to do what Priya said, are we?" Sarah asked as Ethan jumped off the ladder.

"No. I've been thinking. How can your memory of the reservoir be true unless you actually see it? Let's ride past and see for ourselves."

"But," Jack said, "the detective said her partner saw them there. So it doesn't prove anything if Sarah sees them."

"But, if she *doesn't* see them, it proves the memory was wrong and the police are wasting time watching the wrong building."

"I'm not sure anymore what seeing or not seeing them proves. One way or the other, it's a paradox. And Priya told us specifically not to go there."

"I know where the reservoir is," Sarah said. "We'll still be in a public area with Little Brother. We'll ride past without stopping. I need to know if what I'm remembering is true or just my imagination. Please." She reached out and grabbed Jack's hand. "It's important to me."

Jack understood her desire to learn more about her

newfound ability. He also knew her well enough to worry that if they didn't go with her, she might go on her own, later. "Okay. It'll be safer if we go as a group. And faster if we stay underground."

"Are you sure?" Ethan asked. "You're the one who said we should listen to Priya. She said to stay on the surface."

"If we're ignoring her warning about going there, we may as well ignore her other instructions. Besides, we don't have a lot of time. She'll be expecting us back soon."

They rode the empty elevator to the bike garage. Sarah knew her hometown well and led them across several miles of freeway and bike paths before taking a ramp to the surface. A tree-lined boulevard separated the squat, featureless, industrial buildings from a row of taller apartment blocks.

"That's it on the right." Sarah pointed over a short fence, where rows of enormous tanks with domed roofs extended south for a mile. She was still in the lead as they approached the reservoir's business office. Three men were standing by a CorpSec van. "That's them. My memory was real. *I predicted the future.*"

Jack understood she was just happy to be proven correct, but he was only thinking that his parents were in there somewhere. He rode at the rear of the group and stole a quick glance as they passed by. They were far enough away that no one could have overheard Sarah, but close enough to recognize a face. He recognized one—Danny Kou was looking straight at him.

"Time to go." Ethan had also seen Danny. He engaged his bike's motor. "Which way?"

"Follow me." Sarah turned a sharp left, bounced through the landscaped street divider, and sped in the opposite direction. Jack's bike groaned as he slammed it up and over the berm. Ethan was right behind him.

Danny Kou didn't stand a chance of following Sarah. Jack and Ethan could barely keep up as she zig-zagged through parks and alleys, snaking her way back to the freeway.

Jack pulled up beside her when she stopped at a ramp. "I'm pretty sure we lost them."

Sarah leaned over and hugged him. "Take care, Jack. Don't worry about me. They'll be following you, but all you do is take the cross street and then go left at the second intersection. The theater and the Magnolia are on the same road. Call me as soon as you're back on Earth. Goodbye, Ethan." She waved as she rode away.

"She said they're going to follow us," Jack said. "You think she *remembers* that?"

"No, she'd have to use a portal again for that to be true. But yeah, I'm sure they'll be following."

Jack rode for the Magnolia at top speed. Without phones, he wouldn't know if Sarah had arrived home safely until he got back to Earth.

The theater where they were supposed to leave her was an easy building to recognize. Broad steps led up to three sets of oversized doors behind Roman-style columns. The steps resembled cut stone and the columns looked like marble, but—as with everything else in the city—they were printed from a blend of concrete, plastic, and steel. A black van was parked at the foot of the stairs.

"I think we made the right choice," Jack whispered when they stopped for a red light. "CorpSec is here. They could have followed Sarah."

Ethan tilted his head, gesturing for Jack to look at the man standing on the corner across the intersection. "There's another officer on this side."

"They must have been expecting us. How?"

"Priya said that Reynard guy might be a Traveller."

"So then why follow on the street? Why not wait for us at the apartment?"

"Priya's plan must be going to work. He can't wait there because he won't find out that's where we are."

Jack sighed. "I really hate paradoxes." He was also becoming anxious about the crowds as they rode into the downtown core.

They continued along the crowded street, shadowed by CorpSec officers for the final two blocks. At the Magnolia, he dismounted underneath an awning and fed his bike into a slot in the wall, where a conveyor would transport it to the garage.

Ethan watched the men approach as he waited for his turn. "They've stopped." The officer from the far side of the street had joined his partner and was talking on his phone.

Jack hurried through the lobby doors. No one stopped them at the elevator, but that's when his phobia kicked in. *Three, four*, he counted as the elevator filled up. He backed away.

Ethan looked over his shoulder. The CorpSec officers were entering the lobby. "Sorry, buddy. We don't have time for this." He shoved Jack into the elevator and jabbed the button to close the door.

Jack stumbled to the rear of the car, leaned his head against the outer glass wall, and closed his eyes. As they went up, he didn't need to look at the other passengers to know what they were thinking: *Rough-housing in public. How rude. I should call CorpSec.* In his mind, those imagined thoughts were becoming as real as voices. It was hard not to recall the darkened cave he faced in countless dreams. He began to sweat.

"You okay?" Ethan asked after the door closed on the fifth floor, leaving them alone in the elevator.

The voices in Jack's mind faded as the elevator resumed its ascent. "Better. Thanks."

The café on the rooftop terrace was full. Jack waited at the elevator while Ethan pretended to search for someone at the tables.

"There's a camera covering the elevator," Ethan said when he returned. "Do you think it's public?"

"Little Brother is everywhere." Jack motioned for him to follow to the stairs "Let's go."

The zone between the restaurant and the commercial floors was private, with no cameras, but that wouldn't make a difference if a CorpSec officer was coming up the stairs. They ran down to the fifty-second story as fast as they could. Jack opened the fire door to check that the atrium was clear, then signaled for Ethan to follow.

They sprinted past the garden, through the corridor, to their grandfather's door. It opened at Jack's touch. They dove inside and slammed the door shut.

"Safe." Ethan headed for the kitchen. "I wonder if there's anything to eat."

"How can you be hungry again?"

"Welcome home, Jack," Pieter said as they stepped from the hall. "Please, take a seat."

Chapter 37

Jack froze; Pieter Reynard was standing in his grandfather's living room. Behind him waited Danny Kou and a uniformed CorpSec officer. Another man, dressed in a gray suit, lay face down on the rug. Dead or unconscious, Jack couldn't tell. He guessed this was Priya's partner, Davis, who should have been downstairs.

Pieter smiled and motioned to the couch, projecting the false persona he wore for countless business meetings. His expression was carefully sculpted to make the other party feel at ease, as if they negotiated as an equal partner. Danny's face let Jack know he and Ethan had no choice but to cooperate. They sat and waited quietly.

"An interesting man, your grandfather." Pieter wandered the room, examining the furnishings. "He looks a lot like his half-brother, doesn't he? And now he has a portal that allows him to travel between Earth and Cirrus without leaving a trace; *remarkable*." Jack tried to hide his surprise, but Pieter noticed anyway. "That's right. We know it's hidden somewhere in this building. Where is he?"

Ethan lowered his head.

"I only want to talk to him." Pieter's voice was compelling, almost hypnotic. "Tell me where he is."

Though there were only five people in the room—six, including Davis—Jack's phobia kicked in. His throat tightened and he felt lightheaded.

Pieter kneeled in front of Jack. "You want your family to be safe, don't you?"

Of course.

"All I want is to learn how he's shielded that portal. Then you can rejoin your family. You want that too, don't you?"

Yes.

"No harm will come to him. I promise. Where is he?"

"He's—" Jack began, but Ethan flicked his finger against his leg and glared at him with his jaw clenched.

Jack realized he'd been about to answer. *What am I doing?*

Chagrined, he followed Ethan's example, setting his jaw and resolving to say nothing. His anxiety faded.

"No?" Pieter stood and wandered past the bookcases, idly dragging his finger across the books' spines. "Well, he can't be far. And if he uses his portal again, we'll track it by the electricity it uses."

Did Grandpa think of that? Holden couldn't have traveled all these years without upsetting the neighbors if it had the same disorienting effects as a dynamic portal. But the power to run it had to come from somewhere. Or was it like smaller portal crystals? *Can he charge it from just one side?*

"He had us fooled for some time, you know." Pieter stopped in front of the painting and stared intently at the image as he spoke. "In fact, we only worked it out when we couldn't find you in the apartment this morning." He leaned closer to the frame, focusing on the pattern of squares near the charge indicators. He reached out to touch them.

The officer behind Pieter cleared his throat. "Sir."

Pieter glared at the man. "What?"

The officer had been listening to another conversation on an earpiece. He offered his phone to Pieter, who watched the screen for a few moments before passing it back.

"Your grandfather didn't make your rendezvous upstairs. Perhaps our friend here …" He poked his toe at the man on the floor. "Was supposed to make a call. Do we know who he is yet?" He directed this last question to Danny.

Danny also wore a hidden earpiece. He shook his head. "He's got a UN ID. We don't know what department he's with or if he's working with anyone else. I'll have those answers in a few minutes."

"It doesn't matter." Pieter's manner changed from charming businessman to something more feral. "We've got what we came for. Take them away. And find out who the girl is."

Jack lowered his head so Pieter wouldn't see his face. *Sarah was right.* Terrance had hacked her phone to prevent Pieter from finding out who she was. That meant Niels wanted to keep her safe. *What does Niels know?*

The CorpSec officer ordered the boys to stand and walk out the door. A second officer, waiting outside, hustled them into the elevator. He advised them not to say or try anything in the lobby. Then the men pushed the cousins into a CorpSec van parked on the street, leaving them alone in the back. A notice painted on the vehicle's interior wall warned that everything they said was being recorded.

Tiny windows in the rear doors provided the only view of the street, but Jack didn't know Caerton well enough to recognize where they were going. After a few minutes, they entered a parking lot where the gate closed behind them automatically.

"This must be CorpSec's headquarters."

Just when they expected it to stop, the van passed through another gate and turned onto the street.

Ethan leaned to the window closest to him. "What was that all about?"

"Little Brother?" Jack guessed. "Views inside the parking lot are almost certainly blocked. Anyone watching would see us go in and not think to check the other side."

After a few minutes of winding through Caerton's streets, they passed through another gate. The van descended a ramp into a vast underground complex, driving past rows of broad metal cylinders rising from the floor to the thirty-foot ceiling.

"We're at the reservoir," Jack said. The size and number of cylinders corresponded with the domes he'd seen from the street. "I didn't realize the tanks were so big. Most of it's underground."

The van stopped at the far end of the complex, where the guards ordered them out of the vehicle. Pieter and Danny arrived in another car.

Pieter got out and addressed a guard. "Go back to the Magnolia and search the rest of the building. Dr. Marke will eventually show up wherever that portal is." To a second man, he said, "Bring Marke's assistant to his lab and wait for us outside. We'll be there shortly."

Danny motioned Jack and his cousin toward the tank in the corner farthest from the center aisle. Set into the metal wall at ground level was a hatch that resembled a ship's watertight bulkhead door. Danny spun the large wheel mounted on the door and pushed it open. Everyone had to stoop and step over the high rim to enter the tank.

In the center of the space, a cage-style elevator and an adjoining ladder led up to a second level. Ten windowless sliding doors were evenly spaced around the circular room. Each had a keypad fitted next to it.

Prison cells? Jack guessed from Ethan's glum expression that his cousin was thinking the same thing.

"Where do you want them?" Danny asked.

"I don't see why they can't stay together. I'm sure they'll be comfortable here until tomorrow."

At least we'll be together. For now.

Pieter approached one of the closed doors. But instead of waving a card or entering a code, he placed his hand near the door itself. The lock clicked and it slid open, even though Pieter hadn't moved anything or even touched the keypad.

Does his ring work like an access card? Jack wondered as Pieter waved him and Ethan toward the open door. He resigned himself to being locked up.

"*Jack. Ethan,*" overlapping voices shouted as they entered.

"Don't you love family reunions," Pieter said in his fake charming voice. "Now there's just one person missing. And he'll be joining you soon."

He slid the door shut with a solid thump.

Chapter 38

With protesters moving into the city center, the shortest route to Holden's lab at Naef Dynamics became an hour-long drive. Self-driving mode was mandatory in this part of Seattle, but there were so many cars that even the traffic control AI couldn't keep it moving smoothly. Priya could have used her police authority to switch Holden's vehicle into manual mode, except this wasn't an emergency. And it wouldn't have made much difference—most of the protesters were on foot.

She turned the air conditioning to its coldest setting as they crawled across the bridge. "Are you sure you've told me everything?"

"I assure you, detective; I've told you everything I know. Much more than I should have."

"And I appreciate your trust. I won't mention your portal in my report."

"Thank you. If anyone knew of its existence, or even that such a thing was possible, it would only take a few years to reproduce my work."

Priya wasn't sure what she could have reported, anyway; the technology soared way over her head. She only understood that the device was as large as a dynamic portal, as difficult to trace as the smaller static ones, and that it could pass useful quantities of radioactive material without collapsing the wormhole. If Holden hadn't convinced her he'd spent decades guiding other researchers away from rediscovering his techniques, she'd have informed her superiors at once.

"And you're positive that's not where their research is going?"

"The principles of portal merging were in a paper I actually published. Simon could have built a working apparatus from only that, although it still would have taken many years. The theories behind the ultra-stable portal are completely different. There are precursors that must be developed first, and there's been no work in that area for decades. The latest production methods are so efficient that returning to the essential process is no longer an option."

"Simon seemed very focused on efficiency."

"It takes at least six months to grow a crystal. If he can reduce waste by half, that's potentially billions of dollars saved for Armenau. But that's what's confusing about the report you photographed. If those numbers are correct, they're using fifty percent *more* raw materials than anyone else."

"Does that have anything to do with merging?"

"Not at all. Merging is something he could do with any crystal. The most curious thing about these numbers is that they're *exactly* fifty percent higher than they should be."

"What does that mean?"

"I have no idea. But from what you've told me, Simon is doing something new that involves merging. The document suggests Armenau is currently growing at least ten million crystals."

"And the destruction of the portals?"

"It may have been an unintended consequence. Perhaps they have a commercial use for merged wormholes. If not, then they've come up with a way to cripple modern industry."

"There's nothing to suggest Reynard has a motive for that. He might not even be aware of Danny's past. Also, we don't know who sent the arson tip. It may have been Simon himself. Just because he designed Pieter's equipment, that doesn't mean he agrees with how it's being used. I got the feeling he wanted to tell me something the other night but was too scared."

"In science, it can be easy to lose sight of ethics. Sometimes we do things only to see what's possible. My own early research is a perfect example of that. I'm as much to blame for this situation as Simon."

Priya shook her head. "No. This is all on Pieter. And even if Simon didn't send the letter, it's most likely the tipster is working with Reynard."

"Most likely, yes. But not the only possibility."

"You're not suggesting there's another Traveller involved, are you?"

"Perhaps. But maybe they're not *involved*. Maybe they're what you call a Good Samaritan."

"They might also be what we call a pain-in-the …" She broke off before completing her thought, but Holden was smiling and not offended.

Eventually they cleared the bottleneck and made it to the city's industrial section. Holden's building was modern yet plain-looking—mostly bare concrete and glass, no different from its neighbors.

"Good afternoon, Doctor Marke," the receptionist said as he entered the lobby. "I didn't know you would be in today. Everyone's already left—the attack in the Sea of Japan, you know. They were all upset and just wanted to get home. I was about to leave too. Is there anything you need?"

"No, no. That's quite all right. Go home to your family. We'll be fine."

"Thank you. Oh, by the way, your intern didn't show up today. Nobody knows where he is."

Holden wasn't surprised. What with the parties and protests already starting, and himself having been away for the entire week, there hadn't been much work for the younger man anyway. Many of the regular staff, including his two technicians, were away on summer vacation. Most people didn't believe in the Newton prophecy, but weren't keen to hang around if the revelers got out of hand.

Priya followed him up the stairs. His lab occupied the entire third floor, which—from the outside of the building—appeared to have mirrored windows, but the walls, ceiling, and floor were actually several feet thick with solid shielding. The lights were already on when he opened the door.

"Is something wrong?" she asked when she noticed his expression.

"I'm not sure." Lights were also shining in the Archive, on the far side of the workshop. Steel doors flanked the room's sides: six on the left, and five on the right. All were closed except for the first one on the left. "What *have* they been up to?"

Priya peered through the open door. "What are these

rooms for?" A table with a two-inch diameter portal frame occupied the center of the room. A variety of monitors, cables, pipes, and other apparatus hung from the walls.

"Isolation booths. We use them for testing portal crystals. They're shielded so they don't interfere with the other portals or test equipment."

Holden seemed satisfied the room was in order and pulled the door closed. The keypad flashed to indicate the lock had engaged. He drew his identity card from his pocket and moved to the next booth.

"Who has access to your lab?" Priya asked.

"Any of the technical staff. We use chipped cards to record who has been in what room. I'm the only one who knows the codes."

He traversed the workshop's perimeter, pushing open each booth's door and glancing inside before moving on to the next. Each room was slightly different. The second one past the Archive contained a round portal that spanned three feet. The stainless-steel ring—bolted to the floor near the back of the room—had a ramp positioned next to it so a wheeled cart could pass through without having to be lifted over the edge.

The frame's ring was nearly four inches thick, reminding Priya of the one in her department's headquarters in Olympia. "Is that human-rated?"

"No, it's only cargo grade." Holden sniffed the air. "And it's been used recently."

"How can you tell?"

"Ozone. It builds up with extended use. These rooms are airtight, to prevent air from flowing through the wormhole when the pressure is different on the other side." He sniffed again. "I would say this one's been used in the last few hours."

He moved to the next door, which had a keypad like the others. A sticky note on the panel read 'Broken. Maintenance has been called.' He waved his card over the keypad. There was no response. He started to walk away, paused, then entered the code manually. The door unlocked.

Priya followed him inside. "This room is bigger. Why?"

"We also do work for the Department of Defense." He

gestured to racks of equipment around the room. "These are communication modules, essentially miniature switchboards. They'll send over their own technicians to work with us. Otherwise, this room is strictly off-limits."

"What are those containers for?"

"I've never seen them before."

Dozens of unmarked cylinders filled a portable rack leaning against the back wall. Heavy-duty, metal-braided hoses ran from each container's valve into a manifold mounted on a complicated-looking apparatus on the workbench.

Holden inspected the equipment carefully. He lifted a bundle of unconnected cables. "Something has been removed."

One of the comm modules lay disassembled on the table. He flipped over the upside-down cover. The label read: *Property of the United States Navy.*

Even though she knew the answer, Priya asked, "Could this be related to the attacks?"

"It's possible. If they have truly managed to merge multiple crystals into a single wormhole, then it may be that they can not only destroy them, but pass a substance through all of them at once."

"What type of substance are you talking about?" She edged toward the cylinders.

"It could only be a liquid or a gas. Anything solid would be torn apart, divided among all the portals. Even a liquid would be reduced to vapor." He pointed to a part of the apparatus. "This component is a compressor, but the pressure in those cylinders is already very high. There must be a great deal of resistance in their method."

"So, it has to be something that can be used in small amounts." She stepped closer, searching for a label. "Airborne. Fast-acting. Like a poisonous gas."

"An extremely unpleasant nerve gas," a voice behind them said. "Now move away from the device."

Chapter 39

Danny Kou stood in the doorway, pointing a pistol. "Step back."

Priya went for her weapon instinctively, but Danny waved his gun and she hesitated. Holden moved away as instructed.

"You too, Detective," Danny said. "If you damage that equipment and release the gas, you will suffer a horrible death." He stepped aside to allow them to exit.

"Doctor Marke, I'm sorry." The missing intern stood behind Danny; his arm held firmly by a man dressed in black combat gear. "You weren't supposed to be here this week. I didn't know what to do. They were going to hurt my family."

"It's all right, Garett, I understand. It's not your fault."

As Priya stepped through the door, another man in black—one of those from Holden's apartment—pinned her arm behind her back. A third guard removed her weapon from its holster under her jacket.

"You." Danny pointed at Garett. "Open that door." He gestured to a smaller booth.

Garett looked to Holden, pleadingly.

"Do whatever they ask," he said calmly.

Garett swiped his pass card over the panel and pushed the door open before scurrying aside.

"Lock her up," Danny said.

The guard seized Priya's phone, tossed it onto a workbench, then shoved her into the booth and sealed the door.

Danny waved toward the desk with his gun. "Sit down, Marke." He then closed the restricted room and gestured for Garett to open the cargo portal booth. He scanned the room. Satisfied with whatever he saw, he spoke into a communicator on his wrist. "All clear."

One of the guards opened the lab's main door and Pieter Reynard swaggered into the room. Another armed man, Pieter's driver, had followed him but stayed outside, taking a sentry position at the door.

"Doctor Marke," Pieter greeted him warmly. "I'm so glad you could join us for the finale." He waved at the isolation booth where Priya watched through the small window. "Good evening, detective. Comfortable?"

"You're insane," Holden said. "What can you gain from this?"

"What can I gain? As it happens, at least two hundred billion dollars." He turned to Danny. "Get started."

Danny entered the booth and snapped open a panel on the cargo frame. He swapped the address cartridge with an identical one from his pocket, then turned on the power and nodded to Pieter.

Pieter spoke into his phone. "Move the equipment."

The portal flickered. A new room appeared on the other side. A ramp had already been placed on the floor to line up with the one on this side. Someone wearing a lab coat approached, pushing a cart. At only three feet tall, the opening was too short to reveal who it was. The worker began rolling the cart through at a slow, even pace.

Pieter watched the progress with a satisfied grin. "We owe a lot of our success to you, Holden. May I call you Holden, or do you prefer Carl? You recognize the equipment, of course? It's based on your own theories."

"I know what it can do. And I know what it did."

"Ah, yes. Well, I had to run a field trial, you know. I'd originally planned on merging just those portals used on Cirrus, plus a small but important selection from Earth. But then I discovered your rather more impressive collection, and all so very well organized too." He gestured grandly at the Archive window as two of his guards wrestled a table through the door. "Internet, phones, power, fuel—everything our modern world requires, all in one convenient location."

"And you intend to destroy it all."

"Not all of it. And only for a while. I'll rebuild it, of course, better than before. With a few changes." He dismissed this thought with a wave of his hand. "That's not important just yet. We need to get to Cirrus before the main event." To Danny, Pieter said, "Take him downstairs."

"We have the boy, already. He can't stop you now. What do you want the old man for?"

Pieter's surprise changed to anger. "Are you questioning me? He may be useful yet. That's all you need to know. Now take him to my office."

Danny's expression remained unreadable as he used his pistol to gesture Holden toward the emergency exit at the rear of the lab.

Pieter spoke to Garett again. "I want this done in two hours." Then to the guards. "Arm the explosives and make sure you're at the office before midnight."

"What about him?" one asked, referring to Garett.

"Shoot him." Pieter's expression was serious, but then he laughed as Garett paled. "No, put him in the booth with her when you're done. Maybe someone will let them out in a few days." He sauntered out the door, adding, "Or maybe not."

- - - - -

The parking lot at the front of the building was probably empty, but Holden's captors shepherded him downstairs through the back stairwell. In the alley, there was no chance of a witness to see him forced into the backseat of a waiting limousine.

Danny also got into the back of the car, keeping his pistol trained on Holden while another guard took the driver's seat. Pieter entered a second limo with his usual driver and both vehicles headed downtown.

The group drove through the recently expanded International District, past a huge crowd gathering in the park where the metro base used to be. Many more people were moving that direction. Whether they believed in the prophecy or not, there was going to be an enormous party there tonight.

Downtown Seattle was much quieter. As it was mostly business-oriented, and already early evening, most workers had gone home. The limousines pulled into the Armenau building's empty underground parking lot. No one saw Holden enter the elevator with Pieter and Danny.

"You said you intend to make changes," Holden said. "What changes?"

"Please, Doctor Marke. We owe you a debt of gratitude. But your mass-production design has a serious flaw. The world will rebuild, and when it does, it will use crystal pairs that are completely unique."

"And your *field trial*?"

"What of it? It was a necessary step."

Danny stood behind Pieter where only Holden could see him. He deliberately opened his jacket to expose the butt of his pistol in its holster. There was no further conversation.

Pieter wasted no time when they arrived on the executive floor. He dropped his phone on the desk and waved his hand past the blank spot on his office wall.

"Caerton," he said as he entered the chamber. The portal was still powering up when he noticed Danny had left the sliding panel open. "The door," he said with unmasked irritation.

Danny turned around, as if to press the switch, then reached into his jacket and spun again, aiming his pistol at Pieter. Pieter went for his own weapon but hesitated as Danny stepped forward.

"You know you're not fast enough." He raised a phone in his other hand, to show it was Pieter's, then threw it through the now-open wormhole. He gestured to the Earth-side door with his pistol. "Get out."

Pieter kept his hands in sight as he traded places with Danny. "You won't succeed. Whatever you're planning, I'll always be one step ahead of you."

"Not this time."

Pieter didn't need his talent to know what was going to happen as soon as he crossed the threshold, but Danny didn't know Pieter could operate the Cirrus-side door remotely. Even the gesture he normally made was unnecessary—a pretense to mislead an observer. He was already in range of the hidden switch. He activated it with a thought as he stepped backward.

The noise of the door sliding open distracted Danny. A fraction of a second was all Pieter needed. He dove into his Seattle office just before Danny fired, and slammed the door shut.

Holden had not moved during the conflict—he was no match for either of them.

With Pieter gone, Danny pushed Holden into Armenau's Caerton office. After making the passage himself, he shut down the portal and removed its address carousel. Without the cartridges stored in that container, the frame couldn't create a wormhole.

The carousel was too large to fit into a pocket, so Danny ordered Holden to carry it as they rode Pieter's private elevator to the car park. There, he forced Holden into another vehicle and drove toward the reservoir. Instead of following the same route Jack and the others had taken to the lower level, Danny drove to UV Mobile and steered Holden into the maintenance shop at the back of the building. A stairwell there led to an underground corridor that opened in the wall next to the converted water tank.

"I'll take that." He snatched the carousel Holden still carried and then shoved him forwards. "You can join the others."

As Holden stumbled to the cell where his family was being held, he passed an open door. A portal frame—a twin to the one in his lab—occupied the center of the room. Several technicians wearing lab coats were loading equipment onto a cart. On the other side of the wormhole, kneeling before the ring, was Holden's intern. If there hadn't been a gun pointed at his back, he might have laughed at the expression on Garett's face—a combination of surprise and bewilderment at having recognized Holden in a place where he could not possibly be.

Danny pushed Holden into the cell as the technicians watched nervously. He pointed his weapon at them. "There's been a change of plans."

Chapter 40

Emily and Nathan ran to hug their father. "Are you okay?" Emily asked. "Jack told us they were waiting for you at your apartment."

"I'm all right," Holden said. "But we didn't make it there. We went to my lab downtown. Pieter has Detective Singh locked up there."

Jack's mood, already deflated, fell further. "That means no one knows where we are. They got her partner at your apartment. We hoped she'd seen them through the video link and called for help."

Holden was about to speak when a high-pitched hum filtered through the neighboring wall. Grace— who was sensitive to portals—sat abruptly. Like a quarter of passengers on her liner, she'd been *worm-sick* for most of the flight from Earth.

"That started a while ago." She looked as if she was about to throw up. "They've been running the portal every few minutes for the past hour. That room is *not* properly shielded."

"I expect it will continue for quite a while yet. Did the boys tell you about Pieter Reynard?"

"I told them everything you told me," Jack said. "How he intends to hold the portals for ransom."

"I'm afraid there's more to it than just money. Pieter planned to profit from this somehow, but Danny betrayed him and stranded him on Earth. Detective Singh and I discovered cylinders of nerve gas that were almost certainly used in the attack against the Navy. I think Danny was responsible for that and that he's planning more attacks."

"How?"

"Pieter has learned to merge many crystals into a single wormhole. I believe Danny is going to force the gas into one of those portals while they are in phase. It will spread through the entire network."

"How many crystals can he merge?" Jack asked.

"Billions." Holden was silent for a moment. "I don't think Pieter even knew about the gas, although he'll have figured it out by now. When I asked him about the testing, I meant the attack on the Navy, but he was referring to the fires."

- - - - -

The intermittent noise and vibration from the field generator, and Grace's reaction, continued for some time, letting the family know Danny was still transferring equipment.

While Jack sat on one of the crowded cell's three cots, feeling hopeless, Ethan paced the cell.

"Ethan," his mother moaned after ten minutes, "there's not enough room in here for that. Please, sit down."

He slumped onto the cot nearest the door and brooded in silence for another minute with his arms crossed over his chest. Then he fished in his pocket for a coin and began flipping it into the air, catching it and hiding it on his wrist for a second before revealing it. The guessing game seemed to have created an inspiration; his expression changed from bored to puzzled to excited.

"Ethan," Grace snapped. "Stop. It's giving me a headache."

He appeared about to argue but then asked, "Why are we even here in the first place? I mean, why us?"

The noise from the generator ceased. Everyone in the room waited, but no one came to their door. Whatever was happening now didn't involve the family.

"I didn't want to say anything," Holden said, "because I'm not sure myself. Pieter seems to think that you, Jack, will stop him."

"That's mad. How can I stop him? If he hadn't come after us, I'd still be in Fairview and know nothing about this. This is becoming another paradox. These Travellers are insane."

"But maybe you're a Traveller too," Ethan said. "You've used a portal more than most, and you've been through one twice today. Have you had strange memories?"

"No, only strange dreams. But I've always had odd dreams."

"Do any of them come true?"

"No." Then he remembered the one about the cave. "Well not exactly. But those are only dreams. I've never had an ability like Sarah's. The only thing I'm good at is fixing things."

"Too good, actually." Victor exchanged a look with Emily that Jack couldn't follow. They reached a silent agreement before he continued. "We were worried about you when we learned of the problems affecting children who traveled through portals frequently. Your grandfather spent a long time researching the subject. He learned that those who went on to highly analytical careers, such as engineers, showed fewer symptoms."

"My guess," Holden picked up the thread, "was that a mind focused on external objects would be less affected by internal struggles."

"So," Victor said, "I began taking you to the workshop every day. Your toys were tools, motors, gears, and spare parts. You were pulling drones apart and putting them back together before you could read. And that thing you do with the rotors—impossible."

"It's just practice. I bend them a little and feel how they move." His parents exchanged glances again. "What?"

"I'm not so sure," Emily said. "We wanted to understand how you did it, so we replaced those blades with ones that had failed at the extreme range of the testing equipment—ones that probably had internal cracks. When you decided they were fine, we assumed we'd found the limits of your abilities. But when your father checked them later, he couldn't find a problem."

"You think that I …" Jack struggled to keep his voice calm. Being trapped in the cell was bad enough, but he'd just learned that his parents had run experiments on him. "You think I was healing them somehow?"

"We don't know. You've always had a talent for understanding machinery, almost as if you can see right through it."

"And let's not forget the safe," Holden said. "It may be

you arrived at your assumption through logic. It may also be that you *sensed* its presence behind the wall."

"Sensed it. How?"

"Travellers *remember* things from their future. Perhaps you *remembered* the safe, but in real time."

Jack stomped to the door. "Even if I could see through machines or walls, that won't stop Pieter. I want out of here as bad as anyone, but the cylinder in that lock needs to be turned, not healed." He slapped the door angrily, producing a sharp metallic click from the lock.

Everyone froze, staring at Jack. Ethan silently mouthed, *"Try it,"* while gesturing at the door.

Jack reached for the handle slowly, as if a sudden movement might scare it. He eased his fingers around the metal bar, then gripped it firmly and pulled. He was as surprised as everyone else when the door slid open.

Chapter 41

Victor rushed the door and pushed Jack aside. "Stay back." He slid it open an inch and peeked through. Nathan hurried to join him.

"How did you do that?" Ethan whispered.

"I didn't. I was just thinking about what the lock looked like inside and what tool I'd need to force it open. The cylinder moved by itself."

Grace shushed them. "There'll be time to discuss it later. Let's get out of here."

Danny and the technicians had left the lower level. Most of the ceiling was solid steel, except for a sixteen-foot-diameter ring of perforated panels that let air and light pass from the room above. Their voices were filtering through the metal grates.

As Victor and Nathan led the way, Jack saw the technicians' legs and lab coats through the grating. They were facing away from the elevator. *Danny's right above us.*

Holden was last to leave the cell. He stopped midway to the bulkhead door, stretching for a better look at the equipment upstairs.

"Dad," Emily whispered, despite the noise coming from the second level. "Hurry up."

Silently, Holden backed toward the opening while studying the space above.

Nathan crept closer to the central aisle between the tanks. "How are we going to get past the gatehouse? There were guards there when we drove in."

"That's not how I arrived." Holden walked to the door in the concrete wall and opened it, revealing a long, unpainted hallway. "Danny brought me through a different building."

"This must pass under the warehouse Sarah told us about," Jack said. The empty corridor was more than a hundred yards long.

Victor and Nathan rushed ahead. By the time everyone reached the landing at the bottom of the stairs, they'd already tried the maintenance room's door.

"It's locked," Victor said. "Jack, can you do that trick again?"

"Again? I didn't do it the first time."

"Jack," Holden said, "how did you get into my apartment this morning?"

"What do you mean? You programmed my profile into the building's AI."

"No. That's why I came back to the apartment—to let you in. But you were already there. I think you opened those locks the same way."

"C'mon, Jack," Ethan said. "Give it a try."

Jack switched places with his father. He didn't know what else to do, so he just tried the door handle. It didn't move. He shrugged.

"You said you were thinking about what the lock looked like on the inside. Why don't you try that again?"

"I can't. I'd fixed a lock like that one for Stan once. I made a guess based on what I already knew. This one's different. I've got no idea what it's like inside."

Holden spoke from the bottom of the stairs. "I believe I understand. Just like the tractor beam Ethan spoke of, the force you used to open the lock must be present at every wormhole. It makes some people nauseated …" He gestured apologetically to Grace. "But you're able to control it, as long as you're near a portal."

"But I didn't have one there."

"I think you did," Victor said. "The cells look like they were added after the tank was built. There's probably a static portal for power incorporated into the keypad, but the building above must be wired traditionally."

"So," Nathan said, "we need a portal. But none of us have phones." He knocked on the door. "Maybe we can break it down."

Jack was surprised at how easily everyone accepted the idea he could somehow manipulate objects by thought. He was far less convinced and was about to step away when he felt something.

"Hold on." He gripped the door handle harder. "I know what's inside now. It's almost the same as the other one." His earlier doubts vanished under the evidence developing under his fingers. This wasn't the vague pressure he'd felt from wormholes before. It was as if he were reaching inside the lock, touching the cold metal. "I think I can move it." He jiggled the handle. "No, it's like it's frozen or something. Wait, here it goes."

"Jack, stop," Ethan shouted. "There's—"

Someone with a phone on the other side of the door, Jack realized, too late. He'd already turned the handle.

The door swung open before he could react. A hand reached through and seized him by the collar. At the same time, a foot swept his legs out from under him and he was yanked into the darkened office. He hit the floor hard, then rolled to get away from his attacker. He scrambled to his feet as a familiar voice called his name.

"Sarah?" Jack blurted as she pulled him into a fierce hug the moment the lights came on.

Both Victor and Nathan crouched in the doorway, prepared to pounce on whoever stood on the other side. It was apparent they'd only stopped when they heard Jack calling Sarah by name—either that or when they saw the pistol Priya pointed at them. She also wore a bullet-proof vest with POLICE written across it in large letters.

Jack sprang in front of the detective "It's okay. These are our parents. We thought you were locked up in Grandpa's lab."

Priya lowered her pistol and tilted her head toward Sarah, who wore a broad smile. "I was. Sarah let me out and led me here."

"I had to tell her I've been here already," Sarah said. "And also about Terrance and Niels."

"And now I need to get you to safety." Priya signaled Emily and Grace, who'd just entered the room, to join her and the boys' fathers at the back door.

"How did you let her out?" Ethan had reached the top of the stairs.

"When I got home, I used Little Brother to watch the Magnolia. I saw them put you in the van. Then I watched the street in front of the reservoir and saw the van go in there. I knew that for me to have remembered the reservoir, I had to go through a portal again. So I went back to the apartment; someone broke the locks on the doors. When I got to your grandfather's house, he and Priya were already gone."

"But they were at the lab. How did you get there so fast?"

She looked embarrassed but also wore a huge grin. "I drove Priya's car."

"*You drove?*" Both Ethan and Jack said at the same time.

Priya's expression suggested she was having trouble believing it herself. She shook her head before returning to her own discussion.

"I've been there," Ethan said. "That's not an easy building to find. Does your talent give you detailed directions?"

"Well, no. I asked the GPS."

Jack chuckled at Ethan's chagrined expression. But even if Sarah's ability didn't let her remember the address of a place she'd never seen before; he was impressed by her boldness. Not only had she gone to the apartment where she knew Reynard's men might have been, she'd traveled alone across a large, crowded, and unfamiliar city, driving a car for the first time.

"It's a fast car," she said. A hint of jealousy crossed Ethan's face. "It's got four hundred and fifty horsepower." She grinned. Serious jealousy now. "I took the long way around the lake." She giggled.

"Okay, enough of that," Priya said, saving Ethan from turning green. "Luckily, there was no one in the lab then. I couldn't see much from my window, but they worked in the Archive after you left. They didn't put the gas cylinders in there though. I saw Pieter's men move them into the cargo portal room."

"They're here." Holden summarized Pieter's plan to merge and destroy Earth's portals. "He told his men to arm the explosives. I think he planted bombs in his competitor's factories." He also described Danny's betrayal. "I had a better look as we were leaving the tank. There are two racks of crystal testers, identical to my own. From the number, and from what Pieter told me, I believe he has a pair for every type of portal on Cirrus."

"But why send the poison here?" Jack asked. "And why does he need a second resonator?"

"It's Danny," Sarah said quietly. "He's going to kill everyone on Cirrus." Her words made them all freeze; Jack and Ethan had described Sarah's visions to their parents. "At least he'll try. Why?"

"Smuggling," Priya said.

"That doesn't make sense," Jack said. "How would he sell anything if he kills everyone?"

"Not goods, *people*. The corporations control who comes to Cirrus. There are millions of people who'd gladly hand over their life savings to leave Earth. Danny would have an entire empty world to sell to the highest bidder. He'd make ten times what Pieter expects to."

"But then he must be planning to stop Pieter from destroying the portals," Ethan said.

Priya shook her head. "Not necessarily. It'd be better for him to control the only remaining portals. To do that, he needs crystals that aren't in Pieter's collection or the Archive. But he'll need to bring them to Cirrus somehow, and that's not easy. Getting caught smuggling machinery is one thing, but it's a more serious offence to bring in an unregistered portal crystal."

"I think he's already done that." Sarah described the sphere and repeated the story about her escape. "Niels didn't ask me to give the cartridge I swiped to Terrance. Why not?"

Holden was the first to answer. "The wormhole collapsed because the warehouse's cargo frame was a different size from the one it connected to. It *is* possible to sustain an unbalanced wormhole, but it requires an enormous amount of power. With the right equipment, Niels could have detected the collapse from hundreds of miles away."

"And that same signal would be detected on the other side," Ethan said. "So, Niels wanted you to keep it because he knew you'd use it."

"And now," Jack said, "he knows where on Earth one of Danny's portals is. And maybe where the guns are coming from."

"There were at least a hundred cartridges in the sphere," Sarah said.

"Then Danny's got a hundred ways to bring people to Cirrus."

"Not quite." She described the mechanism inside the sphere and how she'd accidentally destroyed his cargo.

Ethan smirked. "I'll bet he didn't see that coming."

"But then neither did Niels," Jack said. "What does that mean?"

"It means he's interfered with Danny's plans," Priya said, "and that Travellers don't know everything."

"There was a second sphere." Jack retold the story of how he found it partially buried. "Could that be how Danny sent the crystals to Cirrus? He couldn't have brought them through the scanners at the ports. Could he have dropped them through the roof?"

"As long as they approach Cirrus slowly, the asteroid deflectors won't stop them and the roof will seal itself. It sounds like the sphere was designed to survive the fall."

"Danny must have made the threats against the passenger ships too," Ethan said. "They're all docked on Cirrus to avoid a terrorist attack, but I bet what he really wanted was to keep them away from Earth. Without crystals, it'll be years before anyone else can get here in force."

Priya pulled a phone—the green, Cirrus-based one borrowed from Holden's apartment—from a pocket in her vest. "I'd better call this in and get a team to the lab to stop Pieter." She dialed a number, then frowned when her phone responded with static. She tried a second one and the same thing happened.

"What's wrong?" Holden asked?

"I can't get through." She entered a local number and heard her own voice asking callers to leave a message. "But only to numbers on Earth."

"That'll be the resonance. Communications to Earth will be the most sensitive and the first to fail."

"All right, there's another way." She opened the door and peered outside. "Jack, Ethan, it's best for you to go to Holden's house in Washington. You can call my office in Olympia from there while I come back to stop Danny. I'll take you to Holden's apartment and we'll use his portal. Sarah, you need to go too."

"Now that CorpSec is looking for me, how will we get there?"

"What makes you think they're looking for you?" Priya's phone beeped. She scanned the screen, then shook her head. "Sarah's mother has filed a missing person report. CorpSec has escalated the case to say she's in immediate danger. They've given descriptions of the rest of you as kidnappers." She paused for a few seconds, then growled, "That changes things. We've somehow got to get to the apartment without being seen."

No one spoke while they imagined ways to cross the city as fugitives, until Sarah asked, "Why is it so quiet in here? The last time I was in this room, the noise from behind that wall was unbearable."

Victor glanced around, reading labels and working out the purpose of the equipment behind the panels. "That'll be the high-pressure valves. Danny must have turned off the water."

"*Water,*" Holden said. "There's another way. We don't need to go to my apartment. The portal in the tank can get one of us directly to the lab."

"That's a cargo portal. It's not safe for people to use."

"If we flood the room, the water will act as a buffer. A person swimming through the wormhole will displace the water, and the change in mass will be slight. I've done it myself, before field stabilizers were invented. It's quite safe."

"Hold on," Priya said. "That won't work. I was held in one of those booths. The doors lock automatically."

"Why?" Ethan asked.

"Customs regulations. Any portal large enough for a person or cargo has to be secured."

"Then how do we open the lock?"

Holden said, "You can handle that, can't you, Jack?"

"*Me?*"

Having only just discovered his talent for locks, Jack had no confidence in his ability to do it again. But before he could protest, Ethan said, "I'm going with him." Sarah added, "Me too."

Chapter 42

Jack wanted to argue that he didn't know how to open the lock at the lab, but Priya was already saying they shouldn't use the cargo portal at all. Both his and Ethan's parents were also voicing their disapproval until Holden interrupted.

"The cylinders are here, not on Earth. Danny Kou will be releasing nerve gas through every portal on Cirrus. We don't know how far it will spread. Right now, there is no safer place, *for all of us*, than Earth."

"Fine," Priya said. "I'll get you into the tank. But if I tell you to, you go back to the maintenance shop. All of you. Is that understood?" She waited until they agreed.

"What about you?" Sarah asked. "Aren't you coming?"

"I have to stop Danny."

There was no point arguing with her. They had to get to Holden's lab to prevent Pieter from destroying Earth's portal network, and Priya was the only one who stood a chance of stopping Danny.

Holden asked the boys to walk with him. "Ethan has been in my lab many times. He knows his way around. Once you get the door open, we'll see what Pieter has done.

"He'll need to use some additional equipment to create the resonance. There will be a large compressor, but I don't know what else. It should stand out as something that doesn't belong. If we can disconnect it, or shut it down, we'll prevent him from overloading the crystals."

Jack wasn't sure why his grandfather was telling them this, although he appreciated finally having some idea of what was going on.

The underground chamber was quiet when Priya eased open the door at the end of the corridor. She crept to the tank and cracked the hatch open. The sound of machinery echoing within made it clear Danny was still assembling his device. She signaled everyone to slip through the doorway, one at a time. Nobody upstairs noticed as they gathered in the portal room.

Victor closed the door behind them. Like the one on their

cell, this door hung not on hinges but slid sideways on a track. There was no way to barricade it, so he and Nathan took up positions on each side of the handle—one prepared to pull and the other to push if anyone tried to force it open.

Holden pointed to the metal ceiling. "There were water pipes in the cell, so I guessed they would be here too. I'll activate the portal first so both rooms fill at the same time."

While he worked, Ethan shuffled around the room. There had been a washroom at the back of their cell, but this space had only exposed pipes and no taps. He rattled a section of plumbing assembled from spare parts. "This place was built by amateurs."

Jack noted the unpainted walls and gaps in the shielding panels. "It's probably difficult to get a building permit for a villain's lair."

As the portal flickered into life, Grace braced herself against the expected effects. Too late, they realized they'd be discovered right away if Danny was also sensitive to portals. Everyone in the room froze at the familiar generator noise.

"The machinery upstairs is louder," Priya said. "They won't hear us."

Jack crouched in front of the opening as the wormhole developed. "I can see the door. It's closed."

Ethan stretched for the ceiling. "I think that pipe will break if I hang on it. Jack, give me a boost." With Jack's help, he gripped the sides of a three-inch pipe and worked his fingers into the gap below the ceiling. The pipe bent but didn't break. He pulled himself up and dropped his weight, then repeated the move several times. "Here it goes. Look out, Jack."

Ethan's warning arrived a second too late. The pipe snapped at a coupling, jetting water against the wall and drenching Jack. "*Yow*. It's cold."

Emily hopped onto a tool cart to stay dry while the room filled. "It'll be even colder swimming in it."

Grace followed her example, then drooped against the wall and closed her eyes. "Trust me; the water's not as bad as the nausea."

"Jack," Holden said once the water was over his knees,

"you should go first, so you have time to examine the lock."

Jack knelt slowly, feeling the cold cut through him. Already shivering, he positioned himself in front of the portal.

"Don't rush," Holden said. "We don't want to create waves. Start counting when you reach the ring. Try to take a full ten seconds to complete the journey. When we're all on the other side, I'll close the portal and you can open the door."

Jack submerged his head and began counting, then crawled forward with his legs stretched out, floating behind him. He wasn't worried about the danger of passing through the wormhole; his grandfather wouldn't have allowed them to do it without a significant safety margin. Even so, he maintained a steady pace, as instructed.

As he passed the threshold, a muscle-clenching prickle sliced through his body at the boundary between worlds. The sensation wasn't painful, but not something he wanted to repeat. The passage through Holden's static portal had been seamless. This one was harsher—like crawling through sand that was slipping in two directions at once. It left him with a touch of vertigo.

He stood, pacing himself to avoid creating waves that might collapse the wormhole. The water had risen another inch while he was underwater. "I'm through."

"I'm next." Ethan was already submerging himself.

Jack turned his attention to the door. The cover on its small window was open and the lab was empty. He twisted the handle and immediately sensed the lock's internal components; the cargo portal was illuminating it like an x-ray. *It's so obvious.* Compared to this, working the lock at the maintenance shop had been like fumbling with a chunk of ice while wearing mittens.

Even though they weren't ready to open the door, Jack decided to unlock it. He wouldn't have the energy field to work with once the portal was closed, to block the gas. Ethan was already rising when Jack worked out that the lock contained a latch he had to hold back at the same time he moved the spring-loaded bolt.

Ethan shook cold water from his hair. "That was nasty. It felt like swimming through an ant hill." He stuck out his tongue and hacked. "Bleh, it even tasted bad. How's it going here?"

"Minor problem. The door will automatically re-lock itself. I've got to bend this plate …" The lock groaned as Jack mimed a twisting motion. "Around the bolt …" He clenched his fingers and the mechanism clicked. "To jam it open."

He was surprised at how naturally the ability came to him and how easily the metal moved. His parents' theory was true. *They were right. The rotors, the winch cable, the door at the train station—I've been using this talent for years.*

"It's not a permanent fix, but the extra friction should hold for a while."

Now that he'd unlocked it, he noticed a second problem. The door opened inwards. There was no way they'd be able to pull it open with a room full of water behind it. The rising water had almost filled the frame when he began shuffling his foot around, searching for a floor drain. He could see the blurred silhouette of someone passing through the wormhole.

"*Hang on,*" Ethan yelled.

A metallic bang sounded through the two-inch air gap at the top of the portal. Ethan seized Sarah's arm as she stood. He also grasped the only other thing within reach: Jack.

At once, the water rushed back through the portal. Sarah screamed as the current pulled her off her feet, toward the ring. Ethan had already braced for this and managed to hold on to both her and Jack. Luckily, Jack was still hanging on to the door handle.

The portal snapped closed. The water that should have spilled through slammed into the higher wall on the other side and recoiled. The wave knocked them off their feet and they ended up lying on the floor in knee-deep water.

Sarah was pale and shaking, and not from the cold; her feet were just inches from the portal frame. If it hadn't been for Ethan, they'd have been inside the wormhole when it closed.

"What happened?" Jack asked.

"Someone …" Sarah crossed her arms to control her

trembling. "Someone was hammering outside the cell as I was going under. They must have forced the door open."

Ethan stood. "With the weight of all that water, the door would have broken off if someone pulled on it. I don't think our dads had a chance of keeping it closed."

"We have to call them." Jack got to his feet and struggled with the door, which was difficult to open even though there was only a small amount of water left. He raced to the desk, slipping and sliding on the wet floor as the flood spread through the lab. He grabbed Holden's desk phone and jabbed the speed dial button with the word *Cirrus* printed beside it.

As with Priya's call to Earth, he heard only static. Only then did he realize the water pressure might have trapped them in the room. Was that why Carl had given him such detailed information? *Did he know he wouldn't make it to the lab?*

Sarah's color had returned. She and Ethan were inspecting the Archive door.

"Big problem." Ethan pointed to the door as Jack joined them. "It's been welded shut."

Jack had never been in the lab before, but one glance through the Archive window was all he needed to see that something was very wrong.

The mainframe computer at the front of the room was a masterpiece of organization. Every color-coded and labelled pipe, conduit, and wire that connected to the huge block of expensive electronics had been bundled in perfectly straight lines and tight corners. All except for a cluster of mismatched cables hanging from an open side panel.

"There are extra cables running to each rack." Jack recognized a powerful minicomputer on a makeshift workbench beside the mainframe, but not the other components. "They're connected to a … I don't know what those machines are, but I don't think they're supposed to be there. This doesn't look like it was well planned."

"Danny must have added a lot more connections than Pieter wanted," Ethan said. "And they're all behind a sealed door."

"Can we stop it from out here?" Sarah asked.

Jack gazed around the workroom. "I'm way out of my depth. Ethan?"

Ethan moved to a workstation. "Without Grandpa, I don't know. I'll log in anyway and see if I can at least figure out what's happening in there. See what you can do about the door."

"It's been welded in a dozen spots." Jack checked the workbenches for tools but found nothing larger than a screwdriver. "I'll need something bigger."

"What about your …" Ethan opened his eyes wide and waved his hands mystically. "Your *thing*. You know. Like with the propellers. Can't you *unheal* something?"

"Dude, I don't know if it works that way."

"What *thing* are you guys talking about?" Sarah asked.

"Jack opened two locks with his mind. It was like magic."

Jack shook his head. "There's a force field … or tractor beam … or something like it coming through the wormholes. I can sense it. And maybe control it. But apparently I need a portal or … you must think I'm crazy."

"I predicted the future today," Sarah said. "*That* was crazy." She brought over a phone that had been left on a workbench. "Will this do?" While she held it near, Jack rubbed his fingers over the welds.

"It's no good. All I feel is hard, smooth metal. I need a bigger portal."

"Can we open the cargo one again?" Ethan suggested as he typed.

Sarah closed the booth. "I don't think that's a good idea. Someone hammered at the door before it broke. If Priya has things under control on Cirrus, she'll turn it on again herself. Also, they'll need to flood the room again. They can't do that with this door open."

Jack spotted a pass card lying on the table. "I'll check the other rooms." He opened the nearest booth. Inside was a pair of stacked, six-inch diameter portal rings, mounted in a rig that held them one above the other, separated by a hand's width. "This'll work."

"What's that for?" Sarah pointed at a large tray of sand on

the floor underneath the apparatus.

"Impact testing. You drop an object through the lower ring. It reappears through the upper ring and loops through, faster and faster until you turn off the lower portal. I built one last year. Well, a smaller version. Mine was a quarter inch wide and could only do five cycles before it was drawing so much current that it burned itself out."

Jack found the controls and switched the device on. He didn't need to use it—simply opening the wormhole was enough. And if his guess about how the field worked was correct, the impactor would provide plenty of energy. Its diameter was much smaller than the cargo portal, but the rings themselves were almost as thick as those on the larger machine; they'd consume a lot of power as the falling projectile accelerated.

Back at the Archive door, he placed his fingers on the welds again. There was an immediate difference. The energy flowing from the impactor wasn't just like a light, but also like a breeze blowing where he willed it to. He directed the flow into the door and felt how the welds blended into the steel doorframe. "This isn't like a propeller. It's a lot thicker and stronger. If I had more time I could … I don't know … chip away at it?"

"The window?" Sarah suggested.

Jack inspected the glass. "It's at least three inches thick. We couldn't lift anything massive enough to break it." He placed his hand on the pane and concentrated, feeling again the breeze-like sensation of the energy field. "I wish we could move the impactor closer, but it's bolted to the floor."

"How does that make a difference?"

"It's like trying to control the wind. It seems to go where I want it to, but the farther away I am, the more it does its own thing." He imagined the energy blowing across the window. The impactor's control panel beeped and a segmented bar lit up to show increased power consumption. Much of the force flowing from the booth faded before it reached him, but there was still enough for him to sense that the window was unusual. "There's a lot of metal in this glass. I wonder if it'll crack?"

He pushed harder and imagined the pane shattering. Three bars lit on the impactor's power indicator. When he pulled his hand away, a vaguely hand-shaped cloudiness remained.

A deep, calm voice spoke from the lab entrance. "You'll need a lot more power than that, Jack."

He spun to face the door. Pieter Reynard stood there, holding a pistol.

Chapter 43

The portal room door had been designed to slide open like an elevator. It also kept the room airtight and provided shielding. It wasn't built to hold back many tons of water.

When the two technicians tried to force the door open, all they had to do was nudge it past the edge of its frame. Without that supporting column, the panel bowed outward. Then the lower guide roller gave way and the door came off entirely. Rushing water swept the technicians away. Victor and Nathan tumbled after them, followed by Priya on her cart.

She remained balanced on the cart until it tipped over as it floated past the elevator. Landing deftly, she drew her weapon before anyone else stopped struggling.

"Get up. Into that room," Priya ordered the technicians, pointing at the cell where the family had been kept for days.

"*Look out.*" Victor pointed to the opening in the grated ceiling.

She spun just as Danny fired his weapon. The echo from the tank's metal walls was deafening. She returned fire, but he'd already retreated to the section protected by a solid floor. Victor and Nathan scrambled to their feet and dashed to the portal room to rejoin Emily and Grace. The technicians also ran to the cell for shelter.

Priya approached the ladder cautiously, keeping her weapon pointed at the opening. "Get out now, while I've got him covered. Hurry up."

"What about the kids?" Emily asked. "We need to open the portal."

"They're safer where they are," Holden said. "If he opens one of those canisters, the nerve gas will fill the tank. If the wormhole is open, the gas will flow through there as well."

"What about them?" Victor meant the technicians huddling inside the open cell.

Priya tossed a pair of handcuffs and growled, "Handcuff them to each other and take them with you."

Nathan shackled them together. He snapped a pass card

off one of their shirt pockets as the family moved to the bulkhead door. They all left the tank while Priya kept watch on the ceiling. The moment Holden stepped outside, she reached for the ladder.

"Shouldn't you wait for backup?" Holden asked.

"There's no time. Seal me in."

"You can't climb the ladder without being seen."

"Officer," one of the technicians said, "there's another way in. There's a second hatch at the top of the tank. You can get to the surface with the elevator by the tool shed."

Priya backed away from the ladder and stepped out of the tank. The reservoir's underground portion was cavernous. Near the ceiling, a network of pipes ran along the aisles between the rows of tanks. Metal stairs rose to a catwalk suspended below the ceiling for access to the control valves. "Are those pipes connected to this tank?"

"Yes, but there's a safety interlock on this door. We can't open the valves as long as it's open."

She called Nathan and Grace back. "I want you to open the upper hatch, then stay out of sight." To Victor and Emily, she said, "I'm going back in as soon as the hatch is open. Seal this door, then open the valves."

Victor started to move, but Emily barred him with an arm across his chest. "You want us to flood the tank with you in it?"

"Danny brought the address cartridges from Pieter's office. He must have planned on leaving through this portal. Now his only escape will be through the upper hatch. I want him to think I'm there waiting for him."

With the plan stated, Nathan and Grace uncuffed the technicians. They went with one to find the tool shed, while Victor followed the other up to the catwalk. Emily stayed at the door with Holden, to seal the hatch.

Several minutes passed before Priya heard the muffled clang of the upper hatch against the dome, then a single gunshot. She signaled to Victor to open the valves, then rushed into the tank, slamming the bulkhead door as loud as she could. Instead of running to the ladder, she splashed through the ankle-deep water into the nearest open cell and hid where Danny couldn't see her from the second floor.

Chapter 44

Pieter Reynard stepped into the lab. "I knew there was something special about you, Jack, from the moment I saw you. In fact, from quite some time before that. You understand what I mean, don't you, Miss Rogers? How far into the future can you see?"

Sarah refused to answer. She backed away from the gun as Pieter advanced.

"There's an interesting thing about our particular talent." He walked to the center of the room. "Have you discovered it yet? The further one sees, the less accurate they become. For instance, even now you're thinking there's a chance to stop this. You're wasting your time. I assure you; it *will* happen."

Jack looked around the room, not sure what he hoped for but desperate to find it. He spotted an open toolbox and edged toward it.

"That's far enough, Jack. And step away from the window too. Even *I* couldn't break through that."

Pieter gestured with his free hand, launching a chair across the workshop to smash into the Archive window. The sudden violence caught them all by surprise. Sarah screamed. Ethan ducked behind his workstation.

Jack ducked too. As he did, he saw the light bar on the impactor's control panel spike. The chair lay twisted on the floor but there was barely a mark on the glass.

"What about you, Ethan? No new powers from your grandfather's miraculous portal?" Pieter stared at him for a moment, then shrugged. "Oh well, too bad."

"How can you let this happen?" Jack asked. "You must know how to stop Danny. Think of all the people who will die."

He dismissed Jack's concern with a wave of his hand. "There will be a certain amount of collateral damage, of course, but only what's necessary. I can't have my new customers dying now, can I?"

"What do you mean customers?" Ethan asked. "Who's

going to buy anything from you?"

"The portal network will be rebuilt, of course. But once the world discovers there's a serious flaw in the design—a design your grandfather helped to create—they won't use the current mass-produced crystals. No, every pair will have to be unique."

"And you have the factories to grow them," Jack said.

"Yes." Pieter grinned. "And soon, the only factories at all." He mimed an explosion. "It will be years before anyone else can produce unique crystals on a commercial level. By that time, I'll have sold at least ten billion pairs. The world will be grateful."

As he spoke, Pieter eased over to the booth that housed the cargo portal. He tried the handle but the door was locked. He held his hand near the latch and Jack felt a change in the energy field flowing from the impactor. After two seconds of nothing happening, he picked up a pass card and used it instead.

Why didn't it open for him? Jack wondered. He also guessed that his own temporary adjustment—bending the lock plate, had come undone.

Ethan crossed his arms defiantly. "When they discover it was you who destroyed the network to begin with, they'll throw you in prison and seize your factories."

"But they won't find out, will they? The only people who know are your family. And they won't talk as long as you three are working for me."

"Working for you?"

"Jack, there is great potential in you. You've only just discovered your abilities and have come so far in a single day. And Miss Rogers, your talents will be very useful to me too. And Ethan … Well, we'll find something to keep you busy."

"Jack." Sarah looked terrified. "My mom."

He understood right away. Pieter wasn't about to tell more people that he was responsible for the destruction, and he wouldn't take the risk of Sarah's mother not cooperating. Jack didn't need her gift to know this wouldn't end well for anyone.

"Now, we're all going to Cirrus." Pieter pointed the gun at them and backed into the booth. "Stay where you are while I set the portal."

When he turned away to operate the frame's control panel, Ethan silently mouthed, "*The door?*"

Jack shook his head—they'd have to cover a dozen paces without being heard. *But Pieter threw a chair across the room without touching it.* He turned his attention to the impactor. *And he lit up the entire power bar when he did it.*

While watching its lights, Jack reached out with his new sense, trying to perceive the isolation booth door. A gentle wave of energy flowed from the impactor's rings. The first segment on the power bar lit. *Got it.*

Just like the locks, he could sense the shielded door, distantly, as if through a heavy fog. He couldn't see it directly because it opened into the booth, but he felt it move slightly as he willed more energy against it. The impactor's power gauge rose to the second level.

I can do this. The door will lock automatically, but there's one thing I don't know. Something I can only guess at.

With a mighty effort, Jack diverted the entire force from the impactor. Its power bar lit to the third segment. Like closing a bank vault with a fire hose, the heavy steel moved slowly. Four lights. It picked up speed. Five lights. Six. The door slammed shut before Pieter could react. The walls shuddered with the impact. On the path between Jack and the booth, loose items rolled off the tables. A clock on the far side of the door rattled against the wall.

"*Block the door.*" Ethan started pushing the nearest table.

"That won't work," Jack said. "It opens inward. If he can throw a chair across the room, he can probably move whatever we put in front of it anyway. Just wait."

Through the small window, Jack saw Pieter laugh and reach for the door handle. It clicked. Instead of opening, the lock clicked again. And again. Pieter's grin transformed to rage. He slammed the door with his fists.

"What's happening?" Sarah asked.

"He was able to open the simple lock at the reservoir, but I noticed he couldn't open this one without a pass card. These locks have a two-part mechanism. He's got a lot of strength, but he can't do two things at once. Let's get back to work. Ethan, what did you find out?"

"Won't he just break down the door?" Sarah asked.

"With the shielding, he only has the power he can draw through his phone." *At least I hope that's how it works.* Having only discovered his own ability, Jack could hardly call himself an expert.

Ethan gestured for them to look at his monitor. "I've got a status screen here. I can check any test platform in the Archive and see what it's doing."

Jack and Sarah joined him at the terminal while Pieter struggled with the lock.

"This icon here …" He tapped the screen. "Looks like a stress gauge." The indicator's needle climbed through the yellow zone.

"Are they all like that?" Jack asked.

Ethan clicked through different screens to find one that showed a grid of gauges. "This is it."

Sarah gasped. "They're almost into the red."

"Scroll down," Jack said. "Let's see what the rest look like."

Ethan scrolled the page. Many gauges were still in the green zone. However, as they watched, more changed, climbing quickly to the top of the yellow. "My guess is his program is adding new pairs to the resonance, one at a time. Once they're all in sync, he'll push them over the edge somehow."

Jack gestured for Ethan to keep scrolling. "How long do we have?"

"At the rate new pairs are being added … maybe fifteen minutes."

Jack read the wall clock—eleven-forty-five. "I think he wants to do it exactly at midnight to make the destruction look like part of the Newton prophecy."

"You may be right," Sarah said. "The Travellers have been saying the world ends at midnight, tonight. What if it's not the end of the world, just the end of portals? For Travellers, it would be the same thing. They need to pass through a portal to close the loop. If Pieter destroys them, it's the end of travelling."

"That's exactly right, Miss Rogers." Pieter had been listening through an intercom. "It is the end of the Travellers. I've seen it clearly. I believe you have too."

Sarah's expression didn't reveal her thoughts, but Ethan said, "He's lying."

"Not quite," Jack said. Ethan seemed about to argue so he added, "I don't know how I know, but I'm certain that's partially true. It's kind of like a flash of déjà vu." He faced Sarah. "Is that what happened to you at the Aviary?"

Pieter appeared startled by the statements but recovered quickly. He spoke directly to Sarah before she could answer. "He's right. It doesn't have to end for you. My own portals will survive this night and I'll still be travelling. I'm going to Cirrus to begin rebuilding. Unlock the door and come with me. We'll be heroes. Or you can stay here and your future will be as dark as theirs. Tell me, Miss Rogers, what do you see happening in the next ten minutes?"

He was using the same compelling tone Jack had heard in Holden's apartment. He sounded sincere, and his promise was almost believable. Jack sensed that the effect wasn't just a practiced voice, but something related to a Traveller's talent for seeing the future.

Sarah picked up a pass card and approached the door. Jack held his breath.

"I see no future with you in it." She jabbed the intercom button.

"I'll be waiting for you," Pieter yelled, his muffled voice barely audible through the thick glass. The status light above the door indicated the portal was charging. "The network will be destroyed. Jack will see to that." He backed away from the window.

Jack couldn't see him anymore, but the light changed to warn of an open wormhole. There was a sudden bang and the wall shook. For a moment, he thought it had been an explosion, until water ran down the window inside the booth. The status light flashed rapidly, signaling that the field had collapsed. Pieter swore loudly.

"The tank must be flooded again," Jack said.

"It's okay." Sarah seemed to read his thoughts. "Your parents got out. I'm certain of it."

"What did he mean about me destroying the network? I'm not trying to destroy it. I'm supposed to be saving it."

The lights above the door cycled again. Sarah peeked through the window into the half-flooded booth. "He's gone. *Oh no.* I just realized what he meant by ten minutes. He's programmed his equipment to destroy the crystals at midnight, but they'll be in resonance before then. Danny will release the gas when that happens. Jack, he means you have to destroy the network before midnight."

"How can I destroy it? We haven't figured out how to stop *him* from destroying it yet. And how will that affect what Danny's doing?"

Sarah considered the thousands of cables snaking across the Archive floor. "There must crystals from Cirrus in there. He's saying that if you want to stop Danny, you have to destroy the network yourself, as soon as they're in sync."

Jack shook his head. "Pieter believes he's telling the truth, but Travellers aren't always correct. Niels didn't know you would ruin Danny's cargo."

"But what if he is? If we're wrong and Danny releases the gas before the network is destroyed, he might kill everyone on Cirrus."

"Pieter may think he's right," Ethan said, "but it doesn't matter. I know how we can destroy it." He beckoned them to his workstation. "Watch. Each time a new pair joins the resonance, the stress level drops on the others. Then it bounces up again. My guess is that if we remove pairs, it'll push the rest over the edge."

"They're locked behind the Archive door," Jack said. "There's no way to disconnect them."

"Your dad said you've been healing cracks in rotors. Can you do the opposite? If you create a crack in a crystal that's already stressed, it might shatter, like hitting it with a hammer. That should have the same effect as disconnecting them."

"I don't know. This is all really new to me."

Ethan thought for a few seconds. "Grandpa also said a crystal would shatter if you passed too much mass or energy through it. Maybe that applies to dark energy too. Try throwing the chair the way Pieter did."

Jack considered the chair doubtfully. So far, he'd moved only tiny pieces of metal and one door. However, he'd seen it fly across the room, so he knew the feat must be possible. "Okay." He gestured for Sarah to join him at the impactor. "But come watch these power lights."

He focused on the chair, but it wasn't as simple as closing the door. To do that, he'd guided the force from the portal as if it were the wind. The chair rocked slightly.

"Keep trying," Sarah said. "The lights are bouncing between the first and second levels."

He concentrated again, thinking of the force as an extension of his arms. The chair trembled, then lifted six inches and hovered for two seconds before clattering to the floor.

"Two steady lights," she said.

"That's it," Ethan said. "There was a spike. A small one, but it was there. Do you think you can do it again?"

Jack took a deep breath, blocking out everything but the chair and the impactor. He imagined grasping the cold metal leg, feeling its weight and smooth surface.

"Two lights," Sarah said as the chair rose. "Three." It dipped, wobbled, then froze. "Four." Both the lights and the chair held steady.

Jack smiled and set it down smoothly. "I can do this."

"Great," Ethan said, "then all we need to do is figure out if Danny has released the gas or if Priya has stopped him."

"How can we tell what's happening on Cirrus?" Sarah asked.

Ethan opened the top drawer of Holden's desk. "Grandpa had phones shuttled back from everywhere." He lifted two phones: one gray, one red. "The Moon. Mars." He put them back and withdrew a familiar green case. "This is from Cirrus." He set it on the desk. "Pieter wants to destroy the crystals in the phone network so he can sell them new ones. Once they're all in resonance, Danny's going to release the gas. If that happens, the gas will come from this phone too."

Jack gaped. "Uh, you're suggesting we wait for poisonous gas to come out of the phone?"

"No." Ethan dug into his pocket for a coin, flipped and caught it, then slapped it on his wrist, hidden under his hand. "Heads."

Sarah snapped at him like he was crazy. "*We can't decide the fate of Cirrus on the toss of a coin.*"

"We're not going to. I'm using it to prove something." He lifted his hand to reveal the profile of George Washington. "I discovered something when we were playing soccer, and again while we were in the cell. Heads." He flipped, caught, and uncovered the coin—heads again. He continued flipping while he explained. "Pieter said the further one can see into the future, the less accurate they become. Tails. Well, Grandpa's portal worked for me too. I can predict a coin toss ... for about two seconds. Tails. I'll know two seconds before the network is destroyed whether Danny has released the gas."

Jack understood but could hardly believe what Ethan was suggesting. "You're trusting your life to the ability to guess a coin toss. That's insane."

Ethan continued flipping the coin. "Tails. It's either that or we don't take any chances and destroy the network now."

Jack certainly didn't want his cousin risking his life. But he didn't want to plunge the entire world into darkness and be stuck on Earth in a power failure that might last for years, either. "Sarah?"

"I don't know. If I try to imagine what tomorrow will be like, I see us back on Cirrus. But I also see us trapped here. I can't tell which is real." She seemed both scared and confused.

"So, we have several choices." Jack summarized the situation, as much for himself as for his friends. "We can destroy the network ourselves or keep working on a way to get into the Archive. If we destroy it, Earth will suffer and we may be stuck here for years. If we disable Pieter's equipment, we can save Earth, but there's a chance Danny will kill everyone on Cirrus, unless Priya can stop him. And if we do nothing, then both those things may happen. Right?"

Jack waited for one of them to say something else— anything—but neither spoke. He could barely comprehend the scale of what they were planning. Somehow, the final decision had fallen to him.

He considered the impactor. Like facing the cave in his dream, he could walk away or face his fears. "Okay, I'll get ready then."

Chapter 45

Danny was at the workstation, watching the icons as each portal came into resonance. He'd been swiping through screens, checking that everything was working as planned when the upper hatch opened. His pistol lay ready on the table beside the keyboard. He picked it up and fired in one smooth motion, without aiming.

The console faced the center of the room. He crouched to shelter behind it. Above, the open hatchway was a black circle against the dome's intensely bright ceiling. He kept his weapon trained on the opening until the lower bulkhead door slammed, then rushed to a position where he could fire on the entrance.

There was no one downstairs, only a few indistinct ripples in the water. The large wheel in the door began spinning— someone was sealing it from the outside.

With an explosive roar, water rushed in through the large pipes near the ceiling. The torrent fell on the other side of the tank, where it shifted piles of boxes and other equipment. From there, it streamed across the floor and poured through the metal grates.

Danny returned to the workstation with an unnatural calm. He pressed a few keys. The compressors whined. The gas cylinder valves opened and locked in place. This was the final step. As soon as the sensors confirmed that the crystals had changed phase, the gas would flow.

- - - - -

Priya bobbed her head around the door frame, ready to fire. She hadn't seen Danny, so she moved cautiously out of the room. She wasn't concerned about making noise—the inrushing water was deafening. The flood from the earlier pipe break was nothing compared to the deluge from the main lines. In only minutes, the water had risen above her knees. She approached the ladder, circling the cage while keeping her weapon trained on the opening.

"You'll never stop him that way, Detective," Pieter

shouted.

Priya spun. Pieter was standing in the portal room's open door. He'd lost his suit jacket since the last time she saw him and was soaked head-to-toe.

She shouted over the surging water. "Drop your weapon."

"I'll keep it, thanks." He held the pistol loosely, pointed away from her with his finger well away from the trigger. "He's a *Hopper*. You know what that is, don't you?"

"I've heard of them."

"Like me and your Miss Rogers, he can see the future, but only half a second of it. That's not much, but he can dodge a bullet. You'll need my help."

"Why should I trust you?"

"I never meant to hurt anyone, Detective. This was all just business."

Priya scoffed. "Some business you've got."

"Danny has taken that away from me now. I can't complete my plans, but I can help you stop him."

"How?"

"I know how to shut down the resonator. Just get me upstairs." He spun his weapon and offered it to her. "Better?" He smiled broadly, employing the well-practiced tone and expression that conveyed honesty.

She took the pistol and put it into her own holster, but didn't lower hers. "How long will it take?"

"Only a minute. I've got to get to the computer behind the elevator."

"All right, I'll get you upstairs. Can you swim?"

"Well enough."

"Wait in the portal room." She gestured for Pieter to walk ahead, then waded after him. The water was now at her hips.

She examined the ceiling. "This room is airtight. There'll be a pocket of air trapped at the top once the water is past the doorframe. We can get up the ladder without being seen when it reaches the second floor." She hopped onto a chair as water reached the cargo frame's control panel.

"It's quite safe," he said. "There's no danger of electrocution. Everything is sealed. The portal will even work underwater."

She acknowledged this with a nod. He started wading the room, searching for something in the water.

"Who is Danny working for?" Priya asked, but he only glared in response. "It's not you. Not anymore. This operation takes more than a half second of planning. How did he end up at Armenau in the first place?"

Pieter didn't answer right away. A rare frown creased his brow as he searched. Finally, he said, "He was working for a VIP protection service in Seoul a decade ago. I recognized him for what he was and offered him a job—Hoppers make excellent bodyguards."

"What are you looking—" Priya began, but Pieter ducked under the water. He came up struggling with a tool cart that had been knocked over when the door broke.

He shook water from his hair and wiped his eyes, then moved the cart in front of the portal. "We could be sucked through If someone opened the portal from the other side. It would be a shame if one of us were to be cut in half when the field collapsed." He affected a look of concern as he spoke, although he emphasized the words—*one of us*.

Priya was freezing, but waited a full minute after the water rose past the doorframe before diving through the doorway. She returned less than thirty seconds later. "It's up to the ceiling now. Are you ready to go?"

"Lead the way."

Chapter 46

Jack kneeled in the tray of sand below the impactor and placed his hands between the two rings. As with the cargo portal, the energy seemed like a bright light. He waved a hand through the flow, sensing an initiator crystal embedded deep inside the frame. "How can I possibly destroy a crystal if I can't even touch it?"

"I don't know," Sarah said, "but you've got to try."

"I can't make something happen just by wanting it to happen."

"But what about the locks?" Ethan asked.

"As far as I know, I was only thinking about the mechanism and it moved by itself."

"I meant the ones in Grandpa's building. You didn't even know you'd opened those. What were you thinking of then?"

"I was hoping I wouldn't have to explain to Sarah that we hadn't stayed there last night."

"See, it's like Niels said about the tractor beam. We don't need to understand how something works to use it. They opened because you *wanted* them to."

"I don't know." Jack waved his hand. The energy field moved with it. "This is too much like magic."

"Try," Sarah said. "We'll let you know if something changes." She moved away to watch Ethan's screen.

Jack turned his attention back to the impactor. He'd always been able to visualize how machines worked and imagine what they looked like inside, and assumed any mechanically inclined person could do the same. That was true for the wall safe too, except maybe his grandfather was right. Instead of working it out logically, he'd used the energy field to sense its presence.

He thought of how he checked rotors for defects: running his fingers over them, feeling differences in texture, aligning components by touch. To him, the process was natural. But locks, doors, and chairs were things he had real-world experience with, things he could hold in his hands. The crystal was different. He sensed its position, but the gem was too small to see—only a bright spark.

I need to do this without seeing it.

As part of the effort to control his anxiety, Jack had visited a therapist who taught him meditation and visualization techniques. He closed his eyes and recalled how he'd learned to walk the thin line between waking and dreaming, to be not only a viewer of his dreams but to direct them. He let his imagination visualize the crystal as being large enough to hold in his hands.

His sense of the energy field helped make the image larger and more realistic in his mind's eye. Then he tried a trick he'd discovered for keeping himself in a dream state. Instead of reaching out to touch the object—something that might wake him if his real arm moved involuntarily—he imagined a mirror.

That's it, he thought when the opposite side appeared. *That's what it really looks like.*

The crystal was vibrating like a window hammered by loud music. But the pattern wasn't even. There were distinct troughs and peaks: weak points. It would take only a small amount of force to push them over the edge. He imagined a crack forming and saw it materialize on the crystal's surface.

"Something's happening," Sarah said.

It is like one of my lucid dreams. It's as if the energy field knows what I want. How? And is one crystal enough?

With this thought, something unexpected happened. He was still awake—he was certain of it—but the daydream took on a life of its own. There were now many more mirrors, reflecting a multitude of crystals.

He allowed his imagination to drift to a reflection and found it to be as real as the first. This was an entirely different crystal: a real object existing somewhere outside of this not-quite-a-dream. A nearly invisible thread attached each new crystal to another.

That's the wormhole.

Jack gazed directly into a crystal, following its thread. He discovered far more than he expected.

Threads crossed and knotted, connecting more than just a single pair. As the resonance created by Pieter's equipment spread, new lines appeared, weaving a gauze-like fabric of connections. The material grew denser with each addition, bunching and folding into valleys and peaks similar to the terrain he'd seen so often in his lucid dreams.

That resemblance was all it took to trigger flight. He soared over the imagined landscape and met strange impressions, things he had no way to confirm but felt were true. This crystal suffered an environment of intense pressure and scalding water—a probe next to a deep-sea vent. Another was colder than he thought possible—the vacuum of space. Still another dispensed a hot, thick liquid, and he pictured a valve in a candy factory.

Something his grandfather had said flashed in his mind; that it might be possible to combine many portals. Holden thought there was no practical application for this, but Jack sensed the collective wormhole taking form and wondered if it would be more stable than predicted.

Recalling the peak of Mt. Rainier, he imagined snow and quickly located a crystal that pulsed brighter, as if calling to him. There was no thread between it and the impactor when he first looked, but one formed while he watched. Still aware of his physical self in the booth, he felt an icy draft across his hands.

Was that real? His skin was cool. *Did I open a new wormhole?*

To prove he hadn't dreamed it, he needed something solid, something he could hold. Shifting slightly, he felt the sand under his knees. *Perfect.* Sand, delivered by portal, was used in construction everywhere. With that in mind, he returned to the virtual landscape and selected one of many illuminated crystals.

He rolled his hand under the impactor's ring with the expectation of grabbing a handful of falling grains. And that's exactly what happened.

It is real. *I can control it.*

Holden had underestimated his own breakthrough. The combined portal could become a type of switchboard, able to pass something from one wormhole to any other. Instead of tapping water from his phone, Jack could draw fire, ice crystals, hurricane-force winds, anything already pushing on the other side of a wormhole. An enormous bounty of possibilities existed. He wanted to keep exploring, to discover what else was out there. To do that, he had to make sure the network didn't collapse.

I need to stabilize it.

He focused again on the impactor, on this one crystal. He imagined clasping his hands around it, reinforcing and calming it. The vibration eased but didn't stop. Another tiny fracture split from the first crack.

That's not enough.

Too much energy was coursing through the system. He returned to the complex of mirrors, feeling his way through the network, searching for a crystal large enough to take the strain. To his surprise, he found one—a familiar, rough and disordered orb the size of a baseball.

That's the industrial-grade crystal in Grandpa's safe. But how? It's not part of the Archive, it's … They're connected. All of them. Whether they're identical or not.

The discovery was startling, but Jack had a goal. He imagined the large crystal pulsing and coaxed it to beat in tune with the others. Next, he merged all the crystals he sensed; a vast, uncountable number. They began to vibrate, sharing the strain.

I did it. With this new resource, it would take a thousand times more energy than Pieter was applying to destroy them. *I can save the network.*

"Jack, what are you doing?" Ethan yelled. "The stress is going down, not up."

Ethan's voice broke his concentration. Somewhere in the building, alarms sounded. The lab's lights flickered. There was even a momentary dip in the flow of energy through the impactor.

Jack knew he had very little time. *Ignore it.* He tried to refocus, but one of the power failure alarms nagged at him—a shrill, pulsing tone.

295

Where have I heard that one before? As he slipped into his meditative state, he remembered when he'd heard that sound. *The dream.*

The alarm doubled, not in volume, but in number. He became dimly aware of the noise coming from somewhere outside the booth. The sound surrounded him in the darkness of his abstract world. Unexpectedly, the single crystal his imagination conjured wasn't the one in the impactor. He floated away from it, getting a larger view. The crystal revealed itself as part of an array. The array became part of a circuit. He receded farther, floating backwards through device's walls. Farther still, he saw a dust-coated power cell with a red lightning bolt, sitting on a rock shelf.

Sunlight flared around him. Water splashed in the nearby creek. Wind rustled the pines. He gasped, drawing a breath of cool, mountain air.

I'm back on the Vault.

"It's time to go, Jack," the man standing beside him said.

Chapter 47

Half a second, Priya thought as she crouched on the submerged ladder. *He'll see me coming.*

Now that water flooded the second floor, the surface above was choppy with a growing layer of white froth. She lifted her feet to a higher rung and prepared to jump. Pieter waited on the ladder just below her.

She thrust herself upwards as fast as she could, raised her weapon and fired. There was no point in aiming. There would still be enough water in the pistol's barrel to slow a bullet, but maybe Danny would react before his talent informed him that her shot was a dud.

The impact of Danny's bullet on her vest felt like a hammer blow. Already off balance, Priya fell to her knees but managed to keep her weapon up. She returned fire without aiming while twisting her fall into a roll. Danny didn't move at all from his position behind the console. He fired again and missed.

Priya recovered, steadied her arm and took another shot. This time Danny dodged to one side. While Pieter scrambled to his feet, she scuttled into a partially sheltered position behind a blocky milling machine and blasted large dents into the back of Danny's console.

"Hurry up," she shouted with little hope of being heard.

Danny popped his head up at the opposite end of the console. Priya shot again, forcing him into hiding. She risked a glance back at Pieter. He wasn't at the keyboard. Instead, he was searching the desk.

"Reynard," she yelled over her shoulder. "What are you doing?"

Pieter found what he was looking for: the carousel with the address cartridges. He grabbed the cylinder and dashed to the ladder. With a mocking wave, he jumped feetfirst into the opening.

Priya turned back to the console. Danny raised his hands, holding his pistol by its barrel.

"Drop your weapon." Priya kept her own pistol trained on Danny as he stood and placed his gun on the table. He edged around the console. "Stay where you are."

"I'm unarmed." He continued inching toward the ladder opening. "And you are out of time. You can shoot me or you can try to shut down the resonator. You cannot do both."

She drew Pieter's pistol with her free hand and pointed it at the cylinders. "Maybe I'll release the gas."

Danny shook his head. "Even if that were possible, we would both die." He pointed to the open hatch above. "So would everyone else."

She glanced at the hatch. With all the noise, there was no way to warn Nathan to close it. Danny took advantage of the momentary distraction to dive into the water, which now covered their knees. He swam underwater toward the ladder. Priya lost sight of him under the frothing surface.

A series of large air bubbles erupted through the floor grating. The water level dropped. The cart Pieter placed in front of the frame had served its purpose. He'd opened the portal without collapsing the field.

Priya struggled through the chaotic waves to check the monitor on Danny's workstation. There was nothing as obvious as a countdown timer, but the changing images made it clear there were only minutes to go. With no idea how to shut down the resonator, she splashed over to the gas cylinders and tried the valves. *Locked.* Danny must have expected that someone would interfere and bolted each valve in the open position. He'd even sealed the mainframe inside a sturdy metal box and padlocked the electrical panel's steel doors.

The water was rising again.

She waded to the racks of portal testers. Braided metal hoses ran from the gas cylinders to a manifold, which split into dozens of smaller lines, one heading to each shelf. Hundreds of circuit boards lined the shelves. Each had a tiny LED panel. One entire rack showed green lights. The second rack was only half lit. As she watched, more green LEDs came to life, advancing toward the bottom shelf at the same rate the icons were changing on Danny's workstation.

As soon as those boards are lit, the gas will be released.

A loud splash caught her attention. Nathan had jumped from halfway up the ladder. The technician who'd gone upstairs with him was climbing through the hatch too.

As Nathan fought through the waist-high waves, Priya pulled on one of the green-lit boards and found it locked in place. Using two hands, she loosened the knurled bolts that secured its bracket, and pulled it free. A flexible hose and several cables connected the board to the rack, preventing her from removing it entirely. The hose could only be for the gas.

Priya leaned closer to Nathan to be heard over the noise. "We should be able to stop the mainframe from merging the portals by disconnecting the data cables."

"I agree." He unbolted and removed another board.

With hands numbing from the cold, Priya wrestled with the connectors for several seconds before the cable detached and the lights went out. Nathan took just as long to disconnect his board.

"This'll take too long," he shouted.

Priya turned her attention to the hose connector. "That's a self-sealing gas fitting." To disconnect it, she only had to pull the locking ring, something she could do with one hand in a fraction of the time. She pointed to the hatch. "Get out of here."

"*What?*"

"I don't know if there's a space between the two halves of this type of connector. If there is, there'll be a small amount of pressurized gas trapped in there. You'll be exposed." She looked for the technician, but the woman had submerged herself after swimming to the console.

Nathan reached for the hose on his board. "I'm not going anywhere."

"*Stop.*" Priya seized his arm and stared him down. "We don't know how long the toxin takes to work." She released him. "I'll do it."

She waited until he stepped back before gripping the hose and locking ring. If there was a gap, the fitting would separate with a pop. *How much is too much?* The nerve gas would work through skin, but she held her breath anyway.

She pulled the ring.

The hose dropped silently.

"You're still alive." Nathan grinned. "That's a good sign."

Priya hadn't realized how tense she'd been. Her entire body relaxed, amplifying the cold bite of the chest-deep water.

"We can't prevent them from merging, but we can stop the gas." She shoved the board loosely back into its slot.

They moved along the line, undoing bolts, pulling boards, and detaching hoses. By the time the water reached her shoulders, they'd disconnected only a few dozen.

The technician—who'd been underwater the entire time—surfaced and swam back to the racks. "I'm locked out." She joined them in disconnecting circuit boards.

Soon, the water was over everyone's head. They each had to pull themselves up, take a breath, and dive to continue working. As the water rose, they had to swim higher for each breath. The technician quit first, when she could only disengage a single board between breaths.

There was just one row of unlit LEDs on the second rack's bottom shelf when Nathan tried to pull Priya's arm away. She shrugged him off and kept working. He clutched her arm again, forced her to face him, pointed upwards, and mimed closing and tightening the hatch. Then he pushed himself backwards and swam to the surface.

Priya drifted motionless for several seconds. The lights continued their relentless march toward the final board. She kicked the second rack, on which they'd only disconnected the top row, then swam after Nathan.

As soon as she rolled over the hatch's lip, Nathan slammed the lid shut and sealed it. At once, the pressure release valve began venting air.

"Shut off the water," Priya shouted, even though the technician was already running to the elevator. "How much time do we have?" she asked Nathan, who was lying on the dome trying to catch his breath.

"Less than a minute." It was a guess, but probably

accurate.

Priya stood by, waiting for the moist air to stop blasting from the vent. The sound of water rushing into the tank below eased off. As soon as the airflow stopped completely, she sealed the valve to prevent the nerve gas from leaking out.

"Half." She slumped onto the domed roof beside Nathan and hung her head between her knees. "We only managed to disconnect half of them."

Chapter 48

Jack sat at the edge of a rocky precipice—the one he knew so well from countless dreams. A man waited beside him, sharing the view.

"I know you," Jack said as he stood.

"Of course you do. We've taken this walk many times, you and I." The man turned and wandered into the field.

Jack followed. "Uncle Carl? Are you real?"

Carl laughed. "I think so. Tell me, what's going on in your life?"

"What's going on?" Carl's casual attitude was such a contrast to what Jack felt that he couldn't stop himself from replying angrily. "As far as I know, I'm on Earth, my parents were kidnapped, and some madman is trying to kill everyone."

"Ah, so we've come to that again."

"Again? You know what happens next?"

"Sorry, Jack. We've shared many variations of this dream, but never beyond this point."

"Shared a dream?" Jack was only just coming to accept that this man was his uncle. The idea of sharing a common dream seemed absurd.

Carl walked on, following the familiar path. "Not at the same time, of course." He pushed through the branches of a cluster of ten-foot pine trees. "Every time I see you, you're a different age. We might be having this conversation decades apart."

Jack guessed from Carl's appearance that he was in his late sixties; older than he appeared in Holden's photo, but much younger than he would actually be at this moment. "Do you know how it ends?"

"Sometimes you try to steer the dream another direction, sometimes you go with the flow. More than once, you've jumped off the cliff to wake yourself up. It doesn't make much difference." He pointed to the rocks ahead. "We always end up there."

"What is this place? How come I constantly dream about

it?"

"I've been searching for an answer to that question for a very long time. There are places on Cirrus where the artificial gravity lines have separated from the main band. This is one of them."

"Icarus Island is another, isn't it?"

"That's right, there are several lines crossing there, a result of the impact that formed the island. You've met Niels, then? He commissioned me to find the lines, although he never told me why. Initially, I used engineering reports to locate likely spots and plot them with a gravimeter. It was slow work. But after a few trips through my brother's portal, I began having this dream whenever I camped near one. Since then, I've wandered each of Cirrus' twelve sectors and found hundreds."

"You're not a real Traveller, then?"

"No, the portal's effects are temporary for people my age. But like you and Sarah, I sense these places are somehow connected."

"So, every time I have this dream, it's because you're near one of the lines?"

"It may also happen when you're near one."

"How come I don't remember any of this?"

Carl pointed to the top of the dam. "Up there. That's where you'll find your answer." He climbed up and gestured to the cave when Jack joined him. "What do you hear?"

Jack crouched to lean closer to the opening. "Voices. I always hear them, but they're all jumbled together. I can never understand what they're saying."

"But what are they feeling?"

"Feeling? How can I tell what they're feeling?"

"Try again."

He closed his eyes and listened carefully. It was still a jumble but he picked out a familiar sound. *Was that laughter?* He concentrated, trying to isolate that single voice, heard it again and grew certain. And it wasn't just one voice, many of them were laughing. There were also shouts of anger, exclamations of surprise, insolent tones, and even crying. It became apparent that each sound communicated an emotion.

They were single, wordless expressions, almost like …
Emoji.

With this realization came the familiar, overwhelming anxiety. He stood and faced his uncle, shaking, then took a deep breath to calm himself. "*Emotion detectors.* They're in every phone. That's why I get anxious around crowds, isn't it?"

Carl nodded. "Demophobia. You've told me about it."

"But if I always learn this, how come I don't remember it?"

"I think you've repressed the memory, as a form of self-defense."

"Against what?"

Carl hesitated. "You were so young. We didn't know about the—"

Jack interrupted. "Grandpa told me. Mental health problems were common among children who used portals. But maybe they weren't hallucinating. Maybe they hear what I hear."

He stared at the cave again. The voices and emotions were clear now, some even seemed familiar. For a fleeting moment, several came through much stronger than the rest. One gave a strong impression of anger, of revenge. *Pieter Reynard.*

Carl spoke again, drawing Jack's attention from the cave. "From what you've told me in past dreams, I'm certain you would have become a Traveller, like Sarah, if not for what you describe as a merging of portals. You said you got caught in the middle of it, and it gave you access to not only your own future memories, but to others' as well. You've learned to block this, to protect yourself from being overcome by emotions that are not your own. Now you can only sense them in your dreams."

"Obviously, I haven't learned well enough. I still get really irritated around crowds. But now that I think about it, it's only when there are a lot of phones around. And the merger is happening right now. I'm trying to decide whether to destroy the portals or save them. What should I do?"

"I can't help you with that." Carl pointed to the cave where the power cell would be. "The decision will be yours."

"Will I remember this? Will we meet again?"

"You've asked the same question before. I'm certain that—when the time comes, when it really matters—you'll remember."

Jack felt no fear as he moved to the opening. He reached into the cave without hesitation, grasped the cell, and was abruptly back in the impactor room staring at his empty hands.

I remember everything.

He also understood it all now. Merging the portals would create something new; something wonderful. He wanted to shout out to Sarah and Ethan and tell them what he'd discovered. There was so much more to the network than they knew. They must save it at any cost.

Sarah stood behind Ethan, looking over his shoulder, unable to tear her eyes from the monitor. "How much longer?"

"They're all in resonance," he said. "It's up to Priya to stop Danny now."

For all his bravado, the fear in Ethan's eyes matched Sarah's. He looked between the monitor and the phone, waiting for it to spew toxic gas.

Without a word, Jack slipped back into his meditation. He had the power to save or destroy the crystals, but his friends and family meant more to him than anything the network could offer. This time, it was easy to imagine the impactor's crystal as a real object. He took hold of it, felt the tiny cracks forming within.

"Now, Jack," Ethan shouted. "*Do it*—"

Jack dug deeply into the crystal and pulled. A pulse of energy burst through the portal before its crystals came apart. As if fleeing from an explosion, the matrix of mirrored rooms and their crystals disintegrated in a rapidly expanding wave. He was plunged into darkness.

When he opened his eyes, he found he was truly in the dark. He couldn't see into the lab at all until the emergency lighting system kicked in. Ethan and Sarah stood in exactly the same spot he'd last seen them.

"You know," Jack said, "if I hadn't been able to do it, holding the phone in your hand was not the best choice."

Ethan laughed nervously and tossed the phone away, as if only now realizing where and what it was.

Jack entered the lab and scanned the Archive. The emergency lights were on in there too, leaving the room dimly lit. He had no trouble seeing the thousands of tiny red lights.

Ethan's workstation was running again. "I need to check something." Sarah gasped when he brought up the status screen. Most icons had only a black bar, but there were still many normal ones. "It's okay. The green ones are portals here on Earth that weren't merged. We only need to be worried about the ones on Cirrus."

He pressed a few more keys, then scrolled through a filtered list. All of them were black.

"We got every one."

- - - - -

Nathan, Grace, and Priya sat on the water tank, waiting for the portals to merge, waiting for the gas to flow. The turmoil going on below was not reflected by the calmness above. There was no wind, very little noise, and the artificial stars embedded in Cirrus' roof added their own serenity to the scene by softening harsh shadows. The others were still below ground somewhere, but Holden was walking toward them from the shed when the entire city went dark.

"It's over," he said. "Check your phone."

Priya pulled out her borrowed phone. "It's dead."

"I believe we'll find they all are." Holden gestured broadly. Every building was dark.

"So, they didn't save the network? They destroyed it?"

"The simplest solution. No portals. No gas."

There were no electric lights at all; only the dim glow of the moon behind sparse clouds, and the natural stars above the broken sky.

Chapter 49

After a few moments of silence in the dimly lit room, Sarah asked, "Well, what now?"

Ethan answered right away. "I'm hungry." Sarah rolled her eyes but Jack laughed—his cousin's appetite might be the one thing they could count on in the middle of an apocalypse.

Jack waved a hand to the door. "Let's go see what's open, then."

He wasn't too surprised when they reached the parking lot. Everything was dark in the immediate neighborhood, even the streetlights. He could see the stars.

"I don't think we're going to find a restaurant tonight," Ethan said.

"Back to Grandpa's, I guess."

Without the normal noise of traffic, the rumble of thousands of people echoed from blocks away. As Jack and his friends got closer to the International District, they were relieved to find these were partiers, not rioters. While some people may have expected the worst tonight, most had come out only to have a good time.

A group of food trucks were parked at the edge of the party zone. Fortunately, Ethan had cash and bought them a snack. It wasn't the fancy restaurant Jack was hoping for, but it was welcome at the end of a long day.

Sirens wailed in the distance, but no cars moved on the streets. On the bridge over Lake Washington, vehicles were stuck bumper-to-bumper.

"It's so calm," Sarah said.

Jack considered the lanes of abandoned vehicles. "From what Priya said, these cars have been gridlocked for hours."

"And with no phones, nobody knows what's going on yet." Ethan pointed at the mix of lit and darkened buildings downtown. "Also, some of the larger towers are lit up. They must have their own fusion generators. People would panic if it were completely dark."

A cluster of flashing lights brightened the far end of the

bridge. Police cars, fire trucks, and ambulances still had power. There were even a few commercial transport trucks running, but no private vehicles at all.

"Is this what Pieter meant by *discomfort*?" Sarah asked. "Or did Danny do this?"

After a long walk through quiet streets, Ethan placed his hand on the scanner at Holden's front door. "Grandpa's fuel cell is still working," he said as the door opened. "The emergency lights are on."

Jack hoped his parents or grandfather would be there, but only Dusty came out to greet them.

Ethan went directly to the kitchen and fumbled around in the darkened fridge. Sarah followed Jack into the living room, where he checked the portal's charge indicators.

"One bar." He rubbed his hand across the mirror's surface and felt the smooth pane. "The crystal is still in one piece."

"We should activate it," Sarah said, "even if we can't get through yet. Maybe they're waiting for us."

He touched the hidden switch. The mirror went completely black. His heart sank. "It's dead."

"Are you sure? Does your grandfather have a flashlight?"

Jack found one in a desk drawer. He pointed it at the mirror, illuminating the ceiling in the opposite room.

"It's not dead," Sarah said, "it's just dark in the apartment."

"That's a relief." He stood on the ladder's second step for a better look. "I can see the city through the window. There's not a single light out there. And no sound either." After a few seconds, he closed the portal and stepped down. "I don't know if the crystal can be charged from the house's fuel cell. We'll check it again later."

Back in the kitchen, Ethan had laid out most of the fridge's contents on the counters. "What?" he asked when they stared at him. "It'll go bad."

"What if we're stuck here?" Sarah asked.

"It won't be so bad," Ethan said. "Some neighborhoods we passed through had lights. That means a few power stations are working. This partial blackout is probably just because communications are down. We'll have heat and running water again when the power is restored."

"What about food?"

"Well, we saw a semi with its lights on. Parts of the transportation network must still be working. Getting food into the stores is going to be a big priority."

"It'll be easier here than on Cirrus," Jack said.

"Why's that?" Sarah asked.

"Back home, *everything* uses portals." He pointed to Priya's car in the driveway. "Here, a lot of vehicles run on gas or hydrogen."

"And our older neighborhoods are still connected by power lines and cables," Ethan said. "We've had power failures here before when someone accidentally dug too deep."

They discussed the situation for a while longer, talking about what they thought might happen and what they were afraid might not. The sky was getting lighter when Jack suggested checking on the portal again.

"Still just one bar," Ethan said. "Who gets to go home?"

"It has to be Sarah, doesn't it?"

"I don't want to go if you two are stuck on Earth."

"But," Jack said, "it might be days, months even, before things are back to normal here. Maybe things will never be normal again. One of us should go back."

Nobody volunteered. Ethan smiled mischievously. "One of us *is* going." He clapped his hands and called, "Dusty. Come here, girl."

Jack and Sarah laughed but didn't argue. Ethan climbed the ladder's lower steps and activated the portal. Dusty, almost a year old, was too big to sit comfortably on a lap, but Jack could easily lift the squirming dog. He picked her up and handed her to Ethan, who set her on the mantle. She licked his face.

"Okay, stop it now. Go on through. Jump."

Dusty sat on the wide mantle and wagged her tail.

"She doesn't want to leave either." Sarah tossed a rope toy to Ethan. "Maybe this will help."

Ethan threw the toy into the apartment. "Fetch." Dusty stepped through the portal, searching for the toy. "Go ahead, jump. It's on the chair." The dog bobbed her head a few times, then leaped down and barked happily from the apartment. "Good girl. Hope to see you soon." He closed the portal.

"Well, now what?"

"I suppose we should get some sleep." Jack dropped onto the couch. "It's been a long day. Is there a bedroom Sarah can use?"

Sarah fell into a chair. "That's okay, this is fine."

Ethan flopped into another one. "Works for me."

After a few minutes of silence, Jack asked quietly, "Do you think dogs can become Travellers?"

This brought another chorus of laughter and speculation about whether Sarah's talent would remain. Ethan brought out his coin to test a prediction, but the room was too dark—he fumbled and lost the coin on the first toss. By the time they settled down, the city's darkened skyline was developing against the brightening sky.

- - - - -

"*You sent the dog?*"

Jack woke and heard Holden saying, "Now, Priya. I'm sure they had a good reason."

"*Priya.*" Sarah sprang from her seat and ran to the ladder.

"Wait." Priya rose into view and signaled her to stop. "It's not fully charged. The fusion plant has only just come online."

"The portal can be charged from one side," Holden said, "but it will take longer. We should be able to bring you across this afternoon."

"Where are our parents?" Ethan asked.

"Everyone's all right. They're downstairs with Sarah's mother. How are things over there?"

"There's no communication, and most of the city is in a blackout." Jack filled in the details of their trek home.

"I'm not surprised," Priya said. "Anyway, there's nothing we can do until we figure out what's working and what's not. You can all go back to sleep for a while."

Happy to know they'd go home eventually, they agreed. Priya closed the portal.

- - - - -

Power was restored to Holden's neighborhood around noon, but failed again within the hour. There was no television, internet, or phone service, although there were a surprising number of older car radios. Jack learned from one of Holden's neighbors what he already suspected—the same failures in Seattle had happened all around the world.

In Caerton, few portal-based services were working. The Magnolia had electricity from its own fusion plant and a piped connection to the reservoir for water, but that was all. With limited power, Sarah was able to go home in the morning, but the boys had to wait for the portal to recharge. They spent the time gathering items from the house to send to Cirrus: clothes for Ethan and his mother, Nathan's fishing gear, and Holden's equipment for creating coin portals.

That afternoon, Jack threaded the crowds on the downtown streets of Caerton. There were more people there than he'd ever seen in one place. Even the masses at Port Isaac's bus station didn't compare to the sea of confused citizens, wandering aimlessly, waiting for their phones to return to life. For twenty minutes, he and Ethan shoved and apologized their way through blocks of disorganized bystanders until they reached the quiet street where the families waited.

"Jack?" Sarah acted surprised as he approached. "There are so many people here."

"Yeah, but they're all calm. I stepped on a few toes and no one got mad."

She grinned. "That's not what I meant."

"Huh?" Jack looked behind—he'd just passed calmly through a crowd of thousands. "Oh, yeah. I'll tell you about it later. Priya's back."

Priya was still wearing her UN Police jacket. "I went to Reynard's mansion. It's deserted. There's no power either; Danny must have included one more portal than Pieter intended. I did find one thing working though." She signaled them to follow.

"Are you staying on Cirrus?" Sarah asked.

"No. Somebody has to explain what happened. I'll tell my boss I came through the cargo portal before the lab flooded. If Reynard has a functioning portal somewhere, or as soon as passenger flights resume, I'll get myself re-posted to Cirrus. It may be a while, but I'll be back."

"What about Pieter and Danny?" Ethan asked. "Will we ever know if they made it to Earth?"

"They did," Jack said.

So far, he'd only told his grandfather about his conversation with Carl, and what he'd learned about the emotion detectors. He wasn't ready to discuss that with anyone else yet, but they all deserved to hear what he knew about Pieter.

"For a moment, when everything was … *connected*, I … *sensed* … people going through portals. Pieter was one of them, I'm sure of it. Danny too."

"We'll find them," Priya said. "Until then, Pieter has no use for this." She leaned against a stretched, six-door SUV and dangled a key.

"Is this his limo?" Ethan asked.

"Eight leather seats and enough hydrogen in the fuel cell to go all the way to Port Isaac."

He held out his hand. "Can I drive?"

Nathan stepped forward and snatched the keys. "Ah, no."

Ethan threw his hands up in mock frustration.

Priya said her goodbyes and walked back to the Magnolia, where she'd travel by portal to Seattle.

Sarah was happy to be reunited with her mother, but more upset than ever about being disconnected from her friends. "A week ago, I was worried they'd separate our classes. How will we stay in touch, now?"

"Things will get back to normal," Jack said, "eventually. We can't grow new crystals, but Grandpa can make coin portals now. I'll get a drone working. There's no GPS anymore, but Ethan thinks he can program one to navigate using landmarks. We'll write letters. People used to do that."

"Letters?" Ethan pretended to be offended. "I've moved to a *space station*, on the *other side of the Sun*, and we're going to communicate using *letters*."

Sarah hugged them both and said goodbye. Then she and her mother cycled home through streets covered in pieces of metal and plastic from the hundreds of drones that had fallen from the sky.

Jack watched until they were out of sight. He'd be going home too, but wondered what awaited him there. Would Fairview feel as familiar now that he'd no longer be able to speak with Sarah every day? He smiled, suddenly remembering that Carl had described her as a Traveller. *He said she felt a connection to Icarus Island, but she's never been there. That means … well, I'm not sure what it means, other than she'll have to tell me someday.*

"Time to go, boys," Holden said. Their parents had finished loading the borrowed vehicle.

"Are you coming with us, Grandpa?" Jack asked.

"Part of the way. I plan to borrow Nathan's fishing gear and go visit an old friend."

Jack hopped into the limo and reclined his seat. The journey home would be a lot more comfortable than the trip to Caerton had been.

Chapter 50

The water was freezing and he was running out of time.

He'd passed through the submerged portal on Cirrus, arriving in a darkened, flooded room with no clue what city he was in, nor even what country.

He found the door again, pounded it with his fists and kicked the handle.

Stop. Panic now would be the end of him. *It's shielded.*

He'd been holding his breath for more than one minute. He wouldn't survive a second one.

Think. Water had filled the room, but there should have been an air pocket. *A vent.*

He swam up, scrabbling for an opening. Something floated against the ceiling: a shoe. Had the previous occupant escaped?

He thrashed his way into a corner. One hand slapped a dead light panel but the other found clear water. Grasping the metal rim, he pulled his body into the vertical duct.

There was no light at the top of the channel. The portal on Cirrus was under thirty feet of water, meaning there had to be at least twenty above him.

He clawed upwards through the narrow pipe with his shoulders and hips binding, threatening to trap him. Still no light.

His lungs screamed. Sharp metal edges sliced his knees and fingers. *How much farther?*

His hands broke the surface as his chest convulsed, drawing a ragged breath that he couldn't have prevented. Spitting and coughing, he dragged himself over the edge and sprawled on a cold concrete floor in complete darkness.

He laughed as he caught his breath.

He'd swam between worlds, escaping certain death with only cuts and bruises. The portals had been destroyed. Soon, the factories to grow the crystals would be too. Nothing could stop him now.

But first, he had to figure out where he was.

His eyes adjusted to the gloom. The room wasn't completely dark. He was on the floor of a forty-foot-tall tower. Dim gray rectangles ringed the metal walls.

Air Filters. A ballast chamber.

He'd climbed into an enclosed volume of air that acted as a shock absorber to pressure changes on either side of the wormhole. The chamber would enable the portal below to remain open for hours at a time for the passage of raw materials. Its configuration was familiar.

I'm in an Armenau factory.

An alarmed voice burst from a loudspeaker. "Evacuate the building. *There's a bomb.*"

BLUE SPELL

Read on for a preview of the second book of the Cirrus
Chronicles

Chapter 1

Jack Scatter balanced at the edge of the two-story roof, practicing magic.

A yellow tennis ball hovered motionless beyond his reach. It was an ordinary ball, one he'd used on his school's courts many times. He moved the wand's tip in a circle to set the ball spinning. The gesture was unnecessary—his thoughts controlled the movement—but the motion helped him picture the invisible energy field.

He released the ball and let it drop twenty feet. Just before it hit the gravel, he flicked the wand, directing a beam of energy to bounce it back to its original height. He stretched out to snatch it, overreached, slipped, and fell.

"*JACK*," his father warned, too late.

Jack flung his arms forward. The tennis ball shot into the sky and he froze at an impossible angle, leaning over open air with his feet glued to the weathered concrete parapet.

"*Hold on.*" Victor scrambled onto the roof through the hatchway.

Jack hung there as if gravity didn't apply to him. *I must have redirected the field instinctively*; a surprising and fortunate discovery. "I'm okay."

With his heart pounding, he concentrated on tilting himself upright. He imagined the energy field as a rising wind, pushing him from below. The movement was disorienting, but the world slowly rotated back to normal.

Victor grasped his shoulder, pulled him down onto the flat roof, and spun him around. "Your mother would've had a heart attack if she'd seen that." His grip, hardened by decades of labor, was firm but not painful.

Jack met his father's eyes and saw concern, not anger. "Sorry. I slipped."

"I saw." Victor's expression softened. "And you shouldn't be playing with that where someone can see you."

Jack tucked the wand into his jacket pocket and gestured at the two dozen neighboring structures. "There's no one here anymore. There hasn't been for weeks."

Victor considered the abandoned warehouses and garages, a mile from town, and didn't argue. "Can you see the drone?"

"Not yet." Jack picked up the binoculars. "It's really late this time."

"They may not have sent it if they saw the storm coming."

"Maybe. I've never seen one like it." It had formed so quickly. Towering clouds lined the entire eastern horizon, but the sun was setting behind them in a clear sky. The missing drone should have been easy to spot against that backdrop, yet there was no sign of it.

Two months ago, locating the drone would have taken only a few taps on his phone. But then Pieter Reynard—well, actually Jack himself—had partially fulfilled a centuries-old prophecy by Sir Isaac Newton to bring about the apocalypse. The world didn't end as Newton predicted, but Jack had wiped out the portal network and most of the services people took for granted.

Portals—tiny wormholes through which power and data flowed—had been part of modern life for decades. There was no longer an internet, no phones or text messaging, and limited electricity. He'd destroyed the portal crystals to save Cirrus, the world-sized space station he lived on, and unintentionally isolated it from Earth. Likewise, his hometown of Fairview felt more cut-off than ever.

The roof they stood on covered the family's workshop. *Before Newton*—the time before the loss of the network—their business had been drone-maintenance and repair. The self-guided aircraft, thousands of them, were essential to the small farming community, and the warehouse below was once filled with them. The few it contained now were lifeless.

Jack was about to give up for the night when fading sunlight reflected off a shiny surface traversing an angry black cloud. "Finally. Uh … that's not right."

"What do you see?"

Jack passed the binoculars to his father. "Look how fast it's coming." Ahead of the drone, which was still miles away, the treetops lashed chaotically.

Victor glanced at the collection of items Jack had been practicing with recently: more balls, a folding chair, books, assorted tools. "We have to clean this up. Now."

The windstorm approached with a roar as they scurried around the roof, gathering and throwing items through the open hatch without looking. Like a vast, invisible river, it ushered a wave of frenzied motion across the yellow-green fields of canola. When the cold front hit the workshop, it pushed Jack backwards, causing him to lose his footing again.

Victor, Jack's height but thirty pounds heavier, helped him stand. "That blasted drone is trying to land."

Jack shielded his eyes from flying debris and looked up. The six-foot wide aircraft had slowed and tilted sharply into the howling wind. Before Newton, a drone would have linked to sensors on the ground and compensated for the gusts, or just waited until the storm passed. But this one was following its limited programming and struggling to stay upright as it descended.

He drew the wand. "It's going to need help."

Victor retreated to the warehouse to give the drone a clear landing zone. "Can you reach it from here?"

Rain fell as Jack sheltered in the hatchway, then turned and focused on the flying courier. "It's about sixty feet up. That's near my limit." He concentrated, sensing the drone's mass and inertia through the wand.

Ethan Marke, Jack's cousin, had dubbed the device a magic wand, although it was really a cylindrical portal crystal encased in a metal tube. The name stuck because, well, what else could it be? Jack had learned to move objects, produce water, fire, light, even unlock doors. To an observer it would appear to be magic, and Ethan had been pestering him for details about it for weeks.

Jack started with a gentle downward pressure, then gripped the sinking drone more firmly. The machine fought, spun, and nearly flipped over once. But as it dipped near the landing pad, the action of its rotors became irrelevant—his control was absolute; he could move it wherever he wanted.

"I got it." The drone's motors shut off as soon as its landing struts touched the rain-slicked surface.

When it was safe, he and Victor dashed onto the roof to tie the aircraft to three anchor bolts. Jack retrieved a handful of papers from the small cargo hold and tucked them into his jacket pocket to keep them dry. Even though there'd been no real trouble in Fairview since the breakdown, Victor removed the drone's power cell.

By the time they finished, the sun had set and the shower had become a downpour. Victor closed the roof hatch and joined Jack in the nearly empty warehouse.

"We're already soaked. There's no point waiting for it to stop."

Lightning flashed as they ran, revealing Fairview's squat, pyramid-like profile. Their home was a two-story townhouse on the outskirts, but most of the town's five thousand residents lived in increasingly taller towers clustered within a single square mile.

The sudden storm was unlike any Jack had experienced. An unseasonably cold wind pelted them with falling branches as they fought their way up the tree-lined street. It was raining even harder when they jogged up the steps to their front door.

- - - - -

Jack's mother, Emily, sat at the kitchen table and read the letter from her father, Holden. "Dad wants us to come tomorrow." She passed the page to Victor.

"Why?" Jack asked as he toweled off his wet hair. "Didn't he originally say next week?"

"Apparently, Niels thinks his fusion generator is failing and wants your father's help to complete the solar farm."

"Is that something he *remembers* or something he *knows*?"

Victor scratched his stubbly beard: a recent acquisition that had more to do with rolling blackouts than fashion. "With Niels, it's best to assume there's no difference. If he says something is going to happen, it will."

Niels, an accomplished engineer, was also a *Traveller*: someone who could *remember* things that hadn't happened yet. He'd warned of turmoil across Cirrus in the months ahead and invited Jack's family to join him and a dozen others in Icarus to ride out the worst of it. Jack's parents had been preparing for the trip for weeks.

Emily rested her chin heavily in her palm. "Are you okay with leaving your friends behind?"

"Yeah," Jack said, "it's fine. Ethan will be there. And I'm bored without school anyway." Saying this, he realized why his mother seemed so tired; his parents must feel the same without their jobs. He'd kept himself busy searching the fields and forests for crashed drones, but they didn't have even that distraction. And he was running out of drones to recover, having to walk farther from town each day. Last month he'd celebrated his sixteenth birthday trolling the bottom of the lake for salvage. "But Icarus is hardly more than a wilderness camp. We'll be roughing it. When do we leave?"

"First thing in the morning," Victor said. "So no one sees that we've still got a working vehicle."

"There's something else in the envelope." Jack removed another slip of paper and recognized Niels' shaky handwriting. "It's a map." He flipped the page around to position north at the top. "Niels sent directions for getting to Icarus."

"Good. I wasn't looking forward to finding it by memory."

"I could find it again. Ethan and I found the lake in the dark."

"We are *not* going over the Spine where you did," Emily said. "With this weather, it's probably buried in snow. We'll follow the highway."

"What's this mean?" Jack pointed to a caption on the map: *Here be dragons.*

Victor chuckled. "It's an expression that was used on maps centuries ago. It meant the area beyond was unexplored, that no one knew what to expect. That's got to be Niels' way of saying not to go off-road or we'll get lost."

- - - - -

There was another letter in that day's delivery: from Sarah Rogers. Jack brought that one to his tiny second-floor bedroom.

5

He was surprised by how much he missed her. Although they'd known each other for most of their lives, they'd spent only a few days together in August. Before that, they'd only ever met online. Now, limited to sending letters, he was frustrated by how difficult it was to communicate.

Sarah was a natural letter writer. While Jack struggled to create even the briefest note, hers were long and detailed. Their correspondence ran on a six-day cycle, the time the drone took to fly a circuit between Caerton, Port Isaac, Fairview and Icarus. Her two-page letter described events in Caerton and how life there was becoming depressingly boring. With no computers, there was no school, and the only jobs were those in the greenhouses.

Her closing line: *See you soon*, made him smile. She'd been dropping hints about meeting for several weeks, which was both maddening and intriguing. *Is that something she remembers?* Or was she making a subtle suggestion so he'd find a way to make it happen?

Sarah, like Pieter Reynard, was also a Traveller, although neither was as talented as Niels. Before Newton, conventional wisdom said that Travellers must pass through a large wormhole to connect to their future memories. Now, *After Newton*, that wasn't so clear.

Niels, possibly the most gifted Traveller ever, had made accurate predictions leading up to Newton, but hadn't left his private island for decades. Things Sarah wrote about in her letters had come true, but even she wasn't sure she hadn't just worked them out logically. The world had changed so much that it was unlikely she'd ever *travel* again.

Jack faced the window as lighting illuminated the cluster of workshops a mile away, across the canola field. The storm was worsening as it settled in, but his mood was lifting. His chance of reuniting with Sarah had just improved; Icarus was on the other side of the Spine, hundreds of miles closer to Caerton.

Chapter 2

Fifty-two hadn't sounded so bad when Sarah started, but each level in the Magnolia occupied two floors and she'd had to stop several times to rest during the grueling climb. Even so, after nearly two thousand steps, she entered the atrium on the fifty-second level with time to spare.

She hadn't encountered any of the Magnolia's residents in the lobby or stairwell. To conserve power, the elevators only ran every second hour. Soon, the tower's inhabitants would emerge from their dwellings to take advantage of another brief window of easy access.

Pre-Newton, the interior garden was a pleasant spot to rest: verdant, fragrant, and brightly lit by floor-to-ceiling windows at each end of the building, with park benches scattered throughout. But now someone might see her. Second-floor windows on the inner apartments, once hidden behind branches, opened onto a thinning canopy of brown and curling leaves.

She hurried past a dozen closed doors to the short corridor that connected the atrium to a parallel hallway and an outer strip of apartments. The address she wanted was straight ahead, at the intersection. Like the atrium, windows flanking each end of the long hallway allowed sunlight to make up for the lack of interior lighting.

Holden had sent a key in the mail drone—not for her to use—for his Caerton apartment six weeks ago. She was meant to hold on to it until Detective Priya Singh came to collect it. That turned out to be unnecessary; Priya had found a spare in Holden's house in Washington.

Following the same schedule as the elevators, Holden's apartment was without power and gloomy when Sarah entered. She slipped off her shoes and crept into the living room.

Two bedrooms overlooked the main level. Their doors were open. Below the balcony, the door to Holden's workshop was ajar. The kitchen and living room were clean, as if the elderly man was still living there, but most of the books had been removed from the tall shelves that flanked the electric fireplace.

A flash of lightning illuminated the painting above the hearth. Still slightly out of breath, she gasped at the sight. *There it is.* Although she didn't appreciate the abstract landscape, it was easily the most valuable artwork in the city.

Hidden in plain sight, Holden's portal could create a passage to Earth with the press of a button. More importantly, the device had the power to connect her consciousness across time. She'd *travelled* through it several times already and received future memories that had come true.

What's the harm in a quick trip to Earth? She leaned closer to the frame, searching for the five inconspicuous squares. Disguised as wood inlays in a geometric border, a gentle tap would trigger a color change to show how much charge the portal's crystal matrix held. *I should at least check that it's still working.* She reached out to touch the frame and heard a soft footfall.

Without hesitation, Sarah spun and struck out with her heel. But the person sneaking up behind her ducked it easily.

"I'm regretting teaching you that move."

"*Priya.*" Sarah's defensive posture vanished and she rushed in for a hug. "You scared me."

"You should be scared. What if I'd been a looter?" Priya, a third-level black belt, leaned past Sarah to check that the hallway was empty. She'd arrived by portal and hidden in the workshop when she heard Sarah. "What are you doing here?"

"I came to see you."

"Who told you I … never mind." There was no point questioning a Traveller.

"You're moving the portal today, aren't you?"

"The storage lockers in my building have power outlets. It'll be a secure place to keep it charged."

"We could store it at my place. It'd be easier for me to pass messages."

"This is still a police investigation. Any messages I need to pass are not for your ears. Besides, I don't think you could resist the temptation of using it."

"But wouldn't that be a good thing? You could tell me where you're looking for Pieter Reynard, and I could remember if that's the place you'll eventually find him."

"We both know it doesn't work that way. Travellers can't fixate on something without their imagination taking over. But now that you're here, I can use your help."

"With the investigation?"

"No, Miss Amazon." Priya handed Sarah a socket driver and pointed at Holden's portal frame. "I can't reach the upper bolts."

The power came back on shortly after Sarah started working, but it took most of the hour to swap the Art Deco frame. Thirty inches on a side, the square, metal-backed wooden frame weighed twenty pounds. The portal crystal itself was only twenty-four inches wide—a tight fit for some Travellers, but large enough to diagonally pass the replacement frame from Earth.

While Sarah hung the new frame, Priya lay the original on the kitchen counter and followed Holden's detailed instructions to remove the landscape print from behind the crystal. What had appeared to be an oil painting on canvas was really a printed plastic film, thinner than paper. Once removed, the polished metal surface under the diamond sheet reflected her image as an ordinary mirror.

Priya handed the print to Sarah to install in the second frame while she adjusted the gap between the square crystal and the metal backing.

"A quarter turn each," Priya recited as she slowly rotated the screwdriver. Holden had stressed that each of the thirty-six screws was to be turned *exactly* that amount, then repeated sixteen times in a pattern that spread the pressure evenly across the crystal.

After turning the final screw, Priya checked on Sarah's progress. "That's upside-down."

Sarah stood back for a better view of the painting. She tilted her head. "Are you sure?"

Priya rolled her eyes. "It doesn't matter."

"Your apartment is five miles from here. How will you carry the frame?"

Priya tapped the hidden switch, vanishing the sheet of diamond and creating a wormhole to her rented accommodations in Olympia. She reached through and lifted a set of foam-padded aluminum tubes. "Davis uses these to carry surfboards on his motorbike. How much time do we have?"

Sarah turned the hot water tap. Without communications, the building's management needed a way to prevent residents from being trapped in elevators. They'd decided on shutting off the hot water as a signal that they'd be cutting the power soon. She ran her fingers through the clear stream that poured into the sink.

"It's still warm. We should have at least five minutes."

As expected, the building's residents remained active as long as power flowed. Priya and Sarah crowded into a full car and rode to the basement. The mirror they carried earned them some unusual looks, but no one questioned them when they recognized the UN Police logo on Priya's jacket.

In Caerton, bicycles had always been the preferred means of transportation. Pre-Newton, the city's underground freeway thronged with hundreds of thousands of commuters. But that was when people had jobs and somewhere to go, and bikes had power for their electric motors. Now, with only skylights to illuminate the tunnels, Priya and Sarah had their pick of hundreds of abandoned bicycles in the Magnolia's garage.

Priya mounted the surfboard rack on a free bike, strapped the mirror to it with elastic cords, then rolled out of the garage towards the on-ramp.

Sarah knew the way to Priya's apartment and so pedaled beside her, keeping the mirrored surface between them. With only a few hundred riders on each block, the freeway was far from crowded. But with the storm raging above, the tunnels were gloomy and they couldn't risk a collision—a four-square-foot diamond sheet was not indestructible.

At the underground entrance to her building, Priya

dismounted and unlocked the door. Sarah held it open for her while she pushed her bike into the garage.

"*Damn.*" Priya scuttled backwards.

"What's wrong?"

"It's Davis." Priya crouched and activated the portal. "He can't know I'm here." She dove headfirst through the wormhole, twanging the elastic cords that secured the frame.

"Why not?" Sarah leaned over, listening to the clamor as Priya struggled to right herself. "You work together."

"Later. Move the frame against the wall."

Sarah swerved the bike and tipped it against the concrete wall seconds before a stocky man wearing the same blue jacket as Priya burst through the door.

Davis, not expecting a bike in the hall, stumbled around her and hurried to the end of the corridor. He scanned the crowd of riders, but there were far too many people to spot an individual. After only a few seconds, he gave up and confronted Sarah.

"Did you see a woman come out this door wearing a blue jacket?" He pulled the fabric straight to display the UN logo. "Like mine?"

"Sorry." Sarah peered over Davis' shoulder, as if she might have missed someone. "I wasn't paying attention."

Davis stood for a moment, looking puzzled. He glanced at the square frame mounted on the bike and seemed about to question it, then shook his head and returned to the garage.

Sarah stooped towards the mirror after the door closed. "He's gone. Why can't he know you're here?"

"If he knew there was a way to get back to Earth, he'd insist on using it. Then everyone would find out, and that would lead Pieter to Holden's—"

Sarah coughed loudly as Davis pushed the door open.

"Hi." She smiled and shuffled to place herself between Davis and the mirror, but the man leaned over for a better look.

"I have a set of racks just like that. I didn't know you could get them here."

Sarah glanced down. A faint rectangle of light shone

against the wall—Priya's room was brighter than the corridor.

"Uh, my mother brought them from Earth."

"Huh." Davis nodded, perhaps wondering why an immigrant had used so much of their limited cargo space for such an unusual item. He shook his head again and closed the door.

"Are all UN officers so … uh … not tall?" Sarah asked when she and Priya were alone. At five-seven, she'd been looking down into Davis' eyes.

"I'm five-three. I'm not short."

Sarah decided that silence was the best response.

"Davis is on the short side, but our other partner, Katherine, is taller than you. Anyway, we can't move the frame inside now. I'll try another day. Just take it back to Holden's building and open the portal when you get to the garage. I'll help you carry it upstairs."

The light against the wall disappeared.

- - - - -

Priya scanned the room. "This isn't Holden's apartment."

Sarah, sitting cross-legged on her bedroom floor in front of the open portal, gestured defensively. "No, it's my place. But just hear me out. This will be a lot easier. We … I mean, you, won't have to climb all those steps at the Magnolia. My mother works four days a week, and this is actually closer to—"

Priya, also sitting cross-legged on her own carpeted floor, hung her head with an exasperated sigh and raised a hand for Sarah to stop. "Okay, okay. It's fine. Just give me your mother's work schedule and keep the frame out of sight until I have time to try again. And no *travelling*."

"I won't." Sarah began writing her mother's timetable on a scrap of paper.

"I'll know if you do. I've moved the Earth-side frame to my place in Olympia." She leaned forward and met Sarah's eyes. "I'll know if you've been there."

Sarah handed the slip to Priya. "I won't use it. Honest."

"Good, because I'm serious. I know you must want to see if you can make more predictions, but if Pieter Reynard survived Newton, he's looking for this portal. He must suspect that I have it. If he finds *it*, he finds *you*."

ABOUT THE AUTHOR

John Harvey lives in British Columba. He trained as an
Electronic Engineering Technologist and worked for decades in
Information Technology and Healthcare Support Services
before turning to writing and freelance editing. He writes
mostly science-fiction and fantasy, but occasionally delves into
humor.

Manufactured by Amazon.ca
Bolton, ON